Dieudonat

BY THE SAME AUTHOR

Illusions of Immortality
Daah: The First Human

Dieudonat

by
Edmond Haraucourt

Translated, annotated and introduced by
Brian Stableford

A Black Coat Press Book

Visit our website at www.blackcoatpress.com

ISBN 978-1-61227-777-6. First Printing. August 2018. Published by Black Coat Press, an imprint of Hollywood Comics.com, LLC, P.O. Box 17270, Encino, CA 91416. All rights reserved. Except for review purposes, no part of this book may be reproduced or transmitted in any form or by any means, electronic or mechanical, including photocopying, recording, or by any information storage and retrieval system, without permission in writing from the publisher. The stories and characters depicted in this novel are entirely fictional. Printed in the United States of America.

Introduction

Dieudonat, roman by Edmond Haraucourt (1856-1941), here translated as *Dieudonat*, was first published in book form by Ernest Flammarion in 1912. It was reprinted in an illustrated edition by Arthème Fayard in 1932. An earlier version of the story was, however, initially published as a series of fourteen "*contes*" in *Le Journal* in 1906, beginning with "L'Enfant doué" on 31 May and concluding with "Dans la rue" on 1 November. Much of Haraucourt's work for *Le Journal*, his principal market for fiction after the turn of the century, was first published in that fashion, including the stories that were eventually combined to make up the classic prehistoric fantasy *Daâh, le premier homme* (1914; tr. as *Daah: The First Human*[1] and several of the novelettes translated in the collection *Illusions of Immortality* (2012)[2], but *Dieudonat*, like *Daâh*, was very extensively expanded and revised for publication.

Because it was published as a series of *contes* rather than as a feuilleton serial, the episodes of the first version of the story of Dieudonat had more flexibility in length than the episodes of a serial confined by the feuilleton, and they could be produced at a much more leisurely pace, at intervals of between one and three weeks. They were, however, still made up as the author went along rather than being planned in advance as an ensemble. The most important precedent for that mode of publication in *Le Journal* had been set by Jean Lorrain, who had a contract to deliver weekly content to the paper between 1900 and his death in 1906, and who mingled articles, short stories and episodic long stories as the mood took him. When those materials were reprinted in book form, however, they did not undergo any revision, save for minor copy-editing. Haraucourt's policy was very different, involving considerable supplementation and reorganization, in order to develop and

---

[1] Black Coat Press, ISBN 978-1-61227-355-6.
[2] Black Coat Press, ISBN 978-1-61227-075-3.

extrapolate the ideas explored in his fiction—much of which consists of Voltairean *contes philosophiques* of considerable intellectual ambition—as well as repairing inconsistencies and supplying esthetic enhancements.

Haraucourt's favorite book when he was a child, at a time of his life when books were exceedingly precious to him, was *Don Quixote*, and *Dieudonat* is, in a sense, "his *Don Quixote*." It is, in consequence, a very personal novel as well as a novel very much of its time; it is *Don Quixote* recast as a kind of modern *Candide*, addressing the problem of theodicy frankly, seriously and satirically, on the assumption that there are some true words best spoken in jest. Like many of Voltaire's own *contes philosophiques* it elects to continue and transfigure the rich French tradition of *contes merveilleux*, by endowing its hero with a supernatural gift similar to the one whose possible consequences had recently been explored, in a superficial manner, in H. G. Wells' cautionary tale "The Man Who Could Work Miracles" (1898; Fr. tr. in *Le Mercure de France*, 1899).

The result of this complex combination is that, whereas *Don Quixote* was a satirical tragicomedy geared to generate relatively amicable laughter and pity, *Dieudonat*, at least in its final version, is a ferocious black comedy that almost prohibits laughing at its own jokes, and which eventually turns to unremittingly bleak tragedy, for which the explanatory excuse provided in the epilogue might well seem cold comfort to many readers. The extended apologue and the elaborate moral drawn therefrom are, however, ingenious and compelling, entitling the novel to be considered as one of the great twentieth-century additions to the traditions of *contes merveilleux*, alongside the near-contemporary *La Révolte des anges* (1914; tr. as *The Revolt of the Angels*) by Anatole France, who was Haraucourt's companion in daily excursions for a while, when both became passionate cyclists during the early years of that hobby's fashionability.

The introduction to *Illusions of Immortality* contains a detailed account of Haraucourt's unusual life and career, some of which it is useful to repeat here in order that the idiosyncratic intellectual perspective of *Dieudonat* can be more fully understood. When the author set out to write his *Mémoires des jours et des gens* (which he never finished, but whose existing text was published posthumously in 1946) he began with the ironic proclamation that he owed his existence to the Catholic Church. His mother was one of seven children of a family surnamed Biet, and was the only one not to be sent into Holy Orders, not because she was insufficiently pious, but because her parents needed someone to do the housework and look after the younger children. While the rest of the Biet children were sent to the Far East as missionaries, where most of them died, Edmond's mother remained behind, but when her own mother died, her father had difficulty adjusting to celibate life, and turned to the Church for help.

The Church not only volunteered to supply Monsieur Biet with a new wife, but also offered to provide his daughter—who would thus be made redundant as his housekeeper—with a husband. Edmond's mother was then introduced to a complete stranger on the day of her betrothal, the banns having already been posted, and was married within three weeks. Haraucourt was thus brought up in an improvised household which was, to begin with, very poor and exceedingly devout. His mother, however, had not forgiven the Church for taking away her six siblings, and she refused to send Edmond to the seminary in which the Church offered him a free education. She also refused to send him to the local community school, as his father wanted, and insisted—although it involved considerable financial sacrifice—that he go to a *lycée* in order that he could learn Latin and Greek, thus being prepared for entry into a profession without being simultaneously indoctrinated and groomed for Holy Orders.

A precocious child who began writing poetry at five years of age, Haraucourt became a dedicated book-lover, in the only way that a child in a devout and poor household could

7

be. Having access to very few books other than the Bible, he treasured the few to which he did contrive to gain access enormously, and he reports in his memoirs that from the age of six to eleven he lived in the near-exclusive company of just one book: *Don Quixote*, which he describes in his memoirs as "the secular Bible of the Occidental world," arguing that Quixote and Sancho Panza are, in combination, the perfect symbols of the divided self, containing between them an entire account of human being.

For the rest of his life, Haraucourt seems to have compartmentalized himself in a similar fashion, creating such a sharp distinction between his Quixotic art and his hedonistic everyday life that no one who knew him could ever understand how such a cheerful *bon viveur* and relentless womanizer could possible write books that seemed so deeply pessimistic and embittered. In his memoir, he explains that, while he had always been grateful for his personal good fortune and fully appreciative of the joys available to him—whose indulgence he did not stint, when he could afford them—far from preventing him from observing the miseries and mistakes of others, the awareness of his own blessings had only made him more acutely aware of their rarity, prompting him bitterly to lament the misfortunes of the majority of humankind. The 1912 version of *Dieudonat* concludes with one such heartfelt lament, extrapolated to considerable length.

Haraucourt reports in his memoir that he attended a different *lycée* almost every year because his father, a civil servant in the Ministry of Finance, was transferred at regular intervals to various far-flung provinces. His final year of school was spent at the prestigious Lycée Henri IV in Paris, and soon after completing his diplomas he assembled his first collection of poetry, modeled on Victor Hugo's *Légende des siècles* and Charles Leconte de Lisle's *Poèmes barbares*, but focusing more narrowly on the subject that most occupied his thoughts and endeavors at the time; it was entitled *La Légende des sexes*. Haraucourt asserts that the collection went everywhere with him for the next few years, and continued to follow him for the rest of his life, but between 1876, when he completed it at the age of twenty, and the day when it finally crept into print, he had considerable difficulty in placing individual poems in periodicals.

He had a vague notion of preparing for a career in law, and worked in a notary's office for a while, but he could not settle there, and tried the civil service—an attempt not helped at all by a brief stint working directly for his censorious father. After various other brief employments, and a few intervals when he occasionally had to sleep rough, he obtained a position as secretary to the Prefect of Corsica, spending a year on the island in 1879 before returning to France for his compulsory term of military service. On his release he stayed in Paris, where he fell in with members of a political group carrying forward the radical ideas of Léon Gambetta, and became the editor of their campaign newsletter. At the farewell dinner of the group—whose candidate had been defeated in the elections of 1881—that the idea was broached of using the group's printing press to run off a few copies of *La Légende des sexes* for private distribution. The copy of the text in the Bibliothèque Nationale catalogue, bearing the signature "Le Sire de Chambley" is dated 1883 and the place of publication is given (probably fictitiously) as Brussels, but if Haraucourt's memory is accurate, that might be one of several pirated editions that appeared because he neglected to register copyright in the work.

Haraucourt then found work as an electrician in a theater, managing the lights—a job that apparently led to a split with the Biet family, who heard that he had been seen hanging out with actors and decided that the black sheep had finally strayed too far; his tyrannical grandfather demanded that his mother cut off all communication with him. His parents disappear from his memoir thereafter, but it is hard to believe that they really never saw him again, and he certainly continued to communicate with his uncle, Félix Biet, with whom he seems to have maintained a friendly correspondence while the latter

9

was the Bishop of Tibet, and with whom he remained on good terms when the latter returned to Paris.

An extraordinary stroke of luck transformed the poet's fortunes in 1882 when the editor of *La Jeune France*, Albert Allinet, was moved by the submission of some of his poems to burst into laughter at their apparent absurdity while Leconte de Lisle happened to be in the office. The great man asked to see the poems, did not laugh—perhaps recognizing his own influence—sternly instructed the editor to publish them, and then sent Haraucourt an invitation to his *salon*, where he introduced him to some of the other grand old men of French letters, including Théodore de Banville and Ernest Renan. The three of them appear to have decided—apparently on a whim—to take Haraucourt under their wing, and to promote him as a promising young poet. Banville published a glowing essay on his work in *Gil Blas*, and within a matter of weeks he had been invited to numerous other salons, including dinner at Alphonse Daudet's house, where he met Georges Charpentier, who took him to dinner at Sarah Bernhardt's the following evening.

Almost instantaneously, Haraucourt became so famous within the limited circle of the Parisian literary community—without yet having published anything substantial—that when Rodolphe Salis decided to save his ailing *cabaret*, Le Chat Noir, by promoting it as the capital's leading literary café, Haraucourt was one of the two young writers—the other was Maurice Rollinat—that he invited to the planning meeting, along with Emile Goudeau, whom Salis invited to re-form his literary club the Hydropathes, with the café as a base. Haraucourt was drafted to the editorial staff of the periodical *Le Chat Noir*, to which he also became a regular contributor, and he joined the café's cast of regular performers of songs. He was also introduced to Victor Hugo, a few months before the latter's death, and became one of his coffin-bearers.

In spite of the critical acclaim won in select circles by *La Légende des sexes*, the book remained virtually invisible in the marketplace, and Haraucourt settled into a clerical job at the Ministry of Commerce, where he was able to do his assigned work rapidly enough to allow him abundant time to write; he composed poems, plays and prose fiction in his office before going off to spend his evenings in Le Chat Noir or at various salons. Félix Biet tried to save him from his "life of debauchery" by arranging for him to go into retreat in a monastery for a while, but Haraucourt loftily informed the prior that, although he considered himself to be a good Christian, he had never felt the slightest need or inclination to believe in the divinity of Christ, and he simply used his cell as another quiet place to write—but the experience doubtless provided some inspiration for the peculiar monastic phase added to Dieudonat's career in the 1912 version of the story.

In 1885 Haraucourt published his second poetry collection, *L'Âme nue* [The Naked Soul], and in 1887 published his first novel, the quirky satirical love story *Amis* [Lovers]. His first play was written for Sarah Bernhardt, whose coterie of male admirers he had joined with enthusiasm; it was a *Passion* in which she was supposed to play the Virgin Mary, but it became embroiled in controversy and the first scheduled performance had to be moved and drastically reduced in scope; some years passed before it saw production in a theater and publication, in 1890. He fared better with a musical comedy based on Shakespeare, *Shylock* (published 1889) with music by Gabriel Fauré, but his next play, *Don Juan de Mañara*, languished unproduced and unpublished for some while, again surfacing in 1890. The critical reception of his "novel in verse," *Seul* [Alone] (1890) was more muted than that of *L'Âme nue*, and he might have felt by that time that a backlash against his initial welcome was beginning to take form.

The first, and one of the most striking, of Haraucourt's *contes philosophiques* was "Immortalité" (1888; tr. as "Immortality"), a posthumous fantasy that reflects his doubts regarding his ability to live up to the reputation he had acquired in advance of any real achievement, but which extends into a meditation on the value of life in Paradise and the challenge of discovering a purpose in life. It extrapolates the philosophical issues inherent in its initial hypothesis much further than is

11

typical of the subgenre to which it belonged, in a fashion that became typical of Haraucourt's prose work, and which permitted both *Dieudonat* and *Daâh* to become highly unusual and remarkable works. Its more immediate successors similarly showing a liking for tackling big themes with bravado, included *L'Antéchrist* (1893 as a booklet; tr. as "The Antichrist") and "La Fin du Monde" (1893; tr. as "The End of the World"), which were included with it in his first collection *L'Effort* (1894), an elaborately decorated book with colored or monochrome illustrations on every page. Unfortunately, *L'Effort* was not a commercial success, and there was a hiatus in his publications thereafter; it was not until he began working on a regular basis for *Le Journal* after 1900 that he resumed publishing prose in a relatively steady fashion.

In that interim, however, Haraucourt had another stroke of luck. In 1894 someone he met by chance in a café while out cycling suggested that he might be an ideal candidate for a vacancy as a curator of the sculpture collection in the Musée du Trocadero. He applied for the post, and got it, at last discovering a job in which he could take a real interest, and in whose exercise he could be content. He spent the rest of his working life as a museum curator, transferring to the Musée de Cluny in 1903. Although he had had no interest in archeology prior to 1894, except insofar as it bore upon his love of Classical art, he took to it like a duck to water. The amenable job and his marriage in 1896 did not change his fundamental pessimism, but do seem to have helped to mellow it somewhat in the thematic collection that he considered to be his poetic masterpiece, *Les Ages. L'Espoir du Monde* [The Ages. The Hope of the World] (1899)—a much closer analogue of *La Légende des siècles* than *La Légende des sexes*—and in the more commercial work that he did for *Le Journal*, to which he remained a regular contributor for two decades.

Much of the work he did for the newspaper consisted of short domestic melodramas and *contes cruels*. He reprinted some of his early pieces, along with a previously-unpublished novella in *Les Naufragés* [Castaways] (1902), and a further batch in *La Peur* [Fear] (1907), both of which volumes reflect the miseries of the human condition in a series of depictions of small-scale tragedies and disasters, often involving an element of physical horror, narrated in a rather laconic manner. Five stories from the former collection and three from the latter were combined with three further items from *Le Journal* in a new collection, also confusingly entitled *La Peur* (1914), but the Great War followed hot on the heels of that collection and he published nothing similar thereafter, much of his work for the paper never being reprinted.

The *contes* with which Haraucourt supplied *Le Journal* became increasingly ambitious over time, including a remarkable trio of futuristic *contes philosophiques* that were split up into several parts: "Le Gorilloïde" (1904; tr. as "The Gorilloid"), "Cinq mille ans, ou La Traversée de Paris (1904; tr. as "A Trip to Paris") and "La Découverte du docteur Auguérand" (1910; tr. as "Doctor Augérand's Discovery") The story series featuring Dieudonat and Daâh are not futuristic, but they are both fantastic, and can be seen as making up a distinctive sequence in company with the futuristic fantasies, all of the stories embracing a similarly sardonic world-view, with variations of tone. Alongside his work for *Le Journal*, Haraucourt published a few longer prose pieces, including the novel *Les Benoît* (1904) and a book containing two short novels, *Trumaille et Pélisson* (1908), all of which were blackly ironic tales of luckless humans implacably crushed by cruel fate and the hostility of their fellows.

Haraucourt offered himself as a candidate for the Académie in 1909, in competition with Henri de Régnier, whom he had met during his first evening at Leconte de Lisle's salon, and Jean Richepin, whom he knew well from the early days of Le Chat Noir, but he lost the election to Richepin; Régnier simply waited for another seat to fall vacant, and was accepted at the second attempt, but Haraucourt never tried again. Perhaps he saw the failure to attain the "immortality" that election at the Académie was proverbially said to offer as a judgment on his career, and perhaps, having published his own judgment on the value of immortality long ago in "L'Immortalité," he felt that it really did not matter, but it must have been at around that time that he set out to rewrite and amplify *Dieudonat*, which, among other things, examines the question of its hero's qualification for entry into Paradise with earnest ironic wit.

In spite of its pre-advertisement in the pages of *Le Journal*, *Dieudonat* does not appear to have sold well. The *Daâh* series was more popular with the newspaper's readers, requiring continuation in response to popular demand, and retained a higher reputation in spite of the fact that the book version, released a few weeks before the outbreak of the Great War of 1914, was prevented by that event from any chance of attaining large sales. Perhaps, if the war had not intervened, both novels might have been reprinted much sooner, and thus saved from a long disappearance, but it was not to be. The war interrupted Haraucourt's career decisively, and, like many other French writers, he was not the same man by the time it had concluded. Although he did go on to publish two more novels, *L'Oncle Maize* [Uncle Maize] (1922) and *Vertige d'Afrique* [African Vertigo] (1922) he dedicated most of his subsequent writing career to the production of a supposedly-definitive historical study of *L'Amour et l'Esprit gaulois à travers l'histoire du XVe au XXe siècle* [Amour and the Gallic Spirit Through History, from the Fifteenth to the Twentieth Century], published in four volumes, after his retirement from the Musée de Cluny, in 1927-29. He lived thereafter with his wife in a cottage on the Île de Bréhat off the coast of Brittany, apparently doing very little until he decided to write his memoirs, and not being able to bring that work to a conclusion.

Although it is arguable that *Daâh* is Haraucourt's most impressive work, that is partly due to the fact that its ambitions are a little more modest than those of *Dieudonat*, which attempted so much that it was almost bound to fall short—a judgment reflected in the moral of the story contained in the epilogue. *Dieudonat* was certainly intended by the author to be his masterpiece, the summation of his philosophy and his art, but one suspects that he was not entirely happy with it himself; one of the sections added to the later version describes how the eponymous hero, during the eremitic phase of his checkered career, sets out to employ his time usefully by sculpting a masterpiece, but eventually concludes, reluctantly, that the completed work has not lived up to his hopes. Nevertheless the novel is a work of such tremendous verve and ambition that it inevitably provokes admiration, and if the nutritive value of some of the food for thought that it contains is a trifle suspect, it is nevertheless a phenomenal feast. It might well be reckoned a flawed work of genius, or even a work of flawed genius, but genius it certainly possesses.

It appears probable, in retrospect, that the later phases of the episodic version of the story of Dieudonat seemed a little too downbeat to command the wholehearted affections of *Le Journal*'s readers, who would have preferred the comical and satirical element to retain more buoyancy. A judgment of that sort might have played some part in delaying the adaptation of the story for book publication, but Haraucourt was obviously undeterred by any such consideration, and the new material added to the full-length version, although certainly witty, taking the author's love of sarcasm and wordplay to extremes unreached in his other works, it is not at all conducive to frank hilarity.

Although the early part of the story is greatly expanded in the 1912 version—the ground covered in the first two *contes* is expanded to thirteen chapters (out of a total of thirty-seven)—the most dramatic shift is at the end of the story, where the brief final *conte* is expanded to ten chapters, which deepen the darkness of the black comedy to Stygian menace. The new text also adds an important additional character to the plot in the embittered poet Calame the Calamitous, who observes Dieudonat's decline and fall with horrified amusement, and ultimately comes to an intriguing judgment regarding the essence of his relationship with the hero. The epilogue, of which there is no foreshadowing in the newspaper version, allows Saint Peter to provide Dieudonat with a supposedly-definitive explanation why everything went awry for him and to sum up his eventual achievement, but the gradual evolution of Calame's somewhat contrasted and mordantly sentimental commentary is equally interesting.

On esthetic as well as philosophical grounds, the author's decision as to how to expand, reshape and finish off the narrative seeded and gestated in *Le Journal* was undoubtedly correct, and the work would not be nearly so remarkable if the author had not followed the logic of his argument where it led him, as far as it could possibly be taken. It is, in that regard, an essentially honest work, and if Dieudonat's hypothetical life story is compared with Haraucourt's actual experience of life, as recorded in his *Mémoires*, the depth and breadth of that honesty becomes appreciable. It is certainly not an "autobiographical novel" but it is a novel fully informed by the author's idiosyncratic experience of and relationship to family, religion, amour and the challenge of maintaining Effort in confrontation with the implacable hostility of circumstance. Haraucourt appears to have met that challenge successfully in life, and he met it in the finest examples of his literature too, as this text, because rather than in spite of its quirky eccentricity, clearly demonstrates.

This translation was made from the copy of the Arthème Fayard reprint reproduced on the Bibliothèque Nationale's *gallica* website. Some sections of the text pose considerable difficulties in translation because their wordplay and their frequent use of colloquialisms loses a great deal in crudely literal translation, but I have done my best to retain the flavor of the original by improvising somewhat in the substitution of appropriate English colloquialisms.

Brian Stableford

I. How Dieudonat came into the world and the strange circumstances that accompanied his birth

The story of Prince Dieudonat is a very fine story. Unfortunately, it is probably nothing but a tissue of lies; many considerations, in fact, encourage the belief that the gentleman never existed, and that reason would suffice to explain why no one can say in which country or century he lived. The most ingenuous contradictions, not to mention anachronisms, abound in regard to the personage. Undoubtedly, some erudite individual will succeed one day in bringing into rigorous accord the events that might never have happened; in the meantime we shall content ourselves modestly with following as best we can the thread of the more or less authentic adventures that several traditions and a few documents propose with enough good faith for the complaisance of our credulity.

There was once a couple of great feudatories, issued from royal stock, who governed an immense fief in the Empire; just like a King and Queen, they had their capital, their army and their subjects The Duke was named Hardouin, the Duchess Mahaut. They were God-fearing, and people feared them almost as much.

They were loved too because of the charity that the wife showed to the poor and the husband strove to render to all. It was said in whispers that he was not often in a judicious state of mind and that he sentenced at random. Equally, the servants at the castle claimed that he was much inclined to anger. They were not lying, but the Duke made it a principle not to make any decision in anger, which is a bad counselor, and the people understood the range of that good intention so well that, in order to express their gratitude for it they granted the lord a magnificent nickname; they called him Hardouin the Just. For custom dictated in those days that leaders were venerated in spite of their faults, just as it determines today they are hated for their qualities.

Everything, therefore, was for the best, save for one detail: the sovereign couple had no heir. That detail was important in the eyes of the people. They became anxious: what would happen when the present masters died? What exotic despot would come to take their place? Might the Emperor not profit from the circumstance to adopt the duchy, as a wolf adopts a lamb? Might he offer it to his son, Galeas? King Gaifer to the west and King Aimery to the east did not dissimulate their sympathy for those future orphans either, nor their intention to take them in guardianship. Now, the province was jealous of its autonomy; would it consent to be subject to a foreign yoke? Certainly not.

Blood would flow, then!

"Who will liberate us?"

There did exist, in the Court, one of the lord's bastards, who was already growing up and whose name was Ludovic. His father had sired him with an infidel woman under the walls of Jaffa, or some other Asiatic city, had baptized him, and then brought him back with his luggage out of the goodness of his heart; but to tell the truth, the child was Christian in name only, and no one doubted that he was possessed by the Devil by virtue of maternal heredity. Everyone knows that the Saracens are the issue of Hell, as indicated by the burned color of their skin, and that the blood of the fallen angels runs in their veins, propagating all the vices there.

The little bastard did his best to demonstrate these known verities. He lived in a perpetual fury, beating his servants, breaking his toys, torturing animals and ripping up his clothes. He rolled eyes as black as coals, and the Duchess never encountered him without trembling. As for the Duke, he testified an alarming tenderness for that child of his sin: Ludovic was handsome; Ludovic was intelligent; everything that Ludovic did provoked tearful laughter or wide-eyed admiration in his father.

The Duke often took the boy with the gilded skin between his knees and gazed into his eyes for a long time without saying anything; it was supposed then that the master was reflecting, although that was not in his habits; in reality, the former crusader was remembering similar eyes, and nights in Idumea, the memory of which rejuvenated him. The sessions of that contemplation never failed to end with a deep sigh, which was attributed to the apprehension of future days, but simply translated a regret for past nights.

Although there was cause for it, the effects of this predilection were feared; if the lord took it into his head to leave his fiefs and his crown to the dark-skinned boy, what a shame it would be for Christians to obey a Moor! Between that threat and the threat of foreign domination, where was salvation?

All salvation is in God. People had the good idea of addressing themselves to Him; on Sunday, and even during the week, thousands of prayers rose toward Heaven, to request therefrom a legitimate heir, an authentic scion of the sovereign and his veritable lady.

The supplications were heard on high.

One morning, the news spread that, in seven or eight months, the Duchess would bring into the world a male child. A daughter would have been no use, at least for what interested the people, and the latter did not hesitate in deciding that Heaven, since it was finally intervening, had the firm intention of being useful to the country.

The bells rang delightedly in the belfries of all the churches and convents; public prayers were organized to encourage God to continue His good work and prescribe that the future child really was a boy. They also wished that the prince would possess all the qualities of an excellent sovereign, and that desire was quite natural.

In order to be a good king, however, more virtues are required than to be a good man. That is why the saints in paradise were individually requested to furnish the embryo in question with the merits by which each of them was distinguished on earth; it was agreed between the faithful that every saint ought to bring his or her personal contribution, and to that end, would be individually solicited by all the Christians to which he or she had already testified a particular benevolence.

There is nothing like being in accord, and union makes strength; that precise organization had the result that was hoped. The saints of both sexes allowed themselves to be persuaded by the touching unanimity of an entire people; they judged that such a rare entente ought to be compensated, if only to set an example for peoples to come, and they interceded.

God listened to them. The child was made into a boy; then, day by day, during the months of the gestation, all the saints, at their annual festivals, brought their own particular virtues to him. Qualities of the mind as well as those of the heart arrived in the little fellow, numbered and classified, even before he was born. He also received the physical advantages: health, strength and beauty. For all these reasons it seemed appropriate to call him Dieudonat.

At the same time, in anticipation of immediate needs, the maidservants of the Duchess dressed a cradle and sewed swaddling clothes.

But the Devil, who never fails to get mixed up in our plans, watched these moral and material preparations; as is only just, he was anxious for his Ludovic, whose affairs were about to be compromised by that birth. For want of being able to make anything, he resolved to spoil everything, and add to the gifts of Heaven a present from Hell.

He drew up his plan: the Duchess would take charge of alerting him herself when the first pains extracted a cry from her, for our cries of pain are the Devil's daily bread, and he does not miss a single one. As soon as she screamed, he came running. Taking advantage of the disorder that reigned in the castle, he presented himself in the disguise of an old beggar woman.

In that era, sovereign ladies gave birth in public, to avoid substitutions of children, and access to the natal chamber was permitted to all. The Evil One penetrated without difficulty into the hall of honor where the chatelaine was lying on her splendid bed. Slipping between the chambermaids he came all the way to the cradle, and there he put his hands together hypocritically, with an expression of admiration, shed two tears on to the wrinkled skin of his cheeks and said:

"I too would like to make you a present, dear child, and this is mine: all your wishes will be granted irrevocably."

Who was very astonished, on hearing those words? The Duke, the Duchess and all the servants. It was thought that the old woman was a fay, and perhaps even the Madonna. Think of it! His wishes granted—all of them! What a gift! Emperors did not have as much, nor the Pope in Rome.

The Duke approached the old woman.

"Did I hear correctly, my Lady? The wishes of our child will be granted—all of them?"

"Yes indeed," said the Devil, "irrevocably."

The word "irrevocably" might have been able to disquiet reflective people, for, if one thinks about it, Death is the only irrevocable thing down here, and adding a second to it is, to say the least, imprudent. But people do not reflect, to begin with; they prefer, as a commencement, to jump for joy or sink into sadness, and to go back on their first impression later.

At any rate, events did not take long to prove that the Prince really did have all the virtues, and the Devil's present into the bargain.

II. Little Dieudonat demonstrates
his superior endowment

From the start, he had all the virtues: superb and plump, he suckled vigorously, digested well, sleep soundly and laughed at everything. In his slightest gestures the nurse and the chambermaids were pleased to admire the intervention of a saint; when his teeth came through he supported that pain with the constancy of a hero from whom plantations do not extract a cry.

"Saint Sebastian is protecting him! And Saint Edmond!"

When the suffering was too great, instead of wailing, he sang.

"Like Saint Cecilia."

When the women washed him, he showed his modesty by not hiding anything of his body, since the supreme chastity is not to know that it exists. If he ran away on all fours, stark naked, across the room:

"Like Saint Agnes, clad in her hair!"

He laughed as he crawled and stood up. He learned to walk very rapidly, and for his first steps he went away on his own.

"One would think he were Saint John in the desert!"

He learned to talk very quickly, remembering all words and their meanings from the outset. "*In principio erat verbum*,"[3] said the chaplain.

He was solid on his legs, and muscular. At the age of five he took pleasure in lifting burdens and carrying them with ease.

"By the will of Saint Christopher!"

He offered his toys to the pages, not wanting to keep any for himself.

"Saint Martin is inspiring him!"

---

[3] "In the beginning was the Word." (*John* 1:1)

He adored animals; he summoned the greyhounds in order to offer them his soup. He threw his bread to the sparrows and the pigeons that fluttered around him; he offered jam to bees on the tip of his little finger, and babbled affectionate speeches as he did so.

"There's Saint Francis!"

A donkey was his friend; he gave it roses to browse, after having carefully removed the thorns.

"Saint Dorothy, my patron saint!"

On the day when he entered his sixth year he was put on a living horse, by order of the Duke, and at the first gallop he fell off in the meadow; in his fall he saw a great light composed of thirty-six different lights.

"It's Saint Paul on the road to Damascus!"

He got up again, slightly dazed, and, like the saint, he understood the revelation; in consequence, he decided never to consent to be put in the saddle again, and no one ever put him on a saddle again, since his wishes were realized.

The Duke was desolate; his son ought to reign one day and lead his people, who could not reasonably be led by a pedestrian; it was necessary to make him a knight, and how can one conceive of a knight without a horse? The idea of that anomaly is still not admissible.

"Well," said the little Prince, "it's quite simple. I won't be a knight."

That scorn for honors disconcerted the nobles, and the townspeople even more so; it could only be explained by the inspiration of Saint Augustine or Saint Radegund, or perhaps Saint Bathilde, or several others who had disdained society; opinions were divided and debated.

The people would have argued even more if they had known what only his familiars were able to observe: at an age when children only ask to play, he played at asking. His questions were often very strange; his responses were even more ludicrous; he gave evidence there of a species of good sense that put him in discord with established usages, received opinions and even current locutions; he would fatally have passed for a simpleton if he had not been the Prince. But he was born in a high place and his ways of thinking came from higher still; people knew that and repeated it, and his listeners inclined instead of protesting, although devoted ears were often offended by his words.

In order to avoid that displeasure, and also in apprehension of the requests that could not fault to assail a young person all of whose wishes would be granted—and also in fear of the excesses that he might imagine if he were informed too soon of his extraordinary condition—the child, as soon as he was seven years old, was consecrated to solitude. All servants were distanced from him, especially maidservants; a law forbade anyone to speak to him, on pain of death; only the chaplain had that right, and was to proceed with the Prince's education.

The task of that tutor was initially too easy; soon, he became inadequate for it. As long as it was a matter of inculcating the child with elementary notions, the work went smoothly; he learned everything and forgot nothing. But Dom Ambrosius was not very knowledgeable, and his pupil very rapidly knew as much as he did; where the knowledge of the master reached its limit, the curiosity of the disciple did not stop, and they entered together into the domain of questions that remained without response—or, at least, any useful response. Understandably, the dignity of the pedagogue did not permit him to remain silent when he did not know how to respond; he therefore spoke, come what may, fatiguing the child with words that did not emerge from his mouth with the desirable facility, and which, once out, only produced around them an apparent satisfaction, because they did not signify anything.

The disciple was not content with those affirmations devoid of evidence, and the master was even more discontented that a nine-year-old boy, even one enlightened by the saints, dared to outstrip a doctor who, save for the vow of chastity, might have been his father, and was, at the least, his spiritual father. The young have the unfortunate tendency to want to go further than the old that is known as indiscipline; Dom

Ambrosius was greatly disturbed by it; he shook his head sadly and labored for hours trying to figure out which of two influences was exercised on the child, that of the Holy Spirit or that of Satan.

It was much worse when the Prince, as he grew older, asked about problems to which the tutor had never given any thought. The priest's perplexity became frightful. It seemed to him that his pupil as a sort of monster, as can be seen on the tympani of cathedrals: a hybrid, incoherent composite presenting the gigantic cranium of a demon over the winged shoulders of a cherub; for he was surely double, an excellent heart and a deplorable head. He gave proof of it continually.

One saw him, in fact, giving evidence of a frank and honest soul, a perfect probity, incapable of lying, and pushing charity to the point of showing himself irremediably cowardly before the dolor of others; he could not see them suffering without being affected all the way to the marrow; as for his own pains, when he had any, which was very rare, he supported them with and equable soul, with a sort of unconscious stoicism, which he owed to his mildness, his resignation and the scant regard he had for himself. In brief, on questions of sentiment, he never hesitated, and his instinct impelled him directly toward love and pity, without him even having to think, with evidently revealed a celestial inspiration.

On the contrary, as soon as it was a matter of knowing, not the Good but the True, the little wretch invented objections and demanded explanations, with ifs and buts, and a candor of reasoning before which no verity received mercy; he demolished them all, and in that, satanic inspiration was much more probable, since Satan is the demolisher *par excellence.*

However, probable as that influence of Hell was, it was not absolutely proven, and the priest, not feeling very sure, abstained from any definitive anathema for fear of offending God by confounding him with the Devil.

That uncertainty tortured him; it lasted for three years.

By virtue of seeing everything round him crumble at the breath of a boy, Dom Ambrosius arrived, involuntarily, at

25

sensing the fragility of even the most solid axioms; everything tottered, he lost his footing, and he was already trembling for the salvation of his soul. The good shelter and the good table of the castle no longer appeared to him to be a compensation for the perils of his charge. He thought about resigning his functions, without, however, making that capital resolution. But it is the rule, in human life, that the most important decisions are provoked by the smallest incidents, and the incident was produced at the moment when the priest least expected it.

III. First contact with the dirigible classes

It was produced in the course of a walk.

Dieudonat had left the castle in the company of Dom Ambrosius and they were strolling hygienically along the high road after the midday meal. It was a fine October day; a sky that was still lilac enveloped trees that were still yellow, behind which a tangle of leafless branches cast a background of violet haze. Mosses made a ground of bronze sewn with gold, and, amid the oblique rays of sunlight, the cold was darting its first arrows maliciously.

"There's a chill in the depths of the air," said the almoner.

"Where are the depths of the air, Monsieur l'Abbé?"

Without responding, the ecclesiastic raised his eyebrows, which is the most discreet way of indicating a desire to shrug one's shoulders.

"Come on, trot, run, act your age instead of walking like a margrave and cudgeling your brain."

"Well, Monsieur l'Abbé, my fur coat is heavy and I'm growing old."

"Eleven years, isn't it?"

"Indeed; I'm a decagenarian."

They followed the road, and suddenly saw, to their right, a little blue smoke rising between the trees. In a forest, the slightest event causes anxiety; perhaps we have conserved a hereditary memory of the times when our earliest ancestors lived in the depths of the woods, uncomfortable and devoid of security; it is even necessary to believe that the human species prolonged that existence for a long time, since fifty more-or-less civilized centuries have not yet sufficed to rid us of our prehistoric terrors.

With an instinctive prudence, the priest and his pupil veered to the left in order gradually to approach the middle of the road, but they continued walking straight ahead. Their courage was compensated and the scene that they beheld reassured them immediately.

In a minuscule clearing, under inoffensive birches, between a lively stream and a small fire of dead branches, a family was gathered, composed of a woman, a man, a donkey and five ragged children; that progeniture was staged year by year: five years old, four, three, two and twelve months, and the woman was pregnant. The father was weaving rush baskets while the donkey was attempting to browse, exhibiting a bare back. Close to the quadruped, a vehicle painted yellow, encumbered by dirty clothes, was somnolent on its rickety wheels.

Charitably, the priest observed: "God blesses numerous families."

"I can see that," replied the Prince.

He had stopped, and the poor children, sniffing the windfall of a rich man, advanced in Indian file in the hope of holding out their hands. The father doffed his cap and went back to work. In the resounding autumn, Dieudonat shouted: "Good day!"

But his tutor took hum by the arm and said to him, in a low voice: "Milord has forbidden you to talk to anyone, and you're going to catch vermin; come away."

The heir pulled away gently and advanced with a youthful smile toward the hearth of the proletarians.

"You must be cold," he said, "for the depths of the air aren't warm today."

"Nor the depths of the water," said the woman, who was extracting a clump of dishes from the stream.

She spoke without amenity, and Dieudonat was chagrined by that. He thought: *The poor lack indulgence for the rich, and perhaps they aren't wrong.*

The woman wiped her wet hands on the fustian of her dress, and the future gentleman was slightly ashamed of his gloved hands; he hid them behind his back. The he saw the mother pick up her youngest child from the grass and install him in the vehicle, bringing the flap of a white sheet over him;

he felt even more ill at ease in his heavy fur coat. At the very least, he wanted to be amiable, and he sought a means of beginning; he had some difficulty finding one.

"Is he comfortable there, the little boy?"

The mother grunted: "It's a girl." Then, without paying any further heed to the youth, she went to stoke up the fire under the cooking-pot.

But Dieudonat wanted to chat. "Does the little girl like traveling in the vehicle?"

"When it goes," replied the father. "Otherwise, she cries."

"Do you travel a great deal?"

"As much as is necessary to sell."

"Do you live far away?"

"We live everywhere."

"I mean, is the house where you sleep far from here?"

"It's there."

"That open vehicle? You sleep there? In the open air?"

"Wherever we happen to be."

"And you can all fit into it?"

"We aren't fat, we pile ourselves up, the heaviest at the bottom, with the sheet on top."

"Oh!" The Prince was profoundly astonished, and the father scarcely less so, on seeing someone astonished by such a simple thing.

The child said: "So that vehicle is like a kind of nest, in the woods, a nest on wheels..."

The man laughed heartily.

"And your children are like chicks..."

"One is what one can be."

The disciple of Dom Ambrosius turned to his tutor, who appeared to him to be the representative of human society on the deserted road, and his gaze implored an explanation of the excessive difference that existed between the sons of Adam.

"It seems to me," he said, "that these people have prolonged a trifle belatedly the mores and habits of the terrestrial paradise. I believe that they are mistaken, for the temperature has changed considerably since our common ancestor, and the depths of the air have become chilly."

Deliberately, he took off his overcoat and he approached the vehicle; the oldest of the children had just climbed into it, in order to demonstrate is talents, and was huddled against his younger sister. Smiling at them, Dieudonat extended his fur coat over them.

"Little brothers," he said, "here's a little down for your nest."

The mother left her cooking-pot and ran to the children. The father dropped his rushes.

"Say thank you, Hans. Say thank you to the lord who has given you a beautiful cloak.

But Hans lowered his nose and did not say a word, he pulled the fine new cover over his shoulder and sniggered slyly.

"Hans!" exclaimed the vagabond.

"Don't spoil his pleasure," said the ducal child, "but I beg you, why do you call him anse?"[4]

"Hans; it's a name."

"In your country, doubtless?"

"Perhaps; I don't know."

"Where did you get the idea of giving him such a name?"

"It's mine, and that of my father and grandfather too."

"Ah?"

"Yes. It's like a rule in the family that the eldest son is always called Hans. The old man told me, and his father told him, and I'll tell the kid when he grows up."

"For what reason?"

"Well, I can't explain it, but it appears that it must go back to another grandparent, in times past, who must have made something good for his epoch; he had that name and then it became a rule that the eldest would have the same name as him, in memory of him."

"You don't know what he did, your ancestor?"

---

[4] *Anse* means handle, or cove.

"No one knows anymore."

"What was his name?"

"Hans."

"I understand that—but his other name."

"Oh, our name? Gutenberg."

"Hans Gutenberg is your ancestor?"

"Father to son. Have you heard of him? What did he make?"

"A world."

The vagabond stated to laugh, and the youth contemplat ed him. He saw a thick and dirty beard, eyes imprinted with kindness rather than intelligence, and a low and already wrinkled forehead.

"Do you know how to read, Hans Gutenberg?"

"Read? How would that help me to make baskets? No, I don't know how to read."

The traveler laughed heartily. Dieudonat felt some unease, and also a slight chill in his back; he no longer had his coat. He turned toward the almoner, pitifully, who concluded: "You'll catch cold now, without a cloak; it's necessary to get moving and go home."

"You're right, Father. Let's go."

The father and mother ran on to the road, yelping: "Thank you very much, my good lord, thank you. Another time!"

The Prince took off his cap. "I salute you, Hans Gutenberg."

Then he set forth, while the couple, leaning over the vehicle, picked up the cloak and weighed it, caressed the fur and searched the sleeves, where they found an Oriental silk handkerchief, forgotten there.

"Necessary to return it," said the man.

"Are you mad?" said the woman. "He has others at home, that fellow."

In the meantime, Dieudonat was walking with his head bowed.

"It's sad, Father."

31

"Trot," replied Dom Ambrosius. "Warm yourself up."

"I think..."

"You can reflect at home. I don't criticize you for imitating Saint Martin, but it's still appropriate not to catch cold. Trot."

In order to conciliate obedience with his personal desire, the adolescent started trotting on the spot alongside his tutor, and while he was hopping he followed his train of thought."

"Why did Saint Martin only give away half his cloak, Father?"

"In order to keep the other half, my friend, and, in so doing, he was obeying the Lord strictly, who recommends us to love our neighbor as much as ourselves, and not more; with the result that those two equal parts are presented to us as a symbol of equality in fraternity."

"One can also suppose that that cloak had no sleeves, for its two halves would have been inconvenient."

"It was a cape. Run now."

"And then, that fraternal equality—I'm running, as you see, Father—scarcely seems to me to exist in people."

"Run, I tell you, and in order that our encounter with a fallen family should be of some advantage to you, you can do your next writing assignment on family heredity and the inequality of social conditions. A debating point, that's all."

The master had the habit of concluding speeches and discussions with that final formula. The pupil lengthened his stride and as soon as he was in his room he started working with a zeal whose results were, in every respect, deplorable.

Departing from the principle that, in order to come into the world, he had needed a father and a mother, who had previously had the same need, he extended his genealogy and discovered, with amazement, that only twenty generations required more than two million ancestors. Extending his calculation to the first century of the Christian Era, he came to observe that, since that not very remote era, he had personally collected eighteen quadrillion, fourteen trillion, five hundred and eighty-three billon, three hundred and thirty-three million, three hundred and thirty-three thousand three hundred and thirty-three forefathers, and as many mothers.

"Wow! I knew that our family possessed a respectable number of ancestors, and that the number in question makes our nobility, but I didn't realize that I was as noble as that. For by myself I have more ancestors than the earth has had human beings since the world began. That's very curious. Not to mention has the priest has as many for his part and that little Hans has no fewer, and that each of our servants, not excepting the scullions, has an equal number."

He checked his calculations, which he found to be accurate.

"There's no error; let's draw conclusions. Since the total of a single family is greater than the total of humankind, it's therefore the case that the same individuals have served several times. Not only must they figure simultaneously in different branches of the same genealogical tree, but they must be represented there with an indubitable frequency; consanguineous crosses and recrosses must be effected in stupefying proportions, and every alliance or misalliance has sufficed to introduce into the closest families an incalculable number of relatives..."

Still ignorant of the existence of illicit amours, he was only tabulating marriages, without any hypothesis regarding the intrusions that hazard, tender grass and travels, might effect, and, in general, all the circumstances foreseen and forbidden by God's ninth commandment.

"We're all cousins, that's evident, and it's even a matter of mathematical necessity that we're cousins an indefinite number of times over. Our groom descends in a direct line from Charlemagne, just as the traveler descends for Gutenberg: a fallen branch And I too am a Capetian. A debating point, that's all."

He closed his notebook.

"Without any doubt, that verity is little known, to judge by the harsh and arrogant relations people have with one another; it would be rendering them a precious service to inform them of the error into which they've fallen in believing in different castes; if they knew their parentage better, they'd treat one anther more kindly, and that would simplify many things."

As little as he had learned about the world and social life, he had divined much more, and his precocious intelligence, connecting effects and causes, saw clearly that arrogance engendered abuses, which caused misery, which gave birth to rancor. His little head started working hard on that theme, for a good hour, at the end of which he wished that he were able to divulge to the powerful and the humble the useful verity that his arithmetic had just put into the world.

A wish? The Devil was only waiting for that.

IV. First contact with the directing classes

Expressly to satisfy his wish, and at the very moment that he formulated it, something happened a few leagues away. Everything is connected down here; the world, which we believe to be very large, is very small, and becoming smaller and smaller. At the moment when we are thinking about it the least, people that are out of sight, whom we do not know, and of whom we have no suspicion, are weaving our destiny without knowing it.

When Dieudonat made his wish, Archduke Galeas, the heir to the Empire, was sitting in his palace, where he had been royally bored for a fortnight. Suddenly, he got up, moved by a sudden impulse; it would have astonished him, even more than someone else, if it had been revealed to him that the impulse in question had not emanated from his own free will, and that a spring had pushed him.

Once on his feet, Galeas the One-Eyed declared his formal intention of undertaking, without delay, a journey through the kingdoms and duchies whose homage he would soon receive; perhaps he would even discover, in the course of that excursion, a spouse capable of curing his ennui.

"We leave tomorrow!"

The decisions of that powerful lord were not among those that one questions; the preparations were ordered immediately, and six days later, His Serene Highness, surrounded by a sumptuous escort, penetrated into the lands of Hardouin, the first vassal of the Empire.

In order to feed his future Suzerain appropriately, the Duke had had hundreds of domestic and wild animals slaughtered, which the cooks butchered. He had also had Dom Ambrosius draft a beautiful speech, which he learned by heart, although the heart had nothing to do with it, in which he expressed his joy at receiving such an august personage.

When the couriers informed him of Galeas' approach, he went out to meet him, in great pomp, but very troubled, having is son to his right and the chaplain to his left, preceded by his men-at-arms and followed by his pages in furbelows. He rode with as much majesty as possible and, while riding, his eyes intense and his lips mobile, he repeated his difficult speech.

Soon, the two troops were in one another's presence, and the trumpets sounded. The old lord got down from his horse, and advanced toward the Archduke, who was waiting for him on foot, beneath his banners.

It's true, though, that he's one-eyed.

That observation occupied the orator so much that it became impossible for him to think about anything else. *One-Eyed... One-Eyed...* The fixity of that unique eye ended up troubling his memory; he recited his compliment very poorly, which irritated him against everyone, especially the chaplain. Galeas' eye only expressed a demi-satisfaction. A second fanfare put an end to the Duke's embarrassment, and the heralds of the Empire invited Dieudonat to present himself for the genuflection.

The later advanced, full of cordiality, and, instead of bending his knee, he extended his hand, saying "Good day, cousin."

The heir to the Empire frowned, and muttered: "Are we in the land of fools?"

Dom Ambrosius shoved his pupil from behind. "Kneel down, then!"

But Dieudonat started laugh. "Why would I kneel down, except to pray to God or play marbles?"

The Archduke turned to his master of ceremonies. "Have I not heard that his fellow refuses us homage?"

A disquieting breeze shook the leaves of the aspens, and very valiant warriors felt a chill at the roots of the hair beneath their helmets.

But Dieudonat paid no heed to that; a more interesting spectacle attracted his attention; he had just perceived Gutenberg's cart on the road, behind the halberdiers, which had just come over the top of a hill. Sergeants-at-arms moved the donkey and the carter off the road, but the oldest of the children, with two of his brothers, slipped under the horses, in spite of thrusts with the hafts of the halberds; in the end, that ragged and pale-faced trio appeared between the thigh-guards of the nobility.

Galeas let fall upon the human ants a gaze as heavy as a sledgehammer. The good Duke Hardouin, furious at the scandal, swore internally to hang the bandits who were giving such a deplorable idea of his people and his police.

It was then that Dieudonat took young Hans by his tattered sleeve and drew him into the middle of the circle.

"My dear cousin," he said, "I present our cousins the Gutenbergs to you."

"What?"

"Yee, yes. yes, my cousins and yours! As much as you and me, these descend from Hercules, and the blood in their veins is as royal as yours and mine; I've discovered that, and will explain it to you this evening, after supper."

The heir of thirty-four emperors did not want to hear any more; he turned his back and shouted: "My horse!"

Everyone understood; a page brought the charger; the Archduke grasped the mane and leapt into the saddle. Hardouin tried to improvise a supplication, but his voice was lost in the clash of iron horseshoes, for Galeas' horse had reared up and pivoted on its hind feet. The Archduke rode away; his men followed.

The fearful Ambrosius made multiple signs of the cross and recommended himself to Heaven.

"What's happening; my God, what's going to happen?"

For a long moment the Duke remained motionless in the middle of the road, abashed, contemplating the backs of the departing escort. Then, whipped by indignation, he climbed on to his mount, as the Archduke had just done, but with less agility. He dug in his spurs, and such was his fury against Dieudonat, Galeas, Ambrosius, travelers and emperors that he bloodied the flanks of his horse, a complete stranger to human affairs. Where was he going? To his manor, in order to hide his shame there; the plumes of his crest fluttered in his wake and a cloud of dust swirled behind him. Road-menders at work watched the master's equestrian wrath go past and shook their heads, thinking: *That's bad. Something's going badly.*

The Duke withdrew to his bedroom, where he broke various objects that came to hand; when he could not find any more, he tore his garments; that initial task occupied him for half an hour, after which, the powerful lord sat down in order to catch his breath, for he had great need of it. Faithful to his principal of not deciding anything in anger, he wanted to wait until his soul was in repose.

Serenity only returned to him at nightfall. Then he summoned the chaplain, in order to demand an explanation from him of the strange attitude his disciple had adopted.

Dom Ambrosius appeared; he had no confidence, and remained on the threshold.

"Advance, Dom Ambrosius. I'm calm; pull yourself together. I like you, you know that; I entrusted you with the education of my son, and that's evidence of my great esteem; but I'm not content. What is he doing to us, and what mania has gripped him? Can you explain that conduct?"

"Milord, I'll tell you; it's because of arithmetic..."

"I don't know arithmetic, but it was up to you to forbid it to him, if it's incompatible with the most elementary duties."

"Milord, that child is too well-endowed. He destroys everything!"

"Bah! It's the Holy Spirit that moves him; but you're his tutor, you ought to direct his mind."

"He escapes me, Milord. He goes too quickly. He only has to say: 'I want to understand,' and he understands. He understands too much; he understands everything, final causes and original causes, consequences and subsequences, everything, Milord! 'I want to understand.' That's it. His wish is granted and nothing can resist it. Doubtless thanks to the Devil, for he reasons, Milord! No verity can stand up to it: heresy lies in wait."

"Box his ears."

"He receives cuffs with an angelic mildness, Milord; he's even delighted when I slap him, because it proves, he says, that I have nothing to respond and that his judgment is sound."

"Prevent him from reading!"

"I assure you, Milord, that books haven't perverted him. I possess very few, but they're good books, and among those I offer him he can no longer tolerate any but geometry and the Gospel."

"You mean the Gospels "

"No, Milord. He has deliberately suppressed three of them, which inhibit his belief in the fourth."

"Edify him with the reading of Holy Scripture."

"He isn't edified at all. He admires the prophets, but if you heard how he judges Abraham and Jacob, David and Solomon, Judith and Delilah! He's always in favor of the vanquished or the lame, and he asked me one day—I scarcely dare repeat such a blasphemy, Milord—whether the Holy Bible isn't the history of all the vices, recounted to children in order to teach them what people ought not to do. Doesn't he imagine that every patriarch incarnates a deadly sin and that the God of Israel summarizes them all in himself. He sustains that Jehovah is the brother of Moloch."

"I don't know this Moloch, or his family, but I know that it's necessary to honor God the Father, and everything you're telling me about that child is evidence of a great deal of pride."

"No, Milord. He's modest and considers himself to be the brother of the humblest animals; he talks to them and listens to them, like Saint Francis, and I imagine that they're the only company in which he takes pleasure—but what I'm very sure of is that he prefers it to mine."

"Is that possible?"

"He converses with ants more gladly than with me, and he draws aphorisms from their frequentation that would make your hair stand on end. To hear him, the beasts possess the maximum of verity permitted to terrestrial creatures, with the minimum of pretention; he concludes therefrom that they obtain thus a relative quietude, which is the maximum of happiness, and that's why. Milord, not only does he admire them but I can assure that, times, he envies them."

"Well, let's be careful. His wishes are realized, and if he has a whim to be a dog or a pig..."

"He won't, Milord. Because his excess of intelligence has allowed him to discover the limits of intelligence, he declares that a limited understanding engenders unlimited error..."

"Ta ta ta... I don't understand any of this nonsense. Speak more clearly, Father."

"In other terms, Milord, it comes down to saying that he couldn't consent to risk, on his own part, the error of making a decision."

"Father, Father! What are you saying? He'll have to make decisions when he reigns in my place."

"I greatly fear, Milord, that that child is too intelligent to accept a throne. He'd judge himself unworthy of it, and resign it out of conscience."

"Father, Father! My people are counting on him, and I've counted on you! You've brought up my son badly, and I'll have you hanged."

"It's not my fault, Milord. It's the fault of the Holy Spirit!"

"Shall I hang the Holy Spirit, and are you advising me to do it, wretch that you are?"

"Please, Milord, don't be angry!"

"That's well said, Father; a judge ought to abstain from all passion, when delivering his sentences. Don't say any more, and let me think."

A few moments went by.

"I've reflected, Abbé. It's quite certain that you've misdirected a well-endowed child. That's a grave fault; I'm a sovereign full of justice, who ought not to leave any fault unpunished; come here, so that I can embrace you, for I love you with all my heart and I'm very sorry about what is happening to you."

He embraced Dom Ambrosius, whom he did indeed like a great deal, and in order to be quite sure that his personal sentiments would not impede the work of his justice, he ordered that he be hanged without delay.

Dom Ambrosius did his best to protest, but with no success. He was simply hung from the crenellations, because his humble birth did not permit him to pretend to the honor of decapitation.

V. How the young Prince quit the castle
of his forefathers

The next day, when he woke up, Dieudonat, who lodged in the north tower, put his nose to his window in order to see the morning, and immediately perceived, under the machicolations, the long body of his tutor, which was hanging at the end of a rope. He was profoundly moved, for his sentiments of commiseration always came to him first, and he wept for that companion of all his hours. Then he was astonished that such a worthy ecclesiastic had been put to death, and wondered what crime he could have committed. Finally, he thought that every living creature is, by definition, a fallible creature, and that Dom Ambrosius had doubtless failed, like anyone else.

Thus, he went to the good lord his father to enquire about the fault, and his amazement became much more considerable when he leaned that the tutor was expiating between two crenellations the deviations of his disciple. He estimated, and declared without hesitation, that ducal justice was mistaken, and that logically, it was necessary to take down the almoner, if there was still time, and very quickly, from the place that was rightfully his.

He went up on to the platform, and perhaps he would have been hanged, since all his wishes were granted, but the priest had died the previous evening; a second execution would not have repaired the wrongs of the first, and the Prince resigned himself to the fait accompli, as he was accustomed to do, already being very wise. He contented himself with taking down personally the old friend who had boxed his ears so often in order to teach him think like everyone else, and had not succeeded..

On going back down the stone staircase he meditated on ill-timed justice; he was compelled to condemn those who permitted others to be condemned, and who dared to take away life, being incapable of returning it subsequently if they perceived that they would have been better not to touch it.

He venerated and loved his father, as God prescribes in the fourth commandment, but no veneration could alter the fact that the father in question had showed himself to be unwittingly unintelligent and ferocious, in the manner of bulls and tigers, which are animals. He declared that respectfully to the author of his days, and, in the same breath, with a gaze full of tears and tenderness, told him that he would always persist in venerating and loving him such as God had made him—which is to say, like a beast.

On hearing those words, the Duke flew into a violent rage and had Dieudonat thrown into a profound, very damp dungeon, where the Prince continued to meditate in the company of rats.

Before the end of the first day, he arrived at the conclusion that power is a very unhealthy thing for humans, which ought to be dreaded rather than desired, since it multiples opportunities for error and sin. In order to ask God to spare him such a mission he threw himself on his knees, taking great care not to crush any rats, and prayed from the depths of his soul.

His prayer was granted, naturally, and this is how. After a week, Hardouin the Just summoned his heir, laden with chains, and called upon him to retract the words that he had spoken and ask for forgiveness for them.

"You ask forgiveness, Father. I want that, and with all my heart, if I have been able to cause you chagrin by observing your lack of intelligence. As for retracting what I said, I do that wholeheartedly also, Father, if I was wrong so say what I thought when my thought was of a nature to cause you pain, and if it is better to lie than to cause chagrin to those I love, as I believe."

"So, you miserable runt, to say that I'm not a beast is lying?"

"That lie, Father, I am willing to tell for you, and to assume the remorse for that sin, so much do I love you and venerate you, for I believe that, in the perpetual conflict of our incompatible duties, the duties that come first and exclude the others are the duties of love."

The Duke leapt from his throne and came in person to slap the heir of a long race; his indignation was even so violent that, at the moment of the slap he forgot to open his hand; that simple distraction was sufficient to make the paternal hand into a fist.

"A fist, that's all," said Dieudonat.

Almost immediately, he felt a tooth that was wandering over his tongue like a pastille; he took it out between his thumb and index finger and said: "I'm quite content Father, for Dom Ambrosius had the custom of striking me on the cheek every time I had reasoned correctly, and I must have reasoned better than usual today, for you strike harder than Dom Ambrosius."

"Execrable insolent, you won't have my crown. I disinherit you!"

"You're fulfilling my desires, Father, in granting me, in exchange for the perilous diadem, the serenity of my days to come."

"Excrement of the earth, get out! I expel you."

"Be blessed, Father, for that word, which makes me a free man."

"Free! I'll imprison you in a convent!"

"I have no objection to that, Father, for you'll only imprison my body. In the week that I've been in prison, I've learned this: the mind travels further when the body remains tranquil. Lock me up, in order that my thoughts will be free."

"Out of my presence, villain!"

"May God keep you in his holy protection and grant you his protection, Father."

"Out! Out!"

"So be it."

The Duchess begged, rolled on the floor, wrung her arms and cried that her son was mad, and that it is necessary to forgive madmen, but in vain; the Duke remained inexorable.

Dieudonat was led away under guard and taken to the convent of Fortunada, which was far away in the mountains. In order to get there it was necessary to go up and down many hills, along paths scarcely frayed between the rocks, and to pass over torrents that rushed into the hollows of gulfs. The Prince had never seen anything so beautiful. Inviolate trees had been growing here for centuries; unknown flowers boomed in peaceful corners; the depths of the precipices were blue, and when a fire was lit in the evening, the smoke rose straight up toward the calm of the sky.

"Oh, what a magnificent country, imposing and pious! Don't you find, Captain, that these mountains, with their summits and gorges, invite the soul to prayer?"

"Silence!"

"They went into the monastery. Along with his guest, the prior received an order to make sure that he did not communicate with anyone at all, and the order added: *Above all, and in the interest of our Estates, it is important not to reveal to the Prince that he has the faculty of realizing his wishes; the prior and his monks will answer for that with their lives.*

In order to reinforce that advice with an argument that had all the vigor of a threat, the Duke sent the good Fathers the mortal remains of his defunct almoner and friend; he asked them to give him a worthy funeral, as he had given him a sound justice, and thanked them in advance.

The venerable prior appreciated the scope of that double advice in its full extent, and took his measures. The dead man had a crypt and the living one a cell.

Nevertheless, in order to forearm the neophyte against the temptations of ennui, he was authorized to borrow whatever he desired from the library of the convent, reputed to be the richest in the entire world, which contained thousands of works.

VI. Dieudonat makes a tour of human science and returns from that long voyage

The well-endowed child installed himself in his next existence with delight; his habitation pleased him, and the idea of being at home, having his own lodgings, an inaccessible retreat devoid of slaps and a tutor filled him with virile pride as well as gratitude toward the benefactors who had made him that present.

"How comfortable it is here! What a delightful little castle!"

The castle consisted of two superimposed rooms communicating by means of a miller's ladder. On the upper floor there was a bed, a prie-Dieu, a table and a chair; on the ground floor, a small table for meals, a shelf, a stool, tools for carpentry and gardening. Aliments came through a hole pierced in the wall, and the only door opened into a square garden—minuscule, to tell the truth, but between the walls of which an enormous expanse of sky was perceptible, in which the clouds filed past in complete liberty.

"Not to mention that I'm in a splendid location! I can't see it, but I saw it when I arrived, and I know its beauty!"

He could not weary of admiring his domain, his wealth and the independent future that all those possessions promised him.

"I'm my own master! So young! I'm being spoiled! What sublime things I'm going to read in those big books! My father was cruel to my tutor, but he's been generous to me; paternal tenderness inspired his heart when he imagined sending me to this place of delights. Isn't prescribing me solitude while permitting me books simply dispensing me from conversation with people who have nothing to say and limiting me to those who speak in order to say something? With Dom Ambrosius I was alone, while I shall now have the society of the noblest minds that existed in all times. A book is a soul

46

that confesses; add that one can interrupt it without having to apologize, one can reply to it without having one's ears boxed, one can raise a objection to a stupidity without being obliged to blush, and one can even shut it, as one can't shut people. It's admirable!"

He set about reading all the books.

In between times, he cultivated his garden during the mild seasons, or worked with wood in the days of winter. Then he resumed reading. At his command, at his choice, philosophers and the Fathers of the Church, scientists and historians, and also poets, filed through his cell and sat on his lectern. He knew all the great men of humankind, the great events and the great ideas; his brain became parallel to the world, and as vast as time.

That task had been fecund at first in intellectual sensualities; every time that beauty surged forth before his mind's eye, every time that the truth lifted a corner of the veil, his entire being was impregnated with glad light, and his eyes brightened with an interior fire.

But so many successive illuminations, provoking one after another an emotion that was always the same, ended up only having the value of a phantasmagoria, and the universal reader became anxious.

"I admire the forms, and the skill that produced those forms or formulae; I admire the subtlety of human genius, an acrobat and conjurer; but it seems to me that in total, I'm not being given very much. Of what am I sure? Very little; and the more I'm instructed, the less sure I am, since, to every one of these beautiful sentences, another replies to demonstrate the contrary to me; when I know them all, they'll all have been belied, and I'll be left without anything.

He was at that point in his thoughts when, one morning, he heard the sound behind his garden wall of stones, hammers, sawn beams, shifted earth, wheeled trucks and voices conversing vigorously, with cries and oaths. Being naturally inclined to pity, he felt sorry for the people who were going to so much trouble while he was so tranquil. The racket lasted until nightfall, and from then on, that rumor of an invisible labor was renewed every day. Undoubtedly, the foundations were being laid there of some building, perhaps a church. The young monk was not astonished by that, having observed elsewhere that priests, much more than the common run of men, are haunted by the passion of erecting edifices, as if their celibacy found in that chaste creation a pasture for the desire to engender and to leave on earth a prolongation of themselves.

The noises continued and they were embellished by songs. Reading and study became difficult, but Dieudonat never became impatient and he was always able to look at the good side of things. In any case, his neighbors interested him, as did their mysterious work; he waited, sometimes looking at the crest of his wall. After some lapse of time, the wood of a scaffolding extended in the sky; later, the heads of masons appeared, and then their shoulders, their torsos, their entire bodies; then a section of wall appeared in perspective above the enclosure, and the building rose up without discontinuity.

Dieudonat became increasingly interested; he saw the workmen adding rows of stones to rows of stones. Indubitably, a church was being born; already, the lateral wall was braced by perforated buttresses from which pinnacles protruded; it was illuminated by rose-windows and ogives traversed by slender mullions; it was displayed in its width, and departed into the air again, still rising. The thing nonexistent yesterday existed today, and the monks piled up the cubes on the masses, and the thing rose ever higher.

On seeing it augmented thus, the adolescent shivered with internal effort and collaborated with all his muscles. Seized by a spirit of emulation and avid to act, without knowing it, he got up from his seat and only came back to get up from it again. He arched his back and stretched his spine in order to pick up folio volumes, with a need to find them very heavy and an air of wanting to pass them to the masons.

He could not hold still anymore; he solicited an audience with the prior and asked him: "Father, how long have I been in this cell?"

"Seven years, my child."

"Can it be? Seven years already? I've lost seven years of my life!"

"The time a man spends endowing his mind is not time lost, my son, and if Milord the Duke, relaxing the rigors of your reclusion, authorized us to utilize your knowledge in consecrating it to the instruction of our brothers..."

"Teach! I couldn't do that, Father; I've read too much. Between so many contradictory affirmations of genius, how would I have the presumption to accord preference to one to the detriment of another, and attest which one is sound? That would have been possible when I knew almost nothing, but at present, I know too much, and I'm not capable of teaching."

The prior shook his head. "What you're telling me there is bad, my child; it is necessary to be sure of the truth and to believe it. I believe the truth."

"Because you only know one, Father, and I have much of which to complain in knowing several, since they are incompatible."

"I'll grant you that Metaphysics provides matter for debate, at least insofar as it does not attain the Faith, but History has procured you certainty, for it relates to facts, and facts are undeniable."

"The number of facts that are uncontested is relatively considerable, yes, Father, and I have not encountered anyone to deny the death of Charlemagne or the ruination of Nineveh, but on the matter of what engendered those events and what their soul was, the profound causes that alone are capable of revealing to us the meaning of life, there is never agreement, and History is nothing without that."

"The testimony of men who have seen..."

"Is error or lies; the explanation of facts is only pure hypothesis; History and Legend are two sisters worth as much as one another, but one speaks and the other sings. I can no longer teach history."

"Fall back on the sciences."

"Oh, science, Father, what an admirable trampoline of enthusiasm and vertigo, and how it launches us to the edge of infinity! But only to the edge, alas, and the very clarity of the conceptions that it permit us renders our impotence to go any further crueler. To everything, a limit exists that human understanding will never surpass, and our heads always bump into the pitiless wall of an enigma that humans cannot penetrate."

"The mysteries..."

"At the terminus of everything I have found mystery! Science only leads us to the inaccessible, and if some genius reached us from a world where minds are superior to ours, in order to reveal to us what we do not know, we would listen to him open-mouthed, and we would not be able to understand."

"Pride is laboring you, I see..."

"Because I have acquired the notion of sitting on the last step of the ladder of thinking beings?"

"You think too far, my young friend, and that is why you have lost your footing. Your ambition is leading you astray beyond your strength, in purely speculative theories, and it's a grave imprudence to want to go so high, for humans can only draw away from the earth without peril with the aid of the Faith, and under its constant tutelage. Let me finish: to criticism I will add consolation, by assuring you that your labors will not remain entirely sterile; they have prepared you for wisdom, for prudence, for the day when Milord the Duke, in quitting his world, will leave you his crown to wear and his people to lead."

"Reign over my fellows? Can you think so, Father? How can I pretend to lead them, when I recognize myself incapable of instructing them? I wonder how Heads of State dare to walk, eat, sleep, go up or down stairs, sit down or get up, when they know that a gesture of their finger, or their abstention from making that gesture, can overturn lives, annihilate forces and stimulate others, engender life or death, and prepare the future!"

"One does one's best; Heaven will enlighten you."

"By enlightening the fors and againsts? For it ought to enlighten both at the same time, since the two coexist and no contingency is completely good or totally bad. And that is what is terrible, Father, enlightening at the moment of action! I imagine that at that moment it is necessary no longer to see anything, and that if you have the misfortune, at that supreme moment, still to be examining the decision to make, with everything that is contrary to it, you would not make it Father. Me neither."

"You would make it, my son, with the aid of God and the firm intention of becoming a benefactor of human beings."

"Yes, indeed! I would form projects immediately deformed by those in view of which I meditated the good, and from which evil would emerge. I know very little of the world, Father, only having studied it in books, but I know enough to glimpse that every idea is perverted as soon as it becomes action. I shall not act. Or, at least, I shall not act in the fashion of kings."

"I understand you, my young prince; you consider, fundamentally, that the authority of sovereigns is a lure of vanity far more than an effective power; you disdain their role, because you suspect their strength of not being real; if I have understood correctly, you estimate that each of their names is planted in history like a golden nail that supports the weight of common actions and the responsibility of all?"

"Perhaps. They direct, but they do not lead; no power is absolute."

"Except for that of God, my son. God alone can do what he wishes."

By way of reply, Dieudonat picked up a sculpted bronze hand-warmer from the table and presented it gravely to the old monk. "Father, could God make this ball cease being round?"

"Assuredly, if he deigned to want it"

"But could God determine that the ball had never been round?"

The venerable priest started with indignation, but made no reply.

Dieudonat added, tranquilly: "I said, Father, and without exception, that no power is absolute."

"And I say that books have done you no good. They have maddened your miserable reason with pride!"

"Very miserable, yes. I know all its misery and sterility."

"Return to your cell. You will not read any more!"

"In fact, I no longer want to read; I believe I even declared that to you, having come expressly for that. For I've perceived your masons, Father, and they're working. Now, after so many lost years, I also want now to devote myself to real work, no matter how humble it might be. You're irritated against me, Father, and I wouldn't be any less so than you if the appreciations of my mind derived from my will instead of imposing upon it, as they do and ought to do. Deign to believe me; the sole role to which I aspire to the render myself useful, in a small way. Send me to join the masons, whom I envy and admire."

"Milord has forbidden you any contact with the outside; his orders are formal."

"In that case, Father, find me a task inside, a true task that serves my fellows, I beg you."

"I'll think about it, and when I've obtained Milord's assent, we'll se. Go."

The Prince went back to his cell, with the satisfaction of a man who has just decided to take the better path.

He closed all his books, saluted them politely, thanked them and bid them adieu.

A monk came to take them away in silence.

VII. The heir presumptive of a throne
discovers a better career

The prior meditated, consulted his chapter, and informed the sovereign that, seven years of solitary study having exasperated the pride of the young prince, necessity imposed recourse to new remedies to bring his mind back to sentiments of a more Christian humility.

That news fell into the Court like rain into a frog-pond; a great racket resulted from it. The Duke's anger had calmed down a little over time, but in the murky souls of fools the rancor of vanity only ever sleeps lightly, always ready to croak at the slightest sound that awakens it; Hardouin's started.

"Oh, the criminal, the miscreant! Oh, the incorrigible heretic! A leper without a rattle! A donkey without a stick, a hood without a head! A runt who isn't even capable of mounting a horse dares to have ideas! I'll give you ideas! I'll show you what kind of wood I warm myself with! I'm Hardouin the Just!"

The bastard encouraged him. "Assuredly, my young brother is burned by pride; all that we can hope for him is that he makes his salvation in a cloister, and even that will be difficult for him, with the doctrines he professes. Outside of that refuge he'll only be able to do harm and spread dangerous errors among your people."

"Horns of Beelzebub, that's certain!" cried the Duke.

"Really?" said the Duchess. "How is that possible for a child endowed by all the saints?"

"Endowed by the Devil, Madame! Know that children too well endowed make the despair of families."

"And the misery of the world," added Ludovic, "as soon as they become men."

He added many other things, talking by turns about royal security, public tranquility, moral outrage, the present and the future, and he spoke so well that the necessity appeared evident of averting so many perils. At all costs, it was necessary to reduce to impotence a pretender who was known to be too inclined to insubordination, and the mildest, most indulgent and most paternal way was to cut his hair definitively, in default of the head.

The Duchess fainted at the idea of the tonsure, and her only son imprisoned forever behind the grilles of a monastery. But nothing could be done about it; the perfidies of the bastard prevailed; the Prior of the Fortunada received the order to shear Dieudonat and attach him to the vilest employments, in order to master his arrogance.

Thus it was done. The eighteen-year-old novice was extracted from his philosophical cell and received a new habit of coarse and solid cloth. The Prior having decided only to confer Holy Orders after a year's novitiate in the kitchens, the Prince was sent there with a broom in his hand.

"Learn humility," the Prior said to him, "and enter into yourself."

Dieudonat was scarcely thinking of entering into himself, since he only aspired to get out of himself; as for feeling humiliated, he did not think about that either. He was not unaware that certain tasks were reputed to be degrading, but that appreciation seemed to him to be erroneous, and his logic refused to admit it; not only could he not conceive that labor could be dishonoring while it is honest and necessary to the common good, but, on the contrary, he judged it honorable, and more honorable still when the task involves few inherent pleasures for the mind or satisfactions for pride.

That is why, when he went downstairs after mass he went with a lively step and a light heart, full of joy at finally feeling useful for something for the first time in his life.

"To nourish one's fellows, what a mission! Eating is a primordial urgency. People can do without books and kings, but not bread. God gives subsistence to his creatures; as a kitchen aide I shall be an aide of God."

He learned his métier quickly. He peeled vegetables, rinsed the spoons and scrubbed the floor-tiles. The monastic rule forbade meat, so he did not have to fear the soiling that horrified him, that of blood; the pleasure that he was able to obtain from scouring the cooking pots came from his liking for cleanliness and purity; the coppers shone.

The lay brothers, initially intimidated by his august birth, became familiar on finding him cordial and devoid of arrogance. He became cheerful.

"I divined correctly. Manual labor is the most recreative employment in the world. At least one sees the result; it's tangible. When I've peeled three hundred carrots there are three hundred, incontestably; when my soup is cooked, it's eaten; that's my work, and there would be a lack if it were not done. Is there a philosopher on earth who could say as much?"

In order to accompany the work, he counted in his head the quantities to do, the quantities done and their mathematical proportion, and he ticked off the unities as they went past. Then, when a need for reverie happened to overtake him, he opened a fruit or a root, a lettuce or a cabbage, abruptly, and quickly looked inside, to see something new that no one before him had ever seen, with the result that he gave a modest satisfaction to the slightly egotistical taste that the makers of the human species profess for virginity.

He had other amusements; the best consisted of following in the sky the ascent of the sketched church, and he was enthusiastic in noting day by day the quotidian progress of the labor.

"Bravo! Well done! Hurrah! Oho! And how they sing, those fecund fellows! I'll wager that they think themselves unhappy because their work is hard, and yet they sing in spite of themselves, so much does joy impose itself on their hearts."

He watched the arms swelling and the stones settling.

"Wasn't I naïve on the day when I took it into my head to feel sorry for those worthy fellows? They're toiling? Who doesn't toil? Now, if I'm not mistaken, the will of a laborer only ever conquers two joys, that of effort and that of the result; we all know the first, but only manual workers know the second fully. Hurrah for the effort that is realized!"

And he laughed

"When I compare the worker who moves stones to my poor father, who moves armies, one making houses and the other ruins, who has the better role, and the more amusing? One is more at ease in clothes that have holes than those that have pearls, and the true misery of the humble is not being warm or cold but being unaware of the sum of happiness that their lot comprises. If one told them, they wouldn't believe it."

In spite of his resignation, he continued to envy the masons, who made more use of their energy than he did; in order to procure for himself the pleasure that he believed them to have, he started seeking out the rudest chores in the convent, deeming that his joy would be in proportion to his effort. He drew water from the wells, he sawed up logs, cleaved the wood, and loaded baskets of vegetables on to his back. Sweat ran down his forehead and his laughter swallowed the salty droplets, the taste of which pleased him like an ordeal.

"Harden muscles! Broaden, shoulders! Let the will of my head tame the cowardice of my beast! I enjoy living when you creak with lassitude. To work, arms! Even if our work brought no other profit, I would still have that of being obliged to you for the effort. Obey! By the victory that it gives us over ourselves, for lack of that of overcoming obstacles, effort carries its own reward!

His joy was great n the day when he was admitted to the honor of kneading the bread; curved over the wooden mortar he plunged his arms into the dough and moaned with a joyful heart; his ideas aided him to push, and he worked like a madman while philosophizing in stammered speech punctuated with groans.

"Dom Ambrosius, my defunct tutor, sometimes reproached me for quibbling like a heretic, _aah!_ I wouldn't want to offend you, Lord, but how is it that in your Holy Scriptures, in the first pages, I encounter a verse in which your anger says the humans: 'You shall earn your bread by the sweat of your brow,' _aah?_ That you said that, I don't presume to doubt, but that you proffered such a sentence as a condemnation, and not as a favor, that's what I can scarcely conceive, *aah!* Certainly, bread is good, but sweat is no less useful, nor less good, *aah!* And if one of them procures us the strength of our bodies, the other maintains the health of our souls; bread is nourishment for the flesh, but action is the hygiene of the entire being, *aah!* Nothing is ennobling for humans except effort, and in condemning us to effort you obliged us to ennoble ourselves, *aah!*"

He interrupted himself in order to draw breath.

"Is it not better to be content with oneself, Lord, after completing a task than to be content with oneself without doing anything? Isn't deserving better than enjoying? And even if one attaches a high price to enjoyment, can one deny that it's more delectable when one has earned it thoroughly? Aren't desiring, willing and hoping, tending toward the goal and dreaming about it, profiting from it in advance, better than not knowing what to do when one has reached it? Isn't savoring the illusion, caressing the chimera, intoxicating oneself in such a manner that the imagination dresses the future with charms that the reality will soon disappoint? By expelling us from the earthly paradise, you opened up the interior paradise to us; why didn't you say so, instead of telling humans that the duty of energy is their punishment?"

He worked harder when his idea was in contradiction to another.

"The fabulous Eden in which idleness and profusion reigned, and that inevitable nausea that satiety gives, *aah!* was the Devil's garden and not the Lord's, for Satan is the proprietor where humans have nothing to do, *uuh!* He invents passions for us to employ our strength, and occupy our leisure, and then we bite the apples that he offers us, *aah!* But the Archangel came to liberate us by throwing us out of the garden, *aah!*"

A fly that took advantage of his occupation to tickle his left nostril constrained him to interrupt himself.

"The more I think about that legend of the earthly paradise, the more I sense that the text isn't written for us; doubt-

57

less that apology for idleness was drafted by and for the Orientals, who like sleeping in the shade during the hot hours of the day: appropriate to Asia. But a man of the North, or simply a man, would not have invented that blasphemy!"

In fact, he took greater pleasure every day in his métier as a monastic scullion, and he devoted himself to it, content with everything, singing, laughing, working as much as he could, thinking just enough to collect himself for a few minutes, perfectly happy and devoid of any desire.

"I've found the world's haven; I'm installed within it for life."

Such an absence of ambitions and appetites disconcerted the powers charged with realizing all the wishes of the fellow. That a favor so exceptional had fallen precisely on the only man who imagined that he had to need of anything was truly a pity! The Devil could not find his due therein. So he therefore stimulated one of those well-intentioned passers-by who rarely fail to come along and spoil life, under the pretext of doing us a service.

VIII. Dieudonat realizes that he is endowed with a virtue
that will prevent him from having any

Among the lay brothers who carried out the inferior labor of the convent, Brother Onesime was undoubtedly the dullest and the most boorish. He swept the cloister, the courtyard and the corridors, because any other task would have seemed too arduous to be entrusted to his intelligence. By reason of that simplicity the fellow was the butt of the jokes of the stupid, who called him Zime, as if to withdrawn something further from the little that remained to him of heaven and the human. As was reasonable, Dieudonat had found a charm in the excessive candor of the simpleton, and the latter venerated him; they took pleasure in one another's company, and when their work was done, they laughed wholeheartedly together.

One day, Onesime, who, among other defects, had a few rotten teeth, began to suffer from a molar and to writhe on the kitchen floor. The event seemed to be of scant importance; nevertheless, because of that small incident, fate was about to change for entire provinces. Hundreds of thousands of people were having breakfast tranquilly in the distance, with no suspicion that they were entering into a fearful phase of their existence because of an imperceptible black spot that had just been revealed in the second molar of a monastery servant!

The lay brothers watched their Zime rolling around on the floor or hitting himself in the jaw with his fist, and they laughed with the good humor that welcomes so gladly the suffering of people that one is accustomed to find ridiculous. When he was no longer amusing them they left him, and his only friend approached him in order to offer him gargles and simples. He caressed him gently with affectionate words; but the patient merely screamed. He howled like that for an hour, mingling his cries with bizarre words, always the same: "It's forbidden...if it weren't forbidden...why is it forbidden?"

He seemed to be struggling against an obsession or a temptation, and turning longing gazes toward his protector.

Finally, at the end of his tether, he murmured: "If you wished..."

"What?"

"Dieudonat, if you wished..."

"What, cousin?"

"To cure me..."

"But, my poor Zime, I'd like nothing better, if it depended on me; I've tried everything; I don't know what more I can do."

"A word, just say a word!"

"I've said so many of them that I'm ashamed of always talking without doing anything."

"You haven't said the right one. Say it, if you pity me."

"I do pity you."

"Say it, then. Aloud, quickly, while there's no one here, say it! 'I wish him to be cured.' Say that, and I'll be cured."

"What folly has got into you? Only Our Lord and the saints can accomplish miracles."

"Say it, quickly!"

"Your childishness is causing me chagrin."

"He won't say it! He doesn't love me! He wants me to suffer! But I can't, any more... Speak, then!"

"I wish you were cured."

Immediately, Onesime stopped writhing on the floor, raised his head and looked at the walls, as if to seek a message there regarding himself; then he stood up with a sprightly bound, his face cheerful, and he started dancing in the middle of the kitchen. The other contemplated him with amazement."

"How good it is no longer to be in pain!"

"You're no longer in pain?"

"None at all! You see how easy it was? But don't tell anyone, I implore you; the Prior will throw me in the dungeon."

"How can you believe that a word from me...?"

"Oh, my good friend, my savior, it's true, then, that you don't know?"

"What?"

"What we're forbidden to tell you."

"I don't know and I don't understand."

"Listen! You've soothed me, and I'm not an ingrate...I'll do you a favor too. But don't betray me, at least. Come closer, so I can whisper in your ear. There's a fatality over you, since birth. All your wishes are granted."

"What a story!"

"No one's unaware of it except you. It's even said that your father locked you up in a convent because of it. All your wishes, you understand? All of them! You've just made one, and here I am, on my feet. Cured forever, you know. If you don't believe me, try something else. Order that...that...that... I can't think of anything myself, when I try."

"You're rambling, my poor Zime."

"Try!"

"Certainly not. I won't try."

Dieudonat went back to work, tranquilly. He refused to suppose, even for a minute, that he could really be invested with a superhuman power, and the mere hypothesis of an arrogance of that ludicrous extent seemed to him to be as culpable as it was grotesque, offensive to God as much as to reason.

"Humans have a singular liking for superstition, and one might think that, the more naïve they are, the greater need they have for mystery; the supernatural attracts them much more than the natural; those who have little understanding of things delight in thinking that no one can understand them, and it's a species of revenge that Heaven accords them when it opens up regions of dream to them that are forbidden to strong minds."

While talking to himself in that fashion, he found some little brown slugs in a very pale cabbage, and concluded: "Happy are the poor in spirit; skepticism is a luxury for the exclusive usage of the rich, rich in intelligence, who ought to hide that luxury, and above all, to refrain from giving it as alms to the poor."

At that moment, he found that he had no water to rinse his cabbage. He stood up, picked up an empty bucket, and, by way of a joke, he exclaimed, jovially: "I wish this bucket were full of clean water."

At the same instant, the bucket became heavy at the end of his left arm. He felt the weight, looked at his hand, saw the miracle, and, in his amazement, dropped the bucket full of liquid. The bucket rolled on the tiles, but the water did not run out.

"You see," said Onesime. "The bucket stays full. Your wishes are irrevocable. I told you."

The Prince had gone as pale as his cabbage. He contemplated fearfully the vertical and tranquil disk of water, with refused to spread out over the floor. This time he understood the truth.

"My God, my God, with what terrible favor have you heaped me? My impotence, which I knew, is overcharged with a power, which I don't know!"

Onesime was baffled by that sadness.

"You're desolate? Why? On the contrary, you should rejoice, and thank the Lord. Haven't you noticed, then, how your coppers shine as soon as you've scrubbed them, how the rust vanishes from the pots, how the chimney stops smoking, as soon as you wish it?"

"As soon…yes, you're right. 'As soon…' And that signifies: 'Too quickly!' For here I am, among all creatures, deprived of the ardor for hope that we call Desire, the ardor for work that we call Effort. Innocent friend! Understand, then, that I am henceforth poorer than the poor, infinitely deprived, since I will no longer desire anything, having the possibility of everything."

"It's very convenient, however."

"I've spent eight years learning that Effort is the unique nobility of human beings, and in a minute, I've learned that effort is forbidden to me. What remains to me, then?"

"You have…you have…you can do what you want, of course!"

"The good and the evil."

"You've done good for me!"

"Are you sure that you won't pay dearly for it?"

"Pay?" said Onesime. "I don't have a sou."

So saying, he burst out laughing, but this time, his gaiety was painful to the young sage, who felt a shiver run down his back, and looked at his humble comrade for a long time, as if he had a presentiment that the fellow would soon pay with his life for the relief of a minute.

He said: "Your designs are impenetrable, O Lord. May your will be done."

He made the sign of the cross, sat down on a stool, picked up another cabbage, sliced it in two, and strove not to think about it any longer.

But the good times of inner peace were over.

From that day onward the Prince was haunted by an obsessive concern: never to formulate a wish, in order to leave himself some latitude for the energy of effort, without which life is not living.

He no longer dared to desire, he no longer permitted himself to want, in the fear of seeing the wish granted before the gesture. As soon as he sensed the embryo of a desire born in his soul, he immobilized it in the depths of his being. Like a young giant afraid of his strength, and even of his shadow, he only walked with the apprehension of brushing people or things, even mentally; and because the action of his excessive power seemed more perilous for him than other people, he began to dissociate himself, separating his mind from his body, distancing the will that motivates from the beast that effectuates.

In vain he persisted obstinately in hard tasks; brutal effort is joyless when the mind is no longer cooperating with it; work lost all its charm, and Dieudonat lost his gaiety. He became an automatic force, and already he sensed the moment approaching when he would no longer seem to be anything but a corpse that continues to move.

IX. Unfortunate consequences of a good deed

At about that time, Duke Hardouin fell gravely ill; the physicians declared that his life was in danger, perhaps in order to have the honor of returning it to him, and the country was alarmed. The idea of seeing the scepter in the hands of the terrible Ludovic frightened the population, and the egotisms in peril remembered the legitimate heir imprisoned in a cloister. As long as it was only a matter of him, they had borne his misfortune patiently, but now that it was a matter of themselves, the captivity of a innocent man appeared intolerable. It became all the more so because the author of such an injustice was about to die. Deputations departed for Fortunada, from which they were determined to bring Dieudonat back.

Their journey was futile. The Prior remembered only too well the example of Dom Ambrosius, hanged from the crenellations of the manor. He watched over his prisoner, preserving him from any communication with the century, and locked him in his cell every evening. He welcomed the deputies with tenderness, caressed them, praised their zeal and that of the Prince he guarded, whom he loved like a son. However, what could he do? He had formal orders and deplored his impotence. He offered, with his regrets, a collation and meager souvenirs, medals and medallions, tin baubles and ampoules to ward off maladies; then, mildly, he sent the worthy folk away, who saluted him—after which, he rubbed his hands, convinced of having eluded a difficult situation.

But human cleverness cannot prevent the advent of evil when the logic of events has rendered it necessary. Is it not for that reason that certain men, made a little more than others in the image of God, are admitted to the sad privilege of foreseeing things that are still distant and prophesying them? Is it not also for the same reason that the Orientals, firmly decided to accept logic rather than to study it, resign themselves to everything, saying: "It is written!"

Nothing, therefore, prevented the heir presumptive from learning the news that people tried to hide from him, and learning it in the simplest fashion. To begin with, he heard the convent bells ringing at an unusual hour; then, in the frisson of the breeze that stirred the flowers and bushes in the garden, he perceived the tiny voice of distant bells, and was able to conclude that the entire country was ringing toward God; then the monks intoned the psalms for the dying, for an illustrious individual whom they did not name. By way of the peasants who brought the tithe and the questing brothers who return to the monastery with their satchels and stories of the world, Onesime was informed, and charitably, he informed his comrade.

"The dying man for whom prayers are being said is your father. You're going to be the Duke; the whole country is demanding you."

At those words Dieudonat put his hands together, moved by filial tenderness, and a cry rose from his heart to his lips: "Let my father be saved, O Lord! Render health to my father!"

The miracle occurred, and the Duke was cured.

As was appropriate, the first actions of the convalescent were actions of grace, and the second, acts of wrath. Because people had, before his death, disposed of his throne and gone against his decisions, that criminal audacity merited a good few gallows.

He was reflecting along those lines when the ambassadors came back from Fortunada and presented themselves very inappropriately at the gates of the castle, with banners deployed, in order to request the recall of the disgraced prince. Hardouin received them with an impetuous face and invited them violently to mind their own business.

In those days, the happiness and unhappiness of peoples was not within their competence; everyone knew that, city-dwellers or peasants, and no one contested an axiom so veridical. This time, however, the subjects protested against the master's decision; Dieudonat, who had been cruelly taken away from them, was their work, they claimed, since God had made him in response to their prayers. In resisting the will of the sovereign, they were conscious of obeying the celestial will that renders men so powerful against their adversaries and so firm in their ideas. They mutinied, therefore, and in order to express their discontentment clearly they strung up the tax-collectors from trees.

To tell the truth, those modest functionaries had nothing to do with the dispute, but their mission down here consists especially of not being liked by anyone in times of peace, and hanged immediately in times of trouble. That is why monarchs justly consider executions of that sort to be an insult to their own person, even more than a prejudice to that of their agents. Hardouin the Just became increasingly angry, and made it a point of honor to avenge his prestige. That vengeance involved further hangings, and things went from bad to worse.

They went all the more rapidly because the bastard employed himself malevolently to maintaining anger in his father's soul. It went to his head, as the petit bourgeoisie are wont to say, although the result is much easier to obtain among the powerful, who already have the habit of holding their heads high.

Since the recent events, Ludovic was execrated even more than before, because the role of his influence was divined, but the hostility of worthy people earned him the sympathy of those who were not. Cut-throats and mercenaries acclaimed that adventurous captain, with whom they went on campaign. Cheers raised in his honor emerged by night from taverns; his glory was written on walls in charcoal or by the points of daggers. Ambition created a party, fear of it constituted another; groups formed, and subdivisions within the groups, with controversies and quarrels over this and that. Some wanted to set Dieudonat on the throne right away, others preferred to wait until the Duke fell ill and was buried; others did not want anything at all, but made speeches anyway. People debated, and argued; discord spread everywhere; the potentate no longer calmed down, and existence ceased to be tenable in the country that had previously been so happy.

Ludovic judged the moment opportune to suppress his brother definitively.

"I don't want to worry you, Your Lordship, but it would be prudent to conceive the most serious apprehensions, now that your second son is aware of the supernatural power of which he disposes, for your misfortune."

"The monks swore on their heads not to reveal anything!"

"They might have forgotten their oath after eight years, and perhaps they counted too much on your death, which was announced. The truth is that the ambitious felon uses his magic on a daily basis to cure scullions and wash cooking-pots. He might also use it against your scepter and your life. You're at his mercy. Whatever chagrin I might experience if I'm troubling your repose, I'm fulfilling a duty in warning you."

Furious, the Duke cried: "Have people forgotten, then, that I'm named the Just and that I make Justice? I warned those monks! So much the worse for them, if they've determined their fate!"

That same evening, a troop departed with orders to occupy the convent, raze it to the ground and kill everyone.

When the men-at-arms arrived, in the middle of the night, Dieudonat, locked in his cell, was sleeping the vigorous slumber of his twenty years; at first, he did not hear anything of the tumult; the mercenaries, in order to be quite sure that the Prince did not escape them in some disguise, murdered everybody; that task had lasted a good half-hour, when Onesime, who was still alive and continued to have the best of intentions, volunteered to indicate to the killers the retreat of the man for whom they were searching.

He ran to the closed door and, hammering on it, shouted to his friend: "Save yourself, Dieudonat! They're killing us!"

The murderers arrived behind him.

"Kill! Kill! The Prince is there!"

They felled poor Zime with hatchet-blows to the head and broke down the door with the same implements; blood and short hair came through the cracks; the Prince was splashed in the face by it. Could he hesitate in such circumstances to use his magic power?

"Let the massacre cease! Amen!" he ordered.

Instantly, the massacre ceased. But the door collapsed; the men rushed into the cell, by the light of torches, and recognized their prey.

"It's him! Kill! Kill!"

Then something strange happened. Those brigands could shout, as before, but they could no longer kill. While howling furiously, they arranged themselves tranquilly in a semicircle behind the Prince without a single hand being raised against him. They stabbed him with grim gazes, but their weapons dangled at the end of their arms, motionless.

Without paying any heed to them, Dieudonat had thrown himself on Onesime's body, and he embraced him, weeping. He heard the warriors sniggering behind him, but the anger that another might have felt was, in his soul, an immense pity for the victim and the executioners. He turned toward the cutthroats, mildly, and asked: "Why have you killed this child, who has never done any harm?"

"Order of the Duke and Ludovic: we're killing everyone."

"Why has the Duke, my father, given that order?"

"To suppress you and those who were conspiring with you."

"Then why not strike me?"

The soldiers looked at one another with stupid expressions, and they all waited for someone else to explain the reason that prevented their actions from being in accord with their will. For want of anything better, they had recourse to a sort of laughter, which at least explained their embarrassment.

"Have you, then, ceased to hate me since you've found me?"

"We hate you. We're friends of Ludovic!"

"And you want my death?"

"Yes, yes! Death to the Presumptive! Death!"

They agitated as they yelled, with ferocious visages, but their bloody hatchets continued quivering uselessly in their fists.

The monk raised his eyes to the heavens.

"Oh Lord, my Lord, with what and power have you equipped the worker of miracles, whom one only obeys against one's will, who can do anything with gestures but nothing with thoughts? I command matter, but souls escape me! But your lesson is all too intelligible, Lord, and I shall not forget it, for I have just learned that men, however brutal or inept they are, cling to their ideas more than anything else, and they will consent to anything except renouncing the form of stupidity or wickedness that they have in their conscience, and want to be inviolable, because it is their very soul—which is to say, their reason for being."

The mercenaries understood vaguely that that harangue tended to treat them as stupid and wicked, not to mention brutes; they were confused; they desired fervently to decapitate the orator, at the risk of making in this world and sending into the next one martyr more, but their muscles persisted in refusing them the satisfaction of that fantasy.

To console themselves, they yelled: "Long live Ludovic! Ludovic on the throne! To the gibbet with Dieudonat and all those who conspire with him!"

The Prince went past them. In order to get out of his cell he had to step over the body of the man who had been the companion of his labor and his quietude for months. He saw on the flagstones the innocent brain that had never thought about anything, and which had been opened nevertheless. He felt his heart lurch, made the sign of the cross, and, turning toward the men-at-arms, he pronounced sentence: "You will never kill again; I wish it. So let it be."

Then, in the shadow of the corridor, he went away, without considering that he had just deprived those brave men of their only means of earning a living. One cannot think of everything, even when one is superiorly endowed.

In spite of their limited intelligence, the brigands took better account of the wrong that had been done to them; they set about pillaging the convent, since they had only been forbidden murder; they discovered the prior, from whom they extracted the secret of the hidden treasures by torture, while taking great care not to allow him to perish on the rack. That game of patience, in any case, appeared to amuse them considerably. The worthy abbot had begged in vain: "Kill me, for charity's sake! Finish me!"

"It's forbidden."

When they saw that he was duly crippled for the rest of his days and nights, thy transported him, with precaution but without tenderness, into the garden of the cloister, after which they set fire to the convent, which had not been forbidden to them by anyone, and they withdrew, laden with booty, gold and gold braid, silver plate, sacred vessels and precious fabrics—everything that people had the custom of taking away, in those ages of profound piety, after every military descent on a religious house.

In the meantime, the heir drew away across country.

"Before anything else, it's necessary to deliver the convent from my dangerous presence."

Not knowing the area at all, he marched at random, following a stony path that led upwards through a large wood.

After he had been walking under the vault of trees for more than two hours, he reached a plateau that overlooked the mountain. At that height the branches were less dense and the traveler could perceive overhead the pink-tinted sky. He thought that the sun was about to rise, and that was why, before going down the other side of the mountain, he wanted to look again at the place where he had lived, in order to salute it with an adieu. He scaled the rock and turned back toward the plain.

Horror! Instead of the dawn that he thought he would see on the horizon, an immense fire was blazing, red and yellow, beyond the blue dome of the forest.

"The convent's burning! They've set fire to the convent! Flames, extinguish! I wish it, I order it!"

The flames died down at his order, and he collapsed on to the rock; he sobbed into his hands, raising his head at intervals to watch the fire diminishing.

"Alas! What remains of the unfinished church of which I admired the brave ascent? And the library, where all the thought of centuries was accumulated? And the cell where the poverty of our intellect was revealed to me, and the kitchens where I learned to benefit from manual labor, what remains of them?"

Wisps of flames and sparks were still spurting from the furnace and swirling in clouds; against the sky, which was beginning to pale in the east, spirals of opaque smoke were unwinding in the breeze and fleeing with it.

"The books are flying away in light! The books are drifting in darkness! The blackened pages are birds! The great ideas are clouds! It is accumulated effort that the win is carrying over my head, which will fall back as dust, disseminated to the four corners of the world. It is thought in ashes, only good now to soil a blade of grass! Oh, nullity, nullity of effort!"

In the ending night, the monk was cold, and he shivered. Finally, the sun appeared; the flames, which had finished dying away, bright a little while ago, became obscure beneath the resplendent radiance that gilded the countryside.

"Yes, yes, that's it. Human thought is only a glimmer for the night, but when daylight falls upon it, it's no more than a dull mist."

He stood up.

"That lesson too, I understand, Lord, and I know where to go."

An exalted soul inspired him. Standing on the summit in his coarse robe, he extended his arms, and his silhouette, with large sleeves, was cut out in the middle of the matinal sky like that of an eagle about to take flight. With a final glance he embraced the land that he was about to quit forever. The convent was no more than a heap of ashes from which a few pink puffs of smoke were escaping.

"Adieu, house...you were a peaceful dwelling...this is what men make of the peace of others..."

He beat the air with his open hands and inhaled the odor of ash.

"The peace of others, this is what I make of it myself! I bring disaster into the homes of those who welcome me, and for that, Lord, it is sufficient that I'm different from your other children by virtue of my birth and your gifts. Misfortune is attached to the man who does not resemble everyone else; he is harmful without meaning to be. Ruins were made within me while I was studying in books, and ruins around me when I peeled carrots. The exceptional being can only live in solitude. Lead me into the desert, then Lord, and permit me no longer to analyze anything, since analysis leads me astray. In order for me to live in peace, enable me to become simple again, and in order that I cease to do harm, enable me to live alone."

His arms fell back, his head inclined toward his breast, and the man who had seemed to be about to take flight like a eagle a few minutes before fell to his knees, like a man.

X. Dieudonat refuses to believe that he is indispensable

Everything encouraged the belief that he was about to weep, for he was sentimental; finally, he stood up and went down the opposite slope of the rock.

"Where am I going? It doesn't matter, as long as I quit my father's realm."

Again he marched through woods for hours. When he emerged from the forest he found himself on a slope in the final foothills of the mountains. At the bottom of the hill, a cluster of roofs was cozily huddled in a nest of orchards, and the church in the middle rose up as if on watch, like the mother of the houses. He was admiring the restfulness of that pretty place when he saw an animated troop of men emerge from it, who ran toward him.

Those peasants were armed with scythes and plowshares, and with the same fury that the exile had already seen in his brother's soldiers they were shouting the same things, except that the name had changed:

"Death to Ludovic! Death!"

A city-dweller, better dressed than the rest, was marching at their head; they reached the monk and surrounded him, all talking at the same time.

"Have you arrived from Fortunada?"

"Is the convent on fire?"

"Have you come through the forest?"

"Have you encountered Dieudonat?"

"His enemies are looking for him, to kill him!"

"I know."

"He isn't dead?"

"No,"

"Long live Dieudonat! We'll make him Duke! We'll make him King! Ludovic will be hanged, and those who conspired with him! We'll find our Dieudonat and seat him on the throne."

"Worthy people," said the Prince, "I know the man you're looking for, and he doesn't want anyone to be murdered in his name. You ought to return home in peace. That Dieudonat doesn't want to be King, or Duke."

Then the city-dweller, a man of short stature and great verbosity, who had come from the city to whip up the country dwellers, advanced toward the monk and spoke under his nostrils. He had raised his right arm and his speech was violent. It began with the words: "Where do you come from, monk, and why are you interfering?" The first part of the discourse, entirely consecrated to irony and insult, delighted the audience. The second part, consecrated to eloquence, began with the words: "And all of you who are oppressed..." Both parts, taken together, tended to demonstrate that Dieudonat was indispensable to the wellbeing of the country.

The peroration concluded: "This monk is nothing but a secret agent paid by the enemies of the people. They want to deceive the people! Long live Dieudonat the Indispensable!"

A frenetic hurrah filled the landscape. The Prince waited patiently for that amorous wrath to die down slightly, and when he thought he could make himself heard he ventured: "Even if I were endowed with the vast genius and virtues that someone has been kind enough to describe to you, that wouldn't imply..."

"It isn't a matter of you, monk, but of the Indispensable Dieudonat! Do you hear? The In-dis-pen-sable!"

"It's a matter of all men, and none is indispensable. I have much to tell you: the most powerful men of genius, and even those who push power as far as becoming what you would call benefactors of humanity, by endowing it with some revelation that changes the face of the world, are scarcely more indispensable than the others. If they hadn't been born, be sure that others would have been born in their place, to do or say the same things, for what is necessary to the progress of the world isn't the individual but the action, and when the action has become possible, by the same token, it becomes necessary. Necessary! And by that, understand that it must be produced, whatever the organ might be that is employed for its production. All progress is a total that is realized in its hour; nothing will prevent that realization when the time has come. Men of genius are those in which is manifest, not their own strength, but that of their race and their epoch; they summarize and they express, condensers of human possibility, and that possibility, or capacity, engenders them spontaneously by the very logic of its normal evolution."

"He's a madman. I can't understand a word."

"Kepler and Newton, in the time of Charlemagne, Harold or Richard, would only have plied the woodcutter's ax or the soldier's pike; but the century in which they were born was precisely the one in which such men could be born, and if they had died in the cradle, their work would have been done nevertheless, and barely delayed; five or twenty years later, their idea would have appeared under another signature, because on the day of their birth, that idea had finally become accessible to human genius."

"He's comical!"

The peasants listened, open-mouthed, nonplussed, not knowing whether they ought to laugh or become annoyed; in order to know their intention, their eyes interrogated the public orator, who set the tone by bursting out laughing. Everyone burst out laughing

The city-dweller drew closer to the Prince, put a hand on his shoulder, gently enough, and tapping him on the clavicle, said without eloquence: "Old chap, you're making us yawn nicely, eh? You're a clown! Damned joker! I don't hold it against you. But it's necessary not to make fun of us any longer. I don't care about Kepler or Newton, or when they were born or will be, but I know that you're making us waste our time, and that time's pressing. Forward, friends! Let's go find Dieudonat!"

"Brandishing weapons, the crowd ordered: "Forward!"

"I beg you to stop! I'm Dieudonat!"

"Peace, madman. Enough! To the padded cell!"

"I'm the Prince, I tell you, and I don't want to be King or Duke! You won't kill in my name!"

He had grabbed one of the men by the edge of his coat and he hung on. A kick in the belly sent him rolling into the mud of the ditch.

"That's for you, Dieudonat!"

Loud laughter saluted his fall, and the band, in a good humor again, drew away singing battle songs.

Still on his back, the Prince raised his hands.

"I forbid you to kill. Amen!"

But the men went on toward their goal, not knowing that the goal had just been forbidden to them. They plunged into the wood, and their elect ceased to see them. The songs only reached him filtered by the curtain of branches, and then faded away entirely. He could to longer hear anything. Again, he was alone.

"Assuredly, no, I won't be the King of those men, and I understand less and less how I could lead them, since I have nothing in common with them. I'll go so far away that they'll never find me."

He set forth again, and entered all alone into the un-known.

XI. In a corner of a wood he encounters the two sovereigns of this world

He went across country, going straight ahead, not knowing where and not caring, only wanting to go further away, and even further, into lands where no one knew his name.

"People will not kill in my name!"

He was fleeing out of charity. He marched all day and all night, only stopping when he ran out of strength, and even then resuming the struggle against his fatigue in order to advance in spite of it.

"Every step I take might save a life..."

He did his best to avoid encountering people, apprehensive of harming them without wanting to. When a passer-by imposed his company on him he submitted to it politely, for as short a time as possible.

One day, he saw a man by the roadside who stood up as he approached and came toward him with a detached air, saluting him with his hand. The stranger was young, with an agreeable face, and was wearing, with elegance, clothes that had once been sumptuous but had been depreciated by wear. He was also wearing spurs, although he had no horse, and his feet trod the ground with so much certainty, his face expressed such a benevolent affability and his gesture opened with such a hospitable courtesy that Dieudonat had no hesitation.

This man, he thought, *is the lord of the vicinity, or at least his son. His attire appears to be a trifle neglected, but in order to accost passers-by with that authority, he must be at home.*

Immediately, he decided, in the depths of his heart, to refuse the hospitality that was about to be offered to him.

At the same moment, the young man cried: "Sire monk, I salute you! Bless me, my father. I am you humble servant. The afternoon is beautiful and it's a pleasure to walk. Will you permit me to solicit the grace of your company?"

He spoke briskly, with the rapidity of a man who asks questions without wanting a response, punctuating his phrases with smiling eyes and drawing breath with a smiling mouth.

"My God, sire monk, I stopped here to pick strawberries; the strawberries in these woods are exquisite. Where are you going at this pace?"

"Elsewhere."

"Just like me. We'll travel together, and I'll be delighted by that. The leagues are only half as long when there are two to make them. Your health, I think, is good?"

"Yes, thank you."

"Excellent? Like mine! I suspected as much just by looking at you. You're going back to your convent?"

"Oh, no!"

"The city, like me? Perfect. No? Too bad! At least you've said the right word, Father. It's necessary to go elsewhere, elsewhere... Elsewhere!"

"I believe so."

"I'm sure of it. It's a region full of future, elsewhere! Elsewhere is the promised land, and you see in me a man firmly decided only to stop elsewhere."

"You're not the baron of this locale, then?"

"This land of savages, clodhoppers and peasants! Baron of this locale? No, certainly not—I'm worth more than that: Vicomte d'Avatar, Gontran, at your service, gentleman in search of fortune, and who will find it, Father, and wants something better than there is among these villains! I'd die of boredom within six months in this mountain décor of precipices and fir trees. I don't like precipices. It's the boulevards of capitals and the splendor of royal courts that my activity requires, and my means—I dare not say my merits."

"Dare, sir."

"Yes, indeed! You're right, sire monk, and whoever wants to succeed should have no fear of affirming his worth. What convinced friend would speak well of me if I weren't the first to do so myself?"

On that, without respite, he exposed his entitlements to admiration; they were of such great number and so various in nature that the worthy monk was initially seized by amazement, and soon by torpor.

This must be what is known as a brilliant man, he thought. *In sum, that faculty isn't to be disdained, for it proceeds from God as well as the others, and given what men are, it might well be that it is able to conquer them a little better than another.*

Suddenly, a disquieting frisson stirred under the branches to the right and left of the road; crawling beings emerged from the thickets, hirsute, clad in rags and armed to the teeth, and came to arrange themselves in a circle around the two travelers, silently. Their silence, however, was very expressive, and it accompanied gestures incapable of leaving any doubt as to the intentions of that small army. In fact, Dieudonat and Gontran had first been seized by the throat, and hands searched them; already, the vicomte had gone paler that his underwear, and the miracle-working monk hastened to reflect before losing his breath completely

Shall I save us? This young fop, if I'm not mistaken, is a useless creature, and as for me, I'm a harmful creature; unless I'm wrong I'm inclined to believe that we could be suppressed without any inconvenience. But do I have the right to allow a murder to be accomplished when I can prevent it? Hola! Oh, don't kill! So be it!

Immediately, the chief of the brigands surged forth from the other side of the ditch. He saw the scene, and with a curt voice, he stopped the imminent decease.

"Peace to these vagabonds! You'd only be taking their breath. Haven't I forbidden you to kill game that doesn't yield fur or feather? Down claws!"

The fists opened, and Dieudonat thought: *There's a very respectable bandit, who finds misdeeds with a meager return repugnant.*

But the captain of the thieves spotted the vicomte and cried, with a loud laugh: "Eh! Gontran the Rogue, is that you? A stupid capture my men have made here!"

"Ruprecht the Pug-nosed!"

"By the horns of the great Devil, I've arrived just in time to save your skin—and your skin, I imagine, is better than you!"

Gontran adjusted his clothing, and did not protest.

"Saints alive!" the captain went on. "You're hooded, my lad, and here you are flanked by a confessor. Good, good, don't defend yourself! I like monks when they're fat; I'll fatten you up, Father, since I have you for an hour, you can share my Spartan broth and the wine I wash it down with. Don't refuse! Whoever breakfasts with Gontran can certainly sup with Ruprecht. And you'll be free after drinking. Let's go!"

Disobedience would not have been appropriate. The Prince ruptured from his throne resigned himself tranquilly and followed the march. The captain had taken his fancy comrade by the arm and was drawing him through the wood. In hearing them chatting, exchanging memories, Dieudonat was able to learn that they had once worked together at University, that neither one of them had had an appetite for study, and that they had both departed for adventure, each by his own way. They were laughing, experiencing joy in having found one another again by chance, but the vicomte's delight remained imprinted with an entire correctness, and that of the highwayman was expressed with a brutal exuberance.

"By the blue blood! The feast would be complete, and our old trio would be reformed for an evening, if we had Calame the Calamitous here, who composed such fine poems, instead of this lugubrious monk!"

They arrived next to a steep gorge. A torrent rumbled at the very bottom; on the slope of the ravine, fifty feet below the edge, a hole opened between the rocks, behind a curtain of holly.

"That's my lair!"

They went down. The brigands' cavern was similar to all brigands' caverns described in books: the successive shelter of troglodyte bear-hunters, tracked bagaudae and vanquished Gauls, it now sheltered he highway robbers, and hearths of the same human misery had smoked its walls for hundreds of centuries.

Dieudonat, who was interested in everyone and everything, went in without displeasure; with the same step he was making his entry into society, and it could not help being a little symbolic. On emerging from a cloistered adolescence he was about to make his first contact with individuals free of any religious or social shackles, and he was seeing Man for the first time.

He inspected the décor, while a bandit servant set the table in haste. That large brute was wearing a lady's surcoat lined with squirrel-fur, which was too narrow for his shoulders, which had been split before being put on; apart from the strangeness of that accoutrement, the lewd individual did not differ much from honest cultivators that one perceived laboring. He was neither more nor less dirty, and his eyes, devoid of ferocity beneath bushy eyebrows, translated a canine soul: just like those of a dog, in fact, one might have thought that they wanted to speak but could not; they examined the monk slyly, but with a persistence that could not help disconcerting Dieudonat, little accustomed to gazes.

The brigand went around him, paused, came back, and finally, taking advantage of a minute when his captain took Gontran to the pantry, he leaned over the table and, while pretending to be moving the goblets and spoons, he said: "You wouldn't care to come into a corner with me before supper?"

"A corner? Before supper?"

"Yes, because afterwards, you'll be drunk, as is appropriate, or even unconscious; our captain has bad wine."

"Oh."

"Very bad. But me, I ought to go to confession while you're here. I have a lot to tell you, as you can imagine. You can give me a little absolution with a flick of the hand. Will you?"

"I haven't received orders. I was an aide in the kitchens."

"Too bad. It would have done me good. In the métier, one doesn't know who's going to live and who's going to die, and when one makes the leap, the less of which one has to render account, the better it is, not so?"

"Change métier."

"Well, it's easy for you to talk. One has to live, eh?"

That idea of washing a conscience as one washes underwear, with a view to immediately resuming its usage, appeared a little ludicrous to the philosopher, whose exile had maintained him until then in ignorance of practical plans. He thought he was encountering an exceptional case, and was amused deep down. But many other revelations were being prepared for his astonishment.

Ruprecht the Pug-nosed and Gontran the Rogue came back charged with victuals; they had unhooked salted meat from the vault and taken dusty bottles from the good corner, which caused laughter. They were laughing in advance. The lieutenant of the robbers called out to his chief: "Before the goblets, Captain, what's tonight's password?"

"Outside society!"

"A good motto for you," exclaimed Gontran, laughing, "and a bad one for me."

The two friends sat down; the monk was obliged to imitate them and took the third stool. Immediately, the solid and liquid items that encumbered the table began to disappear, and everyone strove to hide as much as possible; a noise of chewing and clinking cups rang out without discontinuity. Dieudonat admired the energy of those sonorous appetites. He watched, listened, ate with the tips of his teeth, drank with the edges of his lips, and finally got up in order to go in search of a pitcher.

"A cup of wine, sire monk, to the health of our absent friend: I drink to the immortal Calame!"

Obediently, the monk clinked cups. Ruprecht attacked the red wines; Gontran preferred the white wines, and their tongues were immediately loosened, evoking past days.

"Do you remember, one evening...?"

The past loves the odor of wine; it rises up as soon as it is invited; in the emanations of the reddened table, the memories of the two companions launched forth in gaiety and swirled riotously, dancing their saraband around the smoky candle. In that cavern, which one would have thought so distant from any city, the evocations of the street ran in sequence, and the subterrain was populated with anecdotes in which a horde of creatures swarmed, a temptation of Saint Anthony in which the devils were people. Against a background of darkness, those tableaux of an absent society, enlivened by rich colors, succeeded one another like the images in an exceedingly profane Book of Hours; the seven deadly sins appeared in turn, in abundance, and each of them came back as soon as another left room. A joyful immortality ran riot through the tales and the verve was so warm that Dieudonat, who was drinking water, got drunk on hearing the winy words.

Is this it, then, the world?

When the young friends had emptied seven bottles in honor of the past they started on the future.

"Me," cried Ruprecht, "I'm for the action, you know! A man of action, me! I've always been a man of action!"

To prove what he was saying, he hammered the table with blows of the fist that made everything tremble. His face was congested; his eyes were challenging invisible contradictors.

"It's necessary that people know, and they will know, that I'm a man of action, a man! People will talk about me, I promise! Would you like to see another Mercadier? Look at me! I'll have my fief, like Roger de Flor, my manor, like

Mérigot![5] The Archpriest? He's not worth as much as me. No, my old friend, he's not worth as much as me!"

Renouncing maltreating the table, he was now hammering his own torso, which resonated like another cavern, more formidable than the big one.

"They'll see it, my glory! I'm bursting with strength, me. My strength is a right. You hear me, monk? Repeat that in your convents. Announce Ruprecht to them, who is going to come. He's coming, Ruprecht, and Ruprecht is only coming as a master! Men are cowards, men are dastards, and you're the first, Gontran! They only ask to be flattened under a boot, provided that the boot is solid; they disgust me, men! I don't want to live with them, but I deign to march over them!"

Gontran feared that the vicomte, accused of dastardliness, might take that judgment ill and become annoyed, but the gentleman smiled with urbanity, and his condescension even seemed to be nuanced with disdain.

"You old chap, yes, you're a brave man, and I'm a clever one: everyone makes his life as he can, and according to his means; all means are excellent; the important thing is to attain one's goal. I go there gently, me, and if you have the strength, I have the ingenuity, which is worth as much as all your strength. I'm very intelligent."

"You, the Rogue? You? A good-for-nothing! An ignoramus! At University you were the prince of duffers. The intelligent one, of the three of us, was Calame! Talk to me about

---

[5] Max Mercadier was a twelfth-century Occitan mercenary in the pay of Richard the Lionheart whose depredations in southern France became legendary. Ruggiero da Fiore or Roget de Flor (1267-1305) was an Italian adventurer and Templar who became so powerful in the service of the Byzantine Emperor Andronicus II that he decide to carve out a small empire of his own, but was swiftly assassinated. Aymerigot or Merigot Marches (1360-1391) was a mercenary in the pay of the English during the Hundred Years War who was executed for banditry when captured by the French.

Calame! Of the three of us, he was two men, me and him, me the strength and him the thought. He was a brain, our Calamitous, but you, you're nothing."

"At University, oh, yes, I'll grant you that; but we're no longer at school. We're in the world, and you're talking about knowing while I'm talking about know-how. It's quite different, my friend."

"I pay my own way, me. I spend my own money!"

"I spend others' money, which permits me never to be mean and to make largesse. You'll see, my friend, you'll see, sire monk, which of the two of us is right. I take you as my witness, and even as a witness to my wedding, for I intend, please God, that you'll be present at that feast, since it'll be the first."

"Ah!" said the Prince. "You're getting married, sir?"

"Yes, certainly."

Ruprecht only shrugged one shoulder; his eyes were scarcely fulgurant any longer.

Gontran added: "Yes, sire monk, I've opted for the straight path, me, because the straight path is the shortest route. I'm getting married!"

"Soon?"

"Not for a few months; a semester, I think, will be necessary to smooth out a few difficulties that I glimpse: the resistance of the father, the temporary insufficiency of my situation. It will all work out."

"The young lady is waiting for you?"

"You said it! She's waiting for me, even though she doesn't know me, just as I'm searching for her without knowing her; for I'm categorically resolved to marry her without delay, but it's important that I find her first, and for that I have a very precise description: she's rich, very rich, young, unless she's mature, brunette or blonde, and perhaps a red-head, tall or short, pretty or ugly. There's her portrait, sire monk, a striking resemblance; if you know where she lives, take me here, and I'll take charge of the rest: the child will adore me, for I'm well able to convince her of it. A task all the easier because I don't pretend to eternal amour. Nothing lasts, but everything last long enough, if one knows how to lead one's amours to the altar."

"And afterwards?"

"Afterwards? Come what may, cavalier! In the saddle for life! When a woman has put her foot in the stirrup, I'll have the rest of her."

The captain of the brigands, slumped over the table, his eyelids half-dead, was gazing at his friend with a troubled eye, shaking his head. Through the hair and wine of his moustache, he muttered an insult whose meaning the monk did not understand, heaving only read the substantive in a summary of ichthyology.[6] Instead of taking offense, Gontran d'Avatar clapped his hands.

"I accept the augury, old chap, and in a couple of years, I'll teach you by my example what the métier is worth, when it's professed before God and the notaries. I'll be bourgeois and sworn, administrator of financial societies, alderman and capitalist, Commander de Saint-Jacques. I'll have my valets, my flatterers, my hunts and my carriages; I'll offer fêtes to princes and prizes to inventors; I'll encourage the arts, the sciences and virtue; I'll be considered, my friend, and considerable."

Ruprecht the Pug-nosed was asleep on his folded arm. Gontran the Rogue, whom drunkenness was urging to confidences, fell back on the monk and developed his projects for a further hour. Suddenly, however, he had the sensation of talking to a useless audience and working without profit; immediately, he got to his feet, very politely, extended his right hand, bowed with an abrupt twitch of the back of the neck, smiled, showed his white teeth one last time, and went to lie down on a mat. Dieudonat was left alone in the middle of the room.

"This evening, I've heard the two conquerors of the earth; Lord, you have enabled me to put my finger on the two

---

[6] Presumably *maquereau* [mackerel], the common French term for a man living off a woman.

forces that reign over this world: Violence and Intrigue. I wasn't born for this world."

His heart was beating in his breast: "Outside society! Outside society!"

He drew away from the table and, in the vague torch-light, he began to walk toward the exit.

A seminal stopped him. "Who goes there? Where are you going?"

"Outside society."

"Pass."

He emerged from the subterrain, and was dazzled by the light. The day was ending, however; the sun, having disappeared behind the mountains, was still tinting the sky bronze, but in the depths of the gorge the night was already amassing blue mists, and from one minute to the next it was climbing along the steep rocks. Up above, little trees were designed like lace; down below, others were melting into the haze; a divine peace blessed the landscape. The crescent of the moon was rising above the treetops.

Then the Prince cried: "O Nature, Nature! Before you, I render thanks to God, who has given it to me to see you; seeing is the consolation for hearing."

XII. The anchorite obtains large and small animals,
and some information about himself.

After he had walked for many days through mountains and plains he arrived in a country that was no less savage than magnificent. For a week he had not encountered a man or a woman.

"Here I can live without being harmful to anyone; here I can meditate without the fruit of my deductions contaminating the minds of others; here I can gain a quotidian subsistence without it being necessary for me to have recourse, like the Gontrans and Ruprechts of the world, to violence or intrigue; here I can make in peace my happiness for this world and my salvation for the other."

He installed himself in a nice grotto, which he furnished with sand and foliage. He lacked implements of labor, and also a few utensils of primordial necessity; in spite of the repugnance he had for using his magic power, he did not think it sinful to ask Heaven to grant him the indispensable tools. He had them immediately and set to work with a great joy.

"I've reconstituted the Earthly Paradise, the true one, the one in which a man, in an admirable location, gains his nourishment by the sweat of his entire body."

He worked, prayed, thought, breathed the air and gazed. He did not suffer at all from the solitude, having discovered that it did not exist; deserted mountains are richly inhabited places, much more populous and much more alive than cultivated terrains, and even capital cities. Generally, we pay no heed to them, and doubtless that is out of scorn, but Dieudonat, less proud than a man because he was more than an ordinary man, paid attention to every creature.

Very quickly he had the sensation, among the animals, of living among people. His fellows, whom he had only known until then by reading, he found again here in reality, and he recognized them. All the modes of life in use among us were renewed at ground level and under the branches; there were republics of ants, kingdoms of bees, cities of woodlice, errant insects armored like knights, butterflies dressed as princes, spiders lying in ambush in their lacy fortresses like barons in their towers and more or less poetic birds who sang from dawn till dusk in order to take turns with those who sang from dusk till dawn.

They were friends. In the morning he received the visits of rabbits and hinds, not to mention stags and wild boar; at midday lizards basked in the sun around him, and in the evening wolves came politely to wish him good night; even bears willingly frequented the vicinity of his abode. Large and small animals had promptly recognized him for one of their own, and were no longer frightened of him, for animals enjoy a particular instinct that designates the less harmful people to them; the most timid creatures allowed themselves to be caressed by him, and he took an infinitely sweet pleasure in that confidence of the weak, whom we could crush by closing our hand, who know that, and who go to sleep nevertheless in our hand.

One thing troubled him, however; in that universal fraternity he observed an evident and undeniable lacuna. He lived on the best terms with everyone, but it was impossible to enter into amicable communications with the insects. For his part, he experienced an epidermal repulsion in their regard; he was a little afraid of them, without knowing why; for their part, they gave the impression of not seeing him, and treating him as a slope or a spring; they climbed over him, tickling him as they walked, sometimes sucking a drop of his blood, and going away without apology or salute, quitting the human landscape to go elsewhere. All the polite advances he risked remained without effect.

"Funny people!"

Science had taught him very little about them, and their limited dimensions scarcely permitted study; in the hope of that he might understand them better if he saw them more clearly, he formulated the wish for a biconvex lens. Immediately, a magnifying-glass of compressed ether fell from the sky, ready mounted. It was an article of the first choice, magnifying objects abut two thousand times. The insects entered the field of the miraculous lens.

"Eh…? Ah…! Oh…! Eh! Now I understand why my skin was afraid of them, and my skin wasn't so stupid!"

Dieudonat was amazed by that phantasmagoria of miscellaneous horrors. In taking on the proportions of mammals, those minuscule creatures agitated in nightmares, so formidable that by comparison, tigers and alligators gave the impression of being inoffensive. Eyes launched terror, mouths chewed menace; pincers and claws, saws and rasps, daggers and drills, a whole arsenal of tortures, all the instruments of hate, were exercised under the glass disk with a metallic tranquility, brilliantly deploying the pitiless force of their unconsciousness.

"They're beautiful, yes, truly, with an atrocious beauty, which might well be that of the evil angels fallen into Hell; one might believe oneself in Gehenna, or at least on another planet, if any exist somewhere, as scholars claim, or even in the first days of this one, when the exuberance of a globe in parturition threw out monsters in order to sate its fury to invent perpetually and no matter what. Perhaps the Creator amused himself sculpting in jewels these paradoxes of his genius, to which he refused the honor of normal dimensions. In any case, it's appropriate to thank Him, whose wisdom and goodness deigned to forbid the development of these imperceptible monstrosities, which would terrorize all living creatures if God had made them on a larger scale. God does well what he does!"

He discovered unusual mores. Those creatures lived in a permanent state of immorality; endowed with all vices, accustomed to all crimes, they took pleasure in them with so much candor that the Ruprechts and Gontrans, the tigers and reptiles of human society, appeared in their turn as petty saints.

Every species had its own very characteristic vice, the exercise of which was indispensable to the very existence of the individual and the entire species. He was obliged to observe very clearly that on every creature that lives, a certain form of evil, or what we call thus, is imposed as an essential law of its race, and imposes itself with the ineluctable character of a fatality, against which attempts at disobedience are neither permissible nor possible: such is necessity.

Dieudonat replied: "God does well what is necessary."

But why was it necessary?

"To them, an order to do; to us, an order not to do; and the two contradictory wills emanate from common Master; which is to say, a unique principle. Now, God cannot contradict himself, since he is God; and since I don't understand, it's therefore quite simply that I'm an imbecile; I knew that already."

The certainty of not being subtle has never prevented a man from undertaking intellectual tasks; Dieudonat did what another might have done and resolved, for the honor of the good God, to discover, or at least to investigate, the basis of a natural morality. To that end, he undertook to study with precision and method the mores and characters, not only of insects but of all the animals present around him. Similarly, he surveyed the gestures of plants, and was not very surprised to observe that they possessed, to a lesser degree, sensations identical to those of the animal kingdom, and instincts, volitions and even vices.

"Creation is decidedly very complex."

Thus engaged in his essay on universal morality, Dieudonat got bogged down and the work did not advance. Every time he thought he had edified a general law, based on patent facts, other facts just as patent came along to demolish it in haste, in order to propose a new one, absolutely contrary.

"My word, the animals are treating me exactly like the philosophers; the more they teach me, the less I understand what I've learned."

He bombarded them with questions.

"Why are you? What do you want? What do you prove? Give me the key to your enigma in order that I can see clearly into mine."

The animals were used to the speech of the biped who talked to himself, and were no more concerned about it than any other song.

One evening, when he was reasoning, according to his custom, sitting on a stone outside his grotto, his piteous reflections had inclined his head toward the ground. Then he noticed, to the left of his left foot, a blonde Spider who, taking advantage of the nuptial emotion, was slyly devouring her young husband without the amorous fellow budging from his post. Revolted by such an abuse of confidence, the moralist looked away, and, at the same moment, to the right of his right foot. He saw a Bee who, while drinking the soul of a golden bud, was allowing herself to be gripped from behind by a Wasp, and the later was unwinding her viscera like a tangled skein, in order to nibble more at her ease the golden meanders to which the Bee continued tranquilly to send sugar; and the Wasp, in her turn, was so attentive to that living repast that she did not even deign to notice the indiscretion of a Mantis occupied in gnawing her abdomen.

"That's too much! They're making a chain. They tolerate being eaten, and don't even notice it, provided that they're alimenting their own poor little bodies!"

An amorous Hind that was passing by gracefully placed her delicate hoof on the Mantis, who was cut in two, without that incident being able to interrupt her feast or the others.

"Insects exaggerate, Lord! That one might sacrifice one's life to one's passions I can conceive, rigorously. But that death accompanied by slow tortures appears to be no more than a detail devoid of importance before the double appetite of nourishment and amour is excessive!"

The work of the flesh went on serenely, along with the agonies.

"Let's see, let's see... This is natural, since it exists in nature. Let us take account of these excesses and extract the principle: to nourish the individual and perpetuate the species, by order, such are the two goals of the creature, and hence its morality. The dolors that might result from that do not count in the totality—which is to say, in the universe—which, in consequence, is ignorant of pity and cruelty, corollaries of those sufferings. Modesty or immodesty, purity or impurity, corollaries of amour, count for no more; nothing is either good or bad, everything is, and death is only life in function. Am I right this time, Lord?"

No voice protested; the breeze rocked the Clematis hanging around him, and the Meadow-sweets erect on their stems, and everything nodded: "Yes," swinging their perfumed tresses at the friction, by which the evening air was embalmed.

"Life wants to live, and that is the entire morality of a plant. In other words, the goal of life is life. I've reflected hard to arrive at that sublime discovery. Dom Ambrosius would treat it as a pleonasm or a tautology, and he wouldn't be wrong, but bah! That law has the advantage over many others of being logical, simple to grasp and easy to remember. Shall I leave it at that?

But the torture of animals in the throes of death drew his eye and thought toward it.

"I can't, however, let them suffer indefinitely..."

He did not want to touch the Spider, because of the future she was already carrying in her entrails, but the others? He hesitated for two full minutes; then, suddenly, he stretched out his leg and, abruptly, he crushed with his bare foot, the Mantis, the Wasp, the Bee and the golden Bud; the sole of his foot clenched with horror over the final wriggle of the quadruple death.

"Were they suffering as much as I imagine? Assuredly not, and it's even possible that the patient individuals, all together, were suffering less than the spectator; alone, I was translating ganglionic sensations into cerebral pain..."

At those words, he interrupted himself; a flash of light had just penetrated him, and under that new light, engendered by the words, he believed that he had glimpsed the admirable verity.

"Aha, my comrade! Cerebral, you say? Doesn't the big difference between humans and animals, between their morality and ours, arise quite simply from the dissimilarity of the nervous systems? Our is remarkable among all, and I won't go into the question of whether it was like that from the start or became so gradually, whether we're born monsters or become monsters. Either way, our cerebellum, unique in the sublunar world, pushes hypertrophy to the point of calling itself a cerebrum, and, from progress to progress, that organ of exception has been developed to the extreme by the usage that we have been able to make of it, and which we have made of it.

"Consequently, if I'm not mistaken, we see the manifestation of two series of perfectly logical reactions, on the one hand proceeding from the nerves exasperated by the reveries of the encephalum, and on the other emanating from the encephalum overworked by the nerves. In fact, dear and defunct master—for it's to you that I'm addressing myself, Dom Ambrosius; listen to me without getting impatient—in that precious and marvelously sensitive organism, a phenomenon could not fail to be produced: our purely animal sensations quickly became more subtle, thanks to the intrusion of the intelligence that applied itself to extracting the best return from our senses; appetite was stimulated. The decupled organism decupled its needs, and our mind became ingenious in discovering, within us, as well us around us, subsidies of sensuality.

"We harvest them here and there, by imitation, by assimilation, in order to increase ourselves. While every species had its own instinct, and its predominant pleasure, we wanted them all at once: we would have liked to be all of nature at the same time. Certain capacities of certain animals remain prohibited to us? We salute them with a regret, but without renouncing the hope of acquiring them some day, and our desire invites inventors to supply us with the means; in the meantime, in order to substitute for the absence of the forbidden joys, we multiply to their highest power those that are permitted to us....

"Can you grasp that, Dom Ambrosius? The first result of the cerebrum: exaggerated instincts become vices, since vices are nothing but exaggerated instincts.

"But we made too much of them! We abused the original reminiscences; we exasperated nature in pretending to obey her, we emerged from her in thinking that we were entering into her. The necessity of a brake was imposed, without which the race would not have taken long to perish of exhaustion. And the second result was that the cerebrum itself, that multiplier of the nerves, that provoker of excess, invented what was required to save us from the peril caused by its role, and produced the brake in question: Morality."

The soul of Dom Ambrosius made no reply, and Dieudonat continued;

"You'll tell me that Morality varies with climates, races and epochs. Well, my master, that detail is of no importance. The important thing, common to all men, but belonging to them alone, is their intention to have a morality, their firm determination to apply a brake, whatever it might be."

Content enough to have string out a chaplet of paradoxes, the philosopher stood up.

"O little animals and big animals, my sisters, I am worth less than each of you, since I have taken from each of you, every time that I could, instincts that I have made into my vices. But I am also worth more than you since, by virtue of doing too much, I have been ingenious to the point of conceiving by myself the limit of doable things. A limit that I impose myself, that that is my entire profit, but it is magnificent! While each of you only knows her own right, I have invented the right of others, and I call it my duty!"

He drew breath, as befits orators after a significant pause, while the audience applauds. Nothing applauded, but the solitary had accustomed himself a long time ago only talking to himself. He went on:

"The Nerves of humans determined it thus, when their hyperesthesis had developed to the point of making us sense, as if they were our own, the dolors of that which surrounds us.

And it is thus that nature saw spreading over the indifferent world the flower that emerged from us: Pity!"

At the name of a new flower, the calices agitated in the finishing day.

"More beautiful than all of you is that flower of my soul! The gardens of the Lord have nothing similar. Oh, I would be glad, Lord, to have had the glory of inventing it, but my folly has been seeking it outside myself. A purely human relativity, I know full well that it is in me alone, as if born of me alone, a creation of the creature that I am, a lie that I have made into a verity, since I sense it, a chimera of which I make a reality, since I apply it!"

In the enthusiasm of articulating words that seemed to him to be definitive, he took a long step forward. The young Spider happened to be exactly where his foot came down; she died of it, and her posterity with her.

That murder upset the orator; in order to refresh his emotion, he drank a ladleful of clear water; at a single stroke he annihilated a hundred million existences that were swimming in that water.

"I kill when I drink, I kill when I move; the world that is turning around me mocks my axioms, and puts me to the proof; the law of the universe reigns over me as over all. To do good and abstain from evil is the desire of my unreasonable reason, when the least of my movements multiplies good and evil, without distinction, around my gestures. But so what? I am the master of the intention, the king of my interior idea, and the morality that I am seeking, applies to me in accordance with my rule: if the two conquests of the human intellect really are Thought and Pity, I shall strive to honor both of them."

Dusk fell. The nocturnal animals emerged for the third phase of the quotidian massacre, and fear crawled under the blue-tinted branches, a landscape of prey.

"Enough, harsh mother! You have cried to me loudly enough that my pity will sterilize the world and that God does not want it. But into maintaining it in spite of your order, I shall put my human nobility, and in the universal consciencelesssness, I shall affirm conscience. If Nature has God for her, it is not necessary that one knows it, and even urgent to assert the opposite; that is why we have made our Pity an attribute of pitiless gods. What am I saying? We have made God against the gods."

He made the sign of the cross, raising his eyes toward the clouds, which were still rosy.

"Lord Jesus, I am your disciple and I shall persist in your path, for I know now the double formula of my role: Effort and Pity!"

He went back into his grotto, said his prayer and went to bed, satisfied in the belief that he had found the means to bring into accord the immorality of the world with the morality of Christ.

"The law of Effort and the law of Pity; I now possess the double verity. But, alas, and twice alas, am I not the only one among humans to whom the application of one, as well as the other, is forbidden by a deadly gift? Effort is forbidden to me because my wishes are realized; my pity is dangerous since I harm those to whom I come close. I am the being of exception, the recluse of my privilege, condemned to live alone. Because a power has been put into me that surpasses the human, I am a lesser man than any other, incapable of the human task. Charity orders me to remain here. I shall stay here, Lord, sterilely, I shall remain here, and since nothing more is permitted to me, I shall confess the law of Sacrifice in the heart of the realm of Instincts."

He went to sleep searching for the labor in which he might affirm his faith without harming anyone; he was still searching when he woke up.

"A labor that would be difficult and assiduous, in order to celebrate Effort, but simultaneously platonic, in order to cause no new harm, a material toil to the glory of the Idea... What?"

A block of marble overhung the entrance of the grotto, nine feet high and fifteen wide, assailed by wild plants; as he contemplated it, Dieudonat remembered the masons that he had seen sculpting a church behind his cell.

"A manual laborer of art? That is what would respond to my program... That's it! I'll rid you of instinctive nature, O stone, by removing the parasites that are biting you in order to live, and I shall wash you and polish you in order to make you a symbolic fronton attesting the divination of Man by Charity!"

For several nights he searched for the motto to engrave on the slab when the slab had been cleared; finally, he opted for a quote from Saint Matthew:

BEATI MISERICORDES
QUONIAM IPSI MISERICORDIAM
CONSEQUENTUR

"Blessed be the merciful, for they shall obtain mercy!"

He set to work without delay. But while he bloodied his hands in tearing away the brambles and the ivy, he was already wondering whether the promises of the Evangelist might not be a trifle temeritous, and whether it was really certain that Effort and Pity would be recompensed in this world or the other...

"It might be better to say that they carry their own recompense within them."

XIII. Dieudonat contrives two masterpieces,
one with talent, the other with genius, which disgust him
with the fine arts

Right away, he got a taste for what he was going to do, such that the initial project acquired an unforeseen amplitude from one day to next, even from one hour to the next, and sometimes from one minute to the next.

By the time he had cleared the marble, everything had already changed. The motto that was going to be merely inscribed on the unpolished stone first acquired the modest frame of a border; shortly thereafter, a banderole with beautiful curves seemed preferable. To attach the banderole, two nails were recognized to be necessary, and then two angels offered their collaboration to replace the nails, by lifting the ends of the phylactery; almost immediately, their unimportant wings gained more notably proportions, demanding to be deployed above them, in order to make it understood that they were arriving from afar and on high, which is to say, from Heaven. But a bare interval was displayed between the two divine emissaries; logic dictated the addition of other angels, in the course of travel, smaller because of the distance, closer to God; and the image of God then became indispensable. What if, at the summit of the composition, Christ presented the cross on which he had died out of pity or humankind? That would be good! It would be better still if the procession of human miseries were unfurling in the foreground, in order to serve as a foundation for the ensemble; one could see therein all those who are suffering, and everyone knows that they are innumerable, so that there is no shortage of models...

The author was enthused by his idea; it woke him up at night; as soon as first light he went to plant himself, upright, before his block, and he searched the thickness with the penetrating eyes of his intellect in order to caress in advance the silhouettes of his dream emerging from their matrix and modeling themselves for him alone.

"It will be beautiful!"

He said that with passion, but without vanity; in any case, as a true artist, he only admired his work in the future without ever making much of the present or the results obtained, in which he only saw a preliminary path, a promise.

"What an amusing métier I've found here! It can't be denied: the plastic arts are the integral occupation of humans, the human task *par excellence*, since it requires the collaboration of our double nature, mind and body, mental labor and manual labor. What a magnificent combination! I was wrong not to think of it sooner, and I really believe that, this time, I've finally discovered the best employment of my time."

Under the blows of the mallet, his steel chisel entered into the marble, made fire spring forth, and gave birth to forms.

"Yes, yes, it will be beautiful! It isn't yet, but it will become so. In the meantime, I'm procuring incontestable satisfactions from it: I'm creating! Perhaps one day, later, in passing by here, a soul similar to mine will take pleasure in stopping before my work, as I intend to perfect it.

But the pleasure diminished as the work approached its definitive state.

"It won't be as beautiful as I imagined."

Nevertheless, the wings of the angels were well imitated; their robes fluttered very nicely in the wind of their flight through the air; from the height of his cloud, Lord Jesus looked down with a true expression of pity; in the frieze of the miserable, naked men and children, bitten by beasts and pricked by devils, mingled with crowned kings, draped women and mitered bishops, and they all seemed to be fleeing, some raising their eyes toward the heavens, and others collapsing on the ground...

"It's a little beautiful, but not much."

He worked for an entire year.

"That's singular. I've done everything exactly, or I thought I'd done everything exactly, as I wanted to do it; it promised to be superb, in the time when the mass had neither holes nor protrusions; to prevent it from resembling my idea, therefore, there was only a little excess stone; but now that I've removed that superfluous stone, I can no longer see my dream at all."

He finished off the faces and their expressions, the hands and the feet, the feathers and the fabrics. He took particular care with the Lord's face. It was finished.

"Well, there it is! It's not beautiful at all. Frankly, it bears as much resemblance to what I foresaw as the braying of a donkey to the music of paradise."

That disappointment saddened him, a little because of the trouble he had taken in vain, and a great deal by reason of the wrong that he had done to the landscape.

"I've spoiled the work of God by adding my collaboration to it; that wall was more majestic, incontestably, when the primitive stone was inhabited by moss between the ivy and the brambles."

By dint of having it incessantly before his eyes, he became horrified by his folly, which he found grotesque over the grotto, and which imposed itself there like a stone criticism, a perpetual reproach to his presumption. When he returned to the shelter after a walk in the woods, it was necessary for him to see that ugliness again, even more aggressive than usual, waiting for him and contaminating everything. He wished upon it the invasion of vegetation and nests, and promised himself that he would never again attempt the virginity of a pebble.

Now, he was about to realize his masterpiece on the very same day that he vowed not to attempt it again; furthermore, he executed it very rapidly and in the most unexpected fashion.

Since he had disappeared from the world, the principal concern of the people of his father's Duchy had been to discover some trace of him, some in order to give him the crown and others in order to kill him. Hatred being, in general, more active than amity, his enemies were bound to discover him long before his friends. Ludovic's police brought back items of news to their master that concorded strangely. A certain fugitive monk had once been seen near a certain village and had claimed to be the fugitive prince; in a neighboring region a monk had been received by a man named Ruprecht, and since then, a certain woodcutter claimed to have seen a certain anchorite wandering over a mountain...

The usurper did not want to leave to anyone else the care of verifying an identity that was so important to him. He set forth, determined to encounter his brother, and to stab him with his own hand, in order to be quite sure that, this time, the task would be carried out properly.

He therefore came, alone and well armed, had the mountain pointed out to him, found the clearing and saw the man—and he recognized his rival in a savage sitting on a tree trunk and talking to a turtle dove perched on his index finger.

He ran forward, howling, as was his custom: "Kill! Kill!"

Naively, the anchorite thought that it was the attack of a hunter.

"Don't kill this bird! Stop!"

His order immobilized the assailant, his arm high, his leg stiff, his face contracted with anger, and Dieudonat recognized the Bastard in his turn.

Then, at the memory of Onesime and the other cadavers, indignation stirred his gentle soul, and he could not help crying out: "Wicked child, you kill incessantly! Your hatred claims too many victims! Fratricide! Here you are, fixed in your murderous gesture! I wish, for your punishment, that you might remain in that attitude and that you be changed into a statue, like Lot's wife, in order to serve as a lesson to the wicked!"

Scarcely had he uttered those words than Sire Ludovic was transmuted into limestone and became his own effigy.

The sculptor has only spoken in that fashion because of the habitude of sculpture, and simply because each of us brings things back to the one that occupies him; not for a second had he thought about making use of his magical power, and the abrupt metamorphosis stupefied him painfully. He launched himself toward his calcareous relative with a cry of terror and tenderness, taking Heaven as a witness that he had not wanted the sinner's death, that he had spoken in anger, that he repented...

It was no use. The words that one speaks in anger, even if one does not think them, do as much harm as the others, if not more. He learned that at the expense of his neighbor, as all experience is acquired.

He also tried, in order to restore life to the deceased, to formulate a wish contrary to the first, in all sincerity this time. It was wasted effort; his wishes were realized irrevocably, as the Devil had promised. He tore his hair, circled around the new marble, touched it and caressed it, called Ludovic by name, embraced his sculpted boots, implored his pardon and begged him to come back to life, but even though the statue, with its menacing arm, its braced hamstrings and its contracted features, was "full of movement," as art critics say, it did not move.

While lamenting from the bottom of his heart, Dieudonat could not help casting over the magisterial sculpture a professional and admiring glance; the chagrins of an artists always have one eye open.

"Oh, how beautiful it is! What suppleness in the fabrics! And the hands! It's perfect! The hard bones, the elastic flesh, a skin whose tan one can divine! And that face of bestial fury, with that mouth yelling in silence! What a diabolical appearance! Poor devil, all the same. Yes, poor devil, for he's in Hell, having died in mortal sin, and by my fault."

He recommenced mourning the bad lot, but as soon as he changed place and perceived the marble from a new angle he recommenced admiring it.

"Prodigious!"

It was indeed a prodigy, and the desolate magician knew that only too well; he beat his breast as a sign of remorse. He turned away and drew away, hiding his eyes with his hands in order no longer to see his crime, but he came back immediately, recalled by some detail.

"What workmanship! Discouraging. When I compare this block of life to the worthless product of my patience, it's like red blood beside vegetable juice. However, I applied myself the first time and only succeeded in spoiling the stone; the second time, it's true, I've spoiled life."

He struck his forehead.

"I've understood! I understand! Everything is explicable, and it's obvious: life only exists in works in proportion to the life with which one inoculates them, and talent is merely the implement of transfusion. It's the soul that it's necessary to put into matter, in order that it has a soul, and I've imprisoned one inside this. To make life surge forth can only be done at the expense of life, and someone has to die or extract it from himself in order for something to be born or to palpitate. Every work of great art is made of an existence, or at least a torture, and this is vigor fixed. Art is vampiric: from oneself or one's surroundings it's necessary to draw, to pump, to infuse. Well, that, of course, yes, I understand, and this block is howling at me through its beautiful mouth that the only marble of genius is condensed dolor, just as the only ink is dolor in a bottle."

He swore never to risk himself in the arts again, where the cost was really too dear. He ended up taking refuge in his grotto, in order no longer to see his atrocious masterpiece, and he threw himself to his knees with his nose against the rough wall.

"I have killed!"

He spent the rest of the day in lamentations and prayer. He spent all night there.

At one moment, he went outside. The new statue was very white in the moonlight. He recoiled fearfully, and went back into his burrow.

"I've killed my brother, like Cain. Punish me, Lord!"

He had no need to go to the other world in search of an abode of expiation. He possessed it in his domicile, in the very heart of his little domain; amid the cabbages and the carrots, the excessively beautiful statue replaced the imps, and it made him suffer superabundantly, having all the forks of remorse with which to jab its man. It made itself very evident; at daybreak as by moonlight he found it faithful to its post, and as soon as he reappeared, it welcomed him by crying out, with its ever-open and round mouth: "You've killed me!"

It cried soundlessly, but he heard it marvelously.

Naturally, he thought immediately of seeking another shelter.

"Stay with me, and that will be your penance. Henceforth, the victim and the murderer will live face to face."

"God's will be done..."

The first six months were very difficult. When winter came, the Bastard made a semblance of shivering under the snow and the north wind. When the buds swelled and the flowers bloomed, he changed his theme; perfidiously, he recalled that nature, like art and more than art, her imitator and disciple, engenders life at the expense of life, and only fashions beauty by occasioning suffering.

Dieudonat knew that, and the aphorism was banal, but the formula arrived at the point of spoiling spring; it installed itself as an obsession. Solitude is not good for people whose conscience labors them and incites them to monomania; every time the anchorite's gaze fell upon the petrified man—which is to say, a hundred times a day—the obsession was renewed; the vicinity of the marble ended up becoming a symbol of universal dolor.

From then on, the location ceased to be magnificent; populated by visible or invisible crimes, it gave the impression at all times of a guilty individual caught at fault; serenity was no longer resident there; its meditation became crushing. The months passed, the seasons did likewise. Every day, and during every hour of the day, the thought of the poor ascetic turned on itself like the shadow of a sundial, and no longer marked anything but the passage of time.

That same time passed over the marmoreal brother; the patinas of the heavens had soon burnished it, and the masterpiece obtained its normal destiny; turtle-doves acquired the habit of alighting on it; they adopted as a perch that image of fury, which they insulted with petty excrements, with a perfect tranquility. The other birds imitated them, and the clearing soon became so accustomed to the presence of a sublime morsel that no one lent it any attention any longer. Only the author still had eyes to see it, and those eyes became sadder and sadder.

"That intelligent man is ripe for an important stupidity," said the Devil. "Let's give him some help!"

And the Devil set to work.

XIV. His past catches up with him

People get used to anything, even remorse for their sins; at length, Dieudonat was scarcely suffering any longer from his crime, but he was enormously bored.

"I imagine... I'm imagining? In other words, I'm a scatterbrain. And what am I doing in this oasis? Being happy? No, since I sense the time approaching when I won't have any of that any longer. My duty? Even less, since I've discovered that the superiority of humans is in devotion to charity and I've exiled myself far from people: voluntary isolation, the worship of oneself, is an egotism, and I'd be wrong to dissimulate it from myself; to retire to a desert in order to engrave inscriptions in honor of pity and fraternity there is incontestably illogical, in spite of which I might once have said to excuse myself. God judged it good to invest me with a power, and I judge it better not to make use of it; am I sure that I have the right to do that?

"All the same, when I arrived here and the solitude pleased me I found good arguments to demonstrate that it was imposed on me by pity for others; now it wearies me I find it incompatible with charity and I demonstrate that too. Is my logic, therefore, only the sly advocate of my tastes and preferences, the unacknowledged or unconscious servant of my caprices? Cleverer men than me have said so. I've meditated too much on all these vain problems for years; I've lost myself in them, I don't know any more. Where is the truth? What is it necessary to do? Where is duty?"

He was tormenting himself mistakenly, forgetting two laws of fatality, which were about to take the trouble of remembering themselves to him and tracing his conduct for him.

By virtue of one, any force that resides within us will be exercised, with or without our consent; if it is laudable for us to restrict its usage, it is not our prerogative to abolish its existence, and sooner or later there will be an imperious revolt against which the authority of our reason risks remaining impotent.

The other law of fatality, to which he had given too much care, is one that attaches us indissolubly to our past actions, and which makes our existence into a long chain, each link of which commands all the others. Some imperceptible gesture made twenty years ago, of which we have not retained the memory will soon necessitate the gesture that will be imposed upon us, and which we shall make even if it displeases us, because it is the normal prolongation of what happened twenty years before.

He experienced the effects of both these verities at a single stroke.

One day, he was reflecting, in his fashion, sitting in front of his grotto when he saw a woman at the edge of the wood: a sordid and very mature woman, who came out from between the trees and traversed the clearing; she came toward him, treading down the long grass, where her footsteps left a trail.

When she was close, she stopped in order to say: "It's me. Don't you recognize me?"

"No, woman."

"That's not astonishing; you've never seen me before. However, you're the cause of my misfortune and I've come to tell you that. Let me speak. I had a husband and three children, and we lived in ease. Then you quarreled with your father; with regard to what, I don't care and I don't know anything about it, but after your quarrel, the tax collectors were hanged. My husband was one of them, he was hanged, and I was left alone with my three children, without a sou. The harm you've done, it's necessary to repair."

"I can't resuscitate your husband, poor woman."

"I'm not asking as much as that. Render me what he earned, and I'll call it quits."

"I don't have any money."

"Money? You have as much as you want, and more than you need to live, since you only have to make a sign for anything you wish for to come to you, money like everything else. Make the sign and pay me."

"It doesn't please me to make use of that power."

"Yes? That proves your good heart, in truth. What about your conscience? Doesn't your conscience say anything to you?"

"The harm that I might have done to others..."

"It scarcely counts, eh? And when it's done, you turn your back. 'Goodbye, all, and die at your ease.' You go to the mountain, on the edge of a spring, quite tranquilly, with the little birds. Very convenient! And me, I've come to say to you: 'Where is your conscience?'"

Dieudonat began to lower his head, and became ashamed. The woman took advantage of that, and spoke more clearly.

"This is it: there's no bread in the house. I've sold every-thing in order to feed my children, and I have nothing more to sell except my eldest, who's coming up to sixteen. If she turns bad in order to nourish her old mother, it will be your fault, and you'll take that to paradise, with all rest."

The anchorite started with horror. "How much do you need to save that virgin soul?"

"My husband earned two hundred us a year."

"Have your two hundred écus, then. I wish it. So be it."

Immediately, the widow felt her pocket become heavy and she plunged her hand into her rags in order to draw out the money, which she began to count, crouching in the wild grass. Dieudonat contemplated her sadly.

Finally, the old woman raised her head again.

"Well, my good lord, that doesn't settle the account, you see. My husband earned that per year, but he had another ten years to live, the poor dear man. It's necessary to pay me the ten years."

"You can come back next year."

"And what if you're dead? What if I can no longer walk? Think a little, you who are goodness itself and so learned; who knows where you and I will be next year, in ten years or in twenty? It's necessary to be reasonable, my Prince, and pay me my twenty years right away."

"You claimed that your husband only had ten years to live."

"Ten years? One can see that you didn't know Victor. He was as solid as an oak, and built to last for a century, the stout fellow! I'd be losing out if I didn't ask you for twenty years."

"Be careful; excessive wealth is harmful."

"You ought to blush to bargain away the days of a worthy functionary that you've already caused to die horribly. Reimburse me my twenty years and we'll say no more about it."

So saying, the widow held out her skirt. The resigned prince made a sign, formed a wish, and four thousand écus weighed down the fustian.

"Thank you very much," said the beggar.

She turned her back and went away, limping, because the burden was heavy. For a long time, the prince watched the meager silhouette drawing away with an apron full of future; the figure testified veritably to an ill-contained joy, and the philosopher became slightly anxious.

He became even more anxious when the good women, having reached the edge of the clearing, went into the trees and thought that she was invisible. Then, in spite of the weight of the years and the money, she started to dance entrechats that made the coins sing, and Dieudonat, marveling at that sudden cure, undertook a meditation on the power of metals.

That was a relatively new theme, at least for an ascetic; it amused him momentarily, but desires to move racked his legs, as if the approach of a human creature had awakened in him an appetite for agitation. He started walking, and laughing.

"That excellent dame was scarcely sympathetic, and I dare not affirm that she had a husband, or children, but I'm quite sure that she's joyful, and that joy is my work."

He supped with a good appetite, and lay down with a heart lighter than usual; that evening, his bed of hay and ferns was soft and scented.

"I haven't wasted my day, since I've done a little good, and my day would be better still if it's true that in doing good, I've repaired harm."

A voice whispered to him: "The old woman lied to you, fool."

"No, not at all! I'll believe the old woman. I want to believe her, and I gain by it, for my wellbeing this evening is undeniable, and I'd be ill-advised to spoil it. I've satisfied my conscience, eh? The old woman insinuated it to me just now, and it wasn't stupid; who knows whether our conscience isn't simply the sum of our actions? I glimpse there a plausible definition: 'The conscience is the total of the Past.'"

Delighted to have found another formula, he became drowsy before having debated the matter, and when the time came to discover that the aphorism was just as false as another, he was snoring.

XV. And he manufactures the future

The swing had been set in motion. Five days later a city-dweller presented himself, pot-bellied, puffed up and dressed in great luxury; servants parted the branches ahead of him, and he strode with majesty. He came straight toward the anchorite, who then observed his hooked nose and his face illuminated by satisfaction.

"Good day, Prince!" cried the visitor.

He spoke familiarly, with certainty, and his accent denoted a foreign origin.

He went on: "Bad news, Prince! I'm ruined, and I've come to inform you of it, convinced in advance that you won't tolerate that collapse, which will be a national disaster tomorrow, and which is your past work."

"Please?"

"I'm appealing to your conscience."

"Oh. You too?"

"Me: baron Kraff. I'll introduce myself. My establishment is known the world over. At my bank, as you know, thousands of cultivators, petit bourgeois and meager rentiers deposit their savings, very modest, in truth, but one does what one can and no one can live beyond his means. In brief, my safe is that of the little people, who had confidence in me. But I too had confidence in your father and you, and now, blow after blow, your departure and the disappearance of Prince Ludovic—I'm not reproaching you for anything; everyone defends his interests as best he can—turned the political situation upside-down. The market dropped, I bet on a rise: general crash! I've struggled for eighteen months, having a solid back, but I'm at the end. I've lost forty-three millions, all the money of the petty purses. Your late mother…"

"My mother is dead!"

"Exactly: of chagrin and terror, during the massacres at the convent."

"My mother..."

"Evidently, evidently, it's a very regrettable decease, and no one deplores it more than me, since I was just about to remind you of the concern that the excellent Duchess had for poor people; if we had the good fortune of still possessing her, she wouldn't fail to intercede with you in favor of the poor; for it's necessary not to dissimulate that if I go under definitively, you'll have bankruptcies throughout the country, suicides of fathers of families, the ruination of industry and the famine of those it employs, the cessation of commerce, the death of credit, and a hundred cadavers a day. Will you consent to prescribe that hecatomb? That's the whole question."

"Is it possible that...?"

"I've brought you the newspapers. Consult them; from the present, deduce the future. After which, you decide."

The banker sat down on the somewhat hard stone, and unfolded his newspapers; his index finger pointed to the columns of numbers. He developed a few technical explanations concerning reports, arbitrages, transfers, the raising and lowering of prices, capital and interest, and demonstrated clearly that the Prince had to save the innumerable existences that he had compromised.

By dint of listening to that man, the anchorite began to sense under his cranium the intense burn of numbers, and his thoughts became torpid; he was no longer listening, attentive only to that host of victims, whom he could rescue or allow to perish, at his discretion. Certain people require, in order to resist their pity, as much courage as others require to help people in difficulties. Dieudonat did not have the strength to refuse his intervention; he made a gesture, murmured a wish, and the capital was created.

Sacks of gold appeared in the grass, and barrels full of coins; by virtue of an infernal malice that would have escaped the ascetic, there were also wads of banknotes, but he financier protested against those.

"Oh, pardon me! Not that! Paper money is credit on the Treasury, which would refuse the reimbursement and would implicate me in an affair of fraud. Take back your paper, and please substitute for it an equal sum in coin."

"As you wish."

The magical appearances recommenced in the crushed grass. The Baron, a man accustomed to the return of capital, did not blink before that fortune; from the top of his nose, through his lorgnon, he allowed to fall upon it a gaze of immediate adoption. When he saw that the heap had ceased to grow, he exiled his lenses toward his belly.

"It's all there? No, no, let's not verify it. I trust you."

Incontinently, he pivoted toward the wood, made a sign to his first valet, who sent the second valet to search under the foliage for the first secretary, who ordered the cashier to send forth his agents, who brought the coffers prepared in advance.

"I didn't doubt you, as you see."

He snapped his orders with the edge of his lips, and even the tips of his fingers. Dieudonat admired the briskness that gold gives.

He's as arrogant with his clerks as the Archduke with his pages! That self-made man would be as offended as the son of an Emperor, perhaps more so, if I were to insinuate that he's the cousin of his accountant. I shan't take the risk again.

The rich man honored the removal of the funds with his presence, but did not deign to supervise it. He even affected to turn his back, and, the serious affairs being liquidated henceforth. He perceived the landscape.

"Your residence is charming. Yes, yes, very picturesque. Those rocks, those trees, this tranquility. I envy you. A casino in this corner would flourish. You have a spring?"

He replaced his lorgnon and discovered the statue of Ludovic.

"Damn, Prince! You have a pure masterpiece here. I'll buy it. How much?"

"I don't..."

"I'll give you twenty thousand...? No...? Thirty! Oh! Where the devil is my head? I forgot that you can make gold at will. I regret it: that piece would look very well on my lawn at the foot of the perron. You must do me the amity, some day, of coming to visit my summer lair; it's very comfortable. But how have you been able to transport that figure here? Seriously, do you suspect how admirable it is, and that it's a murder..."

"A murder!"

"To keep it here in this desert, where no one sees it."

"I see it, sir."

On listening to the individual talk, Dieudonat made the reflection that tact is perhaps not a worldly quality, as is believed in manor houses and drawing rooms, but rather a primordial virtue, closely related to what is called in metaphysics the notion of good and evil.

The philosopher could, in any case, philosophize at his ease, for the millionaire was no longer occupied with him; he had approached the beautiful marble, of which he made a tour, sniffing it with his trunk bearing two lenses, not without darting an occasional keen glance at his cashiers.

"No signature? No? Too bad. Do you know the author?"

"Alas..."

"Oh, I can guess: a paltry individual of whom you have something to complain? Eh? It doesn't astonish me. General rule: mistrust artists. But damn it, this one had talent. On the other hand, the big one over the grotto, with the angels...do you like it?"

"Not much."

"Nor me! Your bas-relief, I call that idealist art. Your statue, fine! That's reality! And I know it! I even perceive, in the face and the costume, and in the attitude to, a rather comical resemblance..."

"Comical?"

"To the Bastard. Do you know that malevolent tongues have accused you of having...?"

"Go on, please!"

"I don't occupy myself with politics. That's a principle. Kings, Princes, I tell you, sort things out between themselves. He aspired to the throne, you aspire to it: one crown, two heads a bad count. Bad, above all, for business. One of the pretenders evaporates? I register the result and I don't enquire as to the means."

"Others than you explain it, don't they? Tel me everything."

"Don't worry, no one's talking about it any longer. Your brother wasn't much liked—a small loss. You'll reign in peace: an enormous benefit, for you as for us."

"I shall never reign."

"Get away! When Papa goes, you'll come back. We'll see you again, my Prince, and we'll do good work together, you and I: I sense that. The country has high hopes of your reign, and awaits it with impatience—legitimate impatience, I confess, between us, for the situation certainly isn't brilliant."

In order to occupy his leisure while the loading of the millions was completed, he was willing to continue a conversation in which he had nothing more to ask; gratuitously, and out of pure benevolence, he exposed the facts: the tax-collectors had been hanged, the taxes had not been gathered, and the Duke, in the absence of his ordinary receipts, had had to make extraordinary expenses. In such dire straits, Hardouin the Just had been constrained to rely on exceptional resources, peculations and prevarications, adulteration of the currency, various exactions and arbitrary confiscations, imprisonments and decapitations.

"My father has done these things?"

The Baron strove to excuse the ruling power, which is sometimes obliged to such regrettable measures, but the Prince remained dazed, and could not understand how his noble father, so honest when all was going well, was so dishonest because things were going badly.

Immediately, he resolved to save the paternal soul and to render to honesty the one who had given him the light of day.

"How much does he need?"

The financier glimpsed an unexpected, superb affair. He replied that he was not able to answer, and offered to study the question. He even went as far as to promise to speak to the

Duke, to propose a rapprochement between the father and the son, and to negotiate a non-reimbursable loan from one to the other; he assured him, in addition, that, out of gratitude, he would be content with a modest commission.

The loading was completed. He learned that without having any need to look. At that precise moment he declared that his minutes were counted and that the route was long to the next stopover. He promised to return and repeated that he would see the Duke.

"I'll reconcile you, I tell you, with your dear Papa. I'll take charge of it, and if you're content with my offices, you'll offer me the statue, won't you, in memory of our first encounter? Until we met again, dear Prince, and see you soon."

He extended his hand and retired toward his carriage with the rapid dignity of a man able to earn forty-three millions in as many minutes.

The coffers of gold followed their master. The anchorite found himself alone again, but for several days he retained a very nasty impression of that visit.

Once again, the landscape had changed; miasmas of unhealthy memories floated therein. The foliage murmured terms of agiotage; solar disks fell from the trees in gold coins and disappeared under the thickets as if they were rolling; numbers hooked on to the thorns of viburnum; the thick branches bore hanged citizens or severed heads.

"My father has committed these sins! What a pity, Lord, that I have no influence on human thought! At least the evil will cease, I hope, if we suppress its causes. Lord, let the Duke not reject the Baron's offers!"

Wishes of that sort are realized without the help of occultism; the Devil has no need to get mixed up in them; we are sufficient. After a week, Dieudonat saw Treasury officials appear, who came to take up residence on the mountain and proceeded to load up the subsidies. The good Duke had consented!

He only put three conditions on that favor: he would fix the amount of aid himself without discussion; like the Baron, he would only accept metallic payments; and no one else would benefit henceforth from the Prince's liberalities. He had to swear to those on oath.

Dieudonat was ready to do anything to save his father's soul. That same evening, in order to be rid sooner of a duty that promised few pleasures, he fabricated a great many coins and ingots.

"Is that enough?"

He had to recommence the following day, the day after, and every day.

"More?"

"More."

The sovereign's appetites were revealed to be considerable, doubtless because his needs were great. Dieudonat was able to observe that the administration organized a regular service of transport; he also learned that it was occupied in clearing roads through the forest and building bridges over the rivers; he knew that taverns were being installed along the roads, with stables, for the use of carters and their carriages.

"I'll only have them for a little while..."

Carters were howling oaths and clerks were making puns in areas accustomed to birdsong. Soon, highwaymen appeared, necessitating a militia. From then on, sentinels guarded the vicinity of the factory and patrols made rounds throughout the night. The sound of trumpets rang out unexpectedly and recognition calls were relayed in the silence like stones skipping over the surface of a pond. Sentry-boxes surged forth between the trees.

On the other hand, the doves and finches sought more peaceful abodes; the blackbirds fled, the nightingales fell silent and the flight of kingfishers no longer whistled over the stream. The hinds had disappeared, the lizards were crushed, the spring became muddy, the trampled grass dried out in the clearing and throughout the landscape pieces of paper were seen flourishing at the foot of trees, which blossomed like large white daises.

"I'm beginning to think that they're here for good."

The poor maker of gold had the sensation of being similar to a milk-cow, but his byre resembled a factory complicated by barracks. He thought, sighing, about the good weeks of boredom and remorse that he had savored so peacefully in the exile of a beautiful location.

"I'm deprived of everything, even my own company, although it wasn't amusing."

One day, he saw, to his surprise, masons unsealing the statue of the Bastard.

"You're taking him away?"

"Duke's orders."

He was slightly glad of that separation, but also a little chagrined. He watched that bad companion disappear, laid on a bed of straw, with an envious gaze.

"They've only broken a hand and an eye; he's very tranquil. What if I go too?"

Evidently he could have dispersed the crowd and resumed his solitude by wishing; he thought about it many a time; but those acts of egotism would have appeared criminal, since a great distress had reached out toward him, which he could relieve.

"*Beati misericordes...*"

He therefore remained the prisoner of his power, and thus learned that the elect of this world ought not to pretend to the unique monopoly of poor wretches, which is the right to live in peace.

XVI. In which one sees the depiction
of a fortunate people

The country became prodigiously rich; that affluence of gold had changed the conditions of social life utterly and completely.

At first, the people were very happy, or believed themselves to be, which comes to the same thing, for you are not unaware that our happiness is simply a favorable appreciation of contingencies that are sometimes disastrous.

Now, the social contingencies appeared fully satisfactory. The Duke, in fact, scarcely bothered any longer to collect the taxes that had cost him so many anxieties; he ceased to hang the insolvent and despoil the rich, and even went so far as to decree that no tax or rent would levied until further notice. Bonfires were lit in towns and the countryside and people sang *Te Deums* with *Te Ducems*, and *O Salutaris hostias* that blessed God, the Duke and his son, the national benefactors.

All the auguries were good. An era of prosperity opened. The sovereign was long past fifty, the critical age at which the passion for procreation is transformed in a man, and from carnal becomes simply lapidary; having become almost chaste, the potentate set about building. He knew the love of placing stone on stone, and of the durable thing that rises at the moment in life when the fragile thing begins to collapse. He wanted palaces and churches, fortresses, bridges and aqueducts, canals, fountains, quays and stairways: useless edifices and useful buildings, new monuments surged forth from the ground, to the glory of religion and commerce, great men and small, to the memory of the dead and the profit of the living; everywhere, the Duke erected beauty or ugliness, indistinctly and without preference, as long as they were solid; he possessed the means to offer one and the other, and he did not fail to demand both,

The fatherland bristled with towers and gables, bell-towers and turrets, steeples, arches and colonnades, bas-reliefs and corbels, everything that could be made in stone, in marble, and even in bronze. Statues and domes were decorated with gold—what was the point of depriving them, since gold was so abundant? The clouds, as they passed by, were astonished to see the cities resplendent, and went on their way; in the rising sun and the setting sun, they splashed the sky with their radiance. From the tops of the mountains that closed the frontier, they could be admired, shining in the verdure like diamond brooches on a jeweler's velvet.

The more the Duke built, the more he wanted to build, and he recommenced endlessly. All the young men became masons; the daily wages of a manual worker would have contented a prelate. Apprentices were able to court dancers; on Sundays, carpenters appeared in promenades, sumptuously dressed; the wives of entrepreneurs had carriages with two horses, and their daughters married barons and earls. Carters, stonemasons, plasterers, carpenters and wood-merchants, locksmiths and ironworkers, metallurgists and miners, wheelwrights and shipwrights all grew rich, and their fortunes enriched others.

When construction thrives, everything thrives.

And all went very well—too well, and too rapidly. At first, the people, excited by the new force, had created radiantly, and their fecundity, stimulated to labor, illuminated genius. Great artists, who, in other times, would have remained swineherds, surged forth, rivaling one another in ardor, and that abrupt flourishing of human beings produced a crop of masterpieces. But one does not make well for very long that which one makes for money; behind the true artists, the false ones appeared, and, as usual, they found people who thought them preferable, especially when the sovereign had judged them to be. All the sons of families wanted to be architects, and anyone who possessed any musical or poetic talent hastened to learn to model clay or paint frescoes instead of singing or writing. Art did not gain from that, but the good Duke could not see it, and paid everyone handsomely.

People were paid too much; enjoyment was better than production; drunkenness arrived, and lucre engendered luxury, which engendered lust; soon, young working girls were moving fingers charged with rings.

"Would you like to put that away, slut!"

But the mothers did not become too indignant, and the fathers scarcely protested any more, gold being essential in the new fashions; the amorous put it on all the women as the Duke put it on all the cities; couturiers wove it into clothing, cabinet-makers embedded it in furniture; goldsmiths owned palaces; but the farms no longer had any laborers. All the vigor of the country flowed toward rapid gain—which is to say, toward the city. The fields devoid of laborers were spangled with wild flowers, and crops no longer emerged therefrom. A chicken cost as much as a sheep.

Bah! Everything the country lacked, foreigners would furnish. The wheat and the livestock would arrive from abroad.

They did not come alone.

The Duke, enfevered for grandeurs, took the title of King; sumptuous presents that cost him very little bought acceptance of his crown from the sovereigns and diplomats of the Christian powers; the Emperor approved, having received arguments of the first order before all the others; Rome sent its assent, with the necessary oils; ambassadors made their entrances solemnly. A large army was indispensable to so much majesty; mercenaries came running, attracted by high pay. The riffraff of neighboring kingdoms rushed toward that quarry; the least nasty asked for work, the worst were content with theft; beautiful young women from everywhere brought their lucrative bodies.

Feasting flourished, morality declined. The national soul, disorganized by that foreign invasion, lost its particular virtues, its original faculties and its genius. Peoples that no longer have a morality no longer have anything but talent; the masterpieces of the initial epoch were unable any longer to be born, and art was refined without creating, plagiarizing its past, becoming flaccid and debased. The fine impetus that had previously lifted up the crowd, and the joyous effort that bore them to work, was only remembered in order to be ridiculed. Work, toil? Pooh! Everyone gave as little as possible and demanded as much as possible.

For they demanded; the discontentment of humans is manifest much less in the reality of poverty than before the insufficiency of advantages; so long as they are suffering they weep and collapse, but as soon as they begin to enjoy, they want more than they have, and proclaim their right to enjoy more.

Orators began to make speeches.

The citizens talked so much in order to occupy their leisure that the habit of talking soon engendered the habit of speech-making; eloquences were revealed; the need to sustain ideas made people believe that they had some; they called them principles, and everyone was irreducible with regard to his own. From then on, everyone affirmed them. That country, where everyone spoke so well, was covered with pulpits and podiums, which gave birth to parliaments, and parliamentarians appeared, which gave rise to parliamentarianism. Words reigned.

They reigned to the exclusion of anything else and instead of anything else; formulae substituted for sincerity; as for the cult of the good and the dream of the better, with respect to work or oneself, no one cared about that. All faith was dead. The family scarcely existed any more, by reason of multiple adulteries; husbands scarcely concealed it, having become accustomed to it; culpable liaisons did not last any longer than the others. People theorized about everything, but, fundamentally, laughed at everything, and were even already weary of laughing. Soon, they were content to smile.

Several suicides of young people were symptomatic of that degeneration; the lack of an ideal caused internal distress among people born to hope, and many adolescents, for want of fodder for the irreducible appetite for something beyond, threw away their blasé lives like useless rags. Forces without employment suppressed themselves. Lovers were seen to poison themselves in couples, because they had squandered happiness, and still wanted it, without being able to invent it. Before those quotidian dramas, mature individuals and old people shrugged their shoulders tranquilly and clung on to existence, valuing it more as it gave them less.

That population of rich people, diminished as it was, was not devoid of arrogance. It requires a nobility of soul to possess gold without being scornful of those who lack it; similarly, it requires a real solidity of intelligence not to be intoxicated by suddenly-acquired power. That King and his subjects, by dint of launching commands throughout the world, believed that they commanded the world; in their eyes, licensed suppliers appeared to be wage-slaves, servants of a sort, only too happy to serve; at the precise moment when their incapacity of production rendered them tributaries of other realms, they imagined that they were becoming their masters, and allowed that to be seen. They spoke with authority, and their speech had the tone of indubitable certainty particular to men who are playing a role superior to their intellect.

They were importunate; people thought them grotesque, and then detestable.

In addition, envy had prepared the way for hatred. More than one sovereign, in the depths of his impoverished Estates, kept watch avidly on that prey, as juicy as could be desired, ripe for swallowing, which would fatten his kingdom and his dynasty for a long time. Perhaps it was even important to make haste, for fear that the booty, desired by all, might be taken by another. The suspicious Kings kept watch one another; each of them had decidedly secretly that he would be the first to get annoyed and that he would fall upon Hardouin without warning, and without inviting anyone else

Among them all, Gaifer the Twisted, who reigned to the west, was the most urgent, because he was the poorest; slyly, he organized his troops, and as soon as he was in a condition

124

to go on campaign he complained of a diplomatic impropriety, sent his herald of arms, and crossed the frontier the same day.

He moved rapidly, followed by black bands, pillaging and burning; everything crumbled before him. The defensive armies, splendidly braided in gold, only showed themselves as if for a parade before vagabonds armored in iron, and immediately vanished in clouds of dust stirred up by their flight. The cities with such well-constructed solid ramparts opened their gates as soon as the enemy appeared in the plain, and costumed officials appeared, their faces pale and their hands trembling, bringing the damascened keys on golden trays. Not one hero rose up to cry love of the fatherland, for the fatherland was too rich, and no one loved it any longer, and the fatherland was no longer a mother but a mistress, whose lovers had enjoyed too much...

XVII. Dieudonat decides not to give anything any longer but himself

The work went smoothly. Hardouin was captured and imprisoned, and immediately, Gaifer considered himself to be the legitimate king of an annexed country; from then on, he no longer made haste, and on his orders, his captains destroyed less, careful to conserve the beautiful conquered cities. Even the inhabitants were no longer massacred, except for amusement, for they put into receiving the victors all the good grace of deferential cowardice; they surrendered everything, including their daughters and wives, and accepted everything, including blows, and when they were chased away with kicks like dogs, they smiled politely, in order that their throats would not be cut like pigs. In a week, their celebrated arrogance had disappeared; the masters of the world were now the valets of a corporal in the army, and performed their new role just as congruently as the old one; the transformation cost them little effort, for those people had only been carrying, beneath their garments of mastery, the souls of slaves.

The war and its horrors therefore seemed likely to be of fairly short duration. Unfortunately, Aimery the Simple, who reigned to the east, considered in his simplicity the wrong that was being done to him by pillaging a neighbor that he should have pillaged himself; without hesitation, he protested, in the name of justice and humanity, declared that he would support the weak, and crossed the frontier, as an ally. The war was resumed, more hotly.

Between Aimery and Gaifer, no one could see any difference. Just like Gaifer, Aimery, by right of alliance, demanded in his turn that the cities were opened to him and the fortresses surrendered; that protector, more terrible than the conqueror, obliged the indigenes to go forth and make war, which Gaifer had not constrained anyone to do as long as they surrendered. Whether people liked it or not, it was necessary to kill, ridiculously, on fields of carnage, under the command of uncivil captains who, moreover, spoke a foreign language. And those brutes from the West no longer struck with a dead hand! Mercy of God, what a way to behave!

Between the two armies, the entire country was bloodied; the pillage recommenced with a ferocious hated; Aimery's carts took away to the East everything that Gaifer had not had time to expedite to the West; the country was emptied via its two frontiers; when a troop, allied or enemy, arrived somewhere and no longer found anything to steal, it lit a fire to avenge itself, and hurried elsewhere.

Hardouin I was huddled in a dungeon, but no one was concerned with his worthless carcass. They were much more preoccupied to know who possessed the anchorite Dieudonat, the maker of gold. The example of the disasters of which he was the cause did not instruct anyone, and everyone wanted to have the destroyer of energies in his custody, for his own exclusive advantage.

He was snatched, he was hidden; every fortress in which one of the two sovereigns had imprisoned the precious magician temporarily was quickly retaken by the adversary, and that human parcel rolled from the West to the East and from the East to the West, toward one frontier and toward the opposite frontier, without anyone having had time to do anything within him, indefinitely tossed from one master to the other, and always defended royally by an owner always destined to lose him, so strong is the desire to have an irresistible force in all those who do not.

On the way, he encountered cities in ruins and villages reduced to ash; here and there, he perceived some belated conflagration devouring an isolated farm. Every time he emerged into a plain he saw in the distance, toward the bottom of the sky, like a huge swarm of flies, thousand of crows feasting continually; whenever a gust of wind blew, the air stank virulently; cadavers lay everywhere, representing in the horizontal stance that which had once depicted pride in a vertical station.

"Never again will I make gold, oh, never again!"

While marching at a military pace—*one, two! one, two!*—he meditated, and his meditations were not advantageous.

"In wanting to repair evils, I've created worse ones. My God, my God, is pity, them, also a source of errors and misdeeds? Does the heart lead us astray as much as the head, and do our commiserations lead us as far astray as our deductions? Sentiment allows us to be moved by things that are close at hand and immediate, and only to perceive them; the distant consequences escape its short sight. Love is myopic, but wisdom is for the presbyopic, who look to the future. Woe betide the reckless who mingle in the world's affairs and do not discern the future! Woe betide those who risk substituting their conscious will for the unconscious will of the universe, and who come to trouble history in the design of perfecting it!"

"*One, two! one, two!*"

"If I made the decision no longer give anything that what can be drawn from myself, perhaps I would look further, and my benevolence would be at less risk of being toxic. Strictly speaking, I could also give what serves for human subsistence, for to prevent a Christian from dying of hunger is not bad and cannot harm anyone. Thus let me do in future, Lord, if you lend me life, which I scarcely merit, and which scarcely appears to me to be desirable."

Before the ruins and the cadavers, he beat his breast, to the great amusement of his guards, and proclaimed aloud: "It's my fault! It's my fault!"

The soldiers accompanied the cadence by sending him kicks from behind which arrived about half way up his body, and they laughed wholeheartedly.

He was treated with more deference at the beginning of his alternate journeys toward Gaifer and toward Aimery; then his conductors hoped by turns that he might give them gold, and each of them assured him, in secret, of his cordial devotion; several even offered to facilitate an escape and accompany him in his flight, but he discouraged those good intentions, trying to explain that treason is a disloyal action, and above all by declaring that he would never again make or give gold; the disappointed amities had immediately turned sour and everyone, at present competed in brutality in public, in order that no one would suspect what they had proposed in secret.

"Hup, magician! Forward march!"

He responded to the blows: "Punish me, you who know my power and the use that I have made of it. I have decided irrevocably with a fallible understanding! Let my example serve as a lesson to you and instruct you to doubt yourselves; humans desire at hazard and not otherwise, for the truth is more complex and more deceptive than Janus, and our examination has always forgotten one of its innumerable faces."

"Feel whether I've forgotten your face!"

And the military boot attained him with precision.

"Perfect! My dear cousins, don't stint yourselves, recommence; in giving me the foot, you're only giving of yourselves, and because of that, your action is not very harmful."

"Is he mocking us?" said the sergeant.

"I fear so," said the captain.

"He'll see!" said the corporal.

The boots went to work again, gaily at first. "*One, two! one, two!*" But after a while the warriors discovered for themselves that they were imposing extra work on themselves gratuitously, unhelpful for men charged with burdens who have a long road to travel; they stopped.

"And there it is!" said the philosopher. "When one gives of oneself, one rapidly gets tired, and the harm that one has done stops. Oh, I understand the lesson, sirs, and I'm grateful for it; I swear to you that I'll profit from it, with the exception of foodstuffs, which are indispensable to every creature, I shall no longer give anything but myself.

XVIII. The amazement of an ascetic
rejoining the century

He had been traveling thus for a fortnight when every-thing changed abruptly. His latest possessor had succeeded in taking him over the frontier; a messenger from the Court brought orders from Gaifer the Twisted that prescribed treat-ing Dieudonat with all the regard due to Princes of the Blood.

Among the people, as well as in aristocratic circles, the possession of that captive, whom the sovereign was already wittily calling "the goose that lays golden eggs," was counted as a definitive wealth. The unhealthy intentions of the Goose who no longer wanted to lay had been reported to the mon-arch, but Gaifer shrugged his shoulders.

"I'll be able to persuade him!"

The truth is that he had discussed the case with his con-fessor, a wily psychologist expert in manipulating the mecha-nisms of souls; that director of consciences, without actually giving any advice on a matter so delicate, had indicated in a general and purely theoretical fashion, a means of reducing the determination of a chaste anchorite. In that regard, he had ex-plained how an excessively severe youth, bridled too soon, predisposes innocence to opportunities of the flesh, which is very strong before being so weak; still in that regard, he had cited Saint Anthony, whom the Church had canonized, so mer-itorious did his resistance seem. But had not that great saint been dealing with imps and not real women…?

"Enough," said the King. "I understand."

Exactly as if the King had not opened his mouth, the priest continued: "It is a well-known truth, but which mystics do not suspect sufficiently, that extremes touch. Mysticism confines many points of excessive sensuality, for both proceed from an aptitude to feel keenly and to imagine; look at Dante, who was the most idealistic of poets, and whose biography exposes to us that he was 'marvelously lustful.' Excessively impressionable individuals, whose imagination also works to excess, risk overflowing, in accordance with whether Grace guides them, or abandons them, into religious fervor or carnal passions. Sometimes, they even go from one to the other in different parts of their life, and it is for that reason that frightful debauchees suddenly renounce their disorderly existence in order to take refuge in prayer, ecstasy and the rudest penances; several have become Blessed, not to say Saints; conversely, alas, pious souls find themselves unexpectedly seduced by the demon and fall drunkenly into the folly of sin; on that day, Satan does everything he can."

"I understand, I tell you, priest!"

After that conversation, the monarch had the delightful palace of Armida furnished again;[7] speeches of welcome were also commanded for the person who had the right to them, and constitutive bodies in full regalia came to take up positions at the North Gate in order to receive the ascetic.

When he appeared before that superb masquerade, muddy as he was, clad in rags, funeral oration phrases celebrated his majesty and his power. Words of that sort are not ordinarily heard by the man they concern, since he is dead; Dieudonat knew, while still alive, the shame of being praised for virtues or vices that he did not possess; he drained the chalice to the dregs, and when the official eloquence had finished dripping, the procession set forth.

---

[7] Because the French translation of Torquato Tasso's epic *Gerusalemme liberata* (1581; tr. as *Jerusalem Delivered*) was used in nineteenth-century French *lycées* as a standard text, every educated Frenchman in the early 1900s knew the story of the Saracen sorceress Armida, commissioned to interrupt the progress of the first Crusade by seducing the great knight Rinaldo. Instead of murdering him, she creates an enchanted garden where she retains him with her erotic charms. The garden was transformed into a palace in popular parlance referring to any kind of flamboyant device of seduction.

It advanced, with an orchestra at the head, pompously comical, between two hedges of troops, which presented arms; the people behind the soldiers applauded, uttering cries of delight. Under everyone's eyes, Dieudonat felt that he was grotesque.

Finally, the trumpets stopped outside the palace of Armida; the troop formed a circle.

A group of varlets wearing his escutcheon were waiting for him to the right of the perron; to the left, a legion of chambermaids was lined up, cleverly chosen from among the most beautiful daughters of the realm; and in front of them was a little man clad entirely in white, fat and clean shaven, who seemed to be sculpted in lard. He approached the Prince with three strides, punctuated with three bows.

"Your servant Anoure,[8] chief eunuch, begs Your Highness respectfully to enter his abode."

The prisoner went in. The young women crowded behind him; he heard them whispering; at the same time, he admired the superb dwelling

The King will not treat me as well when he's better informed; and who knows, in any case, what tortures might await me inside?

He advanced courageously, ready for anything. The little troop followed a wide corridor with walls lined with onyx; suddenly, it emerged into a vast hexagonal hall illuminated from above, florid with rare plants, in the middle of which a pink marble pool was hollowed, with a noisy water jet; three niches fitted with divans and hung with tapestries sank into three walls; a perfumed freshness floated in the air. The chief eunuch turned round to announce to Milord that the maidservants were ready to proceed with his toilette, in order that he might have the decency required to be presented to the King. Milord tried to protest in the name of modesty, but Anoure was already drawing away and the young women began to

---

[8] Like several of the more exotic names in the story, this one is derived from the Latin, *Anura* being the order if frogs.

strip the ascetic of the habit that he had been wearing for thirteen years.

At first they appeared to experience some disgust; with their fingertips, they threw his clothes in a heap on the marble floor, and those who were not occupied in undressing the price undressed themselves in order to put him in the bath.

He suffered in his chastity and attempted to struggle, but the maidservants were strong; in order to draw him toward the pool they took hold of him everywhere, enlacing him with their plump arms, pushing him with their bodies pressed against his, and laughing all around him. He saw seven or eight of them at the same time; he did not know how many there were, and did not want to know, and he closed his eyes as one clenches one's fists, with a vigorous energy; that effort was the only one of which he was still capable, and he concentrated his poor petty thought therein, in the matter of children poring over their page of handwriting. His head had become hollow, his ideas were adrift, and he confessed to himself subsequently that throughout that long day, he had been profoundly stupid, understanding things wrongly as soon as he tried to understand them, and only being able to link them by ludicrous reasoning.

At any rate, he perceived that behind his closed eyelids, the living tableaux of the previous minute were persisting in their intention with a terrifying precision; furthermore, every contact evoked an image; he had the illusion of seeing with his whole body, as if his skin had been equipped with eyes. He ceased to struggle, in order not to augment further the touches that did not displease him sufficiently, and, in order to refresh his mind as much as to implore aid in his distress, he entered into prayer at the same time as he entered into the water.

The liquid was soft; in spite of the effort he made to liberate his soul by elevating it toward God, his orison was distracted and scarcely rose at all; contingencies recalled it down below, completely denuded of idealism; among them, a major and obsessive astonishment persecuted him without him being able to avoid it.

Never in his life had he imagined that ladies or damsels were arranged in that fashion; never in his life! No document in the library of the holy monks, no illumination, had ever prepared him for such a surprise. On colored parchments or in the capitals of the church he had perceived, here and there, a spouse of Adam expelled from Paradise, or a few of the damned in Hell, but they had only appeared to him to be worthy of pity. And how little those meager individuals resembled these! In any case, and above all, those copies made by human art did not furnish any idea of the incontestable charm that resides in the originals modeled directly by God: the charm that is divine, because of its origin, and which the Creator has so carefully divided in the ensemble and the details.

After all, one can experience the pleasure of admiring the work of the Eternal under the reserve not contaminating that homage with desires that he has forbidden. In consequence, he opened his eyes again. A hand's breadth away from his face he saw breasts where droplets were pearling; the young women were immersed up to the waist, with the pink scoop of their two hands throwing handfuls of water over the torso. Their breasts were so white that he observed his own dirtiness; he was ashamed of it, and his alarm changed motive, the anxiety of not seeing replaced by the anxiety of not being seen; he closed his eyes again.

That ostrich decision did not procure him the relief for which he had hoped; his shame persisted.

Those minutes were of capital importance in his life, for they were those in which modesty, in changing it object, changed its nature; from being religious, it became human, and by virtue of that, the man had just been born within the fanatic.

But so what? Into that place and into that attitude, God had doubtless cast him, Daniel in the women's den, in order that he should endure the punishment of his errors. Certainly, he merited the cruelest of tortures! His soul resigned and his expression sufficiently stupid, he waited while the little hands, foaming with soap, went to work on him furiously. They ran everywhere, lively and familiar; they ran over the slippery surface, swerving, gyrating, flying away and coming back; there were six of them, there were ten, perhaps more, perhaps twenty, and they chased one another, replaced one another, with a silky sound, so rapid and so cheerful that they gave the impression of laughing at their work.

"What strange torment are you according me, Lord?"

All things considered the torture was bearable, and the constancy of the patient veritably merited a recompense; he received it. From one moment to the next, the anguish of his modesty decreased, in order to give way to a sort of seraphic delight, which descended within him like a benediction, or perhaps a pardon, and he perceived a luminous warmth therein that radiated in the depths of his being; he felt the wings of a mystic dove, still perfumed with paradise, palpitating in his heart, so resplendent that it splashed from the inside to the outside.

The genteel torturers persisted in laughing and soaping; he regretted momentarily that such frivolity was profaning that moment of efficacious grace, but he did not have the heart to criticize those young women, or anyone, while his interior ecstasy fill him entirely with gratitude toward heaven and indulgence toward his torturers.

It was then that he reopened his eyes for the second time, and appreciated even better than the first time how much the person of Eve had been superseded; he thought that perhaps the daughters of Eve were not wrong to laugh, as he had believed a little while ago, for the multiple brilliance of lips, teeth, cheeks, eyes, eyelashes and dimples constituted a harmony that only divine science was capable of conceiving and ordering. Was laughter also the work of God, then? And he laughed, in his turn, but with a stupid expression.

"Thank you, Mademoiselles, that will be enough..."

The chambermaids would not hear it; now they untangled his hair and beard; afterwards, they drew him out of the water and shoved him toward heaped cushions; then they dried his skin with soft cloths, and massaged him with odorous essences; a warmth of wellbeing made his muscles supple. Standing in their midst, his torso seemed broader and his stature straighter; a generous sap was flowing in his conscious veins; he felt stronger and more lucid, enlightened by new but confused notions.

It seemed to him that a world had suddenly opened before him, a mysterious fatherland that he was rediscovering without having known it, but which he had borne within him for a long time—a very long time—and had wanted without knowing it; it appealed to him with its promising horizons, and the dawn rose over them while his past became foggy down below, like a dream...

Under the pressure of the young women, he collapsed among the cushions and remained on his back; the abrupt vertigo of his youth had intoxicated him, and his head was heavy. He passed his fingers over his forehead, trying to reflect. Where was he? Where did he come from? Who was he? Someone else, apparently! He no longer remembered, and truly did not want to remember, himself. He forgot everything that was distant, in order to gaze at what surrounded him, and his gaze was that of a young sleeper waking up.

In a circle, the naked young women were standing up, astonished by their handiwork and admiring his reconquered beauty. To one of them, who was smiling more complaisantly, he responded with a smile. She advanced timidly, as if she feared having misunderstood and daring too much. He continued smiling at her, without knowing why; then the young woman's lips expanded further; they came closer, and he saw them hovering above him like a pink bird, which came closer and closer to his mouth, while two eyes appealed to his soul and drank it through his eyes. He felt the fresh breasts settle over his heart, and above the shoulder of the first lover he perceived the others, who were going away, discreetly and sulkily.

*XIX. He discovers an aspect of divine bounty
and becomes an optimist*

The revelation of amour produced a complete upheaval in Dieudonat. His stupor was indescribable; books of science or philosophy, and theologians too, had denounced to him, it is true, the existence of the inferior sensations that they classified under the denomination of "sensual pleasures," and he had supposed that the label in question designated an ensemble of mediocre pleasures, such as those produced by foodstuffs with an agreeable taste. But about an emotion so intense, no one had warned him, either in writing or verbally. For the first time in his life, after so many doubts and negations, he had finally encountered a decisive verity, absolute light, doubtless ephemeral but the dazzling certainty of which nothing could abolish. The plenary light, he had seen! For a moment, he had possessed the incontestable! He was now able to remember something, and that thing fully merited all the honors of memory.

Now, that sudden illumination having accompanied the loss of his virginity, he concluded, by means of syllogism, that the one was inherent in the other, as the effect in the cause, and that, in consequence, that minute must be unique for everyone, like those of birth and death.

Of the three, that one is assuredly the best.

In order not to trouble the last residues, he remained immobile in an ecstasy that was prolonged in languor, and in that demi-dream he told himself hat God is good; he had never doubted it in principle, even though he had never found many proofs of it before this one; at any rare, it was sufficient! But frankly, why were those same books obstinate in recommending chastity, in praising virginity, when the Church Fathers, in assembling to demonstrate the existence of God, did not have a single argument or a single cry in their homilies the eloquence of which was comparable to the one that emanates spontaneously from those two virtues when they are violated?

I'm inclined to think that there is an error in the inter-pretation of the texts; we are told that virginity is agreeable to God, and I don't dispute that, since it proves God on the day when one loses it; still, it is necessary to lose it, under pain of being impious, and that is quite evident.

In the depths of his heart he formed the firm intention to remember, every evening and every morning, in the course of his prayers, the good moment that divine mercy had just given him. Then he uttered a sigh in thinking about the brevity of that precious moment.

How beautiful life would be, Lord, if your clemency had wanted that sublime invention of your genius to be of renewa-ble usage! Such a decision was possible for you, since nothing is impossible for you, according to the affirmation of our Pri-or. If the intoxication that the ablation of virginity brings were only permissible to us from time to time, this world would be your masterpiece, Lord. Perhaps you conceived the earthly paradise thus, and we have lost it. Who knows whether your angels might benefit from that durable perfection, which is forbidden to us, and whether their superiority does not consist of becoming virginal again indefinitely, in order to recom-mence no longer being, indefinitely? If it is thus, Lord, may I become an angel during eternity. Amen.

"What are you thinking about, prince of my heart?"

Thus spoke, softly, the young woman whose upper body was reposing on the arm of the ascetic, in breach of the ban.

"I'm thinking…about that which is already past…"

She kissed his eyes, laughing with pleasure.

"Do you love me?" she asked.

"Have no doubt of it," he replied. "My gratitude will be associated with your memory and that of this hour, of which you were the emissary and sacred instrument."

"Emissary, my treasure?"

"The unexpected happiness has been conceded to me by you, and you must tell me your name, in order that I can bless it."

"My name is Lelia."

"O Lelia, my beautiful cousin, my grateful soul honors your benefit."

She thought that the foreigner's gallantry was expressed in locutions that were slightly too pompous, and which lacked abandon, but not civility; she attributed that excess of correction to the fashions of a country that she did not know.

"Tell me, darling, do people talk to women like that where you come from?"

"I don't know, but ought one to speak otherwise to the person who was chosen among all to reveal Heaven to a son of the earth?"

She tried to understand, and almost succeeded.

"What?" she said. "I revealed to you...?"

"Infinity."

"Really? You were...?"

"Yes."

"And I..."

"Yes.

"At your age! What age are you, then?"

"Thirty-three years."

She clapped her hands, proud of her collaboration, and called her companions back in order to announce he news to them, but none of them wanted to believe it.

"He's making fun of you, Lelia!"

"Isn't it the case, darling, that you're not joking, and that it's true?"

"My heart is still beating."

"Poor boy, then. He's been locked in a convent."

"He must have barbaric parents!"

The brunette Cleanthis, who had red flowers in her hair and was more daring than the others, drew closer to the master in order to confess. She sat down very close to him. hip to hip; she spoke into his ear and he replied in a low voice, and as they conversed, a double astonishment elongated their faces. Around them, the beautiful maidservants observed, intrigued. With lively gestures and eyes shining with gaiety, seemed to be affirming something, which the Prince still doubted.

Finally, she burst out laughing, and cried: "That's too funny, can you imagine that...he believes that...he doesn't want to believe that..."

She had to try several successive formulae to explain, as best she could, the naïve illusion of the neophyte who thought that he no longer had the right ever to rediscover the vanished intoxication."

"What are we doing on earth, then?"

The laughed uproariously, having lost all respect for a man so naïve, for it is generally admitted that candor is a feminine virtue and a masculine vice. Crowded around him and all talking at once, they offered to prove his error without delay. Cleanthis claimed priority; it was recognized.

With a sovereign gesture, she dismissed her friends, and the proof was administered.

"O beloved master, do you still doubt?"

"Oh!" said Dieudonat. "That changes the aspect of the world notably! Life is not at all what I imagined it to be! I didn't know anything worthwhile, and I've wasted my time. In truth, the Earthly Paradise still exists, whatever people say, and it's an offense to God voluntarily to turn away from the best gift that he has granted us! I was impious, quite simply, and without knowing it; God has punished my disdain; that's justice. It's necessary to observe, though, that it wasn't my fault; the books deceived me. Can you read, Cleanthis?"

"No."

"And yet, you're very knowledgeable, since you've instructed me, who has read everything."

"I know the most important thing."

"Indeed, my cousin, and you've proved it to me well. But perhaps you can tell me why the moralists have been able to put themselves in accord to classify among the sins a fête that

God organized himself, and that it is appropriate for us to celebrate with actions of grace?"

"Don't know."

"I'll reflect on it further at leisure, when calm has returned to my intellect. For a quarter of an hour, it will suffice for me to reprove my error and to renounce the sin of abstinence; I shall not commit it any longer; I intend to reform my life to the extent that it depends on me, and whatever the number of my days might be. For I don't know the designs of our King, but my gratitude to him is acquired henceforth, even if he has my head cut off."

"His Majesty isn't thinking about cutting off any part of you, Milord; the proof is that he ordered us to serve you with tenderness, and promised us anything if were able to render you happy."

"Your sovereign is a philanthropist; I judged him very poorly, only knowing him by his military exploits; but a man is truly worthy of the scepter who applies himself to use it for the good of his fellows. I shall tell him that, thanking him as is appropriate. Since, thanks to him, this dwelling is mine, I shall no longer leave it; my solitude is with you. Here I shall install the convent of which we shall be the cenobites, and we shall celebrate together the works of adoration. Dear young women, I have vowed no longer to give anything but my person; it is a fine vow; much finer than I thought. Recall your sisters, Cleanthis."

"Already, Milord?"

"Don't name me thus, cousin; rather give me a kiss with your mouth. I am not your lord, Cleanthis, but your disciple, and very glad of what you have taught me, very glad, Cleanthis; I shall retain a gratitude to you a thousand times superior to that which I owe Lelia, for she taught me happiness, but I owe to you the knowledge that happiness is innumerable."

At that moment, Anoure advanced, with the regulation salutation, to announce that the King would receive his guest in an hour.

"In an hour!" said Dieudonat. "That's very regrettable, but I'd be an ingrate if I hesitated to obey. Let's go find the King."

He got up, sighing, and the maidservants returned, in order to adorn him, with a view to his reception; they trimmed his beard and hair, and then they dressed him in magnificent clothes, which molded his forms narrowly.

Then, he appeared so handsome that they would have had difficulty recognizing him. Sacred virility had transfigured him. When he appeared on the perron of the palace, a murmur of admiration emerged from the people, and, better than before, the crowd understood that he was a Prince.

The maidservants, hidden behind the windows, watched their master draw away.

"Alas," they said, "he won't come back to us. When the great ladies of the Court have seen him as he is now, they'll want to keep him for themselves."

"The great ladies," said Lelia, "are very knowledgeable, and we can't compete with them."

"Are you sure?" said Cleanthis.

XX. He multiplies with excess the gracious gifts of his person

Dieudonat made a sensational entrance to the Court. On seeing the man who had been depicted to them as a savage, the ladies uttered a little cry of surprise, and the lords pulled faces; his virile and lithe stature, an ensemble of strength and delicacy, his proud bearing, but without arrogance, his pure features, his casual gestures and his generous and frank physiognomy, everything about him, expressed an avidity to comprehend, to live, and need to go forth and to give. A strange ardor was shining in his eyes, at the memory of the fire of youth that had just animated his blood for the first time.

"Well," said Gaifer, "is that my anchorite? Hasn't his journey changed him?"

"He's nice," sad Princess Aude.

"He's better than that," said Queen Gaude.

The maids of honor shifted their honor on the stools.

The newcomer had stopped on the threshold of the Great Hall, and his glance verified the noble ladies, counting more than a hundred. He was glad of that, and approved their presence. Under his circular gaze, they sensed a caress brush them all, and the Prince advanced amid smiles.

In the distance, at the back, was the King, under his gold-fringed awning, enthroned in a semicircle of halberdiers and ministers, who all belonged to the male sex, and thus did not merit any attention. Unhurriedly, Dieudonat walked toward the throne; but there he was distracted, having bared his head, having discovered Princess Aude at the foot of the steps, who was contemplating him with large candid eyes, and Queen Gaude, who was analyzing him with little knowing eyes; they pleased him, and he saluted the King. At the same time, he recognized, to the right of the monarch, Archduke Galeas the One-Eyed, whom he was astonished to find in this place. For twenty years, His Serene Highness had been awaiting the death of the sick old Emperor, who could not decide to pass on, and the humor of the heir had become increasingly caustic; already, three wives had passed from his couch to the coffin, and he was in quest of a fourth fiancée. At the approach of Dieudonat, whose insolence he remembered, he frowned the eyebrow over his punctured eye, which was a bad sign.

However, Gaifer was already proffering, pompously: "Prince Dieudonat, we know that your father has lacked gratitude and justice toward you; Heaven has punished him for it. The paternal bounty that you ought to have expected from him, you will find with us. In adopting his Estates, we are adopting his son. You will be ours henceforth."

Having spoken, the sovereign stood up, descended from his throne, came to his guest and gave him the accolade; his royal moustaches reeked of beer and lavender. Afterwards, he turned to Galeas.

"Serene Highness, I solicit for this man the high favor of your bounty, and I ask Your Highness to consider him henceforth as a member of this household, which Your Imperial Highness has deigned to chose among all for the honor of his august alliance."

Dieudonat advanced toward the Queen with eyes like carbuncles. "Never would I have seen in you a mother."

"Kiss me all the same."

And Her Majesty extended her cheek, which smelled good.

Princess Aude having raised her chin in her turn, her improvised brother kissed her immediately; she blushed, and for the second time, Galeas frowned.

Then the courtiers were introduced, and kissed the hand of their new prince, who found that ceremony absurd and too long; he changed his opinion when the ladies and damsels filed past. A few of them were beautiful, many of them were pretty, and they were all women. The touch of their lips and the current of their breath tickled his fingers delightfully; the inclined curves of their bodies, which he was already examining as a connoisseur, had a moving grace in the genuflection, and the gaze that several raised toward his face entered into his eyes and flowed into him like a warm liquid; many a time, the tips of his fingers were seen to return to render a caress to the face whose contact had caused him pleasure; it was noticeable that the honorific distinction in question was only awarded to the most becoming.

This one, yes; that one, no...

He classified them as they passed by. Still obsessed by his discoveries regarding the collaboration of the sexes, he was incapable of deflecting his mind away from it, and scarcely tried; knowing all those gentle creatures in the possession of latent sensuality, he delighted in thinking that each of them contained infinity, and catalogued them mentally in accordance with their physical advantages, without paying any attention to their hierarchical dignities. He adopted one, dismissed another, and cast his designs like a benediction: *This one, yes; that one, no...* They followed one another; the game amused him; the Devil recorded his wishes, and when the file came to an end, sixty-three elect carried away the sacrament of a desire; Aude and Gaude were among them.

The best endowed of men no longer reason when the concern of amour grips them. Dieudonat, in playing thus, had almost forgotten that he was the individual whose wishes were realized; sixty-three lovers returned to their seats, affected by the contagion and perfectly decided no longer to see any but one romantic hero on earth, Him! To that number were added the persons who are spurred on when they are disdained, and those, more reasonable, who were able to calculate the real importance of a rich man introduced into a good family, adding equally to the dowry of virgins to be married a gentleman full of future.

Already, rivalries were sniffing one another out; a fever of competition electrified the palace, while a fever of amour vulcanized it from below; wives were nervous and husbands peevish; fiancés sulked, virgins dreamed, and mothers looked daggers at one another.

The clan of diplomats was unanimous in criticizing the indecent attitude of the foreigner during the hand-kissing.

"He lacks deportment, that anchorite."

"An impolite donkey," riposted Galeas.

The courtiers deemed that that was what is known as a witty remark; jealousies on the alert caused it to circulate as far as the princess, who declared it stupid, inept and abject.

"Highness, it comes from your fiancé."

"And worthy of him!"

Three minutes later, His Serene Highness was informed of that discourteous appreciation; he was irritated by it; the malcontents applied themselves to exciting him; he seethed; nascent hostilities learned that they had a leader. Hatred germinates in the shadow of amour.

Dieudonat had no suspicion of anything. The King having taken him into his carriage in order to enable him to admire the splendors of the capital, he traveled through the interminable ovation of the boulevards. Affable by nature, he responded with amenity to the acclamations of the crowd. When the encumbrance of the avenues obliged the horses to slow down, he looked at the idlers; he discovered in that way a few hundred adorable women, and wanted them politely for a second before drawing away; a wake of the enamored extended behind the two sides of the carriage, and several of them were sluts who had no appetite for waiting.

Evening arrived, with a feast followed by a ball. Dieudonat, who had never yet seen anything of that sort, was astonished by the young couples who did not fear embracing one another in front of everyone. He coupled, like everyone else. He did not regret it; he took pleasure in flexing supple waists in the circle of his arms, in clasping sympathetic roundnesses to his torso. In the vertigo of quadrilles, pretty mouths murmured close to his ear: "I love you." The more audacious said *tu* rather than *vous*.

He replied: "Me too."

And, in fact, he loved everyone, as befits happy people.

"Handsome nephew," said Queen Gaude, "hold tight, and know that you please me very much."

"Good cousin," said Princess Aude, "make me dance, I beg you." And when they were spinning: "Would you like me, handsome cousin, to love you like a sister or a cousin?"

The One-Eyed watched from a distance.

The celebrations lasted long into the night. When the elect of the women returned to his palace there were his twenty-one chambermaids, who were waiting for him in various poses but with equal impatience; they greeted his return with cries of joy. At the same time, he was presented, on thirteen silver trays, with thirteen piles of letters imploring his amour.

"God! This is a country where people love one another! I shall definitely fix my residence here; the mores are mild, the souls benevolent, and the women give of their person."

"If Milord would care to take my advice," said Cleanthis, "he will content himself with the happiness he finds in his domicile. Let Milord count those trays, the number of which is a bad augury; and let him also count his maidservants, the total of whom is three times seven, a blessed number that ought to content his fantasy."

"It might be," said Dieudonat, thinking about Princes Aude.

He thought about many others and had no need to go in quest of them. The following day they came in a multitude; the day after, even more came; they were seen prowling around the palace or slipping through the darkness. In order to reach him they bribed the chief eunuch; he found them everywhere, at every hour of every day, some heavily veiled, others devoid of veils. Of all statures, all forms, all complexions, blondes, brunettes, redheads, gracile youth and ample maturity, the sentimental and the laughing, the modestly passionate and the violently exasperated, those who were burning and those who pretended to be, all dissimilar and yet all parallel, they succeeded one another, filling the house with a cooing of turtle-doves, and the radiant neophyte did not find that music monotonous.

"Oh," said the chief eunuch, "Milord won't be bored."

"In no fashion, my friend."

The weeks passed. Without changing location, Dieudonat made a tour of the world. That incessant travel had made him slightly thinner, even though he had not been fat, but his beauty did not lose anything by it. His figure was slimmer, his gesture more agile, and his eyes shinier.

"Oh," said the chief eunuch, "I've been serving for forty years, and I'm rich, but I'd give all my wealth in exchange for yours."

"You have, in fact, been subjected to a great wrong, my friend."

He was firmly convinced of that, and considered his purveyor the most unfortunate of men, just as he was the most enviable if them all.

Anoure was holding a ledger.

"I shall have the honor this evening of presenting Milord with the last of the eighth quartile."[9]

Toward the middle of the second trimester, the Prince thought he perceived that perhaps, more than perhaps, his pleasure was beginning to attenuate, and that the perpetual unexpected lacked, in sum, the unexpected.

"Am I getting blasé already? Oh Lord preserve me from that ingratitude towards you, and toward them!"

He was obliged to recognize, however, in the sixth month, that his curiosity was fading. However, as he became less and less interested in that perpetual novelty, he observed that the most recent elect testified an intense joy, much more vivid than the first ones.

"That's quite bizarre."

One day, when one of those women, weeping, threw herself over his bosom, he questioned her. "Why are you weeping, beautiful cousin?"

---

[9] i.e., the two hundredth.

148

"I thought that minute would never arrive! O dear beloved, my beloved, for six months, I've wanted it so much, that minute!"

And her eyes expressed an infinite ecstasy.

That day, he understood.

"There are too many of them, and I don't have time to love them; they come too quickly, and I don't have the leisure to summon them. They concentrate on me the wishes that I scatter among them. While I forget them after having seen them, they're exasperated waiting for me, accumulating desire and hoarding hope. Every day, their patience collaborates with the future joy, and when, at the end of their tether, they come here, they bring me the ripe fruit, swollen with sap and gilded by long sunlight. They give me more than I can render them, and that's why, Lord, you accord them more than me."

He shook his head. "I wanted love too much, and I'm only making the gestures of it."

Slightly perplexed, he went down into the gardens; as usual, he encountered timid women there, who lowered their heads, blushing, and who, having come there in order to see him, dared not look him in the face.

"Who are these?"

"Stupid women who love you platonically, Milord, and who are only soliciting a glance."

He smiled at them, out of the goodness of his heart, and deigned to speak to a few; they went home delighted. But the eunuch mocked those futile creatures who baulked at the true happiness.

"Are you sure, my friend, that one happiness is truer than another?"

"I only know of one on earth!"

"The one that you don't know?"

"The very same, Milord, and that one alone."

"Oho!" said Dieudonat. "We're approaching the truth. A lady informed me just now that realizations obtain value by the intensity of the desire; now a eunuch is informing me that

149

the intensity of desire is in inverse proportion to possibilities..."

He stopped abruptly, as if a crocodile had appeared in the pathway.

"But...what I've discovered there, Lord, I already knew! Thirteen years ago, I explained to the worthy Onesime: 'The man whose desires are all realized is a man deprived of desires.' Am I a dupe, then? And I'm a simpleton too, since I haven't even suspected what I told others, and one emotion sufficed to render me ignorant of everything and of myself!"

At a slow pace, with his head bowed, as if he were carrying a burden, he returned to the palace. For the first time since his arrival, he decided to sleep alone, and when the maidservants protested on the threshold of his bedroom, he sent them away, saying: "Beautiful young women, go to sleep; all happiness is in the idea."

XXI. Whereon the inconveniences of futility become evident

That night, the Prince did not sleep, and although it was the softest suavity, he found it singularly desolating, by reason of its very sweetness. Leaning on his window sill, he watched the stars rotating, and amused himself sadly calling them by their names.

"I give you names but I don't know you, any more than you know the names I give you: I enjoy your beauty as you pass by, without knowing anything of what constitutes it, for the aspects that I suppose of it don't resemble you; I imagine you in my own way without any precise information about you, O beautiful stars, and while, via you, I delight myself with your splendor, we remain strangers to one another, mysterious stars so similar to women!"

Never had he felt isolated to the degree that he did now, either in his cell in the monastery or in the hermitage on the mountain; only now did he discover that there are two solitudes: that of the body, which is the desert, and that of the mind, which is among people.

Facing him, the planet Mars blazed red.

"I have seen you rotate all night, dissimilar heavenly body, and now you are about to reenter the horizon, like the others, you who have nothing in common with the others, poor planet, child of the sun, who make a semblance of being a sun. For a long time I thought you were larger than any, uniquely because you are smaller, like me, and closer to me; I admire you for shining so brightly, when you do not even shine, paltry mirror that you are, decorated prince whose adornment only sparkles by virtue of reflections. Are you alive or already dead? Even that is unknown! I resemble you."

In sum, he was traversing the crisis of a melancholy neatly specified by the medico-moral adage that begins with the

words "*Omne animal*..."[10] Ignorant of the causes of his malaise, he let his fatigued soul drift, with the complaisance that
we put into dying in part, and he was chagrined to see the first
light appear of the dawn that was about to rid him of his pain
by rinsing him in light.

"In only loving a single woman I would doubtless have
been less alone."

He set about searching for which one, without noticing
that he was searching the number of the unexplored. He threw
out names at hazard: "Gaude? Married... Aude? Engaged..."
They were all eliminated for one reason or another, and yet
one among them might perhaps ensure him of paradise.

"You who might offer me a lasting felicity, come to me!"
Immediately, he heard light footsteps behind him.

That's my wish being realized...already!

He dared not turn his head, for fear of finding himself
face to face with the definitive elect on whom his destiny depended.

Who is she? What is she?

He gathered his courage and turned round, sure that he
was about to see the Unique. It was the eunuch.

"Why have you come and who are you? Anoure, are you
yourself or a symbol? Are you appearing like a counsel,
Anoure, at the moment when I an invoking the form of supreme happiness"

"I don't understand what Milord is saying. I've become
because it's my duty, having seen Milord all alone and wanting to ask for his orders."

"I have none to give you."

---

[10] *Triste est omne animal post coitum* [all animals are sad after
sexual intercourse], continued in full *praeter mulierem
gallumque* [except women and cocks] often falsely attributed
to Aristotle or Galen, but probably invented in the 16th century
as a joke. Alternative versions vary the word order and the
detail of the Latin.

"Milord is bored? Would Milord want to see my files, with the lists and portraits of the ladies? My account has presently reached the figure five hundred and forty-nine. And if I count those it was necessary for us to refuse..."

"You've refused some of them, then?"

"Is Milord forgetting that he has formally forbidden adultery, and that I was obliged, in consequence, to send away many amorous women stained by marriage?"

The butler neglected to add that in many circumstances, when the clients were particularly pretty, when they remunerated him with a few liberties or a few ducats, he had taken care to denounce his master's scruples to them; the alerted wives had then declared themselves to be damsels or widows. He smiled as he thought about that, while Dieudonat returned to graver thoughts. Anoure heard him sigh.

"Milord is discontented?"

"I was saying to myself, my friend, that women are truly futile."

"I believe so, Milord."

"Have you ever thought of the etymology of that word? *Futere, futilis*, what is susceptible of being, what must be. How shall I put it? Which exists to be...*futita!*"[11]

"I don't understand Latin, Milord."

"That's a great pity, for you'd understand that one is wrong to speak of 'futile things.' There are no futile things, my friend, but only people; and you would recognize that, by definition, futility is the distinctive prerogative of the female sex."

But the eunuch was scarcely listening; he was looking out of the window, anxiously, and he started abruptly, ex-

---

[11] This "etymology" is specious. The Latin root of "futility" is actually *futtilitas*, related to *futtilis*, meaning worthless or brittle; it is difficult to believe that someone as allegedly well-read as Dieudonat would confuse those roots with derivatives of *futur* [future].

claiming fearfully: "There, Milord, in the patch of mist, that woman who is coming, look Milord!"

"I do perceive one, in fact.

"The Queen, Milord! Queen Gaude, who is as determined as the others! I recognize her under her veil."

Anoure ran away.

The Prince received the Queen with an excessive respect; affecting not to understand the gracious intentions of the matinal visit, he talked about his gratitude for the paternal generosity of his host, the King. In the shelter of that gratitude he felt that he was safe, but the Queen disabused him.

"Have no illusions, handsome cousin; it's gold that is expected of you, my friend...don't interrupt your Queen. In the hope of that gold. Gaifer calls you his son, and he'll call you his son-in-law as well, if the role is acceptable to you."

"I venerate Princess Aude, but I know that she is engaged to Archduke Galeas..."

"Whom she detests, who execrates you, and of whom sausages will be made if that is your desire, on the sole condition that you provide what is expected of you; and since a gesture of your little finger would suffice..."

"Never again will I make gold, never again! I've sworn it. I know the work of that metal too well, deadly because it engenders misfortune, deadly because it procures death. Never again, never again."

"There, there! Don't excite yourself thus and reserve your forces for the moment. In addition, I don't care to see you marrying that little fool. I have something better in reserve for you, my friend, since I'm taking you for myself."

The clarity of that speech no longer permitted any misunderstanding regarding the sovereign's intentions; her eyes were shining and her mouth was very red; all her teeth were visible, gleaming. And her mobile lips were muttering a silence even more explicit than her words. Then she uttered a great sigh, as if the double weight of her breasts had crushed her lungs, and, with her two fists resting on the cushions of the divan, she went on:

"I have acquired an intense liking for your person, my friend, and did so from the very first moment. I wanted to see whether it would pass, and I even resisted, for I'm an honest wife. It persists; so, I'm yielding, and I'm taking you for myself, as I told you just now. But you'll find it good that it will be for me alone, and that I don't admit any sharing. I won't impose any on you either; I'm delivering myself entirely, and I demand everything. You'll learn in my arms, cousin, that there is only felicity in amour in the total gift of oneself, and your entire past will seem insipid by comparison with our erudite passion.

"There is no need to add, after that, that I'm renouncing the King, who isn't worth very much anyway. We'll depose him; everything is ready; my agents have worked on public opinion; the people, knowing the favors with which you gratify your subjects, will applaud enthusiastically; we'll suppress taxes, we'll found hospices, we'll open free theaters; our two names will be blessed and our initials, enlaced like our arms, will decorate monuments. That's the plan, Dieudonat the First. Choose between the throne I'm offering you or the prison that your good friend Gaifer is reserving for you."

The Prince did his best to hide his horror of such wicked perfidies and a Majesty so devoid of moral sense; the Court usages that he had been practicing for six months had sufficed to teach him that an honest man must put on a good face to the dishonest ones he encounters. That is why, while affirming that he was very touched by an excessively flattering distinction, he confessed that his respect for the sacrament of marriage would deprive him of the pleasure with which he would have had in the honor of being Her Majesty's very humble and obedient servant.

His response was poorly welcomed.

"You're making me yawn, my fear, with your semblance of scruples and your belated morality. Marriage! Are its duties more rigorous for me than for others and are you asking us to believe that so many legitimate spouses come here in the hope of hearing a Lenten sermon?"

Dieudonat learned with amazement that for six months he had been committing adultery left, right and center; the sincerity of his surprise was so evident that Queen Gaude became less wrathful in order to stifle her laughter; she rolled on the divan like an ordinary person, without being able to articulate a word. That undulation gave generous value to her natural advantages, and she was conscious of it. But the perpetual lover was in a state of mind only to be able to contemplate the horizontal temptations fearfully, and he suffered from a hilarity that seemed to him to be out of season.

Finally, the beautiful Gaude drew breath.

"O great simpleton, handsome simpleton, it's true, then, that you've been made to swallow these lies? Have you been assured, while they were here, that we're all virgins and remained virgins while awaiting your arrival?"

"What! Not one of the outraged husbands has come to break my head!"

"They had too much to do looking out for their own, impaired as it was, and the King was looking out for yours. Do you think he would have tolerated any attempt whatsoever against his goose that lays golden eggs? The fortunes of the country repose on your existence, maker of money, and your life is as sacred as the fatherland itself. The hope of the fatherland, that's you, my friend. To touch you, or to try to, or even to think about it, is a crime of high treason meriting the gallows or the ax, and the entire nation shares the sage sentiments of the King on that score. Let's take advantage of it. Everything is praiseworthy for you, dear heart! I've told you so, no longer doubt it, and come and sit down beside me."

"My conscience is crushed with shame by the universal debasement that I create without knowing it!"

"There, there! What pompous words! Universal debasement? If that idea offends you, scratch it out; you can: the exceptions have proved the rule."

"Husbands are irritated?"

"And fiancés, father and brothers not to mention a few sons."

156

"So?"

"So they've been put in the shade to refresh their ideas."

"No one has lost his life?"

"Very few; the King takes care of it; the King isn't malevolent, but respect for just laws is only obtained by examples."

"Horror!"

"Bah! The jealous men in prison compensate the jealous men who imprison their wives, and if it has seemed necessary to send a few convicts to the gallows, I don't see that they're any more to be lamented than the unfortunate women expedited to the other world by the anger of their husbands."

"The other world?"

"Of course! So you think, then, cousin, that not one of them has taken revenge? That all of them accepted with a smile the disgrace of their amour betrayed, their honesty mocked and their hearths extinguished? That not one of them has paid his whack, and yours? If you had any knowledge of the world, and above all, if, like me, you had read the police reports..."

"Well?"

"Of the hundreds of creatures that you had, happy and alive, how many are dead at present, and how many others are going to die!"

"Had, alive and happy, and then...!"

"You can suppose all dramas; they happen! All forms of rage and despair, they exist! Husbands that will never be seen again, because they were prowling around your palace, armed; wives strangled on their return, children orphaned, virgins pregnant, families dishonored, fathers gone mad, fiancés and lovers who drink forgetfulness is poison, and lovable damsels who, for the fury of having you again after having had you, or the impatience of succeeding in it, go to seek their peace at the bottom of the river..."

"My God! My God!"

"You're admirable! Unconsciousness or innocence, but assuredly admirable! You don't even imagine that days have tomorrows, that causes produce effects, that sown seeds prepare crops. You sow, come what may, and you say: 'Women are futile.' I don't disagree with you, my dear, and I want to give you the proof of it shortly; but our futility is the thing that is paid for most dearly in this world, even when it's gratuitous. Give the gold or don't give it; it scarcely counts, whatever people say, and tears, my good friend, are the unique ransom of kisses."

The well-informed Queen fell silent, and patted the cushions around her; then, when they were provided with bumps and hollows to her liking, she added: "Now, handsome cousin, come to me, for time is passing and that's enough of thinking about others."

But the Irresistible was no longer even looking at her. He was striding back and forth, lamenting with exclamatory gestures, retrospective phrases and eloquent remorse; he was tearing out his curly hair and cursing the hour of his birth. Her Majesty, during that errant monologue, waited, and became impatient.

"Be careful handsome cousin; you're importuning me."

Finally weary, she stood up, and then, with a truly regal slowness, she replaced her thick veil and headed for the door. On the threshold, she turned round.

"I brought you happiness in glory, and you prefer a dungeon? As you please!"

Insensible to the threat, he continued striding back and forth, striking his breast.

"Assassin! Assassin!"

The Queen had not yet left the house when the chief eunuch advanced his head between two door-curtains and said: "Princess Aude, Milord! Here's the Princess coming, like the others! I recognize her under her veil."

The King's daughter came in like a gust of wind, as in the theater.

"Gaude's here! Don't say no! I saw her come in! I've been watching her! For the others, pass, but my stepmother—I don't want it, you hear! I forbid it! Oh, do me the favor, cousin, of not taking with me the air of candor that scarcely suits you and doesn't deceive me. Don't suppose, under the pretext that I'm an ignorant girl, that I don't understand your game; I know what they come to do in your home, all of them, many as they are! I know exactly! And if you think I take pleasure in it, you're heartless! Yes, heartless, heartless, heartless!"

She started weeping, vehemently, uttering shrill cries, hammering the carpet with taps of her heel, and rubbing her large eyes with her little clenched fists.

"Yes, heartless, heartless, so there! Because I love you, and you know that very well, and I won't permit you any longer to cuddle all those ladies when you're my husband, to cuddle them all day and all night, heartless swine who doesn't love me!"

"I love you like the dear friend, the little sister who is soon to be married, for you're engaged, Aude, the fiancée of another…"

"I will never marry him, that vile man, who's too ugly, and stupid too, and who only has one eye, with one eye squashed. Can you see me, wretch, tell me, can you imagine me spending my life facing a single eye, before a face with red hair, looking at me with his squashed eye? I never loved him before, but since you've come, I detest him! And I've told Papa-King that, and Papa-King says that we'll have war if he sends my fiancé away, but I don't care, about the war to which I won't go, and I don't want that frightful fiancé, because I want another, who is much prettier, and who knows it only too well, the heartless swine!"

She was no longer sobbing, but, still tearful, she was sulking, with a genteel moue, with which she marked the punctuation of her sentences. Dieudonat, who was haunted by the Queen's revelations, and who was scarcely listening, replied: "Yes, truly, I've acted like a man without a heart."

"For sure; and the Archduke is more polite than you, for he does everything he can to please me; he pays me compliments, which are idiotic, but that isn't his fault, since he isn't able to invent better ones, and he sends me bouquets, and gives me rings, necklaces, earrings, and everything, and many others besides, and I don't care, because I'd rather have them from you, and you've never had the idea of the smallest string of pearls, not even a flower, which would have pleased me. Do you call that polite?"

"Monstrous."

"There! You're a monster, and you admit it!"

"And you could love such a wicked individual?"

"Obviously, since I do love him."

"In spite of his heartlessness."

"That has nothing to do with it."

"And why, little Aude, do you love me?"

"You know very well, conceited man, but you want me to say it again."

She took his hands, drew him toward her, and made him sit beside her, on the cushions that the queen had hollowed out with her more ample forms a little while before, and she chirped: "Because I find you pretty, oh, pretty, so pretty! Everyone finds you pretty! There are some who love your eyes, some who love your hands, and for others, it's your voice that they adore, and then others..."

"And little Aude?"

"For me, it's your nose that I'm mad about, and your hair too...when I saw your dainty nostrils, which did *that*, like *that*, I understood immediately that I was going to love you; then, when I least expected it, and it was exactly the moment when you made your reverence to me, I saw there, above your left temple, there, a wisp of hair that was twisted...oh, then I understood that I would love you for life!"

"So, if someone else had my dainty nostrils, which did that..."

"You're funny! Everyone has his own nostrils, and it's yours that I want, this one, and this one..."

With the tips of her pink fingers, with well-polished nails, she touched one nostril after the other, and the beloved let her do it, occupied as he was with the occasional causes of

160

amour, the origins of which are so modest and the consequences so terrible. But the young princess, impatient with
that excessively long reverie, ended up by pinching his nose
furiously. Dieudonat tried to free it, and the virgin became
animated, her eyes shining, her teeth digging into her lip, and
her entire body already twitching.

"Futile child!" said the philosopher. But his pretty voice
was nasal, because the futile child had not let go of the philosopher's nose.

At that moment, the eunuch came running for the third
time, and cried: "The King, Milord! The King is coming!"

The Princess let go of the nose, because she needed both
hands in order to clap them together.

"That's good, that Papa-King finds me here. He'll marry
us immediately, and the Archduke will declare war. Well
done, well done!"

Dieudonat gazed sadly at that joy.

"There's no denying it," he said, "that's definitely the futility that etymology announces. But it's necessary now, if I
can still do it, to dam the torrent of misery that has been un-
leashed thanks to me."

The sound of halberds striking the stones of the perron
could be heard in the distance, announcing the entrance of the
potentate. The little princess, delighted, beat the measure of
that menacing music with her finger, and straightened her
pretty torso, with warrior breasts, ready for battle.

Dieudonat, standing beside her, waited.

*Lord God, in the night of lassitude, alone facing the
stars, I asked you for the supreme happiness of amour and
you've presented it to me in three forms: the continence of
castration, the passion of a mature woman, and the frivolity of
a child. But I think I understand why the eunuch came first.*

XXII. He surrenders, in favor of his neighbor,
a few meager advantages

Queen Gaude had run to King Gaifer.

"Gaude, my darling, I can see that you're very angry."

"I've just left Dieudonat."

"Really? At this hour he's in his palace playing with the ladies."

The Queen was not in a mood for pleasantries.

"Sire, people are making fun of you."

She was not foolish enough to claim that the torturer of amour had solicited her, and had caught her, because the King knew very well that she could have resisted. She said: "Your Majesty is being duped. I suspected as much. I wanted to know. I went. You're not unaware, I imagine, that a scandalous libertinism reigns in the house of that adventurer, and that his morals are the shame of the realm?"

"That's frightful," said the King, tranquilly.

"But you're doubtless unaware that he's determined never to make gold again?"

"So he claimed, once, but I've been able to change his mind."

"You've only changed his morals."

"It comes to the same thing, my darling. You don't understand the affairs of government; I've corrupted that man and I have him in my hand, for among a thousand other gifts, I've given him the one thing from which one never gets free: needs."

"Go and see him, handsome Sire, and if you don't believe me, do as I did, ask him for what you want."

The autocrat, anxious at first, and then furious, buckled on his sword and hastened toward his adoptive son. He was disagreeably surprised to find his own daughter there, for whom he was not searching.

"What are you doing here?"

"Love, Papa."[12]

"We'll see about that detail later. For the moment, I have to settle accounts of a different kind with this fellow. Is it true…?"

But Dieudonat interrupted him without deference. "Is it true, O King, that I have caused so much woe and despair in this country?"

"It's not a matter of that. I don't reproach you for anything to which I consented for your pleasure; I haven't been mean with the women of my kingdom or the men that were too close to them. Let's leave those trivia. I've supplied the goods in advance, and I'm told that you're refusing to pay in your turn."

"The dolor of wounded souls, O King, how does one pay for that?"

"With gold, and you're going to give it to me."

"Never again will my wishing produce a gram of gold."

"For a gram you can rest easy, it's a mountain that I need!"

"I've sworn an oath no longer to give anything except of myself."

"That's good for the women, but your King requires something else."

"The expiation of my sins? I'm ready to submit to it."

"No speeches, metal! Look out of the window and see that mountain with granite summits: order that it be changed into gold."

"And at that price, my crimes will be pardoned?"

"Everything you've done you can do again, as often as you please."

The magician hid his face in his hands. "Just God, who sees this base world, you have taught me in my father's land how gold disorganizes a people, and you have informed me

---

[12] The French *faire* mans "to make" as well as "to do," so Aude is deliberately misconstruing her father's question and answering him as if he were asking her what she is making.

now how it depraves souls. O Lord, supreme conscience who tolerates these things, is your name, then, Indifference?"

"Are you ready?"

Dieudonat's hands slid down his pale face, and he replied: "I'm ready."

"To work, then! Your life will answer to me for your obedience. Your wishes are realized; make your wish."

"This is it: that you sit down and shut up, bad father, bad pastor, and that all your Court come here."

At the same moment, the rumor of a plot ran through the palace. Some said: "Dieudonat has taken possession of the King and the scepter, with the Queen." Others said: "The King has thrown Dieudonat in prison, with the Queen." All of them ran to congratulate the power, whoever it might be.

They entered in a crowd into the onyx hall, and saw the monarch sitting silently, with Dieudonat standing to his right, and Aude smiling in a corner. Their attitude appeared enigmatic; people could not discover any indication that permitted them to know which master it was necessary to salute. In doubt, they arranged themselves against the walls, and no one dared to be the first to risk saying something that might be compromising. Eventually, Dieudonat spoke.

"Men of this land, your sovereign, here, and I, your guest, desired your presence in order to make honorable amends before you for the crimes of which we were the two accomplices; we have scorned or insulted you, by means of my lust and his tolerance; we have scandalized the people, by giving them the aristocratic example of a double ignominy. Enlightened now as to our sins—libidinous egotism on my part, egotistical cupidity on his, we are doing penance by a public declaration, and we very humbly beg your pardon."

The King, mute, agitated in his seat, grimacing with tortured creases of wrath; the courtiers, frightened by the effects of remorse on a royal mask, only watched them covertly, avoiding his gaze for fear that he might remember having encountered theirs later.

Dieudonat went on: "I have lived among you in order to learn here at your expense that amour is a medallion struck with dolor on the other side. At our expense, you will learn that omnipotence is miserable, all the more miserable the greater is appears; for this man is a monarch by virtue of the hazard of destiny, but if, by a better hazard, he had simply been a porter in the port, he would not have sinned more than another; his bad luck and yours caused him to be born on a throne, and because he was able to do more, he did more harm. I have done even more, because I was able to do more; more powerful than a king, I am also more detestable, for I have desolated two kingdoms."

Having articulated those statements, which everyone could, as he pleased, find profound or hollow, he lowered his gaze toward the monarch. Then Gaifer was seen to writhe on his seat, opening his mouth to cry out, shaking his head furiously as a sign of negation, and drawing his sword. still seated, he brandished that invincible blade in the air, to the great peril of flies.

"Don't tire yourself out like that," said the magician. "Your iron is not a proof; it can do nothing against the Truth. Since a favor of fate is permitting you to hear the truth for once in your life, hear it and blush: you shall have the advantage of knowing how little you are worth."

The King uttered howls.

"Be quite, potentate! On your knees before your subjects! On your knees, like me, in order that they might pardon both of us. This I command, and I bequeath you, in leaving, the task of repairing, as much as is possible, the disorder that is our work."

Kneeling side by side, the Prince and the King beat their breasts, but Gaifer, at the same time, rolled his eyes, which were bulging with fury. Several courtiers thought it wise to slip away; two ministers, in low voices, confided to one another that the thaumaturge was committing a dire fault in discrediting the power and those who represented it; an archbishop shook his head sadly.

It was then that the Archduke irrupted into the hall, at the precise moment that Dieudonat stood up in order to say: "Adieu, all of you! I leave you a King diminished and better; as for me, I am going away, more charged with pains, my brothers, than any of you, since I am bearing in my heart all of your pains combined."

He was already heading for the door when Galeas the One-Eyed, desirous of triumphing under the gaze of the beautiful Aude, ran forward, his sword drawn, and barred his passage.

"You shan't go, I'll see to that, and you'll expiate your sins."

"Sheath that sword, my friend. I shall indeed expiate my sins, but not as you think, for we don't think in the same way."

The Archduke tried to stiffen his arm, which was putting the sword back in the scabbard of its own accord, but the arm knew better that the Archduke what it had to do, and sheathed the blade. At least, His Serene Highness estimated, he could strike the hilt violently, in order to give evidence before everyone of his indomitable energy; he executed that noble gesture, then, straightening his torso and, directing the gaze of his unique eye toward the princess, he commanded, in a bellicose voce: "Close all the exits! Arrest him!"

Dieudonat replied, mildly: "No one will arrest me, my friend, and no one will search for me or pursue me, for I forbid it, and you'll be content to see me leave yourself."

"Content no longer to see your execrable face, yes, certainly—and I won't be the only one."

"A certain young woman will be chagrined, however, since she has taken a liking to the face that God has given me. I'll give it to you in my turn, in order that it might please her. So be it!"

Immediately, Dieudonat's features were those of Galeas, and the donor appeared in the form of the Archduke, one-eyed and red-haired, with a skin the color of liquid manure and lips the color of lilac. He retained, however, in the depths of his left eye, an expression of tenderness and intelligence. That rendered the sight of his deformities tolerable; his soul ideal-ized his ugliness, while the other's beauty remained aggressive and malevolent.

Dieudonat who, examined the renewal of the imperial gentleman, was not satisfied with his work; he had had higher hopes of the metamorphosis.

"My poor face appeared more honorable to me in the time when it was mine and when I encountered it in mirrors. I was blind then and I'm only one-eyed now; I've gained."

If the prodigy appeared mediocre to him, the audience was less demanding; a murmur of admiration, and also anxie-ty, ran around the onyx hall; all feet recoiled, crushing less rapid toes behind them; the prestige of the mystery petrified all valor, and warriors who would not have flinched before the points of spears moved aside fearfully to leave a wide passage for the sorcerer's departure.

Princes Aude had held out her arms and run forward be-tween the two rivals; she contemplated them in turn, discon-tented and perplexed, wondering which one was her adored.

Dieudonat saw her hesitate, and smiled; the smile on his mauve lips was hideous and tender,

Then she said to him: "You're vile. I detest you. Go away." Then she drew nearer to Galeas, who had the desired nostrils henceforth, and Dieudonat left.

In the vestibule, he encountered the maidservants, who were lying in wait for news, and who were trembling.

"Beautiful cousins who were so kind to me, I bid you adieu forever."

They responded to him by pulling faces, mistaking him for Galeas, whom they execrated because of his hostility to their Prince. All of them had recognized their master's gar-ments, and several recognized his voice, but not one recog-nized his soul in the depths of his eyes. He felt a glacial cha-grin: a chill descended into his heart, to which he had clasped them. Many a time they had given the illusion of melting two bodies and souls together into a single being possessed of a single soul, Nothing subsisted, therefore, of those sacred moments, not even the instinct of the memory that such a communion ought to have left. The inanity of embraces penetrated him with horror, and he wept for the first time in his life; but the tears only ran from his left eye.

"Adieu, Cleanthis, adieu, Lelia, adieu all of you who will never again see the master who was your friend, and who renounces living. But before I leave, tell me, like the princess, of what your amour was made, since a slight modification of my exterior cover has sufficed to detach you from the entire person?"

They thought that Galeas had gone mad, and, recoiling to the wall, they huddled together in order to avoid the person for whom they were mourning. The Prince went on. Only one person followed him at a distance, skimming the walls, and caught up with him.

"Milord…"

Touched by the courage of that devotion, the Prince turned round, and was glad to recognize the chief eunuch,

"My friend?"

"I heard, back there, the words that Milord spoke to the King, and saw what Milord did for the Archduke."

"My duty, very meanly."

"And when Milord spoke to the maidservants, when I was able to understand that he found amour deceptive..."

"Alas."

"Then, I said to myself…I thought I was able to conclude…"

"Finish."

"That Milord is disinteresting himself…that Milord in renouncing…the joys of this world..."

"I am repenting and going in search of penitence."

"Precisely. And I said to myself: Milord will flee amour henceforth, and women, there's no doubt about it; mow, Milord, who is good and can do whatever he wants, has already given one part of himself; perhaps Milord might deign to recognize the devotion of a zealous servant…by a little souvenir...nothing much...some trinket of which Milord had no more intention of making use..."

"I understand, Anoure."

"Ah! Milord would fulfill the dream of my life!"

"To repudiate the crimes of my egotism and to repair the wrong that has been done to you, I yield to you what you ask. Go, and may your desires be accomplished."

At those words, Anoure's face went crimson; his little eyes, sunk in the fat, glistened with a new brightness. Whatever his contentment, the eunuch, returning to employment, scarcely took the time to say thank you. He ran into the palace, perhaps to verify the magician's munificence, perhaps in the fear that the present might be revoked.

It was on that memorable occasion that Dieudonat was able to see the back of a truly happy man; while that rare object plunged into the shadow of a doorway, he examined it attentively; it was a very round back, tilted forward, as if it were bending under a burden of hopes, head down, running to adventure in the manner of a bull.

Then Dieudonat, his soul lightened a little, turned his back in his turn, and went away from the lovers.

XXIII. The most powerful of men undertakes a task that encounters various obstacles

"Now I'm ugly, and neutered, rid of two advantages that might have served to do great harm..."

He emerged from Armida's palace and went down the steps. The midday angelus was sounding in the belfries and the sun's rays were perpendicular.

As he traversed the square where people had acclaimed him, but which was now deserted, he lowered his head toward the pavement white with light; the cubes of sandstone, worn by the friction of so much weariness, depressed by generations of poor people, impassive under the ever renewed burden of human distress, seemed to exhale toward him the mute confidence of the feet trailed over them, and in the creaking of stones overheated by the sun he thought he could hear the innumerable voice of the past.

"How many people have lived, Lord, how many have suffered here! And you have also wanted them to suffer because of me. Where are you taking me now? I'm going, but where am I going? The days that I live from now on belong to those who have suffered from my errors. But where are they?"

His head was so heavy, so weary, that he took refuge in the shade of a plane tree beside a fountain. He tried to think, and remained there with his head in his hands for a long time. He drank from the hollow of his hand; the ideas leaked out of his head like the fresh water through his fingers.

"Let's go...at random. Let God guide me to my duty, if he deigns to do so."

He started walking. Rare passers-by were beginning to traverse the square. Suddenly, a stranger, richly-dressed but whose garments were gray with dust and whose forehead as damp with sweat, ran toward him and embraced his knees, crying: "Highness! Highness!"

"Doubtless you're mistaking me for Archduke Galeas. I'm not him, in spite of the resemblance that has deceived you."

"Highness, I beg you, don't joke. Your Highness hasn't forgotten that he did me the honor of addressing himself to me when he wanted to contract a loan of a hundred thousand écus on the occasion of the tourney?"

"I'm not the person you think."

"Highness, for pity's sake! I only have hours to live! At sunset, if I haven't paid forty thousand écus, I'll be arrested. Two wretches have reduced me to the distress I which you see me: Vicomte d'Avatar and Prince Dieudonat."

"Dieudonat? What has he done to you?"

"The story is simple, Milord. That Vicomte d'Avatar, whom Your Highness might know, as he's been received at Court..."

"I met him once among brigands..."

"He arrived barefoot sixteen years ago; he interested me, or rather he charmed me, by means of his perverse grace and the elegance of his cynicism. Natures that are too honest sometimes have, once in their life, one on those bizarre tendernesses for vice. He dazzled me, I liked him, I helped him and nourished him, I made him my most intimate companion and I introduced him to my father's friends. It was thus that he was able to frequent the house of a rich Lombard, seduce his only daughter and become his son-in-law, then his associate, and shortly thereafter his heir; today, omnipotent in the square, he has the ear of ministers and passes for an honest man. He hasn't forgiven me for having been the confidant of his baseness and the artisan of his fortune; I could say too much about his life. He hates me. His wife is related to mine and he has all the conduits at the Palace. Both of them have become the mistresses of the filthy Dieudonat. Oh, what a scene when she came to me, who didn't suspect anything, and threw herself at my knees, telling me about the irresistible sin and imploring my pardon."

"So?"

"In order to console the sweet child and remove her from that accursed bewitchment I left everything there. The moment was ill-chosen. The enemy was lying in wait for me; this evening, he'll execute me. My wife has decided to die with me, and she rejoices in it, saying that it's deliverance. Anyway, what would she do on earth when I'm no longer here? Oh, to save her, and still live with her, beside her, for her! Life was so good to us! Your Highness will render us life!"

In a surge of his heart, Dieudonat resolved to do anything to repair the disaster of which he was the author; he formed the wish that forty thousand écus would be in the hand of the expectant man, but the hand remained empty, and the man said: "Your Highness isn't going to give me any response?"

The sorcerer, with all his extended will-power, formed the wish for a second time. He observed the hand with anxiety; no coins or ingots appeared there. Then an anguish gripped his throat. *My wishes are irrevocable*! He understood that his previous wish no longer to make gold had been realized, like the others, and that his own will had given it up forever.

"Alas," he said, "I can't do anything for you."

The man who was about to die bowed, without a response, and then took two steps backwards. "So be it," he said.

"Don't kill yourselves! Don't damn your souls, think of eternal life!"

"Please, since it's impossible for you to save us by acquitting your debts, let us die in peace."

This time, he expressed himself with a calm imprinted with such a noble gravity that his executioner recognized therein the tranquility of the defunct; the condemned man, who had visibly accepted his destiny, was already bearing the seal of death. Dieudonat, struck with respect, bowed his head, and the living coffin moved away along the deserted street.

"That's my fault! That's my fault! Only having done harm with gold, I concluded stupidly that it's evil, and I've abolished it for the moment when it would have been beneficent. I knew, however, Lord, that nothing is absolute, that nothing is good or evil in itself, and that our choice alone decides its virtues. I've commented on that verity in scholarly dissertations, but no more than an idiot did I think of making use of it. What difference have you made, then, Lord, between the imbecile and the sage?"

A voice in the wind replied to him: "Only one..."

Dieudonat slapped his forehead. "I only had to order him to live and I didn't even think of it! Where is he now poor fellow!"

He stated running in the direction that the passer-by had taken. He searched for him to the right and the left, and hastened at random. The river barred his route, but a bridge extended before him; should he cross it or not?

"I want to encounter the individual who is going to die because of me! I wish it!"

At that moment, a woman who was leaning over the middle of the bridge and looking at the water, put her leg over the stone balustrade; he launched himself forward to retain her, and was able to grab the hem of her dress at the same time as he formulated a wish: *Don't jump!*

She allowed herself to be led away, meekly, but she looked at her savior with a desolate expression. He had the impression of seeing that sweet face, those distant eyes, before and of having heard the same voice that was now groaning: "There's no more place for me on earth: I'm going into the water!"

"Are you so desperate, then? Tell me the case, in order that I might help you."

"I was in love. I gave myself. I'm going to be a mother. I'm shamed. My father threw me out. I'm all alone."

"Marry your lover."

"Paupers like me don't marry princes like him."

"He's a prince? His name?"

"Dieudonat."

The crowd, which was gathering, groaned; only then did the young woman perceive that people were listening; she hid her face.

173

"Why did you make me recount my dishonor before these people?"

"You'll marry your prince, I promise."

His audacity seemed grotesque; a worker started laughing. "Perhaps it's you who can marry them by force?"

"Me. I'm Dieudonat."

The hilarity was general, and the dolorous young woman was immediately forgotten. A fishwife yapped: "Dieudonat? Everyone knows his face. Haven't you ever looked at your own profile?"

"He can't—he only has one eye."

"And he's saying that with the voice of a eunuch!"

"I am, indeed, castrated, and I resemble Galeas, but I remain Dieudonat, in order to repair my sins; I'll answer for you and for your child. Come."

The unfortunate woman set forth obediently, but wrung her interlaced fingers and lamenting: "It isn't you I love! I've never seen you before! Leave me alone!"

The worker elbowed his way forward. "That's enough, now! If you don't leave that girl in peace I'm going to get mixed up in it and throw you in the water."

That energy obtained the approval of the people. A short petty bourgeois, aging and carefully shaven, advanced behind his spectacles and, looking at Dieudonat from chin-height, said: "Permit me to tell you that if you're veritably a eunuch, it's inconceivable that you can claim paternity of a child or that you can propose marriage to a young woman, but one can easily conceive that she rejects your civilities and complains of your persistence. It's necessary to leave her alone; that's my sentiment."

"That's good, that's good!" cried the worker. "Trot along, beauty; we'll take care of the eunuch. Go on!"

"Go away? Where can I go? I no longer have a home, I no longer have a family. I wanted to go into the water, and now I can't any longer..."

She shook her hands above her head. Women drew her away. Dieudonat searched for his duty.

Gradually, the crowd dispersed behind him. The sun was already declining toward the horizon; the glorious river was heading toward that light, pushing its heavy waves like golden lava.

"That would truly have been a fine funeral bed!"

He watched the waves flowing, always the same, always the same.

"Oh, I'm weary Lord! How weary I am, and yet I'm beginning to hurt. I talk about repairing, and that's how I repair! A happy couple, a wife and a husband, might have continued to bless life, and I let them die! A pair of wretches, a mother and child, will drag the ball and chain of the years, and I condemn them to live. I didn't know! With a charitable intention, I prevent a woman from drowning, and when I've constrained her no longer to attempt to take her life, I glimpse that the tomb would be her only refuge; I didn't know! In repenting of my faults, I've separated myself from that by which I sinned so much, granting my beauty to one man, my virility to another, and that double abnegation prevents me from saving a life broken by my caprice; I didn't know! I never know! I only want to do good and I do nothing but harm! The best sentiments procure me the worst results. Everything is error; I heap stupidity upon stupidity. What difference do you make, then, Lord, between the imbecile and the sage?"

"Only one," repeated the voice.

XXIV. The superior man gets rid
of what he had in his head

The pitiful philosopher turned round in order to see who had replied. He found no one behind him but the neat little old man, fully occupied for the moment in spreading the mist of his breath over the lenses of his spectacles

"What did you say?"

"I didn't breathe a word; I was breathing on my spectacles, and I think I have the right, yes, sir, the right, without having to account for it."

"I'm far from contesting it, and I only regret that you didn't say anything, for you were speaking just now with a tone of certainty..."

"Know, sir, that no one has ever accused me of having any secret, and that I haven't just arrived from my village; I know the world, sir, and as for certainty, I possess just as much as a man who has nothing for which to reproach himself. That's my response, sir."

"Nothing for which to reproach yourself? Truly?"

"Know, sire, that my name is Leonard Dubois. Dubois, Leonard, yes, sir, and I've kept the State ledgers for thirty-five years, and no one, sir, has ever, not ever, done me the insult of doubting that I'm an honest man."

"In that case, do you know where duty lies?"

"Duty, sir, how could I be ignorant of where duty lies?" The little old man adapted his spectacles slowly to the bridge of his nose, hooking the arms behind his ears, lowered his eyelids, and, with the tips of two parted fingers, made sure that the lenses were in front of his eyes, which he opened again with dignity. "Duty, sir, is doing what one ought to do. I know no other."

"Ah! But how does one know what one ought to do?"

"An honest man is not unaware of what he ought to do, sir. That's my sentiment." He expressed himself with severity, and the intellectual effort had doubtless fatigued his brain, for he removed his hat in order to sponge his cranium, which was elongated in the form of a marrow, smooth and white. Dieudonat could not help admiring that object and finding it enviable. He said: "Note, however, that I was obeying a duty when I sacrificed myself in order to bring Princess Aude and Galeas together; now, that duty has made it impossible for me to fulfill another, which reveals itself to be more imperious, and of which I was unaware."

On hearing those words, Master Leonard drew away slowly, moving backwards, as prudence counsels in confrontation with a lunatic. Ready to withdraw, but polite, he bowed, and thought that he had got out of it when Dieudonat retained him by the sleeve.

"Don't touch me, I beg you. I don't accept anyone touching me; that's my sentiment."

"I only desire to ask you a question."

"Ask, sir, but at a distance; I won't refuse you my illumination."

"So far as I can judge, Master Leonard, in accordance with your own eminently judicious words, I imagine that it must have happened to you many a time, in the course of your career to encounter uncouth individuals..."

"Sometimes, sir, even too frequently."

"No doubt, these coarse fellows, having heard the admirable good sense of your reflections and your deductions, have replied by comparing your intellect to various terrestrial or marine animals, such as the donkey, the calf, the goose, the oyster and the mussel, or even parts of the male and female body, or common to both sexes, such as the foot, the..."

"That has happened to me, in fact, sir, but such base insults cannot afflict me."

"I'm entirely convinced of it, and, if I'm not mistaken, you console yourself without delay, in thinking that your interlocutors are mere imbeciles."

"Idiots."

"You should be able to tell me, then, what distinction you make, Master Leonard between intelligence and imbecility."

"Imbecility was them."

"Indubitably: the imbecile is always the other, but the intelligent man, of high intelligence, is, therefore, Master Leonard?"

"The contrary of the imbecile."

"Are you very sure of that, and don't you think that, far from being the contrary, he's simply the exaggeration? The wind said just now that there is one difference between them, only one, and I've glimpsed it since then in comparing myself to you."

"Excuse me, sir, I'm awaited..."

"You don't have to hurry, then; and I conclude: the thinker is the man who thinks the most stupidities, since he thinks more than others. For it is necessary to recognize, sir, that men of the highest intelligence and the most vivid imagination are at risk of committing monstrous stupidities of which idiots cannot conceive. Certain heights of aberration demand faculties almost of genius, and a profligacy of ideas that initially supposes a wealth of ideas, and which, for that very reason, is prohibited to average souls. Imbeciles remain struck by stupor in the face of those prodigies, which far surpass them, and they shrug their shoulders in pity. They are not wrong."

"You're not wrong, sir, I bid you good evening. I'm awaited."

"Await also, Master Leonard; I would like, as a souvenir, to give you a present."

"A gift, sir?"

The petty bourgeois approached with an agreeable expression; lunatics sometimes have abrupt generosities, from which honest men can draw profit.

"Yes, Master Leonard, a gift. I know a man whom Heaven has endowed, it appears, in a very exceptional fashion, and who has been cursing it for a quarter of a century; his mother received the assurance of the genius that he would have; he has read innumerable books and retained what he read; his brain is a encyclopedia, and if you have the slightest desire to possess that magisterial cranium, instead of yours, you see me entirely disposed to make you a gift of it.

The worthy retiree, what had been vaguely hoping for a snuff-box or a cravat pin, and to whom intellectual treasures were offered, recoiled in fear; he looked the madman up and down, and fled.

"There's a sage," said Dieudonat. "That's assuredly a sage, since he refuses; the first act of incontestable sagacity that I've encountered in the world, it's a cretin who has accomplished it."

He turned back toward the river, the waters of which continued to descend in the same splendor, with the same certitude.

"They go to their goal, without error, and your force directs them, Lord. They have the divine science, and I only have the human science. I've exhausted it, in the end, so much have I abused the right to deceive myself, and I'd like to be ignorant of everything, in order only to be guided by your sagacity, like them, Lord, and like the humblest of the earth."

A small boy, noticing that he was speaking aloud, came curiously to stand to his right, and examined him from below with a cunning eye. He had a schoolboy's satchel slung over his shoulder; his calves were bare, and a pen had leaked ink on the sleeves of his checkered shirt. As soon as he saw that he had been discovered by the lord who was talking to himself, he sent his gaze to admire the horizon, and, involuntarily, laughed at the landscape.

"You're cheerful, my little friend?"

"Yes, sir."

"What is your name?"

"Onuphre."

"How old are you?"

"Eleven."

"I was our age when I met Gutenberg and inaugurated that series of deadly cogitations."

"Pardon?"

"You're coming home from school? Does studying amuse you?"

"Yes, sir."

"Much?"

"No, sir."

"What is your favorite game?"

"Running."

"And what day do you like best?"

"Thursday."

"Why not Sunday?"

"Sunday there's mass, and then I go out with Papa, and Mama, and my sister, all dressed up. Thursday's more fun."

"You like amusing yourself, then?"

"Yes, sir."

"More than studying?"

"For sure."

"Yes, yes, but it's necessary to work, all the same, isn't it? And to prepare for examinations, and competitions, to make a position and to earn a living, later, when you're grown up, when Papa is old?"

Dieudonat's voice quavered in his throat, with the anxious tremor of the honest man who is about to commit a bad action and is preparing for it. At the same time, the schoolboy had taken on an almost anxious expression.

"Does it trouble you, what I said just then?"

The schoolboy shrugged one shoulder, slowly, to express some impotence, and the philosopher sensed a secret misery there; immediately, he forgot his own."

"Something's worrying you? Tell me. I want to know."

Slightly astonished by his obedience, the boy, all in a single breath, confided that he would doubtless be unable to continue his studies, that his father, a shopkeeper's clerk, was about to lose his job because of an imminent bankruptcy, that his mother was in despair, and that they would soon have no more bread.

The momentum of recounting and the occasion of interest, in exciting his young brain, illuminated his brown eyes, and he narrated the lamentable story cheerfully. As he listened, Dieudonat remembered the sacred words: *If you do not become like children, you shall not enter the kingdom of God.* And he thought: *I've finished with the kingdom of earth; I no longer have any hope except in Heaven.*

Suddenly, however, newspaper criers went past at a run. They were proclaiming the suicide of a rich merchant and his wife, their domestic disgraces, with which Prince Dieudonat was mixed up, their ruination, and the miraculous disappearance of the Prince.

The child went very pale.

"Papa's boss is dead..."

"The man who has just killed himself was your father's employer?"

"Yes... No more bread...Mama's weeping... Goodbye, sir!"

"Stop! Listen!"

"I no longer have the time, sir; Mama's weeping!"

"Two minutes to gain twenty years of your life! Onuphre, you've heard mention of Dieudonat, who can do anything he wishes?"

"Yes. Papa detests him, and says he's the cause of all our woes and many others."

"Your father is right; that Dieudonat does a great deal of harm, and yet he isn't cruel; he'd repair it if he could. Listen to me with all your might; that man, my little friend, has studied a great deal, a great deal, and he knows more than all your masters put together; he's reflected on each of the sciences. Well, since your parents can't send you to school any longer, and since Dieudonat is the cause of your misery, he'll give you the fruit of his labor, if you wish, and you'll be very knowledgeable all of a sudden, tomorrow, if you like; without having the need to learn anything, you'll pass the most difficult examinations, you'll be able to teach, to preach from the pulpit or speak in the theater, and you'll be a child prodigy, famous in every city, apt for any employment, an you'll earn as much in one evening, if you want to, than your father does in a year. Would you like that?"

"It isn't a joke?"

"You'll have his mind and he'll have yours. Do you want that, Onuphre?"

"I'd like that very much."

"Since you consent I..."

At the moment of formulating his wish, the magician, seized by a scruple, raised his arms toward the heavens.

"Lord, will I not do more harm by passing to another that of which your favor gave me too much? The goods whose usage no longer tempts me might nourish a family, ameliorate the lot of this child, who will soon be a man, and lighten his existence as much as they have overburdened mine. I'm getting rid of them, it's true, but don't you think, Lord, that it's high time for me to live without thinking, and that it's time, too, that I stopped doing harm by thinking wrongly, while this child won't be able to do anything more than a man?"

The sun had just disappeared at the horizon; Dieudonat interrogated a majestically desolate sky, for nature is a mirror in which we discover the prolongation of our souls.

Before the splendid embroidery of crimson-fringed cumulus, he thought that clouds are the breath of the planet, a vapor exhaled by the earth where people suffer, a mist of sighs that strives to rise toward the placid azure, but which cannot reach it, and which bleeds at the end of the day.

"Oh, sir, can you see?"

"What, light soul?"

"The cloud. One might think it's a golden eagle attacking a sitting bear; it's attacking it from behind, and the other is lifting its paws; it's comical, do you see?"

"Not yet... But you, do you persist in wanting the gift of an infused science and a brain that understands everything?"

"It would be too lucky, sir."

"To nourish your mother and our father, say that you want them, and you'll have them."

182

"I want them!" snapped the child, bursting into laughter.

"Let me be Onuphre, then, and you can call yourself Epagomene henceforth,[13] as befits you; I give you my science and my thought in exchange for yours. So be it!"

Immediately, the schoolboy's expression darkened; in his eyes, as profound as wells, a heavy fluid of ideas gleamed mysteriously, and his brows were barred by a grave energy.

But at the same instant, Dieudonat, delivered of himself and his philosophies, ceased to take notice of those sorts of things; he pivoted on his heels, and quickly, pointing his index finger toward the west, he started to exclaim: "No, but, I beg you, look at the bear stretching out his paws. He can no longer sit still. Look at him falling on his nose. He's funny. Do you see?"

The child replied, with condescension; "I can no longer see it, sir." After which with a ceremonious air, he took off his cap, took a step toward the Prince, and looked him straight in the face.

"Will Your Lordship have the kindness to excuse me," he said, "if I don't stay any longer in his august company; my father and mother must be tormented by this evening's news, and I'm late rejoining them. I salute Your Lordship respectfully."

Dieudonat retained his laughter and thought, privately: *He's ridiculous, that kid playing at being a man.*

With a second pirouette, he got rid of him definitively, and forgot him; then, without any longer worrying about peo-

---

[13] From the Greek root *epago*, meaning "I bring in," most familiar in the reference to "epagomenal days" introduced into Egyptian 360-day calendar to adjust it to the actual number of days in the solar year. The name Onuphre, that of a famous Christian anchorite saint who lived in the Egyptian desert in the fourth century, is derived from an Egyptian word meaning "eternally good"; his legend is connected with that Paphnuce, the protagonist of Anatole France's novel *Thaïs* (1890).

ple, happy or unhappy, he leaned on the parapet of the bridge and settled down to watch the amusing clouds.

XXV. Dieudonat's debuts in the career of an inferior man

Let us not try to dissimulate; before that splendid sunset, the altruist had just committed an egotistical act of the worst species; in giving himself airs of liberality, and in prefect cognizance of the cause, he had ceded to his neighbor a bad business, which had inconvenienced him for a long time, and he had taken something excellent in exchange. Those sorts of transactions are much sought after in society, and well noted, but if it is true that they are honored, they do little honor. At the very least, it is necessary to add that Dieudonat had the excuse of discouragement, and that that circumstance is the only one in which we surprise that worthy man *in flagrante delicto* in cunning and perversity; what is more desolating, from the moral viewpoint, is that an act so base was also the only one, among so many fine actions, of which he never had to complain or to repent.

Entirely to the contrary, he immediately entered into the happiest period of his life.

He had said to Galeas: "I will expiate; I'll take charge of that." One must suppose that, at that moment, he projected sacrificing himself without reserve to the good of others in order to punish himself for having sacrificed others to his own pleasure. But he truly went to work a little rapidly, and, in sum, his first day of expiatory sacrifice had been singularly advantageous, since he began by giving away that which enables suffering.

Imagine, in fact, what a state of insouciance and good humor would spread over the earth if one abolished the amplification of woes that we call thought. He gave away his intelligence! Imagine also in what blissful calm the days of the world would go by if one withdrew therefrom the dramas and the comedies that are stimulated everywhere, among people and animals, by the involuntary desire to propagate the species to which they belong. He gave away his virility! Delivered of both of them, he was rid of the thousand cares that they entail—which is as much as to say, of all cares.

Did he regret them, at least? Not at all, and every regret of that nature was forbidden to him, for those two prerogatives enjoy a truly exceptional privilege, since it is indispensable to posses them to the highest degree in order to deplore their insufficiency. On the one hand, in fact, only excessively intelligent individuals are anxious about not being intelligent enough, and on the other, the libidinous are the only ones to complain about the limit that their forces impose on their appetites.

As for the abandonment of his beauty and his left eye, he counted them as trivial, his pretty face never having occupied him much, and since he had acquired the habit of making use of it to the exclusion of the other, his right eye appeared to him to be sufficient for seeing.

A great child of a meter seventy-six, with the vigorous body of his thirty-fifth year and the serene soul of his eleventh, he went forth to adventure.

"I want to see things!"

And his wish was realized. In the twilight he emerged from the city; he slept under a large tree and woke up in the sunlight, just in time to crunch apples that were still fresh, and set off again family, a radiant wanderer, a vagabond devoid of needs, going straight ahead, at random, having neither a goal not a purpose, careless of tomorrow and forgetful of yesterday.

If it is necessary to believe the plurality of philosophers, he ought not to have remembered anything, since the notion of our identity resides in the memory, and he had given away the treasures of his own. But who can say whether the gods have not established a distinction that escapes us between the memory of learned ideas and that of our own actions, between science and conscience, one ephemeral and the other less inalienable?

At any rate, the new Dieudonat, for one reason or another, remembered confusedly a few fragments of his past, as one recalls the incidents of a dream on awakening; he knew his name, his origin and his magical power, but he only attached a mediocre importance to those things, and above all, did not take any vanity from them. Of his anterior existence he retained just what was necessary to enjoy having changed it; his subjects of remorse no longer tormented him, they trailed behind him in the dust of the roads or the mist of the horizons, and when he made the gesture of wanting to launch himself forward he liberated himself from them in the manner of children avoiding importunity, and who, while galloping, expel their cares and strew them along the road.

The sparrows saw him gamboling in the dew, laughing at the trees and the clouds, sleeping in the woods, taking a siesta on the edge of a ditch, playing with beetles and chasing butterflies. When he was hungry or thirty he wished for fruits on the branches or a spring in a ravine, and he found them immediately.

He was intoxicated by landscapes, savoring the distances, swallowing the light, which descended into his heart and dilated his life; the harmonious warmth of hues enlivened the blood in his veins as the warmth of a wine would have done, and voices sang within him in unison with the colors.

How beautiful the earth is, and how little we know it! How lively it is in its immobility, under that envelope of vibrant air! He discovered it and invented it for his usage. Until then, in regarding it as a thinker, he had not seen it, only seeing himself therein; now, he searched the corners where masterpieces were hidden, lay in wait for it at the bends in roads, surprised it on the other side of a hill, a hedge or a rock, always ingenious and always new; he loved it with a juvenile and recent love; he communicated with it.

By night he loved the stars; he no longer knew their names or their distances, but they were all the more easily accessible for that to his childish reverie: of the enormous poetry of terror and vertigo that makes suns rotate, he no longer knew anything, but he had reconquered the naïve admiration of that which shines; lying on his back, he enjoyed being dazzled by that celestial jewelry, and went to sleep trying to count the Holy Virgin's diamonds in their case of nocturnal velvet.

He was free, he was alone, and he savored his solitude and liberty candidly. He loved life for the life's sake, and it was the first time.

"I don't want anyone to find me!"

And he went forth, using up space, expending hours, days and weeks, a rather grotesque silhouette in his Court clothing, whose satin was torn by brambles, splattered with mud and gray with dist; the tattered plumes of his toque dangled pitifully over his ear, and people would have taken him for an acrobat in distress rather than the son of a king making his tour of the world. Who would have recognized him? Of the old Dieudonat he no longer wore anything but the rags, and he scarcely resembled Galeas anymore; his beard had grown; his unkempt hair extended over his neck; his natural health and savage existence had purified the Archduke's complexion; the lips became red again and their rictus relaxed into benevolent smiles; the menaces of the unmatched eye were velveted with tenderness; the brow of the One-Eyed, once furrowed by anger and calculations, was smoothed out like a lake after a storm and shone ingenuously; the whole of that once-disquieting face opened now like a frank book in which passers-by could read the probity of a happy soul.

In fact, everyone was his friend, so much did he need to be liked and so much did he radiate tender benevolence; because he had renounced his mind, his heart filled him entirely, and overflowed from him in sudden commiserations, desires for offerings and perpetual sympathies. He accosted people without knowing them, and immediately he had known them for months. He escorted the travelers who unwound the long ribbon of the roads and cheered up their journey by chatting or singing, while he chased away the gadflies that bloodied the rumps of the horses with handfuls of ferns.

Nothing pleased him as much as giving: a facile joy for that rich pauper, a joy sometimes doubled, for his new childhood had just discovered a game and a gaiety therein of which he never wearied. The game was simple and quotidian; one invites some carter to share a frugal meal, and the fellow never fails to say, after having eaten: "A good cup of wine, with that, that's what's needed."

"I just happen to have a very old bottle hidden in this thicket."

One dives into the thicket, one pretends to search, one curses, one delays, and when the moment arrives when the traveler begins to mock, one reappears with the wine! On another day, it is a slice of lard, or an aune of black pudding that emerges triumphantly from the deserted wood. People open their mouths wide to marvel before opening it to eat.

"You're not a sorcerer, at times?"

"Perhaps so, perhaps..."

As for saying what or how, the great child will not consent to that, so good does the farce seem to him and so funny are the expressions of his stupefied guests.

Those companions of an hour disappear; one will never encounter them again; they leave nothing behind them, not having hollowed out in the memory any furrow of pain or having sown any seed of care. In any case, Dieudonat is very often alone, for there is always something unknown or marvelous over there, tempting him and calling him away from the high road. If the solitude ceases to please him and he has a desire to see faces, he has soon made his entry into a farmstead or an inn.

At the farm, his accoutrement initially amused the young men and women, but he was scarcely moved by that, and his good humor soon disarmed the mockery. In the inns the adventure was more scabrous; the innkeeper and his prudent wife were suspicious of a fellow so strangely clad, who exhibited neither money nor luggage, and who held out a ham or a fat goose as payment for a night in the barn; they sniffed a thief; more than once he had to make himself scarce under the threat of archers. He ran away then without sadness or rancor, avoiding the police as one avoids the rain; insults and downpours are accidents of the journey, and life is good anyway.

Off to elsewhere! As soon as he was over the hill he forgot the country, the people or the shower; a gust of the breeze swept away the past and a ray of sunlight gilded the whole future, the future being of such short duration!

One day, however, he espies a girl sitting on the edge of a ditch; she is very young, with the stature of a woman and the gaze of a child; over her forehead tanned by the sun, her chestnut-colored hair has metallic reflections, and her face shines, with a patina of sunlight varnished with sweat, and her features are immobile in the heat, with the consequence that she gives the impression of a statue made of bronze. Her profound mouth and her enamel eyes are open in an astonishment mingled with languor, and under the thin shadow of a hawthorn she is dappled by light. Her cows are grazing in the sunlight nearby, russet between the green of the meadow and the blue of the sky.

Dieudonat stops and contemplates: has that grave child, with eyes as stupid and dreamy as those of her animals, so chaste in her brutality, so poetic in her coarseness, whom one senses to be almost saintly by virtue of ignorance, not emerged from a missal or a legend? She resembles the Shepherdess of France,[14] who was dazzled when voices came to speak to her in the tree...

"Good day, girl!"

He approaches, and the candid child, under the gaze of a man, lowers her eyes like a sly dog, peeping from below and laughing underneath. But he does not pay any heed to that, and draws nearer.

"Tell me your name..."

"Clementine."

---

[14] Saint Genevieve, the patron saint of Paris, was conventionally imagined to have been a shepherdess, although the historical individual was not. The reference to voices in a tree might, however, indicate that the person the narrative voice has in mind is Jeanne d'Arc.

"I perceive in your basket there a raw onion and hard bread; that's a meager feast, girl, and I have a pullet in my satchel that's much better, with wine—not to mention apples. Shall we eat together, eh?"

He installs himself beside the cowherd, who makes room for him, and the provisions appear; a gleam of covetousness light up in the child's angelic eyes; she squints at the victuals, and when her young teeth sink into the soft flesh or make the bones crack, when her unctuous lips kiss and suck the golden drumsticks, she blinks her eyes voluptuously, and all of human animality spreads over her visage of a virginal brute. She drinks, and her cheeks light up. Laborers pass by in the distance. She crunches the apples, shifts her legs, laughs, showing the depths of her red gullet, and her clogs bump into one another on the slope of the bank. The bushes behind are a convenient hiding place; the laborers in the distance and up above are silhouettes who see nothing, and thousands of bees are buzzing infinitely over the hill planted with vines. If Dieudonat wanted...

But he no longer wants, and does not even understand that the shepherd's hour is sounding in the shepherdess.

She lies down on her back, and her eyelashes come together like diaphanous wings; they are still fluttering slightly. One might think that she is waiting: for sleep, perhaps, or a dream? Dieudonat thinks so, at least, and nothing more; sitting two paces away from her, he admires with delight the ephemeral wellbeing that he has put into one of God's creatures.

But suddenly, God's creature, without saying what fly has stung her, leaps up, uttering loud cries. Her shrill voice springs forth, pierces the landscape and flies like a volley of arrows through the vertical rays that are falling from the sun. Fear or pain? That call of a wounded animal has ripped through the calm of the distances; the curbed countrymen have raised their heads and are searching.

"Help! Help!"

Dieudonat leans toward the girl, who is writhing in the grass and whose feet are agitating furiously toward the little

191

white clouds stationary in the blue sky. From the summits of the nearby hills, peasants armed with pitchforks are running with long strides, and the girl is still howling.

"It's Clementine, with a vagabond!"

The men, congested by running, their brows sweating, arrive and surround the couple; the bare legs of the young cowherd are beating the grass, outside her tucked up shirts. No need to be a sorcerer to work out what has just happened; everyone divines it except the sorcerer. Blows rain down on his back and shoulders; rustic fists crush his face; then he begins to understand.

"Sirs, I assure you..."

"No one is listening. The virgin of the fields gets up, with the aid of women who had arrived belatedly, to pull down her skirts, and she moans, she hides her eyes behind her fists, she strives to weep, to speak, and stammers words salted by tears.

"Is this what it looks like? Say?"

"Yes, that's what it is."

The vagabond tries in vain to deny it; his victim only cries louder, affirming, swearing, that she is a woman and is desolate in consequence. The matrons interrogate her; then she recounts, with precision, how the thing happened and how it went; as the details are narrated, the women and the men shake their heads and simulate anger, but their blood is up and, for want of anything better, blows are expended on the face of the innocent man; he bleeds, and the blows are redoubled; the sight of blood always stimulates the indignation of consciences.

Dieudonat, soundly beaten, partially bruised, was put in handcuffs, and, in stages was taken all the way to the town where human justice sat.

The judge was dressed in a black robe bordered with fake ermine, in which the tails flowed like equally black tears, to demonstrate to the accused that mourning is being worn for them in advance. The good vagabond was able to observe that the preliminary mourning in question is worn for a long time, for he waited two full months while his case was investigated. He did not complain, having a docile humor, adapting to everything and finding a new pleasure in each new condition; his prison reminded him vaguely of a certain cell in a monastery where he had once lived.

"As far as I remember, I stayed there for seven years; it must have been monotonous, seven years always similar. Here, at least, one has the unexpected."

The pomp of justice obtained his admiration, He also admired the perspicacity of human justice, for it was demonstrated to him as clearly as daylight that he was well known, and that his name was Onuphre.

But the major astonishment came to him from learning that the young virgin with the limpid eyes had neither exaggerated nor lied when she had denounced the irreparable loss of her virginity; the sweet child was pregnant! The physicians attested it, and she wept a great deal in front of the judge, of shame, chagrin and anger; she wept and cried, showing her fist to the malefactor who had got her drunk, forced and beaten her, and she recounted the episodes of the drama with such a furious conviction that even the innocent man was moved by it.

In spite of his candor he soon divined that the virgin had probably lapsed before knowing him and that she had denied her voluntary sin in order to replace it with another for which she was less responsible. The idea did not appear to him to be stupid; in any case, he was touched by the trouble that the child was giving herself in order to save her rustic honor; he felt pity for her distress and approved of her energy.

Poor thing, she's quite right; she's sparing herself miseries...

He encouraged her with his gaze and, smiling at her in worthy amity, he confessed everything for which she reproached him.

What can they do to me?

They did not take long to furnish him with that information; there and then, he was sentenced to be hanged, after having made honorable amends on the parvis of the cathedral.

It was thus that Dieudonat, who had possessed so many ladies and damsels, without anyone seeking to quarrel with him, in the days when he was a prince, was judged good for the gallows as soon as he was a eunuch and poor.

XXVI. He encounters charity

He emerged from the tribunal with his eyes cheerful and his heart at ease.

"You see how everything works out? If I remember correctly, I had promised to expiate a heap of abominable sins, and in truth, I didn't give them any further thought! Thanks to that shepherdess, I'm going to settle my account and keep my promise, without having to do anything myself. The good judge has taken charge of everything; it's very convenient. When shall I be hanged, sir jailer?"

"Tomorrow morning."

He was moved to another cell, which he observed with pleasure because of the novelty. As soon as he was alone and imprisoned, he inspected his penultimate dwelling; the lodgings lacked comfort; light, although it cost nothing, was eked out there parsimoniously; it fell from a ventilation shaft pierced near the vault; the walls of sticky stone were oozing; for furniture, a bed of straps with a staved-in mattress and a brown blanket, a full pitcher and an empty ladle. He smiled benevolently at those things, which represented destiny.

"It's claimed that the last night of those condemned to death is terribly spent; perhaps phantoms, devils and remorse come? We shall see."

He sat down on his bed and waited curiously. Nothing came. He raised his unique eye toward his skylight and judged from the pink tint that he discerned in a tiny path of sky that the sun was setting; that example appeared to him to be a good example to follow; he lay down. Gradually, the pink patch turned gray, and the gray turned blue; then the dungeon became completely black.

"It's necessary to admit that if this eve is stirring, as is assured, I've scarcely perceived anything so far. Bah! Let's be patient."

He went to sleep. The rats trotted around his slumber, and he had already been snoring for several hours, dreaming of the earthly paradise where the animals strolled in amicable promiscuity, when a fantastic screech woke him with a start.

"Here come the specters!"

The lock alone had uttered that shrill cry of pain, which was still grating in the darkness. The door opened slightly; a shaft of light, sprung from some muted lantern, cut through the darkness; a human silhouette penetrated into the cell, and the door closed again.

How emotional I am! And how well I've done to accept my fate without saying anything! Nothing is more amusing than a prison door.

The lantern was unmasked and placed on the floor, and the phantom entered into the luminous sector. It was a woman of young but lugubrious appearance, enveloped in a wretched mantle; without saying a word she came to sit down on the bed beside the prisoner, and turned toward him.

"Are you alive, Madame?"

Without responding, she began to smile slowly; the lantern illuminated her fully. Her face would have been ugly without the benevolence of that smile, very soft and very humble, which rose from the mouth to the eyes like a ray of sunlight climbing a hill after a storm. She had dog-like eyes, round and devoted. She unfastened her mantle, which slid from her shoulders toward her hips; underneath it, she was only wearing a woolen skirt over a chemise of coarse fabric, tied around the neck, which her two breasts caused to bulge; her rump hollowed out the mattress.

Finally, she said: "Good evening."

"Good evening," he replied.

They looked at one another amicably, but in silence; she appeared to be experiencing some embarrassment.

"I've come."

"I see..."

"You were asleep?"

"I was asleep."

"I woke you up?"

"I'll have plenty of time to rest; I'm dying tomorrow morning."

"You don't seem sad."

"Sad? No...why would I be?"

"Because of...tomorrow."

"Because they're going to hang me? Well, I've done all sorts of things in my life, but never that; the opportunity has presented itself; I'm taking advantage of it. And then, I'll tell you: I need to expiate; I promised."

"You're funny! I've often seen condemned men..."

"Oh?"

"Yes, masses! I'm the jailer's daughter...Gertrude..."

"Oh?"

"Yes. My father is the jailer, and I'm his daughter, you understand?"

"Perfectly. You're the jailer's daughter and you live in the prison."

"That's right."

The silence that followed denounced the difficulties of the conversation. The visitor, who apparently had other things to say, waited to be aided; while waiting, she caressed her knees with a circular movement of her open palms, and contemplated the lantern with a blissful expression. Finally, she decided to cough. Out of politeness, Dieudonat coughed too. A new silence fell in the dungeon. The rats observed from the edges of their holes.

The young woman gathered her courage and turned to the man.

"So, just like that, you were condemned to death?"

"My God, yes."

"It's a moment to pass. It's necessary to be reasonable."

"As you say; it'll be over quickly."

"Oh, yes, it's very quick. He knows his job, the executioner, and he isn't malevolent. Only I've seen a great many of them, over time, and I can't get used to it, and it troubles me, the idea that there's a man in the house, fully alive, and that soon he won't be anyone, nothing but a heap."

"That's known as 'mortal remains.'"

"Exactly. So, every time there's an execution, the night before, it's stronger than me, I turn back and forth in my bed, and I think about the poor fellow who's all alone in his black corner, like a sick dog, and who's waiting for the moment without a soul to talk to him, all alone. Then, by necessity, I decide to come; so, I come, like this."

"To keep him company?"

"Exactly."

"That's kind of you."

"No, it's something else, inside me, which commands me..."

"That's known as 'the heart.' You have a good heart."

"I don't know how I have a heart, but I believe it's a heavy heart; no one would ever be hanged, if it depended on me. All the same, a woman, there are little favors she can offer, aren't there, if she cares to? Even if one were a princess, one wouldn't have anything more, and it would be just the same."

"The most beautiful woman in the world..."

"I give what I have; I'm not a beautiful girl."

He coughed again, but he understood quickly that that response was not enough; he searched for another."

"You're charitable..."

"It doesn't cost me anything, and it passes their time."

"Does it give you a little pleasure too?"

"No, to tell the truth; of pleasure, I wouldn't have any, without the idea that a poor fellow who'll never have any more is getting it from me."

"It's unnecessary to feel sorry for yourself; the happiness that one gives is as much happiness that one obtains, isn't it?"

"Exactly. I think like you, and I wouldn't exchange my pleasure for theirs."

"The more one gives, the more one has."

"Exactly! And when I'm the most content is when they seem well content. Although that, you see, one finds it when one's like me, and doesn't have a liking for the thing; but them, it's in relation to their worry, or because they're afraid. Necessary not to hold it against them, don't you think? They weep when one talks to them. Then, I weep with them; it makes them a sort of sister, you understand?"

"A species of angel."

"Necessary not to say that, because, after all, it's a mortal sin—fornication, so the almoner says..."

"I know."

"But, you know, one confesses, before going to the gibbet; then the sin is removed."

"And the consolation remains."

"Exactly! The almoner says exactly the opposite, and threatens me with the devil if I do it again, but I do it again anyway, and it doesn't enter my head that the good God will get angry when one is doing what one can for people who are in pain, and when one can't do otherwise."

"Your father doesn't get annoyed?"

"I don't tell him anything, for sure. I've only told him that I don't want to marry."

"That's true; you can't any longer."

"Right! It isn't suitors who are lacking, but, once married, I wouldn't be able to come any longer; my husband would oppose it, probably, and coming anyway would be deceiving him."

"Lying isn't good."

"It causes chagrin; I'd be ashamed. And then, in my idea, I'm more useful here. And then again, to say everything, there's the malady."

"Oh?"

"Yes. Among murderers and thieves, as you can imagine, one encounters some who aren't honest, as everywhere. They don't tell, in order to take advantage. So, they gave me the disease."

"Oh?"

"Yes."

"Poor Gertrude..."

"That's the way it is. Nothing to be done about it."

"But tell me, the disease, you're giving it to others?"

"You're silly. Since they're going to die..." She laughed, and added: "As things are, I'm in prison, like them; they only have me, I only have them. That's it." She was no longer laughing.

They fell silent again momentarily, and then she went on: "I've come to sleep with you. That's it."

He scratched his head, a little behind his right ear; she was not unaware that in cats, that gesture is an announcement of rain, and among men, a sign of indecision.

"Kiss me," she said. "It will distract you."

"I'll kiss you with great pleasure, because you're a good creature. As for the rest, to say everything, I no longer have any means."

"Oh?"

"No. I have the air of being a man, when one sees me, like the others. It isn't true; I'm not a man."

"What are you then?"

He replied, in a low voice and very modestly: "A eunuch."

Gertrude's gaze requested, in the semi-darkness, a supplementary explanation.

"If you prefer, I'm gelded..."

She had never heard mention of such people; it had to be the name of a people, doubtless a distant people, and probably unhappy, a vanquished nation, since the poor devils were humiliated in pronouncing the name of their fatherland...?[15]

He corrected her misapprehension, and furnished a few elementary items of information on the condition of castration.

"Necessary to say that right away! I know that; it's me who clips dogs and cuts cats at the prison door."

---

[15] The French for "gelded" is *hongre*, whereas the French for "Hungary" is *Hongrie*; the wordplay does not translate.

She commiserated with him unreservedly; that individual diminution seemed to her even harder to support than a national defeat, not to mention that it was a ludicrous invention to treat Christians like capons, oxen, pigs, or even cats, since one ought not to eat them.

"But... Eh...? What...? You're telling me stories because I displease you. Liar!"

"I'm not lying."

"That story! You weren't a eunuch with Clementine, whom you raped in a wood."

He confessed his innocence.

"You were condemned, and you didn't defend yourself? When you had the proof? The alibi, as they say..."

"That's because...the thing is...that poor little shepherdess, it's necessary to know that she was pregnant. She'd have been whipped, drummed out, imprisoned in an Abbey; they'd have given her shoulder-knots and an armband. In order to spare her that, I said what she said; everyone's content."

Gertrude admired that abnegation, but she could not help launching indignant epithets against the cowherd and against her bad morals, her libertinage of a girl who sinned for pleasure, and her cruelty and her lies, and also against the magistrate, whom she detested, whom the whole town detested, because he was unjust, wicked, miserly and content when he caused suffering, and a robber, and a cuckold like his father and mother, furred in ermine as he was. Exactly! Her scorn was relentless, with regard to that last grievance, for women, who are able to excuse all crimes, refuse their mercy to the fault of being deceived.

Until dawn, she remained sitting on the edge of the bed, chatting with the condemned man, sometimes caressing his hands or his hair; they addressed one another as *tu*, talking about incoherent things with the gravity of children.

Suddenly, he burst out laughing.

"You know what, Gertrude?"

"What, my darling?"

"I no longer have any desire to go and die now, none at all. And for some time I've been repeating to myself: 'No, I don't want them to hang me.' It's your fault."

"Mine?"

"For sure! Why wouldn't I stay for a little while longer on earth, where there are worthy people like you? For you're a good girl, Gertrude."

"You too."

"That's it! I want to stay."

"Poor fellow..."

She gazed at him with pity, and their innocent eyes, which had encountered one another, began to dream together. They felt sorry for one another, and did not hide it, even though they did not say anything about it. But suddenly, an idea was born in each of their heads, and the two faces took on a joyful expression at the same time; but neither Gertrude nor Dieudonat wanted to say what they were thinking. From them on, they spoke less; they seemed preoccupied or impatient; covertly, they darted sly glances at the ventilation shaft, as if to provoke some signal therefrom.

Finally, a little daylight blanched the ceiling. She thought: *It's now*. And he thought: *It's now*.

She kissed the man who was due to die in a little while tenderly, and two large tears drowned her canine eyes. Then she got up to leave.

"I'm in a hurry; I have something to do right away."

But he retained her by the wrist.

"Gertrude, we won't see one another again, I believe, in this base world, and I'd like to leave you a souvenir of me. Listen: you're good and I like you a lot. However, you haven't even asked my name."

"You're the condemned man."

"But also?"

"They call you Onuphre."

"Have you heard mention of a certain Dieudonat?"

"The one whose wishes are granted and who has gold whenever he wants it?"

"He has better than gold; you too have better, for you have a heart of gold and you've sacrificed your health to console the unfortunate; he's giving you his. So be it! Kiss me now, and go; but in future, spare yourself in order to keep what I've given you. Adieu, Gertrude."

Scarcely had he spoken than he felt a languor making his limbs heavy; he felt a chill all the way to the marrow of his bones, and nausea filled his mouth.

The girl, by contrast, had straightened her torso and her neck; her hamstrings flexed under the rigid weight of her body, and she breathed easily, deeply, as if spring breezes were blowing through the cell.

She did not understand very clearly what has happening to her, but they looked at one another; she was blooming with life, he was radiant at having given it to her, and one minute of happiness floated divinely between those two naïve souls.

XXVII. He is prey to justice

Dieudonat had spoken his secret idea, and had even realized it, but Gertrude was still ruminating hers.

"Necessary to make that happen, but there isn't a moment to lose."

She ran to her kitchen, took her broom, spat on her hands, and drew the bolts on the doors.

"I feel light this morning, I no longer feel my burden. I don't know what's simmering inside me, but it's many months since I knew so much ease. Am I cured of the disease?"

She left the prison, broom in hand, as she was accustomed to do.

"Today, it's necessary to see about making more noise than work. Hup!"

The town was still asleep; the paving stones of the street were damp and devoid of footprints. In the early morning mist, Gertrude's broom set about scything through the silence, tracing broad arcs on the stones, and the dust rose from the ground effortlessly, to fall back in heavy sheaves.

"Oh, how well I feel, and how I'm breathing! Are people never going to wake up today? It's urgent, though."

She kept watch on the surrounding houses. Finally, somewhere in the distance, a shutter clicked against a wall; elsewhere, a window grated, and then another; a rumble of wheels sounded in the distance; a door opened slightly; someone coughed; windows opened everywhere. Housewives in short skirts appeared on the thresholds; the shutters over the shop-windows began to grate on their hinges.

"They're taking their time!"

In order to be seen, Gertrude swept vigorously, and started to sing.

"You're very cheerful, girl!"

"Haven't you heard the news? The vagabond they're going to hang is innocent. They've just undressed him to put the penitent's chemise on him, and they saw that he couldn't have raped Clementine, who lied, because he's a eunuch, as they call it, as one says a neutered cat."

"And does the judge know that? It's necessary to tell him."

"Tell him? He doesn't care!"

Gertrude resumed weeping. From the corner of her eye she watched her story launch forward into the town."

"A eunuch who's going to be hanged for rape?"

"No?"

"Yes—they're going to hang him."

"He's gone," said Gertrude. "It's just a matter of time."

From one group to another, from door to window, the story ran, along the sidewalks, skimming the walls, leaping over the gutters; it raced, the morning's good story, turning the corners of the streets, radiating over the crossroads, spreading over the squares, lingering on the parvis of every church where the angelus was being rung, stopping the milk carts and the dung carts, frightening the maidservants and going up with them to the bourgeois bedrooms, where their employers became indignant in the name of justice and Truth while drinking their milky coffee.

"Are they going to let an innocent man die?"

"It isn't possible!"

The ingenious Gertrude had not lied, exactly; she had simply anticipated the inevitable. In fact, the executioners had presented themselves soon after the crack of dawn in the cell of the condemned man, garnished internally with hot soup and even hotter spiced wine; they had found him in good humor.

They spoke amicably to their client of a day, and nothing in their words reeked of the arrogance that is customary to subalterns when they become masters for a moment. They joked with the vagabond about the rape of which he had rendered himself culpable in the woods and which he was about to expiate under the wood; without vain prudery they informed him of the honorable effects of hanging; their laughter was sonorous, full of health, and Dieudonat, out of politeness, strove to laugh with them, but had no great desire to do so.

The idea of being hanged had decidedly ceased to please him; his appetite for new adventures no longer excited him at all that morning. To begin with, he was feeling ill; the strange malady he had just acquired as chilling his blood and his bones; his immortal soul was exhausted by it; he no longer had any appetite for anything, for living or for dying, although the latter is the final fantasy of discouraged people; his arms were dangling under the weight of his hands, his head was tilting over his shoulder and his skin was prickling with cold while the benevolent functionaries took off his clothes in order to put the penitent's chemise on him.

His torso was already half-naked; he said, quietly: "I'm not very warm."

"It's fear, comrade; have a drop of this."

He drank from a leather bottle a fiery liquid that made him cough, for the lack of habitude, and the executioners slapped his back gaily between the shoulder blades. One of the aides unfolded the ample back robe in front of him, making it click; it seemed to him to be shameful and sad.

"Nothing in all of this amuses me, and I regret giving you needless trouble, but I don't want to be hanged; so be it!"

"You're a good one, my lad!"

They continued their work; his shirt was removed; they saw him without any veil; their hilarity was enormous.

"A eunuch!"

"Who rapes girls!"

"How do you do it?"

"Give me the chemise, please; I'm not warm."

"You know," said the jailer, "this might be what they call a judicial error."

The executioner protested: "You believe in judicial errors? I don't believe in those tricks—they're inventions of criminals to discredit the law."

"Well, perhaps this fellow didn't rape the girl, since he's castrated."

"It's necessary all the same that she was violated, since she's pregnant."

Between these two incompatible arguments, the worthy fellows reflected as best they could, very embarrassed, and Dieudonat shivered, as naked as a worm in the damp cell.

"The chemise… I'm cold…"

"What are we going to do, then?"

The jailer ran to the judge's house.

The man of the ermines was still asleep next to his wife.

"Wake up, sir!"

In those days, the most noble people, even kings and duchesses, who slept without nightshirts, saw no inconvenience in receiving visitors in the bedroom, as we receive them in the dining room; modesties vary. At the noise that was made around his slumber. Master Touillechair opened an already surly eye. A chambermaid drew the curtains at the windows and light poured in.

"What's happened?" What do you want with me?"

Standing at the foot of the bed, vaguely disturbed, the turnkey searched for words and only found ideas, because of the snores emerging from under the sheets of the wife, renowned for her adulteries. He succeeded, however, in exposing the facts.

"What are you telling me? A eunuch? You're mad!"

The citizen sat up, and upper body, covered in black hair, rose up between the green bed-curtains alongside the conjugal mass; majesty was in default. He scratched his ribs vehemently, and his fingernails left long livid streaks on his yellow skin.

"A eunuch? You're sure?"

"I saw it as I'm seeing you."

Disquieted by that comparison, the judge lowered his gaze upon himself, and pulled up the quilt. But his wife shifted everything, cursing in the hollow of the pillow. "What's going on? Are you issuing verdicts in your bed now?"

"Hold your peace, wife; you're strangely mistaken if you believe that a bed isn't a place befitting judiciary labor. Our venerable ancestors didn't think in that fashion; to hear a case and deliberate on it, the kings of olden days lay down on their couch, the bed of justice, and doubtless wanted us to understand by that symbolism that quietude is of primordial necessity in the workings of justice; doubtless also, it's in memory of the royal bed, and by virtue of an exaggerated interpretation of the symbol, that some of us go to sleep on their seats."

"It's well worth the trouble of waking up an honest woman for a eunuch! I ask you whether it can interest you if such a fellow is dead or alive, and what can he be useful for?"

At these revolting words, the magistrate started with indignation, so violently that he had to pull up the quilt a second time. "I'm ashamed, Madame, for you're erring more and more. Know that our tribunal is neither a stud-farm not a harem, where generative virtues have weight; the subjects of the king, however diminished they might be, all have an equal right to hope that, without distinction of persons, our verdicts will be inspired exclusively by social interest and public morality. The problem that is posed to our conscience, Madame, is of a higher nature than you imagine, in accordance with your narrow views, for it's a matter for us, not only of punishing the guilty, when they are encountered, but also and above all in moralizing the people committed to our paternal wisdom, of maintaining them in confidence, and ensuring that the serenity of their minds and the security of their quotidian existence are untroubled by any doubt or molested by any scandal. I am speaking to you as I think, Madame: woe betide the judge who fails in his essential duty and who troubles public consciousness by permitting notorious errors to spread through the city even the shadow of a suspicion against the King's justice."

He paused for breath, and, satisfied with himself, he turned to the jailer, whom veneration had immobilized like a boundary marker.

"For those reasons, a solution is entirely indicated in the present difficulty, and I'm astonished, my friend, that you have been able to hesitate in conceiving it and applying it yourself, since it is incontestably the only one to which our tribunal can have recourse without failing."

"I thought so, but if Your Excellency will excuse me, I'm not permitted to release a man legally condemned without orders..."

"Release him! Who mentioned releasing him! This vagabond is, as you say, legally condemned, and we'd be mocked in the taverns and the papers, and people would jeer us, if anyone knew that we'd released a fellow duly condemned. No, since good fortune permits us to discover in time detail, which would be of a nature, if it were divulged, to disconcert the respect of citizens for the law, we must, above all, make sure that that detail remains absolutely unknown. That is why I am recommending that you take the greatest care in enclosing your eunuch securely in the penitent's robe and making sure that it is not removed at the moments of hanging and burying him. If he keeps it on his body, no one will know what there is underneath it; a robe will be lost, it's true, but we will have avoided the major disaster of provoking a perturbation of consciences, which is the most important thing of all, my friend, and justice will be satisfied. Go, my friend."

The jailer seemed perplexed, torn between his admiration for judiciary wisdom and the scruples of candor. But the judge sent his two legs out of the bed one after the other, and repeated: "Go, I tell you. In any case, I'll join you in the main square in order to make sure in person of these important measures. I'll have breakfast, because it's necessary not to respire the morning miasmas on an empty stomach, and I'll be there."

Having spoken, Master Touillechair collected his chemise from the pillar of the conjugal bed and began to get dressed calmly, with the intimate glorification of a man who, from the moment of his awakening, has done his duty.[16]

---

[16] This chapter of the present text and its immediate predecessors are each derived from a single episode in the 1906 serial version. The last episode of 1906 version, however, begins with the first words of the following chapter and concludes with the penultimate line of chapter XXXVII, galloping from one to the other at a furious pace, without most of the charac-

XXVIII. He makes the acquaintance of the soul of crowds

Master Touillechair walked through the streets pompously, his bile yellow and his coat black, his toque straight, his tread heavy and his heart light; his robe ornamented with fake ermines hung in noble pleats, billowing in the wind at the intersections.

When he emerged into the square he perceived with displeasure that the crowd noise had an excessive animation; he had always prescribed decorum around executions, which ought to be a moral lesson, and he reproved tumult; he frowned. Then, convinced that his presence would restore good order, he amplified his stride, and sensed that he was becoming august.

No one perceived him to begin with; all eyes were turned toward the gibbet.

A somber mass of backs and heads were swarming around the masonry mass that dominated the three gallows, and whistles, cries and jeers were emerging from that opaque mass. Behind the crowd, like sheepdogs around her flock, young boys were running back and forth yapping: "Quick, quick! Come hear the last sigh of the eunuch!"

Eh? What! They know, then, the wretches! Those wretches have no conscience, and have divulged what they should have kept quiet.

Anonymous voices were shouting: "Down with the judge! Down with the judge! Boo!"

Are they talking about me, by chance?

Other voices , in the same vein, were intoning a variant: "Cuckold, the judge! Cuckold, the judge!"

---

ters and most of the events featured in the present version; the expansion gives the ensemble of the text a very different balance.

It really is me they're talking about. Damned gutter-snipes, the cuckold will bring you into line! Bu it's very disa-greeable, when one represents a symbol, to have a flighty wife, and the law would have been prudent if, in order to remain venerable, it had prescribed celibacy for judges, as for priests.

He stopped, raising his right hand in order to reconquer, by the nobility of his attitude, the dignity that the accident of marriage had partially depreciated. Then, bravely, but with a shrill voice, he articulated: "Make way for Justice!"

Then he was perceived, and, heavily, spontaneously, the brown crowd opened up like the Red Sea; a human pathway was hollowed out between the judge and the gibbet. At the end of that avenue, the vagabond, in his black chemise, was strug-gling with the executioners at the foot of the ladder. Firmly determined not to die, he was giving evidence of it in his ges-tures.

The magistrate started walking toward the group; head held high, he entered the moving alley, as a Pharaoh had done before him. At the same moment, throughout the square, an enormous silence spread, a stormy silence emerging from five hundred breasts and which crushed the air; but it only lasted momentarily before resolving into a rumble of distant thunder, which rose from the four horizons.

Already, the human flood had closed again upon its prey; a storm of clamors swirled, sweeping heads and raising a swell, from which agitated hands emerged, like foam on the crest of waves; flotsam of arms launched forth from the sur-face; eddies of fleecy heads inflated in order to roll forward or withdraw. The judge saw peevish forms unfurling toward him, faces in front of his own, eyes confronting his eyes; a rhyth-mic movement carried him away in its cadence.

"The innocent! Hoo! Hoo! The innocent! Hoo! Hoo!"

In less than two minutes, Dieudonat was freed and his escort dispersed; the unfortunate administrator of justice, tossed like a package devoid of weight, rolled from grip to group and from hatred to vengeance. Hatless and shredded, bewildered and ragged, bleeding and moaning, but not feeling the blows, he reached the base of the scaffold and collapsed. Behind the mob, and too far from the quarry to seize their share, frantic voices were shouting; "To the gibbet! To the gibbet!"

The judge, collapsed at the base of the platform. His forehead applied to the upright of the ladder, his two fists on the ground, he was panting and trying to get up.

"To the gibbet!"

All the riff-raff of the dens of vice, pimps, prostitutes, deserters, escaped and liberated prisoners, with rage in their eyes and drool on their lips, jostled one another over the vanquished man, and ill-clad rancor spat threats at him that reeked of wine and onion. A trickle of blood ran from his temple to his throat; spittle shone on his cheeks and hung from his eyelids.

"You won't play the trickster any more, with your white rabbit skin!"

"Go on, then, vermin fur!"

"You've flattened enough of them!"

"And sent innocents to the shovel!"

"This morning's vagabond, you knew he was a eunuch, didn't you?"

"But you said to hang him anyway!"

"You've woven his rope, he'll cede it to you!"

"It's necessary that you hang by his hand!"

"Yes! Yes! Where's the eunuch!"

"Bring back the eunuch!"

Dieudonat was running away, glad to be out of it, but frightened by the tumult.

Oh la la! he thought, *I believe they're going to kill that poor judge, and it's my fault, for sure. Because I stupidly formed the wish not to die, my wish has been realized to the detriment of another. Should I go back?*

"Bring back the eunuch!"

A vigorous fist seized him by the elbow; he recognized Gertrude, who was utilizing her new strength; she shouted to him: "Go hang him, then!"

212

"I don't want to."

"He wanted to hang you, hang him!"

"Is it you, Gertrude, so charitable when you're on your own, who says such things when you're in the street? How is that possible?"

"I don't know; it takes me over. Come on!"

Arrived at the foot of the gallows, he looked so awkward and crestfallen in his penitent's robe that people around him were already beginning to laugh; he cut an even funnier figure when they placed the rope with a noose in his hand. His bewildered eye interrogated the crowd.

"Put the rope around his neck!"

"Hurry up! Don't you understand anything?"

"Yes, yes, I understand. But where is the judge?"

He was pushed toward that bloody rag, whose prestige he had admired at the previous day's tribunal. He did not meditate, as he would once have done, on the fragility of grandeurs or the inconstancy of the fabrics that serve to specify the distinctions of the social hierarchy; he simply saw a suffering, and drew nearer to it, with the naïve commiseration of the humble, who know how to feel better than how to think.

The rope slid from his fingers without him even perceiving it; he bent down and picked up the flap of the robe in which he was due to die, and made a tampon of it. He knelt down carefully, and the people were able to see a condemned man staunching the wounds of his judge.

He murmured: "Poor fellow!" Then he raised his head toward the people; his face was pale and his eye imploring.

"Please don't do him any harm because of me..."

The crowd is mobile, because it is human being with excess; Dieudonat had scarcely formulated his plea than the contagion of his pity immediately transformed the anger, and the nervous tension that was demanding death became the human emotion that is passionate for life.

"You're right, all the same," said Gertrude.

She wept involuntarily; immediately, her neighbor wept; a third clapped her hands. "Bravo, eunuch!"

That was enough; the entire circle of the front rank applauded with that woman, and the enthusiasm gained the second rank, from which it was propagated all the way to the spectators who could not see anything, and who applauded more frenziedly than the others in order to occupy their muscles. As for those who would doubtless have preferred to offer themselves, without peril for their skin, the spectacle of a Christian dancing a jig at the end of a rope, they dared not protest, because they were cowards.

Dieudonat tried to lift up the patient, who cried out in pain; a carpenter came to his aid; they took him under the armpits and stood him up, but he collapsed again; a veterinarian advanced, palpated, and pronounced: "Fractured kneecap."

Dieudonat had a tear in his eye.

"You see, the poor fellow has a broken knee, now, and again because of me, because I didn't say that I'm a eunuch when it was necessary to say it. I've been stupid, and I beg your pardon, your honor, but it can be sorted out...

He put his hands together, raised his unique eye to the heavens, and prayed: "My God, permit me to repair my sin and make the wounds of this poor fellow pass from his body into mine. So be it!"

Immediately, his wish was granted. He fell on the cobblestones, uttering a little cry, his face bloody and his leg broken. Gertrude ran to him.

"How did you do that trick, then? You're in fine state now... Can he be a sorcerer, as he says?"

He was picked up in order to carry him to the hospital, while Master Touillechair hastened back to his lodgings, striving to gather up the shreds of his toga and those of his ideas.

No one any longer thought of retaining him; the tempest had blown over, the common soul had dispersed, the individual souls went back into their shells, the social ermines resumed their prestige, and Master Touillechair, scarcely having escaped the mud, was aureoled in glory, for the rumor was already circulating in the upper town that Our Lady had just accomplished a miracle in the magistrate's favor.

XXIX. He frequents the two dolors

Dieudonat, under the name of Onuphre and on the stretcher of the gibbet, made his entrance to the hospice. Poor people were hardly ever collected except to torment and aggravate their condition. The lame and pregnant women, small-pox sufferers and the wounded, typhoid fever victims and consumptives, the dying who cried too much and the dead who no longer moved enough, cohabited in the same rooms, not to mention the same beds. To tell the truth, those fifty-two-inch beds were not designed to receive two people, but when the number of invalids was augmented without discretion, what could be done? They were heaped up five or six at a time, any which way, the feet of one on the shoulders of another, all naked under the same sheet, and the bedsheets were then called shrouds. Immobile for lack of room and also by their own fault, since they would not have been if they had not been so numerous, they exchanged their vermin and their diseases in that sweat-bath of common warmth, and with more or less patience they waited for their death, or that of their neighbors.

The Prince was attributed to the seventy-seventh bed, which only contained two patients any longer, the third having died that morning. The two survivors were already rejoicing at being more at ease, but whoever rejoices too soon welcomes a newcomer poorly. Immediately, he had the sensation of being an intruder. His head at the foot of the bed, with the heels of one man under his right armpit and the toes of another under his left armpit, he remained still in order not to inconvenience them, and he saw in the distance, at the end of his own limbs, their reproving faces. One, skeletal and jaundiced, with skin like vellum and excessively bright eyes, assassinated him with his pointed pupils; the other, hirsute and massive, menaced him with his violent beard.

He tried to smile at them, by way of apology, but without any success; they even applied themselves to make him under-

215

stand in detail the reasons for the antipathy they experienced toward him, and exchanged their grievances above the tips of his feet. He listened without protesting, suffering from his wound, and even more from the embarrassment that he was causing the first two occupants. The mildness of his patience ended up calming them in their turn. They interrogated him about his case, and told him about theirs.

The skeleton with the glittering eyes was a lyric poet who lived in his art, and whose stomach was dilapidated by virtue of not eating; he was dying angrily of an incurable gastritis. As for the colossus, a roofer by trade and the father of five daughters, he fell down with grand mal seizures, and also from roofs; his last fall had cost him three ribs, if not more.

Dieudonat listened.

The dyspeptic poet never let up, and his sarcasms vilified humankind; the epileptic explained that the ribs would mend, thanks to God, who had decided thus in time of the terrestrial paradise, when he broken one in the breast of the first man; but the worst thing was not being able to go back on roofs in order to nourish the kids. That pair of unfortunates had the wherewithal to touch the charitable vagabond, who felt sorry for them with all his heart, although, for the moment, he could not hear them very well; more atrocious scenes solicited him from elsewhere.

On penetrating into that hospital ward, he had only experienced at first the repulsion of an ox entering the abattoir; a stink that he swallowed by the mouthful as soon as he crossed the threshold filled him with horror; afterwards the hostility of his neighbors had taken charge of distracting him; but now, he could see better, and could even see too much.

Five paces away, directly facing him, a typhoid fever sufferer had just thrown off his shroud, and, stark naked, with the face of a demon, he was kneeling on the naked breast of a consumptive, stifling him frenziedly; two other, companions of the fanatic, were stunning him with blows of the fist in order to keep him quiet; a fifth had rolled off the foot of the mat-

tress and was gasping weakly on the cold paving stones, cooing like a pigeon.

In the middle of the room, surgeons were sawing through
the humerus of a soldier, and the screams of the wounded man
accompanied the squeak of the saw in the bone; the soldier
who was due to be operated on next, mad with terror, was
running away, and his great hairy body was running along the
aisle, pursued by the warders; driven into a corner he grabbed
hold of a stool with his valid hand in order to defend himself.

Orderlies passed by, carrying by the head and ankle a
choleric who was evacuating his bowels. Thousands of flies
swirled over the excrements, the pus and the invalids.

The poet watched the terror becoming precise on the
newcomer's face and burst out laughing.

"Ha ha ha! You amuse me, comrade; you're ready to
vomit, eh? That's the first impression. We've all passed
through it; you get used to it. I'll wager that you didn't imagine these fashions of reducing suffering, eh? Me neither, for
everything they're doing there, you know, they're doing for
good, and I recommend that point for the solicitude of your
admiration."

"Yes, sir."

"Have you read Dante, my friend, and the *Inferno*? No?
Yes? Dante thought he was inventing fine horrors, but observe
and compare; compare the discoveries of human genius and
those of human stupidity, and tell me, I beg you, whether the
second isn't by far the more ingenious?"

Dieudonat replied, piteously: "I'd like to go away…"

"Not me! I'm recording. The world has made me die, for
I'm dying, and everything that it attempts in order to preserve
life, I observe; it's my vengeance."

At that moment, the soldier on whom they were operat-
ing stopped screaming; he was seen opening and closing his
mouth by turns, in an impotent effort to swallow his life.

"Is he dying?" said Dieudonat.

"I fear so, for he's yawning like a carp; see how well he
imitates a fish out of water. Look, there he goes!"

The Prince made the sign of the cross and said: "God has his soul."

"His immortal soul, no doubt?"

"Assuredly. You're laughing?"

"At your simplicity. Have you ever wondered, my lad, why innumerable simpletons, who were good for nothing during their life, should be indefinitely conserved after their death? Can you glimpse the purpose of that eternal museum? Do you know what need those collections of souls might serve, and what God might do with them?"

"Justice, sir! The notion that I have of my immortal soul..."

"Is a nominal brake, very useful, in truth, upon your passions, your vices and your instincts, and as long as you have that notion, it has served its function as a brake, which is sufficient. To affirm the immortality of the soul, that is what is indispensable; but to realize it...what would be the point, my friend?"

"You're speaking like the Devil. If the poor people could hear you..."

"They'll hear me, one day or another, and it'll be so much the worse for them, for they'll lose a hope, the most consoling of all, and it will be so much the worse for the world, for it will lose a brake, the only one that's truly solid."

The surgeons had just dragged the corpse of the operated patient to the floor, and their aides, who had succeeded in taking hold of the next one, were extending him on the bloody table in his turn.

"You see, their charity is going to come to the aid of that one now, and they're doing good."

The patient howled, maintained by the wrists, and fixed his crazed eyes on the multiple steel implements that were about to penetrate him without anger. On all the beds, haggard spectators raised their fearful faces.

"I want to go away," said Dieudonat.

"Egotist! Don't you see that the comrade has no more desire to be here than you? He's staying, though; do as he does, and learn."

"I don't like to see pain."

"Simpleton! It is, however, the best means of feeling your own pain less."

"It's true that I feel that I'm almost no longer suffering, as soon as people scream around me."

"Unlike other men, who no longer hear screaming as soon as they're suffering."

"Oh?"

"Understand, then, that the two alternatives of life are suffering and seeing suffering; as soon as a poor devil is liberated from his woe sufficiently to look around, what does he see, except for physical and mental misery? And when does he cease to see it, if not when he's recalled to himself by the imperious urgency of recommencing whining on his own account? Your gaieties are only respites or relaxations, minutes between parentheses, blind minutes, which your health necessitates and your unconsciousness permits."

"Eh?"

"Fortunate are the unconscious, because serenity is only permitted to them; but they're only human figuratively."

"Huh!"

"Don't laugh. To be conscious is the rare virtue and the execrable gift."

"Oh!"

"It's sad to say, lad, but undeniable: it's necessary to choose, to opt. Be stupid, if you like, stupidly emotive and candidly tender; then you'll be able to love, without suffering from it, and even without pleasure. Or, on the contrary, be an intelligence, if you can, but dry, pitiless, open to ideas and mature in emotion, a solitary, thinking egotism; then you'll be able to enjoy your intellectual exercises. But don't be an intelligence and a heart at the same time, because that's abomination."

"Eh?"

"The abomination of desolation for the complete man, of both head and heart, the image of God, as you say! Now that, take note, leads us straight to the conclusion that the most unfortunate of all is God himself, total intelligence and supreme goodness. Oh, that poor devil God! I pity him."

"And I pity you. You're talking impiously."

"Look at the nincompoop who dares to accord me his pity!"

"I know that I'm stupid..."

"If you know it, you aren't,"

"And I can't always grasp what you're saying..."

"Don't worry about it; when I talk to you, it's for my sake that I'm talking."

"But if there is in what you say a heap of things that escape me, there's one, at least, which I'm sure of having understood."

"Bah!"

"I think that you're not happy."

"Certainly not! But I no longer aspire to be. That's progress."

"You're alone in the world, perhaps?"

"I have my pride to keep me company."

"Uh..."

"In any case, I remain literally denuded of glory. I don't lament that; I have the right to it. Every man who creates a work has a right to injustice at first; the justice only comes later."

"Yes?"

"Have you even understood the octosyllable of my name. It's very fine but unknown: Calame the Calamitous."[17]

"But I know it, your name!"

"Impossible!"

---

[17] A *calame*, from the Latin *calamus*, is a reed sharpened to a point in order to serve as a primitive pen, and hence signifies "writer."

"What...yes...I remember...one day, I even drank to your health, drank wine, with men who praised your genius."

"Oh?"

"Bad men! Brigands...two brigands, Ruprecht the Pug-nosed and Gontran the Rogue, one ferocious, the other genteel."

"The more to be feared! Avoid them both, especially the second. As for me, if I have any advice to give you, only remember of me my name; the rest will do you harm."

"Ah! And the bearded roofer, what do you call him?"

"By a terrible and generous vocable, Polygene. And you?"

"It's Onuphre, people tell me."

"Well then, we know one another. Good night. Let me sleep."

XXX. He acquires amity for the poor in spirit

They knew one another even better after thirteen days and as many nights spent in the same shroud. The philanthropist had quickly perceived that the misanthrope, in spite of his bitter words, was anything but a bad man, and he had arrived at no longer hearing the sarcasms of that voice as anything other than the exhalation of a perpetual suffering; it no longer shocked him, but caused him a god deal of chagrin. Little by little, he passed from pity to affection, and gave it more frankly every day. Calame, for his part, savored that conquest; he found a charm in it, and although he was careful to let nothing show, he became attached to the modest and mild individual who knew, at least, how to listen.

Ordinarily, they chatted, in order to abridge the long hours; Dieudonat, who was worried by the memory of the judge maltreated because of him, had a strong desire to confide his perplexities to his new friend; he thought that Calame, such a subtle mind, might be able to give him some advice as to how to avoid similar blunders in the future. But would not revealing his name, his origin and his magical power thus be boasting? He refrained, while sensing that he would not resist forever.

He sensed that all the more because the misery of the roofer and his lamentations began to solicit his pity in too pressing a fashion. Between attacks the poor man scratched his beard and picked his nose, but was only able to open his mouth to mourn his wife and the kids without bread: "They have no more bread…no more bread…"

"He's in pain," said Onuphre

"He'll have nothing more than that in his life, unless he also has more brats."

"Poor folk…one would like to try to do something for them."

"Indeed! You're sensitive?"

"My God, yes."

"And you wouldn't hurt a fly?"

"My God, no"

"And suffering attracts you more than happiness?"

"My God, yes."

"And yet you can't bear to see or hear it?"

"My God, no."

"I'll even wager that you strive to help your neighbor?"

"When I can."

"And you go as far as granting him what belongs to you?"

"When he has more need of it than me..."

"And you give don't you? And it's stronger than you, for it's necessary that you give? And in so doing, you believe yourself to be a good soul?"

"I don't know."

"What about the well?"

"Pardon?"

"It also gives. It gives water, the well, and lead gives the colic, miasmas give fever, walking gives appetite, a dog gives chase to a quarry: they all give! They must all be good souls! You give with full hands, when you have full hands, as the river fills buckets and the wind fills sails, always generosity, no?"

"You're a joker."

"So are you, but you don't perceive it. My poor boy, giving isn't synonymous with being good. How can obeying an imperious destiny constitute a virtue? I imagine, for my part, that two sorts of goodness exist, and that they have nothing in common except their apparent gestures: one is virtue, which is to say, thinking and acting strength; the other, yours, isn't a strength but, on the contrary, a weakness, a way of being, intuitive and quasi-pathological, more animal than moral; it's benevolence, if you wish, but don't tell me that it's a virtue, for the essence of all virtue is knowing and willing...are you asleep?"

This time, the listener had not heard anything; he was holding himself motionless on his back, and his gaze was obstinately drilling into the eighth knot of the sixteenth beam, of which he was fond.

"I'll wager that you're reflecting?"

"I'm trying."

"Difficult, eh?"

"A little; I'm wondering whether it's necessary to do something..."

"Would it be disagreeable for you?"

"Rather..."

"Then don't hesitate, do it; and remember this criterion: when you ask yourself whether or not it's appropriate to do something that costs you, your hesitation alone proves to you that you ought to do it."

"This one would cost me greatly…"

"Are you very rich, then, little vagabond?"

"I'll explain it to you. My wishes are realized; it's a power that I've had since both. Does that astonish you?"

"A sage is never astonished to find power in incapable hands. Continue."

"So, when I see you so sad, and so harsh in your words, I think that deep down, you're not nasty at all, and you're only making a semblance of it because you're unhappy, and I think you'd become pleasant, intelligent as you are, if you were no longer ill, if you were no longer alone, if someone showed you amity and proved it to you…by taking your illness, for example."

"You could do that?"

"I can."

"And you would do it?"

"If you wanted."

"And my stomach cramps, the contortions of my intestine, the colics of my liver, you'd have them instead of me?"

"You wouldn't have them anymore."

The poet coughed in order to dissimulate the emotion that he felt. In silence, he looked at Onuphre tenderly. Then, abruptly, he burst out laughing.

"Oh, you'd like to take my old gastralgia! And I'd no longer rage, or curse, or suffer, when I'm rejected or whipped? The stupidity and villainy of the world wouldn't make me indignant anymore and I'd contemplate life with neither disgust nor anger? I'd see everything rose-tinted, ignoble life, and I'd savor with amenity the sanies of the human species? Very well—but what would remain to me then? What would I do with myself on earth? What good would I be if I became good? You're joking, comrade!"

"And you're being serious?"

"One can't be more serious! Since I've lost candor, at least let me keep speech; it's my treasure."

"Your treasure?"

"You don't know, then, that it's necessary to suffer to cry out? My most sublime discoveries and my most beautiful verses are the offspring of my constipation, which makes me see life in black—which is to say, in its true color. Melancholy! Melancholy! An admirable word, that, to express the desolation of immortal souls, since it means black bile in a black intestine!"

"So you don't want to give me your illness?"

"What use would you make of it, you who aren't endowed with any formulatory talent? Let's not talk about it anymore, and let's remain what God and men have made us. No matter: you're a brave little fellow. You've given me a good moment. I'll inscribe you in my tablets. My gratitude will take charge of your epitaph: when the surgeons operate on you, I'll compose verses about it, which I promise you will be marvelous, and which I'll engrave, for centuries to come, on the fresh sand of your tomb."

"Thank you, but I have no desire to be operated on."

"They'll do it without your consent, unless you scarper."

"I'd rather do that, and I feel, merely at the idea, the bones in my leg sticking together again."

"As to that, my good man, tell me: if our wishes are realized, why not formulate that of being cured and getting out of here?"

"I'll tell you: my wishes are irrevocable, and I've taken the judge's knee."

"Why didn't you relieve the fellow of his wife? You might be less deteriorated."

"And I've made an oath no longer to ask for anything for myself, except for food when I need it."

"Bread" cried Polygene.

"Victuals!" exclaimed the Calamitous

"Ah!" said the roofer. "If it's true that you can do such things without it costing you a sou, send a loaf to the house!"

"It's there," replied Onuphre, "and a quarter of meat as well: every morning, in accordance with my prayer, I send provender to Dame Polygene, who finds the loaf in her kneading trough and the piece of beef in her cooking pot; she must be wondering where it fell from."

He laughed, but Calame interrupted him. "This is something else! I refused your stomach, but if you can garnish the one I possess, go ahead! Since the age of reason I've labored in the desire for a quail roasted in a coating of lard and a vine leaf. Prove your magic power to us by procure me that marvel."

"When its dark. At this hour, too many people would see us."

"Rather confess that you're boasting."

"Say 'chick' and you'll have a fresh egg in your hand!"

"Chick!"

The sorcerer stammered the necessary words, and the troubadour's right hand laid the egg. Calame, as a good poet, had a liking for the marvelous; he registered the prodigy and swallowed the egg.

"I believe you. I doubted, and I repent. But by Saint Thomas, patron of miscreants, you can prepare the resources of your magic! Until this evening! I've been hungry for twenty years, and I only have four hours left to make the list for my first feast!"

"Will I also have roast quail?" asked the roofer, humbly.

"You'll have them."

Calame turned his back and closed his eyes in order to reflect in darkness on the harmonies of taste. On the wax-coated tablets that he had habituated to receive his rhymes he inscribed the names of dishes, lined up one beneath the other like poorly rhymed verses, which nevertheless seemed admirable to him. Night was slow in coming.

Finally, the last light was extinguished; only a night-light was burning in front of the crucifix at the back of the room.

"Are you ready, Onuphre? This is the hour propitious for orgies. Pay attention, I'm reading the menu. Listen carefully, and repeat after me: fillet of carp with eggs, sprinkled with marjoram, rosemary and basil; little beef meatballs with raisins, lark's tongue pâté and lamb chitterlings; veal stew in rose-water, well sugared. Roasted goslings with the Duke's powders,[18] not forgetting my quail, with a nice cameline sauce, flavored with cinnamon and ginger. Entremets, fried pike's eggs with orange apples, jacobine pie with aromatic verjus. Wines of Saint-Pourcain, Meulan and Sezanne, and strawberry beer. Chailly bread. For desserts: parsleyed cheese and Normandy angelot cheeses; milk larded with saffron, warmed, and various baked custards, Corbeil peaches, Tours perdrigon plums, hazelnuts and Maltese figs. And we'll see about the spices!"

Dieudonat took the tablets and reread them in a low voice; as soon as they were called by name, the dishes were juxtaposed on the bed, crushing legs and bellies with their weight; it was necessary to arrange them between the bed and

---

[18] I have translated *poudres du Duc* literally, as the phrase does exist in English; it is a misrendering of *douce poudre* [sweet powder], which referred to a Medieval blend of spices. Many of the other items on Calame's menu are also derived from Medieval cuisine.

the wall. Polygene's eyes widened, Calame's sparkled and Dieudonat's were moist with the pleasure procured for others.

At first they ate in silence, dipping the thumb and index finger into the dishes, concentrating on savoring soundlessly, giving evidence of their delight in whispered approbations.

"Fine cuisine!"

Each in accordance with his fancy they attacked the stews and the roasts, bit into the unctuous meats, sucked the juices, licked their fingers, lapped the jellies off the trenchers. The roofer chewed with frenzy in the shelter of his thick beard, ingurgitating rapidly, without breathing a word, in order not to lose out in the division; grease coated his cheeks and oozed between his hairs. The poet sampled with curiosity. Between that gluttony and that Epicureanism, Dieudonat found a charm in eating and drinking.

"Half a liter of old Cyprus with that seems indispensable!"

"Indispensable!" hiccupped Polygene.

"Hey, sommelier, the doyen of your Cyprus!"

The dusty bottles circulated from hand to hand, and lips took long swigs from the bottlenecks. The guests' reserve soon evaporated in the warmth of the wine; they evoked dishes aloud, laughing, exclaiming, clinking bottles, spoons and goblets.

"Sire crier, your banquet lacks poultry and venison! Waiter, look after the high table! Cup-bearer, bring the golden and the life-and-soul, let's sample your hippocras and your eau-de-vie!

With the voice of a cantor, the roofer intoned a canticle with licentious variations; the troubadour, suddenly inspired, improvised stanzas, but started to weep, so beautiful did he find them and so profound was his pain on thinking that tomorrow he would no longer know them, and that humanity would lose them forever. In despair, he threw his sauce-soaked trencher at the ceiling; the father of a family, in order not to be left behind, threw a pheasant drumstick to the fever-sufferer in the next bed, who had dared to complain about the racket.

The warders ran forward; the three diners hid the remains of the meal under their mattress. Calame, with a ham under his arm in the manner of a folio, ran away across the room. Polygene howled drunkenly; they tried to take hold of him; he fought, his lips foaming, and he had a seizure. Quickly, they brought him the relic of Saint Mathurin, sovereign for cases of demonic possession; as soon as it was brought he nearly smashed it to pieces; then the victim of possession was tied up and two men dragged him away, bound with ropes, while a priest pronounced the formulae of exorcism over him. The holy water did not work, and he was plunged into cold water; that calmed his demons down, but a congestion choked him; a surgeon ran forward, declared that he was about to die, and bled him.

Calame did not fare much better; his stomach, astonished by the unusual windfall, protested and made restitution; his livid head nodded toward his sternum like that of a hanged man hesitating to die; he fell on the floor, writhing; the surgeon came running, declared that he was about to die, and bled him.

"Oh, my God!" said Dieudonat. "So that's what I've given them for a feast! I've killed them with meat and wine, just as I induced the shepherdess to the sin of lying with my victuals. Let this serve as a lesson to me! I swear never again to ask for food for myself or anyone else! I make the wish! Everyone ought to earn his subsistence, otherwise he has too much and he harms himself with it. There!"

XXXI. He finally decides to live the good life

Neither of the two dying men died that night. On the stroke of midnight, the physician declared that they would escape if they took the emetic powder; Calame was forced to ingurgitate it and it was slipped to Polygene without him perceiving it, but both of them, without distinction, nearly rendered their soul along with their medicine. Dieudonat held their heads, and the lyric poet swore the great oath, by all the gods, to flee his tormentors as soon as he had regained his equilibrium on his legs.

"But will we be allowed to flee? Our case merits examination. Did that heap of meat arrive by theft or magic? The Inquisitors will be after us, that's for sure."

The imagination of the Calamitous worked on that theme, glimpsing interrogations, initially paternal, whose scarcely reassuring mildness would be promptly followed by the ordinary question, preliminary to the eventual pyre.

However, the day ended without encumbrance. As soon as night fell, Calame communicated his fears to the sorcerer in a low voice, while Polygene was snoring.

"We need to escape from here, and without delay; the place isn't safe. Can your leg carry you? Yes? Let's go into the woods, the mountains, the caves; you have the wherewithal to eat anywhere.

"In truth, no, I don't have it any longer."

"Since when?"

"On seeing you so low, you and the other, I made a wish never again to ask for nourishment for myself or anyone else."

"A plague on the idiot! Impulsive soul that you are, couldn't you consult reasonable people before making a wish that concerns them? No matter; I'm habituated to living without roasts and I'm not at all certain of living if I'm roasted myself. But it's going to be necessary for us to take this dimwit with us, who'll pay for the three of us. Let's shake him. Tickle his feet."

The man with the thick beard, woken up with a start, did not want to hear any of it.

"I'm not going as long as they haven't cured me. I'm certainly not abandoning my kids."

"Your kids and your wife will join you where you are."

"We're used to being here. I have my old man's cottage. I'll die here and not elsewhere."

Without admitting it, Dieudonat thought that well said, and that Polygene was not so stupid. He almost admired him. Timidly, he ventured: "I don't want to abandon this fellow, if you say that he'll pay for me. I have to stay with him."

"You're right and I'm right. Goodnight. I'm evaporating. Goodbye, my lad. You're a fine little fellow; it's been a pleasure to know you. I won't live much longer myself, and perhaps we'll meet again in the common grave. I've promised you your epitaph; I'll bring it to you. Think of me one Sunday, if the Office gives you the time."

The Calamitous grabbed a few clothes and dressed himself as best he could. After a brief embrace, he slipped away into the night, stealthily. Dieudonat wept on seeing him leave, already swallowed by the darkness, and Polygene stretched himself with delight, thinking that they would only be two in the bed henceforth.

The affair had consequences quite different from those the intelligent man had imagined. The Inquisitors did not appear to be concerned, or they employed clemency; timid voices recounted that the judge, in his goodness, had deigned to cover up the scandal. However, Dieudonat and Polygene, incriminated with making a din, were gently expelled; they were deposited on the edge of a stinking gutter and the doors of the hospice closed behind them.

The roofer protested. When he thought he had hammered on the iron reinforcements of the door sufficiently with his fists, imploring his cure, he sat down on a boundary-marker and started to moan.

"What will become of the little ones and the wife if I can't work any longer? You had to make me eat quail!"

Dieudonat contemplated that despair.

"I've made a fine mess! How am I going to repair this? I can't even send them bread now."

He twiddled his thumbs and, planted straight in front of the gross beard, from which futile words were emerging, he appeared to be on the lookout for the word that would give him a good idea—but the good idea had already occurred to him.

"I'm not a roofer; I'm not at risking anything falling down with seizures; in any case, I'm alone; I have no wife to nourish, no children; those I might have fathered in King Gaifer's house, I've abandoned in a cowardly fashion to the care of others. Here's a compensation offered; by placing this father in my path the good God has wanted to indicate my duty."

He leaned toward Polygene. "The physicians haven't taken away your illness, but perhaps I can do it. You can begin climbing on to roofs again, earning bread for your daughters. Your lady will be content."

"You won't make me pay too dear?"

"Nothing at all."

The fellow was suspicious; a cure that costs nothing cannot be worth very much; and when a merchant offers his merchandise gratis, it is because he has a hidden means of charging dearly. The fellow eyed the sorcerer. "Fair exchange; I want to know your price in advance."

"I don't need anything."

With that boastful pronouncement, all his needs became apparent. *What am I saying? I'm bragging. Don't need anything? The persistence of his worthy man is evidently another advice from Providence. I've been a prince, a monk, a scholar, an anchorite; I've had palaces, treasures books, women; I've known everything. Except the good life of good people. What if I were to ask...?*

He hesitated, breathed, and spoke: "Since it's absolutely necessary to ask you for something in exchange, well, in truth…what if we were to be friends, like two brothers; we could live together, in your house; I could enroll at your workplace. I haven't been taught a trade, but I can do the simple work, mason's assistant, mortar layer, whatever's wanted; since the convent I've always wanted to be a builder. I'd bring my pay back to your household, and I wouldn't take up much room in the lodgings; a corner and a straw mattress would be sufficient for me."

"Do you eat a lot?"

"Not much."

Polygene thought: *There might also be a roast quail occasionally, or even a goose.* Shrewdly, he kept that codicil to himself, and said aloud: "Put it there! It's done: but I won't take a traitor; if your remedy doesn't work, you'll be thrown out. Cure me, and let's go home."

Dieudonat extended his hand, but as he was about to proffer the sacramental words he saw once again the ugly grimace that the roofer made when his demons ran wild; the idea of introducing devils into his entrails made him nauseous; perhaps also, the fact of concluding a bargain, for the first time in his life, was sufficient to take the edge off his ordinary altruism…

"Well," said Polygene. "I'm waiting."

The Prince made the sign of the cross in order to regain courage; with pursed lips he murmured the prayer.

The worker immediately got up. "It's true that I feel better!"

No more was required to put Dieudonat's mind at rest. His soul was content, but his body was gripped by a strange lassitude. He sat down on the boundary marker that the other had just quit.

The roofer cried to him gaily: "Let's go!" And without further ado he started striding through the cobblestoned streets. The Prince had difficulty keeping up with him, and his head was vague.

"I'm exhausted all of a sudden."

"Trot; it'll pass."

In that hope, he trotted in rear, but the route was long, through the outlying districts; Polygene's cottage was outside the town. The fellow went forth toward the horizon, singing at the top of his voice; the false notes emerged from the bushy mouth and bounded over the road, forward, ever onward. Sometimes, the villain deigned to turn round.

"Hey, slowcoach, you're not walking?" He laughed vigorously, and Dieudonat, comforted by so much good humor, put his best foot forward, repeating, in order to give himself courage: *I'm going to know good people, the good, simple and laborious life. That's what poor Calame needed, to give him back a little aplomb. I'm going to know good people...*

XXXII. The Prince finally knows good people,
and the sweetness of amity

Finally, they arrived; they recognized the spouse long before seeing her, by the cries she was uttering, which could be heard from outside.

"Ah! It's her! She often raises her voice against the brats; don't worry about it, and thump her if she annoys you. I warn you that she's a strapping woman, and her name is Melanie."

She wore than name worthily, black of skin, hair and gaze. With a bark of joy she threw her arms around her man's neck, and then looked the intruder up and down, who collapsed on the bench.

"Who's this?"

"A worthy fellow; he's cured me."

"He'd do well to cure himself too; he's breathing and staring the way you did when your devils were about to come."

"He's a friend all the same; we've made a bargain together; he's going to live with us. He'll be our cousin."

"Where's he going to sleep? What about food?"

"He has his bread. In fact, you've found a loaf and meat in the pot while I was in the hospital?"

"Yes! An angel I never saw brought me that, every morning. I've thanked Our Lady, who had mercy on us."

With masculine scorn, the peasant listened to feminine ignorance until the end. "It was him who sent you the food."

"A sorcerer! Holy Virgin, a sorcerer!" Melanie made the sign of the cross rapidly, recoiling all the way to the wall. "I don't want a sorcerer in our house to attract misfortune! Outside, man, outside!"

"I tell you that we've made a bargain."

"Make him go away! I don't want him!"

Polygene marched toward her. "Repeat again what you don't want!"

"I don't..."

A sonorous slap cut off her speech and her breath; the wife remained open-mouthed with admiration, scratching her head at the place where it had just slammed into the wall.

"Oh!" she said. "I can certainly see that you're cured!" Then she rubbed her cheek and looked at her palm to see whether her nose was bleeding. "It's a long time, Ygene, since you've given me one like that. It's better then, for good? And it's him who cured you?"

"Give him a kiss for his trouble! I don't admit that my actions by judged. Call the kids and let's thank my bonesetter."

Dieudonat no longer recognized the moaning Polygene, to whom an abrupt health had rendered so much vigor. He stood up, confused, to receive the welcoming kiss that the wife and the daughters had brought him. In the meantime under the mantle of the fireplace, the worker hugged an old woman in rags and shouted in her ear: "Mama! He's cured me! I can go back up on the roofs! It's going to be good to live, Mama!"

The good friend of the beautiful Aude approached in order to kiss the old woman, but he hurried slightly, for she exhaled a bitter odor of boiled urine from her entire person. The politeness complete, he stood there, arms dangling, and Melanie examined him.

"He isn't pretty to look at," she said. "Truly, he doesn't look like a sorcerer. What's his name?"

"Onuphre."

In order to give himself countenance, cousin Onuphre was looking at the grandmother, and he suddenly saw the two old shoulders jump spasmodically in a little bony laugh; the eye, lively amid its gumminess, designated the staircase in the corner of the room. Polygene had gone up there, and from the height of the grain-loft he summoned his other half in order to make a sixth child with her up there, on the straw, in honor of his return and his cure.

They supped politely on leftover broth. Onuphre was radiant. He repeated: *Here I am in the home of good people...*

Then everyone went to bed. Dame Melanie had installed her guest in a redoubt under the staircase; a straw mattress thrown on the beaten earth, with a bale of oats for a pillow, and a blanket with large holes, composed the whole of his bedding. The damp in there was so cold that he had to lie down there fully dressed.

Everything is simple among these good people...

But the hours passed without him being able to go to sleep, in spite of his fatigue; a new agitation labored his nerves; in his insomnia he experienced a strange difficulty in following the thread of his ideas; the thread broke continually, in order to curl up and become entangled with other filaments of thought, emerged from who knows where, and which floated in an incessant draught.

For sure, it's the roofer's malady that's causing this restlessness; he could no longer sleep, poor fellow; he must be very glad to be rid of it.

At daybreak, he was beginning to get drowsy when a loud voice woke him up. "Get up, idler!"

They swallowed warm soup and went to the work-yard.

"I can't keep up; I feel very ill."

"Me, it's marvelous how well I am!"

"My knee hurts so much when I walk…"

"No, no: necessary not to listen."

Polygene's return was greeted with acclamations.

"It's me! A bonesetter has taken away my evils by blowing on them. Here I am, ready to climb all the way to the cocks on the steeples!"

"Hurrah for Polygene!"

The new arrival obtained no less success, but as a comical individual: red-haired, one-eyed and lame, his skin imbibed with poison by Gertrude and bile by Galeas, bewildered by the roofer's epilepsy. and timid into the bargain, he immediately became an object of amusement for the time of the snack break; the people lack sympathy with regard to malingerers, and it is their fashion of being Spartan in all lands.

"A fine recruit you've brought!"

"Pay no attention; I picked him up at the hospice: a sufferer who needs to earn his living…"

He was enrolled, and while agonizing people, out there beyond the frontier, were desolate at being unable to put the royal crown on his head, he put on a crown of straw in order to be able to carry slabs of stone on his head.

He was as proud of that as a king, with the conviction of finally devoting himself to useful work. Everything came back to him in that place: people and things; everything seemed to him to belong and to be put in its place; in the midst of workers covered in white dust, and similar to them, he felt at ease; he found their faces open, open through the eyes, through the mouth, which could be entered without any obstacle, much better than the faces in the Court, where all the bays were closed, padlocked with lies or mistrust. When it was necessary for him to buckle under an amicable blow of a fist, he straightened up again laughing, even though, in sum, he would have preferred not to receive that sledgehammer of flesh and bone.

In the world, it's always necessary to put up with something bad, isn't it? A bruise doesn't last long.

His passivity soon wearied a few hearty fellows, who left him in peace, but it encouraged the imbeciles, who delighted in having, ready to hand, a victim more stupid than them; in order to amuse themselves with him they invented jokes like taking away the stool when he was about to sit down, tripping him up when he was carrying a basket of plaster, or replacing the cup of wine from which he was about to drink with another from which they had already drunk.

Approving that, and the rest, he liked his companions indistinctly, save for a preference for the most fraternal of all; that friend was a dog, a poor dog without a master, somewhat eaten away by mites, but with such an honest face. He had large maroon eyes and yellow fur; his name was Noiraud. He hung around the work-yard regularly, guarded it by night, and in the morning wished the arriving workers welcome; he knew everything, understood everything, watched, observed, frowned, wrinkled his nose, wagged his tail and ran around relentlessly, attentive to his perpetual duty of cheering up the men and encouraging the horses by barking; he announced the hours five minutes before the monastery bells; he witnessed the masons' meals, sitting on his meager backside or running from one to another, sometimes catching a blow and sometimes a morsel, receiving the former with indulgence, the latter with joy, and everything philosophically.

In the roundness of his frank eyes one read the memory of kind treatment and the forgetfulness of offenses; all that he was able to retain in his memory of ill-treatment was limited to a prudence devoid of rancor, but sufficient to keep at a distance people who hit him; he liked nothing better than to abolish that distance, and the slightest amenity of word or gesture immediately brought him back to the knees of someone who had beaten him. Onuphre considered him to be sage and good; he would not have hesitated to recognize him as a beautiful soul if he had not known that the soul is immortal by definition and that dogs are deprived of them. He regretted that, for, in sum, could find nothing to hold against the creature but an absolute lack of modesty and religiosity, while for everything else he showed himself frankly superior to the average of human beings.

The fallen prince and the dog had divined one another from the start; immediately, Noiraud, with the penetrating psychology of his race had recognized a brother and acted in accordance; at moments of rest he came to place his warm neck and heavy jaw on the thigh of the immortal brother, and from below, he contemplated him from the depths of his circular eyes, ready to weep with admiration and bliss. Every evening it escorted his friend to Polygene's house and installed himself on the threshold, fixed until Melanie came out with a stick; he learned by that gesture that the day was finished; all the quotidian rites were accomplished, and he retired tranquilly, walking at first and then trotting back to his work-yard.

Onuphre would have been surprised if anyone had told him that one of his worst woes would come to him from that friendship. Nevertheless, it was thus, and the thing happened in the time that it takes to count to twenty. One day, at the midday break, Blaise the Joker broke his wine-bottle on a stone; as he liked to laugh and even more to make others laugh, he decided to hide his embarrassment by showing good humor; to do that he picked up a sharp shard of glass, wrapped it in a piece of bread, started rubbing the ball against his lard and squinting at Noiraud, who was already drooling hopefully. Everyone had understood the joke and was enlivened by it.

"For pity's sake," said Onuphre, "don't give him..."

He did not have time to finish; the bolide described its curve and disappeared into the dog's maw.

"Spit!"

Good dogs cannot spit, and that is another difference from us. Onuphre saw a bump descending along the poor neck, and he recognized the death that was entering into his friend. He burst into sobs, threw himself to his knees, took the neck in his two arms and inundated it with his tears; behind him, a loud hilarity formed a chorus to his grief; he turned round, his face scarlet and wet, with the grimace of a little child cutting his teeth, and he murmured, in a soft but broken voice: "Wret-ches...wret-ches..."

Then, as everyone was still laughing, he turned back to hide his face and his pain in the rough hair of the canine shoulder.

In the course of the day, Noiraud acquired a grave gaze and red spectacles; sometimes, he lowered his head with an expression of astonishment and examined his belly; not perceiving anything unusual, he gave the impression of reflecting on something incomprehensible. A little later, he started licking his skin, which he rasped with persistence, slowly, always in the same place, in the pit of the stomach, and by turns, he tried to lie down, to get up and to sit down; feeble groans swelled his oblique cheeks.

"Friend...poor friend..."

Onuphre was no longer working; the bell and the repeated calls, the gibes and the reprimands all failed to reach him;

immobile before a parcel of suffering, he forgot everything else and repeated: "Friend…poor friend…"

The dog drew closer to that pity and responded by eye: "Don't be upset; it will pass. I'm ill, but I love you." Then, with a stroke of the tongue over the invisible wound: "There's the place. But no one's thrown a stone at me. I don't understand it at all."

Dieudonat caressed the belly and Noiraud licked his hand. The dog's nose became dry and hot; pink saliva appeared at the edges of the chops.

"He's going to die! Poor fried, who is so poorly…"

It was much worse in the evening, when the animal squatted on his hind feet and stuck up his tail with an evident intention of expelling the interior torturer; he had hesitated a long time over that act of courage and he was still delaying under the pretext of finding a good place, the best place; finally resolved, he bent his legs and chose in the distance a point at which it was necessary to stare during the pain; then his furry mask was immobilized energetically, like that of a mariner at the helm looking out for the leaps of a storm, and the work of stoicism commenced.

Without even perceiving it, Dieudonat had crouched down opposite, his hands on his abdomen, and he positively felt claws of glass carving his entrails; he uttered sighs: "Oh la la…! Oh la la…!"

From the height of the scaffolding the masons launched gibes at the grotesque face-to-face. Crimson drops fell from the dog; the earth became sticky with blood.

"Friend…don't strive…you'll do yourself more harm."

In order to remain brave, Noiraud refused to hear him, and no longer saw him; sudden spasms made his yellow fur undulate like a crops in a squall.

At that moment, the companions having finished their day's work, descended from the wall; they formed a circle.

"Oh, good people, it's the shard of glass laboring him!"

"Bah!" sad Polygene. "Let's go, crybaby. To the soup!"

The dog stood up in order to follow, but was no longer able to put one paw in front of another.

"I can stay with him, can't I?" said Dieudonat. "You'll permit me to stay with him?"

Then he perceived the Joker, who was holding his sides.

"Wretch! It amuses you, then, to see everyone suffering? It's you who gave him his pain."

"So what?"

"What if I passed it back to you, to teach you a lesson?"

"What do you want to teach me, you?"

"Justice! Yes…justice! And it would be one, to put the broken glass in your body, since you put it in his!"

So saying he stood up, shaking with menace, and ready to make use of his magic power; for three seconds, he had the appearance of a statue; but his irrational words only obtained the result of raising a few shoulders and dispersing the audience. Polygene, as he turned his back, pronounced: "A dog isn't a man."

The Joker mocked: "Justice."

Then the entire band disappeared, before the sorcerer had made his decision, and dusk fell upon the abandoned pair.

Triangles of shadow were already settling between the cubes of stone. Onuphre's indignation was obstinate in repeating: "Yes, justice!" And he started marching back and forth, with the stride of a warrior.

The general disapproval had disconcerted him a little, however, and in the twilight he became less and less sure of himself.

"Justice? Perhaps they're right. To return evil for evil is to recommence doing evil, and that can't be called justice; at the very most, it would be vengeance. I was about to do something stupid again. By taking glass out of one belly to put it in another I'd be displacing the pain but I wouldn't be suppressing it, and that's what's necessary. Justice! It's easy for me to talk. A man, a dog, I see them as equal, but what if I'm wrong? Now, for having pronounced that treble word 'Justice' I no longer know anything at all, but..."

For want of anything better, he started scratching the top of the head that Noiraud held out to him.

"In truth, Calame's words were golden on the day he said: 'To be good is very easy, but to be just—that's difficult!'"

XXXIII. He experiments with gratitude

Onuphre had already been lodging with Polygene for three months. He was considered as one of the family, and to prove it to him, he was given the job of scouring the cooking-pot and rinsing the spoons after the evening soup. When he had finished his chore, the five little girls climbed up his legs or on to his back in order to play at biting his ear. The game recommenced every day, without becoming monotonous; he laughed at it, but not as much as the old grandmother, whose hilarity turned to spasms when the little teeth hooked on to the living flesh and made it bleed. If the pain sometimes extracted a cry from him, the mother snapped: "Don't hurt the children, eh?"

He was careful not to do that. They loved him. On Sunday, he sat outside the door and took them between his knees, one after another, in order to search for lice, as noble damsels do for their knight when he returns from the war.

But all is not play in life. At the work-yard, Onuphre only earned a sol a week. He brought it faithfully, in its entirety, to Dame Melanie, who never failed to weigh it in the palm of her hand.

"You eat more than that!"

By reproaching him for his nourishment, at every plausible opportunity, she hoped that the sorcerer might finally take it into his head to introduce into the house the plates of victuals that he had the power to create by magic. But the candid fellow did not understand the hints.

She soon became indignant.

"He's too stupid! Too selfish as well!"

Suddenly, in the middle of a night when she was sleeping badly, the housewife had a brainwave.

"What if we set up a rotisserie, or an eatery, where I sold cooked meat? It would be a masterstroke; the meat wouldn't cost me anything and him hardly anything. We'd make a huge profit!"

Right away, she woke up her man, who admired the project, but, scratching the nape of his neck, gave birth to objections: "Sure, that would be a windfall, although…it isn't in our bargain."

"Capon! I'll talk to him myself."

Until morning she dreamed about the hostelry where she was enthroned before a file of servants, victuals and clients; she meditated on it throughout the next day, and organized minutely the future enterprise that ought to enrich her; then, that evening, after supper, she spoke, her fits on her hips, standing in front of the sorcerer.

He admitted his recent vow no longer to ask for foodstuffs; Melanie's dreams, the inn, the stews and the bags of gold, collapsed noisily.

"Oh, the stupid wretch! He must be stupid and malevolent to make such a wish. Now he's a burden on the needy instead of coming to their aid! He can say that he's put one over on you, my poor Ygene, and you're his dupe!"

She grumbled on that theme for an hour. Finally, she slapped the children to make herself feel better and put them to bed. The kids wailed. The deaf old woman, divining the racket by the movement of mouths, took the opportunity to complain about it, and her furious daughter-in-law reproached her for her infirmities, her years and her odor; in order to bring peace between the women, the head of the family threw a jug at his wife. Crestfallen, Onuphre remained on his end of the bench.

"It's all his fault!"

He sensed it only too keenly. After that, every time Melanie talked about people who lived at the expense of others, he was able to divine without effort to whom the criticism was addressed. In vain he tried to think of a means of repairing his wrongs, so he was glad when one evening, after washing the utensils, under the pretext that it was raining, he was sent to the ditch to throw the refuse into it. He went back the next day, although the rain had stopped, and, the habit having been acquired, he went back every evening while the others went to bed. Shortly afterwards, he received the early morning mission of going to draw water from the river while the others got up; he was glad about that too, but people continued to declare nevertheless that he was living at the expense of poor people. That obsession ended up installing itself under the cranium of the housewife, who started to suffer from it; the notion of being exploited by an idler caused her heart to lurch with an anger that came back every twenty-eight days, like the moon.

It was even worse one day, when he suffered a grand mal seizure.

"That was all it lacked! Now he's possessed too! And then, you were my man!"

The epileptic foamed at the mouth, writhed in a semicircle, had contortions and broke everything.

"And that, Ygene, was that agreed on the bargain?"

"Did I do the same myself?"

"Exactly the same."

"Not astonishing, then, that I was exhausted the next day."

His pity did not go much further. As soon as Onuphre recovered consciousness, he was shown in detail the damage he had caused. His host deigned to console him.

"Don't worry, comrade; I promised you hospitality; you have it. If I've made a fool's bargain, too bad for me."

A better consolation was due to the saintly man; he had it twenty-four hours later; still exhausted, he was taking the air outside the door when he saw the tall thin body of Calame passing along the road. He called to him and embraced him.

"Is it really you, my lad? And not entirely dead? Explain this prodigy to me."

Dieudonat, stammering, recounted as best he could the exit from the hospice, but carefully neglected to mention that he had then taken on Polygene's malady. He narrated his life at the work-yard and among the good people, not forgetting the dog Noiraud. He concluded by affirming that he was very happy."

"You only give the impression partially. You're having great difficulty finding your substantive nouns and the means of articulating them; your tongue is furred, your ideas are stumbling and you're lying. Yes, you're lying, and it's quite futile, for I can see lies in the middle of faces as clearly as holes in noses. Dramas have happened that you're hiding from me; come on, cough it up!"

Dieudonat ended up admitting how he had rid Polygene of his epileptic fits.

The Calamitous protested: "Are you mad? I only recognize one sole philosopher on earth capable of such an aberration, the so-called Dieudonat, celebrated for his altruism and his misdeeds."

The other lowered his head and stammered, in an apologetic one: "That's me."

"You? Dieudonat! You're...you're...Prince Dieudonat!"

"Unfortunately, yes, I have been."

"Is it possible that I have the inestimable good fortune of talking to Prince Dieudonat? There are so many legends running around about you, and I'd be so glad to hear them narrated by the hero of such a poem!"

The convalescent could no longer contain himself; he had so much need to unburden himself to a slightly fraternal soul. He related as well as he could an abridged count of his adventures. The poet listened standing up in an attitude of respect.

"Rest, Milord," he said, "you're tiring yourself out."

A tear appeared in Dieudonat's unique eye. "You're no longer cling me *tu*, Calame? That's because you no longer love me because you know my crimes..."

"I no longer love you! On the contrary, I adore you! And if I abstain from addressing you as *tu*, it's because I'm a fool, unworthy of the honor that has fallen to me, a man, my friend, a man in spite of myself, a man—which is to say, a being much more dazzled by the favor of conversing with a prince than the good fortune of encountering a saint. But you're only giving me crumbs! Go on."

Dieudonat resumed his story; he concluded it by confessing that, since the roofer's cure, he no longer enjoyed his full intelligence, but he hastened to add that the loss was mediocre.

"I see: you're an idiot instead of the other, and the other's using it to the point of abusing you. You do the hard work here, of course? You double up: savior and servant."

"It pleases me to make myself useful."

"And their recognition smacks of ingratitude."

"They don't suspect what I've done for them, the worthy people."

"Sublime cretin! Simpleton of genius! He devotes himself to the point of giving away his flesh—the height of absurdity!—and at the same instant—the height of sagacity!—he avoids rancor against his debtors by taking refuge in their indifference!"

"I haven't thought so far."

"You're all the finer for it. But what you haven't said, it's me who'll say it!"

"I beg you…"

"I'm the administrator of justice! The Kings your ancestors bore the hand of Justice? I bear the feet. Look at these two, mine. They've come to earth precisely to be put into things. It's their mortal mission, and I'm proud of it."

Calame seemed strong in wrath. Hoisted up on his toes, with his two arms extended, one toward the cottage and the other toward the town, he shook his fingers with agility, as if electric maledictions ought to have fallen from his papillae, and he cried: "O all my peers, big and small, carnivorous race, sons of Adam who eat your bread on the sweat of others' brows, shrewd guests at the banquet, you plunge your hands into the dishes in order to pull out the best morsels? I shall plunge my feet in, which are not grasping, with the sole aim of splashing you with your wretched cuisine!"

"You haven't changed."

"Scarcely more than the world. And look! Here's your manual laborer returning to the manor on cue!"

"You're not going to reproach him…?"

"Certainly not! I'll do worse."

The roof recognized Calame with a mitigated pleasure. With a virile handshake he dislocated the troubadour's shoulder, and then leaned toward Onuphre with the condescension of strength for weakness, and pinched the skin of his neck.

"Well, weakling, are you feeling better?"

At the sound of that voice, Melanie appeared, a reproach in her voice as others chew a flower stem.

"Don't touch him so much, you'll catch your disease!"

Calame advanced immediately, and the words emerged from him like a trumpet blast.

"Your wife is right, comrade, take care! That disease is contagious, since he's caught it from you. You're laughing? How right you are to laugh! Can you imagine, my good people, that without knowing it, you've been sheltering under your roof the martyr of charity. This scantly representative fellow, such as you see him, is the son of a King."

"Son of a King!"

"Even better, he works miracles!"

"Onuphre?"

"By means of a miracle, he put you on your feet. You believe you owe your cure to a bonesetter or a sorcerer? It came to you be the intermediary of a saint, who has taken it on in your stead. You needed a health that you lacked to nourish your children; this man has given you his. Hey presto! You have it, but he has your disease in exchange! And that's why you honor him, why you bless him, why you kiss the ground on which he walks?"

Calame was speaking dryly, and suddenly fell silent. The healer looked at the ground with the consternated expression of a culpable confessing. The healed man scratched the back of his neck,

"That's not stories, that?"

"It's quite simply your story. Does it bore you?"

The silence recommenced, and as it dragged on. Polygene judged it necessary to formulate an opinion. "Well!" he said. "Well..."

Afterwards feeling a little embarrassed he added: "Are you supping with us, Calamitous?"

"No, certainly not; I'll leave you in the company of your benefactor. Do you hear? Benefactor!"

Then he went away, giving voice to an utterly satanic laugher.

The son of the King went back into the house, hampered by his old crown and his new aureole, which deterred proximity, even though they were invisible. The meal was as dismal as could be. Everything seemed to have changed in the room, where there was nothing additional, except for the notion of a benefit. That was sufficient; one might have thought that an abnormal presence, such as that of a creditor or a judge, had dislocated the family. An atmosphere of malaise hung between the soup tureen and the beams; a constraint camped gestures; even the grandmother contained her emissions and the brats their clamors; the mother, while squinting at the spoon of the enigmatic guest, was eating as if at the holy table.

"Mother, where is he, the Benefactor?"

"Peace!"

Finally, Melanie got up to go and scour the utensils herself. The saint, deprived of his work, had two hands too many, not knowing where to put them, and Polygene thought: *It's not going to be amusing, life, with a benefactor in the house...*

XXXIV. The holy man is in a mess

The housewife sighed all night at the idea that she no longer dared ask anything of such a high-ranking person. As long as she had thought she was only giving hospitality to an invalid, something of a sorcerer and a miscreant, a future damned soul, she could abuse him and exploit him without scruple, and make his life hard in preparation for Hell; that was fine, and even pious work. But to have in one's home a representative of Heaven, who watches everything, notes everything and will repeat everything! What might come of it?

That Onuphre was also the son of a King she scarcely believed, and Polygene did not either; it was sufficient to look at the runt to understand that the Calamitous was telling them tales: the sons of King are not built like that. As for Saints, that was a different matter; one knows those of all appearances; Saints willingly disguise themselves; more than once in various places, people had seen the great Saint Joseph, or even the Good God in person, coming after curfew to knock on the door of a cottage to ask for something to drink, or a bed; almost always, besides, those adventures turned out badly for somebody; no more than the earls and barons down here, the great lords of Paradise are not the sort of people to hang out with poor people; it's better not to get too close to them. Each to his own! When one wants to live tranquil, the wise thing is to bury oneself in one's hole, among equals, with one's family.

Those thoughts were reasonable, and did not procure happiness. Two weeks sufficed to demonstrate that a deplorable era had just been inaugurated. Calame presented himself punctually, every three days, to take note of the progress of a malaise that he had anticipated; he observed visages, and with his sharp eyes he pinned the minutiae of the soul, as a collector pins butterflies. His silent irony made the embarrassment more precise, and augmented it.

"Are we going to see that imbecile all our lives, then, with his mocking airs?"

She called him an "imbecile" to avenge herself for a superiority that disabled her; then, in order to affirm in the face of the enemy her power over others and her misunderstood capacities, she handed down injunctions, in authoritarian terms, to her brats, and information too.

"Look at her," said the poet. "Listen to her, above all. Register the orders that she hurls at her children, with conviction; wouldn't you swear that she's tossing a coin in the air to see whether it comes down heads or tails? But hazard seconds her so poorly that the prescription always come down on the inverse side of good sense. And that's the rule, my friend, the ordinary rule: you can't imagine how many young existences are irremediably compromised by the tutelary care that parents take to inculcate in their offspring the precious education of error; with the same care and the same conviction the children transmit to their children the legacy of hereditary stupidity. It's a great pity, my friend, for certainly, she-cats, sows and lionesses, instructed by instinct, don't impose such harmful nonsense on their progeniture. How many generations of such beings will it take to raise them as far as the dignity of brutes?"

"Melanie isn't stupid, you know."

"Alas, no, and that's precisely what spoils her; for, in order to constitute a stupid individual, it only requires stupidity, but to obtain a perfect fool, it has to be combined with human pretention."

"You're exaggerating, Calame. One would only have to say one word to confound you."

"Say it!"

"I'm searching for it."

The mother of the family, under the gaze of the satirist, lost all her means and became foolish, heaping stupidities on stupidities with a sort of vertigo, as if she needed to give further reason to that attentive malice, and that amused him greatly.

For fear of exploding, she fled, as soon as she saw the accused Calamitous approaching; she took her two buckets and went to the river. The dog Noiraud watched for that exit and rapidly, shaving the walls, slipped into the house.

"Good day, Onuphre!"

"Good day, Noiraud! Is it better, poor doggy?"

"Well, yes," noted Calame. "He's making amends for men."

One Friday, it happened that Onuphre had hidden an old piece of bread under his coat, and he was offering it to the dog when the housewife came back in.

"My children's bread he's giving to animals! A big slice of corn bread! And I should slave away, for that!"

"Cousin, it's a bit of my share."

"Your share? Is it you who've earned it? You're the benefactor! We do the rest! Better not to abuse it, all the same!"

In her indignation, she had only set down one bucket; with a heroic gesture, she emptied the other over Noiraud.

"There, filthy beast!"

The water ran across the room and the dog on to the road; Dame Melanie had to return to the river

"This can't go on!"

The misanthrope beamed; the philanthropist sighed.

"In a sense, you're right, Calame; they're not as nice as I thought, good people..." After a second sigh, he added: "For that, too, they're to be pitied." With a third sigh he concluded: "One would like to be able to do something to relieve them."

"Haven't you done enough?"

The opportunity came that same day. Melanie had not long returned from the river bank and she was chopping the cabbage into the cooking-pot when her man was brought home on a stretcher; having fallen from the scaffolding he had broken both his legs above the knee.

The despair of the wife was, inevitably, sincere and resounding. Her cries flayed the walls, rebounded in the street and frightened the chickens. Suddenly, however, she discovered Onuphre, whose tears exasperated her.

"It's good, your work! Without you, would the misfortune have happened? Misfortune came into our house with you! Get out. You have no more wrong to do here!"

Calame intervened: "Come on, it isn't his fault..."

"Not his fault? He cured my man expressly so that he could go up on the roofs again, and you say that it isn't his fault! Would poor Ygene, stupid, have been able to fall from a roof if he hadn't been able to go up there?"

That logic pleased the poet, but it devastated the saintly man. Calame saw him lower his head, ready to sink under remorse and already beating his breast: "It's my fault."

He observed for a few minutes, while Melanie returned to sob over the body of the injured man. At that precise moment the miracle worker moved his lips like a man praying; he friend jogged his elbow.

"Hey, you!" he cried, "Hey! I can guess what you're thinking."

"It's my fault..."

"You're not going to do what I think?"

"Yes. Let me be. I'm repairing."

"I forb…"

He did not have time to finish; Dieudonat collapsed, unconscious, his legs broken above the knee, while Polygene got up from the stretcher shaking his legs and cried: "Oof! I'm better!"

The witnesses only showed a mediocre bewilderment; the liking for the marvelous was so pressing in people in those days, and their mysticism was characterized by such a voracious appetite for prodigies that the intervention of a supernatural force appeared to them to be the most natural thing of all. Some made the sign of the cross, others dispatched an *Ave*, and no one thought of coming to the aid of Calame, who was buckling under his heavy burden.

"Help me, then!"

The taker of the broken thighs was laid down instead of the roofer. Polygene lent a hand with that; then, slowly, escorted by a crowd that commented on the event and recalled similar ones, the Prince was taken back to the hospice.

This time, the surgeons cut off both legs, but he did not even die.

In the meantime the town continued to discuss his case, and when his wounds had scarred over he found himself both legless and famous.

Two parties had already formed, one crying miracle, the other sorcery; as there were men in that land incapable of professing an opinion without transforming it into anger, a few blows were exchanged. Finally, the physicians judged that the stump of a Christian was good to be put outside, and they had him hoisted on to the cemetery tumbrel in order for him to be transported to the roofer's house.

"It's him! There he is!"

People came out of the houses.

The cart jolted over the cobblestones of the narrow streets; the recent amputee, still unused to his new platform, clung on to the bars. A multitude of people gathered in doorways followed him with terror or veneration. The cortege went through the outlying districts. It arrived. Melanie came running at the noise, recognized the Benefactor, and was not content. She had been living so well for a few weeks!

People of good will, desirous of being able to say that they had touched the saintly man, took hold of him like a sack of wheat and carried him into the house, bumping him as little as possible; the inevitable dispute was relative to the choice of the best place; the human parcel, pulled right and left, oscillating, deafened, saw himself planted alternately here and there, against the wall, against the dresser, against the leg of a table; finally, it was decided that it was appropriate to wedge him in the kneading trough, with a truss of straw, like a baby Jesus. Melanie was less and less content; she threw the people out and bolted the door.

"Where am I going to knead my bread now?"

When Polygene returned he found that surprise, and words of frank cordiality.

"You're my benefactor. I'll never forget what you've done for me; you can stay here as long as you want, even if you're going to inconvenience us."

So saying, Polygene walked across the room.

"I'm limping now, you see."

"Because my left kneecap was split since the other time."

"It's mine now."

"It pains me, only to have been able to offer you a damaged kneecap."

"One isn't reproaching you for anything, damn it! You had a rotten kneecap, you passed it to me, and that's it. Doesn't alter the fact that you're my benefactor. You're going to be cared for here, you'll see: worse than a brother."[19]

The roofer did not dissimulate the importance of his own person in the least; he was no longer a common manual laborer but a beneficiary of a miracle, a man in favor whom the celestial powers had deigned to put in motion twice in succession. *Noblesse oblige*: he abstained from all oaths, talked loudly and spat a long way.

He summoned the work-yard and the companions came in chorus to render a visit to the shortened comrade. Then, before all of them, in a solemn voice, he awarded him the title of Benefactor and gave orders to his family to care for him worse than a child.

The good people congratulated Polygene unanimously, for everyone knows that it is scarcely agreeable to keep an impotent individual in one's home.

"Especially," said Melanie, "when he has his needs. He can't be left in the kneading trough, that man. It's necessary that I carry him outside, such as you see me, and that I hold him."

Onuphre became red with confusion. That delicate affair, in fact, constituted his quotidian misery; every morning, dur-

---

[19] The word *pis* [worse] is used here, as it is a little further on, in a colloquial fashion that signifies the opposite—except, of course, that the author is being sarcastic…

ing hours of retention, he envied the nature of the angels, and it was always necessary for him, in the end, to implore the aid of the housewife, who made it a vengeance never to offer it.

"Fortunate man!" said Calame. "Since you're in the bread box, they treat you like a chick in a nest."

The fact is that Dieudonat found himself too favored; his peers nourished him without him doing anything; the girls disputed as to which of them would bring him his food; when the sun shone they planted him like an espalier in front of the house or sat him in the middle of the road to that they could dance around him with the neighborhood children. And treats! They multiplied them especially when people came to see him. To whoever would hear it, Melanie repeated her formula: "He's our benefactor; we're not ingrates; he can have anything he wants here."

When the visitors were wearing fine clothes, the hope of a gratuity rendered her more loquacious and she deigned to explain: "He produces miracles of a sort when he has his idea, so we pamper him, you see. He's a saint."

Calame glimpsed a long future of gaieties.

"Rejoice, my children! Courage! I'd despair of Melanie if she weren't able to extract a profit from the windfall that God has provided in you."

"What, then, is the windfall?"

"Having a saint in the domicile! Don't you know that in our centuries of faith, the possession of a saint is an excellent means of making money, so lucrative that churches and convents dispute the fragments of the Blessed One, which are torn into strips, stolen by night, and for which people murder one another in order to have them? Do you not know, O Melanie, that monasteries are rare that conserve the totality of their saint, and rarer still are those can display him alive, as you're going to do? Wealth has entered your home, O Melanie, better than if you kept an inn!"

In fact, Polygene's house did not take long to become a place of pilgrimage; initially from the surrounding area, and then from further away, devotees of both sexes acceded to it in order to refresh themselves in the contemplation of an elect. Incurable cripples brought their legs to be cured, beautiful ladies gave their lovers a rendezvous there. Palfreys were seen on the road led by multicolored pages, with varvels and little bells tinkling; then candles were often burned before the door and on the sides of the kneading trough, where the trunk of the man gave the impression of a Buddha. To all these faithful, Melanie gladly sold, as is ordinarily done, medallions and small insignia with the effigy of her guest, molded in lead or tin.

"At least cede them relics," said Calame. "It's a great pity that you didn't reclaim the cousin's legs. Isn't it possible to recover them?"

For want of anything better, the housewife started to cut little rectangles of cloth from the amputee's hose, of which he had no further need; afterwards, she cut up his surcoat, and after that, discreetly, the grandmother's garments, to whom it was high time to offer a new dress. The roofer's old clothes, this wife's and those of his children went the same way in their turn, and when the family's rags ran out, more were discovered in second-hand clothing shops. Melanie bought some well-used garment, put it on the holy man, and cut it up before the eyes of the client.

"Very good! Very good!" cried Calame. "But you're forgetting his hair and his beard, which can be sold like bread. Not to mention that I can see a tooth in his mouth that is loose, thanks to Gertrude, which will be worth its weight in gold."

The best day of the week was Sunday, when idlers wander around in crowds and are inclined to devotion; in addition, the roofer remaining at home all day, the pilgrims had the double advantage of being able to contemplate both the healer and the healed. They were abundant; the commerce prospered; the matron got a taste for it. The entire household was now dressed in new clothes; the house itself was replastered, repainted and rethatched, and its mistress wore around her waist a demi-girdle of silver-plated metal from which a chaplet and a bunch of keys hung, as from the belly of a bourgeois wife.

Suddenly, in the manner of Saint Agnes, a miraculous cure was produced; in the presence of thirty-seven witnesses, a virgin who had been lame for thirty-four springs, fell in ecstasy, threw away her crutches and danced before the kneading trough, like David before the ark. Her sticks were hung on the wall, and, the good example having been provided, more cures followed in the next fortnight. Under the row of lined-up crutches, Melanie hung a collection-box for offerings.

Onuphre was desolated by all of it.

"I'm not a saint! I'm just a humble sinner overwhelmed by the weight of his sins."

The hostess pinched him covertly in order to impose silence on him, and Calame battled with her against the simpleton's scruples.

The old disagreements between the harpy and the clerk had vanished in prosperity; Melanie renounced treating as an imbecile a man who was able to find such good arguments to defend her purse; she valued his ingenuity, consulted him, listened to him, and even invited him to supper, for he paid his whack in kind. Every afternoon, the troubadour came to amuse himself at the expense of the crowd, savoring the credulity of the idlers, encouraging the tricks of the tradeswoman and delighting in the sad faces that his friend pulled in the midst of his adorers. He also invented embellishments, sometimes costly but always of great effect, such as gilding the kneading trough, decorating it with images, planting flowers in the straw and burning grains of incense in the grandmother's foot-warmer.

At the beginning of lent, the clientele increased further. Calame composed a canon of little Latin verses in honor of the Blessed Onuphrius, and the little girls, arranged in front of the fireplace, intoned canticles and sang in chorus, with voices so falsetto that Melanie wept in admiration.

"One might think we were in a real church, eh, Ygene?"

"It's bad, what you're doing," said Onuphre. "We're deceiving Christians..."

"Deceiving them, you say? We're selling hem hope, and you say we're deceiving them? Name me one food more comforting for irredeemably anemic souls! Being happy is believing that one is, and above all that one will be."

Melanie nodded her head in approval. "How well he speaks, all the same!"

"Calm your conscience, Dame Polygene: you are, with your relics, an incontestable benefactress of men, even if this fellow isn't their benefactor."

At such words, the slattern hiccupped with laugher, which made the keys on her belly rattle; and in the evening, the family counted the receipts. Everyone blossomed; even Noiraud was tolerated in the dwelling, and figured at the foot of the kneading trough; he owed that favor to the intervention of Calame, who had invoked the precedents of Saint Roch and Saint Anthony; hieratically seated on his hindquarters, the pooch watched the pilgrims file past like an attribute of his master. People said "Onuphre and his dog," and the people, in passing, patted the dog's head, hoping to get closer to the saint via the beast.

*XXXV. Having already lost his legs, he is disposed
to lose his footing*

In the middle of Lent, however, a malevolent preacher
sent by Milord the Bishop, one of those black and white
monks always ready to thunder against something or someone,
surged into the pulpit to denounce the impostures that were
scandalizing the region, devilments that would soon lead their
man to the pyre. His precise information caused the entire
town to tremble.

Calame hastened to bring the news.

"Beware, good people! Beware! The torch is burning!
The wind is turning! Onuphre, you're no longer worth more
than your dog's four horseshoes. Fanatic, miscreant, demon-
possessed, sorcerer, you're all of that at the same time! Highwayman, cutpurse, eunuch condemned to death for the rape of
a cowherd, hanged man escaped from prison, you've been
seen, at the hospital, picking up the leg of an amputee in order
to transmute it into a ham, and Polygene ate it! Beware, beware! You were alone in the kneading trough before, but
you're all in it now!"

Onuphre wept large tears; Melanie was devastated; Polygene scratched the back of his neck; Calame rubbed his palms.
They decided in haste to take down the compromising crutches and the collection-box, de-gild the kneading trough and
unstick the pious images. The brats were amused by the panic,
but they wailed when people outside began to throw pebbles at
the door and the windows, not to mention cobblestones and
the excrement that, even better than stones, is appropriate to
express public opinion.

"Stupidity has turned its coat! Who feeds you, stones
you. *Vox populi, vox Dei!*"

The distraught housewife ran around the house, only
pausing to implore the advice of the shrewd clerk: "What do
we do now?"

"Wait, and live in apprehension."

The family had no lack of that; Inquisitors clad in black came, frowning, posing questions to which they trembled to respond; at nightfall, the passers-by on the road hastened their steps, making the sign of the cross, and darkness soon effaced their frightened silhouettes. Onuphre no longer dared budge, desolate at a common peril of which he was the unique cause.

Once, however, he beamed at an unexpected face; a young woman has just come in, ugly of face but rich in youth and buxom. She ran to the kneading trough, where she embraced the human stump as if he were a real loaf of bread.

"Gertrude!"

"I recognized you by the stories they're telling. I said to myself: 'If they're going to burn him, I ought to kiss him one last time beforehand.' Well, my poor fellow, things have worked out badly for you! You've lost even more things!"

"Little by little..."

"It's almost a coffin, your box. You were more comfortable in the cell, for sure."

Melanie approached, intrigued.

"What's that you saying, in the cell?" Then, looking the stranger up and down: "Wait a minute...I remember you. You were the jailer's daughter once."

"Yes, indeed."

"The one who clipped dogs and cut cats at the prison door."

"Exactly."

"Then, this one was in prison?"

"By error; he's taken the place of another there."

"Holy Virgin! That's all its lacked! He's been in prison!"

"Bah!" said Gertrude. "Like Saint Peter."

"And all the saints," added Calame.

The housewife grumbled for a long time, shifting her buckets.

"Is he going to bring us the girl now? The poet wasn't enough, it seems. In prison...!"

The confused benefactor gazed, by force of habit, at his absent feet. The jailer's daughter came to his aid. "Would you like to get some air, perhaps?"

"Oh, yes!"

She lifted him in her left arm, like a bundle of laundry, and carried him on to the road.

"Oof! It's better in the street. You've got a shrew of a hostess. You must have a hard time in her house."

Onuphre protested, praising Melanie, her domestic virtues and her fecundity. Calame, standing up, watched the lovely young woman install herself on her buttocks beside the amputee, holding him against her torso; she took his hand and laughed near his ear. Noiraud sat down on the other side of him; between the two of them, Onuphre, wide-eyed and beaming, gave the impression of contemplating the angels. The Calamitous went away, and the three simple souls began chatting together very quietly.

After an hour, Gertrude said: "I have to get back, my friend." She replaced him in his kneading rough and kissed him on both cheeks.

"A fine day you've made for me, Gertrude! Will I see you again some day?"

"I promise you that; every time I come to the neighborhood I'll come to see you, and if I don't come, I'll come anyway."

Scarcely had she gone out than another face appeared: clean-shaven and green-tinted, brows furrowed and dressed entirely in black, the magistrate was standing on the threshold.

"Outside, the rest of you, while I talk to this man."

When he was alone with the sorcerer, Master Touillechair went to shoot the bolt.

"Recognize me, I'm your judge. Reasons that I don't want to dwell upon incite me to benevolence in your regard. In favor of a tumult, you were able to escape the gibbet, but not without the crowd having molested you harshly, and even, I believe, breaking your kneecap; that chastisement by God appeared to us to be sufficient; I abstained from reclaiming you from the physician in order to return you to the execution-er; furthermore, after the feast that scandalized our hospice by virtue of an evident character of sorcery, I succeeded in de-flecting the curiosity of the Tribunal away from you.

"If, therefore, I owed you something, understand me well, if you estimate that I owed you something, I have paid my debt. At present, I no longer owe you anything, except justice. Now, you have put yourself in further peril by a recid-ivism of your faults, and the secular hand will soon weigh upon you and our accomplices."

"On the good people, Milord Judge!"

"On all the makers of impostures! But the parables of the Gospel teach us clemency, and when we see that a sinner, hav-ing given himself to evil, testifies a repentance and devotes himself to good, our paternal indulgence is always ready, not only to welcome him, but to aid him in the work of redemp-tion. That is why I have brought you a means of repairing your crimes by a benevolent act."

"If I could, Milord Judge..."

"Since I know that you can. There exists in this town an unfortunate soul who is losing her eternal salvation by the incapacity of any resistance to the demon, who labors the flesh of which she is the slave. The wife of a man upright and ven-erable among all, a judge who places above his own joys the care of protecting against Satan and against themselves the beings that Our Lord Jesus and our King has confided to his care, she desolates him with the spectacle of her intemperance, and he has deliberated conquering paradise for her. Since within that person the soul is the victim of the flesh, it is im-portant to separate them from one another, and to abandon the wretched body to the Spirit of Darkness, in order that the lib-erated soul can rise up to the Spirit of Light.

"Now, listen carefully; in thirteen days, on the holy occa-sion of Easter, by the double sacrament of penitence and communion, that woman will have obtained remission of her sins, and in that state of grace, which will not last long, she will find herself temporarily in a position to appear before the

Divine Tribunal. Heaven will be grateful to you for sending the stray lamb there at such a moment; by an action so favorable you will have redeemed your sins. Here is a lock of the lady's hair; here is a wax figurine modeled in her image. You know better than I do what it remains for you to do. Operate.

"I am quitting you now. You have thirteen days, and you will save yourself by saving that poor woman. But if, on Easter day, or Monday at the latest, we do not see her called to render her account to the Supreme Judge, those who represent him down here will summon you to render yours, and you ought not to hope from their justice a mercy you will not have had for the distress of your neighbor. You've understood me? Don't respond. Hide this."

Master Touillechair deposited a little packet wrapped in cloth in the kneading trough; then he made with his hand the gesture that imposes silence, and he left.

Polygene, who was coming home, and who saw the magistrate on the threshold of his house, recoiled in fear. Melanie took charge of explaining the detail of things to him.

"He's come out of prison! He hid that from you! Fine company, eh! And he passes himself off as a prince. You don't seem to understand. He's come out of prison, I tell you."

Onuphre stammered: "By error, cousin..."

"For sure there was an error in letting you out. And for a start, I'm not your cousin. Everyone in our family belongs to decent society, know that! In prison! And he brings loose women here, into the bargain—yes, loose women! A whore who kissed him In full, in front of the children. What did he say to you, the magistrate?"

Dieudonat dared not think about that; he lowered his head without replying. The father of the family waited for a moment, and then rendered his verdict.

"He doesn't want to say anything; he has his secrets. Let him be. He's my savior, isn't he? He has a right to respect. He's put us all on the road to the pyre with his simulations of a saint, and now he's dishonoring my roof with his mistresses, but that doesn't alter the fact that he's the Benefactor, and he'll stay with us as long as it gives him pleasure to do us wrong."

He crossed the room lengthways—one, two, three—scratched the back of his neck, crossed it again sideways—one, two, three—and resumed speaking.

"There's also news, Onuphre, that I've just learned myself, and it isn't good. They don't want me on the roofs anymore because of your rotten kneecap. I'm no longer a roofer; I'm no longer anything. That's it."

"God in Heaven!" cried Melanie. "How are we going to eat? And now we have a man with no legs on our hands, for life!"

Onuphre could not sleep. He thought by turns about the injunctions of the judge, Polygene's kneecap, Gertrude's benevolent eyes and all the disasters of a day that he had thought a little while ago to be the sweetest of his life.

"Send me Calame, great God, in order for him to advise me."

But the thaumaturge had abjured the right to ask for anything for himself, and Calame did not come; impregnated with a poem by the charming April, the troubadour was striding through the spring

Every morning, after his prayer, Onuphre repeated: "Perhaps it will be today…only nine more days and the magistrate will come to fetch the good people in order to burn them..."

"Only another seven days…have pity, my God, and send Calame!"

He had hidden the evil wax figure under his surcoat. The hours were very long, and existence became hard; Polygene, having become a manual laborer, was carrying burdens as Onuphre had done previously; the man earned less, the wife grumbled more. She still had coins gathered in the time of pilgrimages in an old sock, but her heart bled when she touched it.

"Since we have no more bread, because of that kneecap, it's necessary to return the kneading trough to me, you!"

266

He was taken down permanently from his once-glorious couch, like a saint extracted from his niche. He was planted in a corner of the room, and then in another, under the pretext that he was cluttering up that one, and then in another, and incessantly from one to another, since he was in the way everywhere; he alone enjoyed all four corners. Since he resided at floor level, the housewife was able to bump into him by chance with a few particularly hard objects; the girls played at imitating Mama.

"You couldn't go outside, instead of remaining under our feet…?"

The human stump dragged himself like a worm, or dug his fingers into the greasy soil; Noiraud, leaning toward him, followed him step by step, frowning and breathing on his spine to help him. In the house, one of the girls wailed, demanding bread, and her mother replied: "Necessary to keep it for the Benefactor."

It was thus that the grandmother got the idea of whining every ten minutes: "I'm hungry…"

"Ask the Benefactor to send you a roast goose."

"Dirty Benefactor!"

When he had crawled as far as the edge of the road, he raised himself up on his palms, looking into the distance, at the bend in the road.

Calame did not come into view; it was Gertrude who appeared.

She was carrying an immense wooden hat on her head, as square as a crate and decorated with four castors by way of plumes or frills.

"It's to take you for a walk, Onuphre, so you can get some air. You need a vehicle, since you no longer have legs. A prisoner made it for me, for the pleasure, with old pieces of wood. What do you think?"

"I think that I've had a great many things in my life, and that I've made a few little deals here and there, but this is the first time that I've ever received a gift."

"Really? Oh, how glad I am!"

"You love me, then, a little."

"Yes, of course, I love you a lot."

"And I also believe that no one has ever loved me, and that you're the first, since my Mama."

She seemed so happy, and for his part, he felt an emotion so sweet that the loss of his limbs appeared to him to be a blessed event, generously compensated by the joys of that minute. He asked for his vehicle, turned it in all directions and made the wheels rotate.

"Do you want to try it out," said Gertrude, "so I can teach you how to use it?"

"Oh yes!"

The party commenced: the big girl and the little ones, pushing the amputee around, laughed until they cried; He was tipped into the ditch, pulled out, replanted covered in dust, and off again! Everyone sweated, and Noiraud danced around, barking with a furious joy. The grandmother, on the threshold, held her sides.

Finally seeing people happy Dieudonat forgot his worries.

Eventually, he tried to walk with his wrists, and when Gertrude had gone, Melanie, her fists on her hips, shouted to him: "You'll have to go and beg now that you have your carriage."

He went, meekly, thinking it a good idea, but the children in the streets threw stones at him; pious people, on recognizing the sorcerer and his dog, made the sign of the cross and ran away; he did not bring back a sou.

By way of compensation, he found that Calame had returned.

"My God! My God! Only another five days!"

But he did not have the leisure to lament for long on that theme; what he saw on the doorstep caused him a very different emotion. The eldest of the little girls, leaning against the jamb, was swaddling and rocking the wax figurine, and her younger sister was demanding the doll with screams. Melanie arrived, drawn by the noise of the quarrel, seized the object of litigation, undressed the minuscule female, was astonished by the immodestly excessive organs, and enquired: "Where did this come from?"

"It's mine," yapped the younger sister. "I found it in the ditch where Onuphre fell."

"Witchcraft! It's yours, this horror?"

He only just had time to reply: "Yes, cousin." His emotion was so great that he was immediately gripped by a seizure.

When he recovered consciousness, the Calamitous was standing beside him. He raised his bleak eye toward him.

"Calame…what day…is it?"

"Wednesday."

"One, two, three, four... Lean over, so I can talk to you."

"Take him away, rather!" cried the harpy, "And may we never see either one of you again!"

As soon as they were alone, Dieudonat made a supreme effort with his head in order to tell the story of the magistrate.

"Bad," said Calame. "Doubly bad. Master Touillechair is ambitious to be elevated to the rank of widower and he's charging you with the task; beware of him if you don't obey, and beware of Melanie, who has finally found a weapon with which to rid herself of your carcass."

"You can believe…?"

"Oh, the good people! Their natural amenity, excited by their gratitude, is making daily progress. They detest you, at present. Are you weeping?"

"Why did you say that to me? It wasn't necessary to tell me that. I didn't want to see it, myself, and now I won't be able any longer not to think it."

"Come on, come on, calm down."

"They are as they can be, the poor. They aren't able to command themselves. It costs them to nourish me, you understand? And now I've become dangerous, into the bargain."

"So beware; by taking the priest the proof of your witchcraft, the worthy woman is exonerating herself and getting rid of you at a single stroke: a double profit."

"Denounce their friend? The worthy Polygene will oppose it."

"As soon as he's no longer angry, his wife draws him by the end of you know what."

"The end of the nose?" said Onuphre, through his tears.

"Yes, my innocent, the end of the nose. You don't want to be burned, do you?"

"If that will sort things out...but I don't want them to sell me, like Judas; that would be too nasty a sin; it's necessary to spare them that, Calame."

"Make a wish."

"No, it's necessary that that comes from their good heart, and I'll disencumber them afterwards, I'll disencumber you all, since I'm still a danger. Talk to them a little, Calame..."

The poet went back into the house, but he did not stay there long. Dieudonat saw him come out again at a run, holding is back and opening his hands above the nape of his neck in order to protect the box of poems from the blows of the firetongs applied by the wife and the blows of a cudgel applied by the husband; the couple pursued him until they ran out of breath.

When they came back, a large tear rolled down the benefactor's cheek.

"Filth!" howled Melanie. "Now he's weeping, so that he can say that we martyrize him"

"Shut up, wife!" ordered Polygene. "He's the Benefactor; he can do anything to us."

Then she served the soup.

The amputee remained outside, in order to be less alone, and he stroked Noiraud's back, sometimes looking him in the eyes.

XXXVI. The heart goes on

The next day, Calame returned courageously to Polygene's house; he found that his friend was no longer there.

"Where is he, then?"

"Don't know. He didn't say."

"When did he go?"

"Yesterday evening. He didn't come back."

"You haven't looked for him?"

"He's his own master, isn't he? We don't ask him to account for himself. I don't have any rights over his liberty."

"In brief, he's run away?"

"If he's done that, after the trouble we've gone to for him and what we've endured because of his magic, he's an ingrate."

Calame ran to the prison door.

"Have you seen him, Gertrude?"

"Yes. He came yesterday at nightfall, very plaintive and crestfallen, with his dog; he told me that he was going far away, in order to disencumber the good people, who have difficulty living; he hid it from them, because they would have retained him, so he said. He came to kiss me before leaving forever, and he told me to give you a big kiss, but that he has to hide from you as from the other, because he does wrong to everyone."

"Truly?"

"You should have heard him when he said: 'Far away! I'm going far away!' It wasn't his ordinary tone; with all his little strength, he shouted: 'I wish it!' He even added: 'So be it.' And then he left."

"But how will he live?

"Oh, I foresaw that, in a way; I was suspicious. He has his means: dog-clipper-and-cat-cutter, like me. I showed him the implements and how to make use of them."

"What about tools?"

"Mine, of course. My big scissors, my new knife, and a nice box to put them in, lined with leather, with big brass nails. It's pretty, though! It opens, it shuts. He admired it enough, turning it every which way. Since the preacher, I've been nailing it expressly for him, for fear of what might happen, but I didn't have time to finish it, as evidenced by the fact that here are the rest of my nails. They're shiny, eh?"

"Magnificent."

"They cost a lot. I've saved, on food. I said to myself: 'It'll be for my little Onuphre.' And every time, I laughed, and my soup tasted better, for not having any butter or lard. Do you believe me?"

"Yes indeed: you deprived yourself. And to give, truly to give, it's necessary to deprive oneself, undoubtedly."

"For sure. When one isn't depriving oneself, one isn't giving, eh?"

"One is rendering, isn't one?"

"Exactly."

"I've always thought that too: giving something of which one has too much is only rendering."

"Exactly! And there's no pleasure in it, don't you find?"

"In that case, good Gertrude, offer yourself the pleasure of giving me the nails you still have."

"I'll wager that you want to go finish my box? You want to catch up with him?"

"Perhaps… one day..."

"Right away, then! It's necessary. He's all alone, and he's so good! You'll catch him up quickly, at the pace he can go."

"Which way did he go?"

"Through the East Gate and straight ahead, following the King's highway. I'll put you on the road." She ballasted him with a soup and guided him outside the town, to make sure that he left.

Calame set forth; he too went straight ahead, eastwards, and followed the King's highway while chewing over the lines of his poem and throwing rhymes at the landscapes of spring.

"Bizarre, how I miss him, that stump of a man, a trunk without legs and almost without a head; it's as if we completed one another, him the heart and me the brain."

The trail was easy to follow; in traversing the hamlets he asked about a legless man escorted by a yellow dog.

"Yes," replied a peasant, "we've seen him. He cut our little cat and he said to him, softly. 'Let me do it, puss, it's for your own good; in this base world, the less one has, the better; the less one is, the happier one is.'"

"He said that, did he?"

"We had a good laugh, and he got himself scratched. We gave him a chunk of bread for his trouble."

Calame resumed his route. "Is it possible that the boy talked like that? Has he deciphered the key to life?"

People always affirmed to him that they had seen the legless man and the yellow dog.

He continued to advance along the King's highway, but he hastened in vain; the days succeeded one another, and Calame never caught up with Dieudonat.

"He the heart and me the brain..."

He searched with his eyes along the thin thread of the King's highway and the edges of the horizons.

"Is it possible that he could walk so quickly?"

Sometimes, he thought he perceived him in silhouette on the skyline.

"Is it possible that he climbed so high?"

He climbed the hill and did not find anyone.

"Devil of a little man who rolls like a giant. I can't do any more!"

As he exhausted himself in his vain pursuit, the inaccessible Dieudonat grew in his thought, until he took on the appearance of a symbol: colossal and transfigured, the image of the disappeared smiled blissfully, and the poet contemplated it in the depths of his memory, believing that he recognized half of himself, and that he no longer had more within himself than the other half.

Finally, one morning, he discovered the imprint of four castors in a rut; it was dry and already old.

"The heart is going on, the heart is going faster. Will I ever catch up with it…?"

On the evening of that day, having reached the crest of a hill, he saw down below, in the violet mist of large towns, roofs without number and the bell-towers of an immense city, astride a red river, and he recognized King Gaifer's capital.

XXXVII. In which Dieudonat loses the little confidence that he still had

After a few weeks of searching, Calame found his prince again one morning, under the porch of the cathedral, wedged against a pillar near the right-hand door, at the feet of the second apostle. To his right, Noiraud was holding himself severely seated; to his left a box covered with leather was ornamented with nails that shone like fine gold. Whether by fatigue, malady or meditation, the group seemed petrified, and the figures of painted stone, in their niches, coated with azure and silver stars, were scarcely more motionless.

"Oh," said the amputee, "You've come to join me, Calame? You've made that long journey!"

They embraced; Noiraud wagged his tail, rubbed his nose against the poet's cheek, and passed politely to the blind side, in order to leave the better place to the new arrival.

"You're very thin, Calame. We live well. In the morning, we stay here; people give to us; people are charitable, and give more than you'd think, especially the poor. With the result that we often have enough to offer a nice morsel to the more wretched, don't we, Noiraud? Not to mention that one doesn't get bored on the parvis; there are celebrations of every sort, marriages, burials, baptisms, *Te deums*; one sees everything, the great and small of the earth, because everyone comes to the house of the good God, don't they, Noiraud? There's also the master of the chapel, who likes us, and who never fails to stop, and talks to us politely; he's a little hard of hearing, and doesn't hear what I reply to him, but he tell me stories about the city. That prevents thought. You used to tell me stories too, didn't you, Calame? When the hour of the offices is past, I go in my vehicle to the river bank, against the abutment of the bridge; there I clip dogs and cut cats—for I have a trade, you see? And a pretty box! It was Gertrude again who gave me all that! When clients come to us, and a little dog wants to move too much, or a little cat isn't content, Noiraud plants himself in front of them, and you ought to see him making wide eyes at them, telling them to remain tranquil! He's a big help to me, the good Noiraud. And then, in the city, we have other friends, other stray dogs; we say hello. Don't we, Noiraud? I'm happy. I believe that I've never been as happy..."

He was exaggerating. With an infantile cunning, he had hastened to affirm his material good fortune, in order not to be interrogated about his mental state, which was not as good. Since his precipitate adieux to the Polygene household, dull and mute sadness had inhabited the depths of his inner being, a lassitude, a discouragement that he did not want to admit to anyone, not even to Noiraud, much less to himself.

It was like a bad fog in which one can only see things vaguely, which move, without one knowing why they are here rather than there: uncertain ghosts, the ghosts of people, the ghosts of ideas, good, evil, unknown beings that are the present and are already blurring, known beings that are the past, which one can scarcely discern any better. From that swarming fog, an insipid odor was exhaled, perhaps the odor of death; and when it rose in gusts, Dieudonat turned away with an abrupt torsion of the neck, as if the poison had veritably been in his heart.

He was no longer exempt from the miseries that immediate contingencies procure; they came to him every day, at a mixed hour, from a friend who detested him. Opposite him, under the same porch, was an old blind man, who carved little deformed animals in white wood, sold very few, and attributed the decline in his industry to the competition of the amputee.

"I can no longer earn my living since you've been there."

When the exit from mass had been poor, he blamed Dieudonat for it, hurling, from one pillar to the other, names that the sanctity of the location ought not to have permitted. In vain the Prince responded with conciliating words; in order to gain indulgence he admired loudly the wooden rabbits or sheep, and signaled their beauty to Noiraud; often, too, be profited from his adversary's blindness to throw a coin into his wooden bowl; the blind man, alerted by the keenness of his hearing, was never duped, but affected to thank an imaginary passer-by, in order to retain his entitlement to rancor intact, a right all the more precious because every recrimination had the result of procuring a donation. Noiraud, sniffing a vile soul, growled continually at the artist, who pretended to be afraid, and Dieudonat took great pains to restore peace between the two enemies.

Calame's arrival brought the carver of images a new opportunity to complain.

"Are you going to draw all the beggars in the city here? Is it a place for repairing old shoes? You haven't finished planting nails?"

The first concern of the Calamitous was, in fact, to finish Gertrude's box. Dieudonat and Noiraud were very interested in that decorative work, which lasted all day, and gradually, they saw a coat of arms appear on the leather of the anterior panel

"Look," said the Prince. "My father's arms. I'd very much like to know what had become of my father..."

Calame went to obtain news, and the following day, he said: "Hardouin died some time ago. Gaifer had him deposed by the Emperor and decapitated by the executioner, in order better to ensure the annexation of the kingdom."

Dieudonat said a prayer for the repose of the paternal soul, but his orison was insufficient to calm his mind. He accused himself of parricide, and from then on the idea haunted him; twenty times a day he beat his breast while praying for his father. Facing him, without respite, a voice sang: "My work... Have pity on a poor blind man..."

"All the same," said Calame, "you're a King now, the legitimate King, for your people persist in searching for you, in hoping for you; they ask for you, refusing to believe in your death. What do you think about going to reconquer your scepter? With two or three wishes, one could see the farce through. You could appoint me prime minister."

In order to complete the decoration of the box, the clerk disposed three copper nails in the form of a royal crown above the escutcheon.

But he was only amusing himself. Dieudonat became increasingly bleak; by virtue of contagion, Noiraud became more severe; the Calamitous could not succeed in making either one of them laugh.

His own life was not cheerful either. To kill time, he recommenced frequenting the mountain of the University; without pleasure, he listened to the lessons of the masters in the public squares, and without success, he climbed on to the boundary markers of the crossroads himself to recite his verses; he had composed superb ones in the Alexandrine mode, recently invented by the clerk Alexander,[20] but his poems were veritably too superior to the mind of the century, with the result that few alms flowed into his wallet. He rarely supped; his hours of gastronomy were spent outside the shop-fronts of rotisseries, where the odor of goose substituted momentarily for the smoke of metaphysics; after that ideal repast, he drew away with a sigh and, if he did not die of hunger, at least he lived in it.

His most reliable bread came from clipping dogs, which earned more. In exchange for some meager meat he brought to the common meal his contribution of intellectual fodder, relating anecdotes about the capital. Unfortunately they saddened his audience more often than they cheered him up.

"This morning, they took to the plain a man named Anoure; his story is comical. Can you imagine that the clown passed himself off as a eunuch and took advantage of the gen-

---

[20] The tern Alexandrine derives from the twelfth-century *Roman d'Alexandre*, which is a romance about Alexander the Great, not a romance by a "clerk" named Alexander, as the author knew full well. If taken seriously the reference would date Dieudonat's adventure to 1165-1200 or thereabouts, although the story is full of anachronisms, as dutifully pointed out in the first paragraph.

eral confidence to lure into his lair prey of a very young age, who were never seen again; in truth, he was abusing it. He was hanged..."

"Alas!"

The lack of success of his tales did not discourage the storyteller.

"Today, you'll laugh, I hope, for the adventure is joyful. I encountered, with his escort of squires and pages, a rich imbecile who was once my comrade at school, Gontran the Rogue. Do you remember him? You met him in the brigands' cavern, with Ruprecht the Pug-nosed, and I told you that in our youth, the three of us were inseparable: Ruprecht, the adventurous brute, Gontran the adventurous fool, and me, the man of genius. Gontran seemed to us to be the least well-equipped, but he had more than us, since he's the only one who has prospered; he's known as the Vicomte d'Avatar. He married the only daughter of a Lombard, successively rendered her an orphan and a mother, and conducted her to the grave; sumptuous henceforth on the heritage of his own child, he struts in the face of the universe. From him I learned that Ruprecht got himself captured last year and quartered. The vicomte told me the details in person, In spite of my rags, or because of them, for he felt visibly magnified by our failure almost as much as by his own fortune, and he showed himself to be candidly proud of the contrast that his cleverness had been able to put between his destiny and ours. He pushed the demonstration as far as to give me a handful of coins, not to mention that he's promised me more. You can see that it's a good day!"

"No, Calame, and your story is vile; that money wouldn't be worth anything to us."

"You're never content: one offers you the picture of a man who succeeds..."

"Alas!"

The voice of the blind man opposite yelped its request to the passers-by.

279

"Share your coins with that fellow, will you? And tell us another story quickly, so that we can forget that one."

"Do you prefer politics? Grave news. The old Emperor has decided to die; he's just entered into death-throes, it's said, for which the Archduke has been waiting for fifteen years, with an impatient patience."

"Then little Aude is going to be Empress?"

"Little Aude? But she's dead. He was very jealous, she was very futile: one day, he dragged her so rudely by the hair that the brain came away with the scalp. It's claimed that she'd married him for love."

"Alas! My pretty nostrils..."

"In fact, there was an entire drama at the Court. That Galeas, whom people continued to call the One-Eyed, was a seductive fellow; Queen Gaude was smitten with him."

"Alas! My resemblance..."

"As the Emperor was taking a long time to die, the two lovers made a plan to dethrone Gaifer in order to offer themselves a kingdom while awaiting the empire..."

"I knew of a similar plot..."

"But what you doubtless don't know is that this one was discovered by a stupefying young lad whose gaze nothing escaped: a fellow named Epagomene, then still a page of the King and now his private secretary. He emerged from no one knows where. His age is unknown."

"He must have reached sixteen."

"He has the figure of an adolescent and the face of an old man. Endowed with omniscience and devoid of illusions, he has read everything, he weighs everything, and sees everything in depth; instead of looking at the effects, like a man, he only looks at the causes; he understands everything, so that he gives the impression of understanding nothing by dint of remaining impassive; he's so shrewd that he doesn't even take pleasure in the honors he's awarded; by virtue of the favor of his master he possesses everything, and by virtue of the excess of his intelligence, he doesn't enjoy anything. He has never been seen to laugh; he has never be seen to get angry; in spite of his age, he isn't known to have had any amour, and although he lives surrounded by hatreds, he isn't known to have had any rancor. Either he doesn't deign to, or he can't."

"Alas..."

"A jolly gift to give a child! Anyway, Galeas has gone away; his betrayer Epagomene will probably perish under the dagger of vengeance."

"When did the Archduke leave?"

"This morning So long as he stayed here the King didn't dare to do anything against the Queen, but the future Emperor no longer cares about her, and Gaifer is already talking about imprisoning his adulterous wife in a convent, not without obliging her to make honorable amends on the parvis of the cathedral: a Royal spectacle that Your Majesty will be able to watch delightedly from here."

"I'd rather not see that. And please, cousin, don't tell me any more stories; I've had my fill of them."

Dieudonat became even sadder; his had inclined toward his breast, and his eyelid lowered over his unique eye. He fell into long silences, during which he evoked his actions of old, for the sake of penitence. The present slid around him without provoking anything in him but a voluntarily vain and totally desolate commiseration, for the notion of real things no longer permitted any hope of remedying the evil of imminent things. All his strength had ebbed away.

Every day, on arriving under the porch, Calame found him similar; standing before him, he contemplated him without daring to say anything to him, and every day, on seeing the dwarf motionless, he remembered the saying of Paracelsus: "All those who have surpassed the measure, no matter in what way, fall into despair."

Afterwards, he sat down. Dieudonat in the middle, Calame to the right and Noiraud to the left, they stayed there for hours without moving and without speaking. Sometimes, the sovereign without a throne uttered a sigh; in the intervals, the voice of the blind man intoned his anthem...

That languor lasted for a month, at the end of which there was a great noise in the square; troops were arranged in front of the parvis; the crowd hastened from all the streets.

"What is it?" asked the Prince.

"They're coming for the honorable amends of Queen Gaude."

"No, no! I don't want any more! I don't want to see that!"

At that moment, the sculptor repeated: "Have pity on a poor blind man!" But almost immediately, he cried: "I can see!" And a moment later he added "I can see with one eye."

Frightened, Calame leaned over King Dieudonat, placed a hand on his forehead and tipped his head back: two empty orbits gazed at the starry vault of the porch.

"Wretch! What have you done now?"

"Nothing good, doubtless. I've unburdened myself."

Dieudonat did not see Queen Gaude on her knees on the parvis; but he heard her sobs, the liturgical chants, the prayers, the responses, the large and small bells; the Calamitous explained the episodes of the scene to him.

"Please, Calame, I'd rather not hear that."

The poet fell silent; but the blind man, ecstatic at the spectacle, continued to describe it. Finally, the ceremony ended; the audience withdrew; Calame's voice called out to one of them, saying: "Good day, Gontran!"

Another voice, heard before, responded: "Oh, there you are, comrade. Beautiful ceremony, you must admit. I was its organizer. But the one who laid the foundations wasn't able to enjoy is triumph; little Epagomene stupidly allowed himself to be poisoned. Between us, he was a fool. I'm replacing him next to the King, but I'm adopting another title, more in rapport with the importance of my role: Comte d'Avatar, Minister of the Court. I have everything in hand; I'll finally be able to show what I am."

And the poet's voice replied softly: "As long as it doesn't constitute a crime against modesty."

Those words were the last that Dieudonat heard the indomitable Calamitous pronounce; a few minutes later he could still hear him, but he was no longer talking, he was screaming; the men of the watch were taking him to prison, by order of Lord Comte d'Avatar, Minister of the Court.

From that morning on, the Prince knew no other speech than that of the carver of images recriminating against his bad luck. The old man had reason to complain, in fact; since he could see clearly, he applied himself to finishing his works carefully, which had lost all the charm of their naivety; furthermore, the public found them devoid of interest, since they were no longer sculpted by a blind man; he sold fewer and fewer, and the beadle wanted to have him removed.

"Now that you've recovered your sight, it's necessary to go away; you no longer have any reason to beg."

At that injunction, the expelled did not fail to observe an expression of triumph on the face of the amputee; he shouted at him: "It's your fault! You've had me chased away, for sure, in order to be alone!"

Every day, all day long, chronometrically, while whittling his pieces of wood, he grumbled: "It's your fault! I can no longer earn my bread!"

Pretending to be still blind, he drew nearer to the stump of a man, and walked over his fingers, by mistake.

"It's your fault!"

The indignant Noiraud bit him.

"That's your fault!"

And Dieudonat thought: "Alas, yes, it's my fault, and even more than he thinks; all the same, I'd like no longer to hear that...."

"It's your fault!"

"Everything is my fault, always, except the fate of poor Calame, who made his own misfortune; and it's a little curious that the only creature for whom I never attempted anything has as much to lament as the others..."

The invisible Noiraud pushed his oblong skull with its unique bump under his hand; smiling, he caressed that warm box, which he sensed to be full of love, and an idea of the dog's entered into him via the fingers: "No, it's not your fault; it's necessary not to believe them, it's necessary not to believe yourself. Misfortune comes on its own, and you have nothing to do with it."

"You think so, Noiraud? Thank you, Noiraud..."

"Modest dogs know that. All life is misery. Bells also know it. Listen to them, what they're saying..."

From one hour to the next, the bronze of the bells coiffed him with a heavy cope of sounds, which fell upon his cranium and his shoulders; they enveloped him with a tremor that penetrated him through all his pores; his breast swelled with those renewed rumblings, and it was as if he had sensed, hour by hour, in his meager body, the gross heart of the city beating.

"All the same, I'd like no longer to be able to hear that..."

One autumn evening, the master of the chapel stopped before him; he spoke in a sad voice: "Oh, life isn't droll! Now I'm completely deaf; the churchwardens are going to replace me; I no longer have anything to do but die of hunger."

The King did not reply; he gave him his hearing.

At first, he had the sentiment of a new deliverance. Then an immense desert extended in the silence, and a boundless solitude.

Calame had not reappeared. Even the organist hardly ever stopped any longer and ceased to address words to the poor devil who could no longer perceive sounds. Since he had been deaf, Dieudonat had lost speech. He still said: "Noiraud... Noiraud..." Or again, when someone threw him a hunk of bread: "Thank you.... Thank you..." But nothing else.

No one looked at him any longer. At the foot of his pillar, he slumped like half a statue.

More than before, Noiraud came to huddle against him; under the windy porch, they pressed together for warmth, and without bending down, the legless man could find, at the end of his arm, a fraternal head, full of mute thoughts, like his own.

But the hours were very slow, and too numerous, even in winter; in order still to count them, he tried to divine them, for want of hearing them rumble above his head. More and more, he withdrew into himself, and diminished.

One night, when it was snowing, the dog started to tremble with fever and his teeth chattered; he licked his friend's hand slowly, and in his manner he said: "Adieu, I'm going to die, I regret it..."

The King gave his life to the dog.

But the sacrifice served little purpose, for Noiraud accompanied the body, and let himself die on his brother's grave.

Epilogue.
In which the deceased learns that he possessed
thirteen senses and practiced two virtues

The late Prince Dieudonat, in the thirty-ninth year of his age, arrived, very perplexed, at the gate of Paradise. Doubtless he would not spontaneously have had the presumption of heading that way if some occult force had not guided him there; he even made the journey so slowly that Noiraud had the time to catch up with him on the way.

On seeing them together, so hesitant and so crestfallen, Saint Peter took pity on them and emerged from his lodge. Standing on the threshold, he smiled, a little ironically, but benevolently, shaking his head with an expression of tender reprobation, as an old grandfather might do facing a child who has not been good.

Dieudonat recognized him immediately by his mariner's beard, his baldness crowned with wisps of hair, and above all by his keys; before that colossal apparition, and although he had recovered the integrity of his person by virtue of death, he felt infinitely smaller than on earth, and more heavily laden with sin.

"Excuse me, great saint, I see that I've mistaken my way. I was looking for Purgatory."

"Behind you, my friend."

The deceased turned round, but only perceived the earth.

"That was it; you've just emerged from it. Haven't you been there long enough?"

"Long enough for others, whom I never ceased to harm! Father, I confess to you: all those I approached have suffered by my actions."

"I like to hear you talk that way, my son, by let's not exaggerate, I beg you; there's a pride in exaggerating anything, even the sentiment of your responsibilities, since it is, by the same token, exaggerating your importance. Don't persevere any longer."

"All along the road, I've seen my works rising up against me. Everywhere, I've spread dolor and death."

"Like every creature, solely by virtue of the fact that it exists and that it moves."

"I've done more harm than any other!"

"Because you could do more, my child. The least harmfulness coincides with the least action. To be able to do more than other men is to be able to do more harm. The Devil certainly thought that when he ceded you the possibility of acting beyond human limits."

"Dolor lay in wait for my every action. From the good I tried to do, nothing emerged but evil."

The effects are not your work, but the sum of the innumerable forces that your movement was sufficient to trigger; they are the cooperation of the universe. What would become of us, great God, if it were necessary to demand that good intentions only produced good results? Paradise would be deserted. Not one saint, that I know, could resist the examination of the consequences that his dream and his role provoked behind him. Would I be here, myself? Could Our Lord himself have entered here, given how often evil has been done in his name?"

"Oh."

"By the mere fact of being placed in the hands of crowds and centuries, every idea is depraved and ceases to be understood, and ceases to be admirable, or even desirable. It is necessary to be able to confess it, young man: to want to do well is a beautiful dream, but to serve it is a chimera."

"I have lived badly!"

"To live better, it would merely have been sufficient to marry a worthy young woman, to have children and to dig your field in order to nourish them. The entire secret is there, and also the moral of your story."

"However, Heaven heaped me with magnificent presents..."

"Magnificent? Magnificent? Evidently, we heaped you with them, but to excess. In seeing you emerge from Limbo, when everyone charged you with his gifts, and when you set forth toward the planet, so small, so crushed under the burden of our future capacities, God is my witness that I felt sorry for you in advance. 'Oh, poor lad, what are you giving him there? What will he become, poor little thing?' A victim! And you were, much more than culpable."

"Sometimes..."

"The exceptional individual is always a victim! You were endowed? Well, there you are! Superficial endowments are causes of joy, I concede to you, but profound endowments are sources of pain."

"It's true that I've suffered in my heart from the evil that I've done, and that I've suffered in my mind from the good that I've conceived; because of the power that had been put in me, all my heart has bled, and over my impotence, all my mind has lamented."

"A battlefield on which the forces of Heaven and Hell clash, that's what you were. The presents with which we heaped a pitiful Prince, Satan topped off by saying: 'Your wishes will be realized.' God had given you a conscience—which is to say, the notion of your human incapacity—and the Evil One, with that, granted you extra-human power, with the result that you became a hybrid creature, omnipotent and warned of your impotence, a derisory knight of love who, among the desolations of the earth, paraded the deceptive motto: *Able to do everything and knowing that one cannot do anything.*"

"Is suffering, then, the ineluctable law of the world? O my father, when I summarized my life under the porch of the church, in the apparent humility in which I was then crouching, more wretched than Job, I consummated the supreme act of pride: at the same time as judging myself, I judged God, and I condemned him! Why has God put dolor on the earth?"

"Out of pity, my son, in order to save you."

"Useless and cruel dolor?"

288

"Attentive and very benevolent dolor! You believe that you only have five senses, and that excessively naïve error comes from not having understood the purpose they serve. Like children, you believed that they were given to you as playthings, for your pleasure. Their role is much vaster; they were given to you, in appearance for your joy, but in reality for the needs of the universe."

"My senses?"

"Oh yes. Life is conceded to you as a transmissible deposit; it is therefore important both that you preserve it and that you transmit it. In that double design, Nature equips her children with alarm systems that remind them of their double duty: those guardians are your senses. But in order to animate your attention further, it was determined that they would be elements of sensual pleasure as well a counselors of prudence, and that is certainly very ingenious, since in promising you pleasure they excite your individual egotism to the accomplishment of the common mission."

"I can glimpse..."

"Exposed as you are to ambient perils and exterior perils, you have your special informers for every eventuality: against whatever menaces you from a distance, sight and hearing; against what might wound you, touch; against what might poison you, smell and taste; in order to awaken your vigilance against the known or the unknown, you have fear, and against the inconveniences of gravitation you have vertigo. Thus warned about your surroundings, there is only the further matter of defending you against yourselves: hunger, thirst and suffocation advise you of internal expenditures, with the injunction to provide for them, and those are the ten senses that watch over the creature. But if it is appropriate for the universe to safeguard the individual although in sum, it is negligible in itself, it is above all because it needs to perpetuate the species; in consequence, Nature has provided you with a propagatory sense, amour, to which she attaches for you the maximum of sensual pleasure, since it comports for her the maximum of utility—to such an extent that, with a view to

289

satisfying that imperious sense, you go beyond any consideration of personal sagacity..."

"Armida's Palace, O my sin..."

"But it was not enough to incite you to joys; in order to
forearm you against the dangers of your carelessness, excesses
or failures, a truly tutelary solicitude has taken care to enrich
you further with a supreme sense that combines all the others,
in admonishing you with a pressing voice: dolor. That sense is
the early warning system *par excellence*, a manometer with an
alarm bell, the one that sounds the alarm in urgent circumstances and which reveals your enemies, overt or covert, those
within as well as those without, and which indicates to you the
limit of your resistance: brutally, violently, it rings, loudly,
and with increasing loudness. The ringing is painful? It has to
be, in order to make you listen, and obey; against your apathy,
the rigor of that inexorable summons is necessary, which con-
strains you to combat the evil in order for the alarm bell to fall
silent."

"And since we discover, in each or our organs, the possibility of an abuse—which is to say, a vice—it gives rise to
dolor like the other senses; thus we can conceive the monstrous sin of cultivating it for its own sake or of setting it in
motion with the unique desire of hearing its beautiful cry of
appeal, the cry that is suffering?"

"The liking for martyrizing the weak is innate in all creatures."

"To such an extent that we invent tortures, instruments,
and even professions in order to obtain Dolor in itself!"

"Is that all, my child? Are you going to forget that the
appetites of torture are so morbidly inveterate in humans that
they even dare to attribute them to God, in imaging a Hell
where defenseless victims are torn apart endlessly by joyful
torturers?"

The deceased had turned back toward to earth, and he
perceived it, deplorably alone and round in space.

Then Peter said to him: "If it is true that human beings
stray further than the beast in the ways of depravity, at least

they have had the honor of imposing limits on themselves, and it is those limits that Satan solicited you to surpass, my prince, when, by a perfidious favor, he gave you omnipotence."

"I have known that only too well."

"Never enough; humans do not know what an interest they have in dreading power. One can never repeat to them enough that more power is the surest means of multiplying not only opportunities or self-deception but also those of falling."

"Alas..."

"The human conscience is not solid enough to risk with impunity the danger of triggering an uncontrolled force; inevitably, in humans, power diminishes its enemy, conscience—and what makes you great is your conscience."

"My father..."

"You were very small, Dieudonat, because of your immense power; but you have grown by virtue of diminishing yourself."

"My father..."

"To grow, my son, is not to gain grandeur, but to increase one's conscience, and you have understood that."

The apostle was speaking in sure terms. Dieudonat, who was listening to him, lowering his brow under the praise, raised his head again and perceived, with amazement, that the saint and he were now face to face, of similar stature.

Peter smiled at him and said: "You have understood, and you are delivered. Like me, you were in bonds, and like me, you have emerged from Herod's claws. Come, my brother, that I might embrace you."

The grand old man opened his arms; the dead man threw himself into them, weeping; the former fisherman of Galilee caressed the shoulder of the former amputee gently.

"The same Angel has extracted us, you and me, from the same jail, and he had two wings: Effort and Pity. In spite of Satan, like me, you have resisted, in order to celebrate Effort-even-so and Pity-even-so. Like me, too, you have failed, and that was the day when, like me, you renounced Effort and Pity."

"I remember; that was the evening on the bank of a river; in a cowardly fashion, I abdicated my soul and denied my duty..."

"The cock spoke to me three times. You took pity on yourself, like me, and that was the sin."

"Then I traveled the roads, and I no longer thought...and I also remember this: it as the happiest time of my life."

"That is the truth that it is necessary not to tell people, in order not to take away the courage from those who do not have much. That time was the one when you applied the theory of the least effort, so dear to Satan, to the brutes and to the generality of humans. You then had nothing good, except your happiness. That is a great deal for a beast; it is nothing for a human being."

"Yes, I failed."

"You redeemed yourself. The task was hard, because we have a limit placed on our strength. To do one's duty with regard to oneself is to do what one can; to do one's duty with regard to others is to do more than one can."

"More than one can..."

"That is why, in recompense for long effort accomplished by the race in the course of laborious centuries, we have succeeded in adding to ourselves a faculty that other species do not have. Just now I affirmed to you the supremacy of a twelfth sense, Dolor, which warns all animals of what they ought to dread for themselves. There is a thirteenth, charged with warning you of what you ought to read for others; and that one is the property of humans. You alone possess it. It is your conquest and your nobility; it is your work. It is the spiritual brother of touch; its name is Tact. For Tact is a sense, but a moral sense; it is the gift of perceiving that which would be dolorous to one's neighbor, with the attention to preserve him from a surplus of misery; it is the antenna of your souls, which warns you of ambient distress, and by which you take care to spare neighboring souls; it is the sense of the other."

"The Others."

"You glimpsed that truth in the clearing of the insects, on the day when you said to the beasts: "While each of you only knows his own right, I have invented the right of others, and I call it my duty."

"The Others..."

"It is from the human brain that that concept was launched across the earth and all the way to the heavens: the Others! And that word is the most beautiful of all those that have vibrated in space. To the immolation of the Others, which the universal law of life preaches to us, we have opposed the immolation of the self. We humans, alone against nature and against all the gods, have erected it as a dogma, and that was the Good News, the Gospel: Man has made God!"

"But in order to be understood by those who would not have understood, you said: God has made Man."

An infinite dawn rose gently over the gardens of eternal peace; the light sang.

Saint Peter extended his right hand.

"My brother, the double sanctity of human being is Effort and Pity. You have practiced both. Enter, you are at home."

SF & FANTASY

Adolphe Alhaiza. *Cybele*
Alphonse Allais. *The Adventures of Captain Cap*
Henri Allorge. *The Great Cataclysm*
Guy d'Armen. *Doc Ardan: The City of Gold and Lepers; The Troglodytes of Mount Everest/The Giants of Black Lake; The Abominable Snowman*
G.-J. Arnaud. *The Ice Company*
André Arnyvelde. *The Ark; The Mutilated Bacchus*
Charles Asselineau. *The Double Life*
Henri Austruy. *The Eupantophone; The Olotelepan; The Petitpaon Era*
Barillet-Lagargousse. *The Final War*
Barbot de Villeneuve.*The Naiads/Beauty & The Beast*
Cyprien Bérard. *The Vampire Lord Ruthwen*
S. Henry Berthoud. *Martyrs of Science; The Angel Asrael*
Aloysius Bertrand. *Gaspard de la Nuit*
Richard Bessière. *The Gardens of the Apocalypse; The Masters of Silence*
Chevalier de Béthune. *The World of Mercury*
Albert Bleunard. *Ever Smaller*
Félix Bodin. *The Novel of the Future*
Pierre Boitard. *Journey to the Sun*
Louis Boussenard. *Monsieur Synthesis*
Alphonse Brown. *City of Glass; The Conquest of the Air*
Émile Calvet. *In a Thousand Years*
André Caroff. *The Terror of Madame Atomos; Miss Atomos; The Return of Madame Atomos; The Mistake of Madame Atomos; The Monsters of Madame Atomos; The Revenge of Madame Atomos; The Resurrection of Madame Atomos; The Mark of Madame Atomos; The Spheres of Madame Atomos; The Wrath of Madame Atomos* (w/M. & Sylvie Stéphan); *The Sins of Madame Atomos* (w/M. & Sylvie Stéphan)
Jean Carrère. *The End of Atlantis*
Charlotte-Rose Caumont de La Force. *The Land of Delights*
Félicien Champsaur. *Homo-Deus; The Human Arrow; Nora, The Ape-Woman; Ouha, King of the Apes; Pharaoh's Wife*
Didier de Chousy. *Ignis*
Jules Clarétie. *Obsession*
Jacques Collin de Plancy. *Voyage to the Center of the Earth*

Michel Corday. *The Eternal Flame; The Lynx* (w/André Couvreur)

André Couvreur. *Caresco, Superman; The Exploits of Professor Tornada* (3 vols.); *The Necessary Evil*

Gaston Danville. *The Perfume of Lust*

Camille Debans. *The Misfortunes of John Bull*

Captain Danrit. *Undersea Odyssey*

C. I. Defontenay. *Star (Psi Cassiopeia)*

Charles Derennes. *The People of the Pole*

Georges Dodds (anthologist). *The Missing Link*

Charles Dodeman. *The Silent Bomb*

Harry Dickson. *The Heir of Dracula; Harry Dickson vs. The Spider*

Jules Dornay. *Lord Ruthven Begins*

Alfred Driou. *The Adventures of a Parisian Aeronaut*

Odette Dulac. *The War of the Sexes*

Alexandre Dumas. *The Return of Lord Ruthven; The Man who Married a Mermaid* (w/P. Lacroix)

Renée Dunan. *Baal; The Ultimate Pleasure*

J.-C. Dunyach. *The Night Orchid; The Thieves of Silence*

Henri Duvernois. *The Man Who Found Himself*

Achille Eyraud. *Voyage to Venus*

Henri Falk. *The Age of Lead*

Paul Féval. *Anne of the Isles; Knightshade; Revenants; Vampire City; The Vampire Countess; The Wandering Jew's Daughter*

Paul Féval, *fils. Felifax, the Tiger-Man*

Charles de Fieux. *Lamékis*

Fernand Fleuret. *Jim Click*

Charles-Marie Flor O'Squarr. *Phantoms*

Louis Forest. *Someone is Stealing Children in Paris*

Arnould Galopin. *Doctor Omega*; *Doctor Omega and the Shadowmen* (anthology)

Judith Gautier. *Isoline and the Serpent-Flower*

H. Gayar. *The Marvelous Adventures of Serge Myrandhal on Mars*

Louis Geoffroy. *The Apocryphal Napoleon*

G.L. Gick. *Harry Dickson and the Werewolf of Rutherford Grange*

Raoul Gineste. *The Second Life of Doctor Albin*

Delphine de Girardin. *Balzac's Cane*

Emmanuel Gorlier. *The Nyctalope and the Tower of Babel*

Léon Gozlan. *The Vampire of the Val-de-Grâce*

Jules Gros. *The Fossil Man*

Jimmy Guieu. *The Polarian-Denebian War* (2 vols.)

Edmond Haraucourt. *Daah, the First Human; Illusions of Immortality*

Nathalie Henneberg. *The Green Gods*
Eugène Hennebert. *The Enchanted City*
Jules Hoche. *The Maker of Men and His Formula*
V. Hugo, P. Foucher & P. Meurice. *The Hunchback of Notre-Dame*
Romain d'Huissier. *Hexagon: Dark Matter*
Jules Janin. *The Magnetized Corpse*
Gustave Kahn. *The Tale of Gold and Silence*
Gérard Klein. *The Mote in Time's Eye; Starmasters*
Fernand Kolney. *Love in 5000 Years*
Paul Lacroix. *Danse Macabre; The Man who Married a Mermaid* (w/Alexandre Dumas)
Louis-Guillaume de La Follie. *The Unpretentious Philosopher*
Jean de La Hire. *The Fiery Wheel; Enter the Nyctalope; The Nyctalope on Mars; The Nyctalope vs. Lucifer; The Nyctalope Steps In; Night of the Nyctalope; Return of the Nyctalope; The Nyctalope and the Tower of Babel*
Etienne-Léon de Lamothe-Langon. *The Virgin Vampire The Mysterious Hermit of the Tomb*
André Laurie. *Spiridon*
Gabriel de Lautrec. *The Vengeance of the Oval Portrait*
Alain le Drimeur. *The Future City*
Georges Le Faure & Henri de Graffigny. *The Extraordinary Adventures of a Russian Scientist Across the Solar System* (2 vols.)
Gustave Le Rouge. *The Dominion of the World* (w/G. Guitton) (4 vols.); *The Mysterious Doctor Cornelius* (3 vols.); *The Vampires of Mars*
Jules Lermina. *The Battle of Strasbourg; Mysteryville; Panic in Paris; The Secret of Zippelius; To-Ho and the Gold Destroyers*
Maurice Level. *The Gates of Hell*
M.-J. L'Héritier de Villandon. *The Robe of Sincerity*
André Lichtenberger. *The Centaurs; The Children of the Crab*
Maurice Limat. *Mephista*
Listonai. *The Philosophical Voyager*
Jean-Marc & Randy Lofficier. *Edgar Allan Poe on Mars; The Katrina Protocol; Pacifica 1, 2; Robonocchio; Return of the Nyctalope;* (anthologists) *Tales of the Shadowmen 1-14; The Vampire Almanac* (2 vols.)
Ch. Lomon & P.-B. Gheuzi. *The Last Days of Atlantis*
Charles Malato. *Lost!*
Maurice Magre. *The Marvelous Story of Claire d'Amour; The Call of the Beast; Priscilla of Alexandria; The Angel of Lust; The Mystery of*

the Tiger; The Poison of Goa; Lucifer; The Blood of Toulouse; The Albigensian Treasure; Jean de Fodoas; Melusine; The Brothers of the Virgin Gold
Victor Margueritte. *The Bacheloress; The Companion; The Couple*
Camille Mauclair. *The Virgin Orient*
Xavier Mauméjean. *The League of Heroes*
Louis-Sébastien Mercier. *The Iron Man*
Joseph Méry. *The Tower of Destiny*
Hippolyte Mettais. *Paris Before the Deluge; The Year 5865*
Louise Michel. *The Human Microbes; The New World*
Miral-Viger. *The Ring of Light*
Tony Moilin. *Paris in the Year 2000*
Michael Moorcock's *Legends of the Multiverse*
José Moselli. *Illa's End*
John-Antoine Nau. *Enemy Force*
Marie Nizet. *Captain Vampire*
Charles Nodier. *Trilby and The Crumb Fairy*
C. Nodier, A. Beraud & Toussaint-Merle. *Frankenstein*
Oksana & Gil Prou. *Outre-Blanc*
Henri de Parville. *An Inhabitant of the Planet Mars*
Gaston de Pawlowski. *Journey to the Land of the 4th Dimension*
Georges Pellerin. *The World in 2000 Years*
Ernest Pérochon. *The Frenetic People*
Pierre Pelot. *The Child Who Walked on the Sky*
Jean Petithuguenin. *An International Mission to the Moon*
J. Polidori, C. Nodier, E. Scribe. *Lord Ruthven the Vampire*
P.-A. Ponson du Terrail. *The Immortal Woman; The Vampire and the Devil's Son; The Police Agent*
Georges Price. *The Missing Men of the* Sirius
René Pujol. *The Chimerical Quest*
Edgar Quinet. *Ahasuerus; The Enchanter Merlin*
Jean Rameau. *Arrival; in the Stars*
Henri de Régnier. *A Surfeit of Mirrors*
Maurice Renard. *The Blue Peril; Doctor Lerne; The Doctored Man; A Man Among the Microbes; The Master of Light*
Restif de la Bretonne. *The Discovery of the Austral Continent by a Flying Man; Posthumous Correspondence* (3 vols.); *The Fay Ouroucoucou* (2 vols.)
Jean Richepin. *The Crazy Corner; The Wing*

Albert Robida. *The Adventures of Saturnin Farandoul; Chalet in the Sky; The Clock of the Centuries; The Electric Life; The Engineer Von Satanas; In 1965*

J.-H. Rosny Aîné. *Helgvor of the Blue River; The Givreuse Enigma; The Mysterious Force; The Navigators of Space; Pan's Flute; Vamireh; The World of the Variants; The Young Vampire*

Marcel Rouff. *Journey to the Inverted World*

Marie-Anne de Roumier-Robert. *The Voyage of Lord Seaton to the Seven Planets*

Léonie Rouzade. *The World Turned Upside Down*

Han Ryner. *The Human Ant; The Superhumans*

Henri de Saint-Georges. *The Green Eyes*

Louis-Claude de Saint-Martin. *The Crocodile*

X.B. Saintine. *Jonathan the Visionary; The Second Life*

Frank Schildiner. *The Quest of Frankenstein; The Triumph of Frankenstein; Napoleon's Vampire Hunters; The Devil-Plague of Naples*

Nicolas Ségur. *The Human Paradise; Penelope's Secret*

Pierre de Selenes: *An Unknown World*

Norbert Sevestre. *Sâr Dubnotal: Vs. Jack the Ripper; The Astral Trail*

Angelo de Sorr. *The Vampires of London*

Brian Stableford. *The Empire of the Necromancers (1. The Shadow of Frankenstein; 2. Frankenstein and the Vampire Countess; 3. Frankenstein in London); The Wayward Muse; Eurydice's Lament; The Mirror of Dionysius; The Pool of Mnemosyne; The New Faust at the Tragicomique; Sherlock Holmes and The Vampires of Eternity; The Stones of Camelot* (anthologist) *News from the Moon; The Germans on Venus; The Supreme Progress; The World Above the World; Nemoville; Investigations of the Future; The Conqueror of Death; The Revolt of the Machines; The Man With the Blue Face; The Aerial Valley; The New Moon; The Nickel Man; On the Brink of the World's End; The Mirror of Present Events; The Humanisphere*

Jacques Spitz. *The Eye of Purgatory*

Kurt Steiner. *Ortog*

Michel & Sylvie Stéphan. *The Wrath of Madame Atomos* (w/André Caroff); *The Sins of Madame Atomos* (w/André Caroff)

Eugène Thébault. *Radio-Terror*

Edmond Thiaudière. *Singular amours*

C.-F. Tiphaigne de La Roche. *Amilec*

Simon Tyssot de Patot. *The Strange Voyages of Jacques Massé and Pierre de Mésange*

Louis Ulbach. *Prince Bonifacio*
Théo Varlet. *The Castaways of Eros; The Golden Rock.; The Martian Epic* (w/Octave Joncquel); *Timeslip Troopers* (w/André Blandin); *The Xenobiotic Invasion*
Pierre Véron. *The Merchants of Health*
Paul Vibert. *The Mysterious Fluid*
Villiers de l'Isle-Adam. *The Scaffold; The Vampire Soul*
Gaston de Wailly. *The Murderer of the World*
Philippe Ward. *Artahe; Manhattan Ghost* (w/Mickael Laguerre); *The Song of Montségur* (w/Sylvie Miller)